Heart of Sacrifice

Cindy Koepp

Des Moines, Iowa, USA

Heart of Sacrifice

© Copyright 2025 by Cindy Koepp

For permissions and queries, contact the publisher at:
C_Koepp@yahoo.com

PRINTING HISTORY
First Edition
March 2025

Paperback ISBN-13: 979-8-9903197-2-1
eBook ISBN-13: 979-8-9903197-3-8

CREDITS
Cover Art by: Rowell Cruz

PUBLISHER'S NOTE

Chapter 1

Erin shifted the bundle of sticks in her arms and looked for the sun through the leafless canopy of the trees. With a heavy, exasperated sigh, she continued her search for the wood she needed for the cookfire. She had to hurry. According to the sun's position, afternoon would soon give way to evening. Connor would be home demanding dinner, and she'd have hell to pay if he had to wait for it. Her earlier trip into town had taken far longer than she had anticipated. Wasn't that just her luck? On the day she was in the biggest hurry, she'd had to go on a merry chase from vendor to vendor to find what she needed. To keep Connor from going into a rage, everything had to be just perfect, though that wasn't always enough.

As she gathered larger twigs and dead wood, Erin heard a cry from somewhere nearby. Discounting it as some odd animal or bird, she shook her head and stooped to get another twig. She heard the call more clearly. The voice belonged to a man, not a wild beast. Looking for another piece of firewood, she ignored the sound. There wasn't enough time to investigate and get back home again. Setting her jaw, Erin went back to her work. Each renewed scream caused her to cringe. What was happening to the poor man to make him cry out so?

She stopped. With one last look at the sun, to confirm that she might spare a minute or two to look into the matter, Erin set down the bundle she was carrying and clutched her threadbare cloak tighter around her in a feeble attempt to ward off the cold. Dreading what she might find, she followed the sounds.

The closer she drew to the gut-wrenching screams, the harder her heart pounded. The hairs on the back of her neck stood on end. Pressing in on her, the air seemed heavy and hot, and the light distorted, as if it came through warped, red glass. As if nearby, children were laughing, but they weren't. Of that she was certain. Like most people with falling sickness, Erin was familiar with both signs. Faeries, both sidhe and fey, were near at hand. Unsheathing her steel knife, Erin held it firmly. Fey were sometimes helpful, but the sidhe were ruthless. If the Unseelie Court were playing nearby, the steel would give them pause, she hoped. They might just as well look at the little blade in her hand, laugh, and kill her with a spell from several feet away.

She came to a small clearing and crouched behind a tree in an alcove of scraggly brush. The screams came from an elf bound to the tree almost directly across from her. He was thin and tall, maybe a third again her height, though she couldn't tell for certain because of the way he slumped against the odd dark cord that bound him across the chest. Except for his piercing violet eyes and pointed ears, he almost looked like a handsome human. His tattered, blood-soaked clothes revealed more cuts, bruises, and burns than she could count. Her heart went out to him. More than once in the last five years, she'd felt every bit as helpless as he looked right now.

Two others were in the clearing. One was shrouded in a black leather cloak, so she could tell very little about him. The other was a sidhe as tall as she was, and just looking at it set her heart racing. Every bone in the creature's body stood out under its mottled red and gray skin. Its disproportionately huge, triangular head sported a ring of fierce-looking horns. Long arms ended in hideous claws, laced and dripping with the elf's dark blood. Three pairs of bat-like wings issued from the center of its back.

"Tell me, *señor*, is this gift to your liking?" the cloaked man asked in heavily accented English.

The sidhe turned to him and bared spikelike teeth in a grin that sent a shiver up Erin's spine. "Oh, a most gracious gift. You must tell me how you managed to capture this one."

"Another time, *señor*. Shall I tell my employer we can count on you?"

The sidhe clapped the Spaniard on the shoulder, nearly toppling the man. "Yes, I believe I'm convinced of Luis's good intentions. I'll come visit him to finalize everything as soon as I've finished with my gift."

The cloaked man nodded. "Luis will be pleased to hear it. We will await your arrival."

As the Spaniard turned to leave, the sidhe caught his arm. "Won't you stay? I'll even let you participate."

"Thank you, but no." He jerked his hand free. "I must return to the continent. Luis will be anxious for news, and I have other duties to perform as well."

The sidhe shrugged and released him. "Next time, Joaquin. Next time. I insist."

Without another word, the hooded man turned to leave. Erin gritted her teeth. Unless he changed his direction, he would pass within yards of her. Keeping the cloak around her, Erin curled up on the freezing ground as near as she could to the brush, wishing she could become invisible. When she heard the footsteps growing nearer, she held her breath, certain that at any moment, the sidhe or its ally would yank her to her feet. Her heart pounded so hard in her chest she knew they could hear it. They'd do to her what they'd done to the elf, or worse. She should have stayed away. The affairs of faeries were not her concern. The way her life was going, there were more than enough of her own problems to worry about.

The crunch of dead leaves under booted feet went past her and kept going. Erin stayed statue-still well after she could no longer hear the footfalls retreating into the distance. She carefully peeked out of her cloak then slowly sat up, worried even the slightest sound would draw unwanted recognition.

Another agonized scream from the elf brought her attention back to the clearing. Giggling like a child, the sidhe withdrew a smoldering stick from the elf's arm. Stepping back into the middle of the clearing, the grotesque thing loaded a small blowgun with a tiny, glowing ball. With a puff, it shot the pellet at the elf, who squeezed his eyes closed and clenched his jaw. The dark creature laughed and danced around the small fire between them, then shot the elf twice more.

This couldn't be allowed to continue, but running for help would take too long. What could she do? Sidhe had magic, and Erin had nothing but a silly little knife. This wasn't even her business. No one in the world would fault her for walking away right now. The elf was no one to her, and she had her own problems. No sane person would expect her, a woman, to do battle with a sidhe. A knife against spells was hardly a fair match.

If he did manage to help him, what if the fey turned on her and vented his frustration and anger in her direction? They might not be as universally evil as the sidhe, but who hadn't heard stories of fey changing allegiances or laying traps for humans?

Still, she couldn't tear her eyes from the battered elf. Hearing his screams and seeing his wounds reminded her of all the times she'd cowered in the corner of the house trying unsuccessfully to ward off Connor's blows. Every time she became the target of his fury, she desperately hoped someone would come rushing in to save her.

Be for others the help that wasn't there when you needed it.

Father had taught her that years ago.

She looked down at the dagger she carried; Erin took several deep breaths to calm her nerves, then left her hiding place. To block her quivering hands and the knife from the sidhe's view, she pulled her old, worn cloak closed in front of her. Her heart drummed in her ears and rabid worms ate her intestines. She had to be losing her mind.

Once in the clearing, her resolve to help the victim wavered. Erin froze when the sidhe turned and looked straight at her with bright yellow, slit-pupil eyes.

"I see you, little human." It fluttered to halfway between her and the elf. "Have you come to help me kill this Great Elven Lord, or do you perhaps think you can save him?"

Erin took an unsteady step forward. The thing could cut her to ribbons in a second, she knew, but the elf needed her. "L-leave him be." Her voice quavered.

The beast laughed even as it looked at her knife and backed away. "'Leave him be.' Or you'll what? Do you think I fear you, human? I am a Great Prince among the sidhe. I fear no one. Least of all a pathetic creature like you. You don't have even a mere fraction of my power. You are nothing. You can't hurt me."

She had heard such words before from much less supernatural lips, and she ignored the insults this time, too.

As it turned away from her, Erin looked past the sidhe to its captive. The elf weakly lifted his eyes to meet her gaze in a silent plea for help. Never before had she been so close to faeries, no matter what their disposition, and the thought of going near froze her to the core, but she was committed now. Even if she turned to run, the sidhe could leave its victim bound and helpless while it pursued her. In any case, living with the elf's death on her conscience would be worse than anything the sidhe could do to her.

The beast loaded another shot into its blowgun. Before it could shoot a pellet at the fey again, Erin charged at the sidhe and plunged the steel blade into its back. Black ichor oozed from the smoking wound as the sickening smell of burning flesh permeated the air. The dark creature shrieked and clutched uselessly at the blade in its back.

Erin quickly stepped back out of range of the sidhe's flailing hands. Mixed feelings of remorse, horror, and relief filled her. The sidhe would die now from both the mortal wound she had dealt it and the effect of the steel blade on its flesh. Any pretense of innocence had fled with the fatal blow. She had succeeded in saving the thing's victim, though. Surely that balanced everything out again. Saving another's life atoned for murder, didn't it?

Convulsing and screaming, the dark creature fell to the ground. When it was finally still, she slowly walked toward it, expecting it to open its eyes and strike at her. Her fears were unfounded. It wasn't even breathing now. The blade came out with a sickening, slurping sound and no trace of the gooey, black blood. The odd distortion of the light and the heaviness of the air quickly faded, leaving only the sound of laughing children, which grew ever so slightly quieter by the moment.

The elf shivered, whether from fear or the cold wind she couldn't tell, and constantly looked between the knife in her hand, the creature she had slain, and her face.

Erin looked at her knife then at him. "I-I-I won't - I won't hurt you. I'm-I'm here to help. Please d-don't hurt me."

For no reason she could see, his body tensed and a tormented scream escaped him. She rushed to untie him from the tree. A thin black cord, that absorbed all light, held him so tightly to the tree she wondered how he could even draw breath. Another, more natural rope bound his hands. She untied the rope and cast it aside.

Standing in front of him with an arm poised to catch him, Erin cut the cord. She'd been ready for a tough job of sawing at it, but as soon as she touched the cord with the knife, the magic dissolved.

Before she was ready, the elf collapsed on her. Desperately trying to hold him up with her left arm, she kept the dagger as far away from him as possible. His fingers dug into her back as he hung on to her to break his fall. Between his greater size and her precarious hold on him, Erin and the faerie fell in a heap on the ground with a loud groan. Erin carefully rolled him onto his back as she sat up and cradled him in her lap. Even that small movement made him tense with pain.

"I'm sorry," she whispered.

After removing her cloak and folding it double, she covered him. Without the meager protection the thin cloth had provided, the bitter cold nipped at her. She could do nothing for that. The elf's clothes were shredded. If for no other reason than modesty, he needed her dingy gray-brown cloak more than she did.

Taking the linen kerchief from her head, Erin used her knife to start tears in the cloth, then set the blade aside where the wounded fey wouldn't accidentally brush against the steel. With the strips of linen, she bound a horrific burn on his arm, a cut on his forehead, and some of the more severe wounds to his arms and legs. With the last, otherwise unusable scrap of linen, she carefully cleaned the blood from his face. While she ministered to him, he watched her, wincing when her efforts caused him pain.

As she inspected his wounds, she pushed aside the cloak as necessary. Most of the injuries looked much more painful than dangerous, which meant the sidhe obviously wanted him to suffer at its hands for a long time. The most curious of the injuries were three grayish bruises with dark lines coming from them. What were those? What could have caused them? They were the result of sidhe magic, Erin suspected.

Managing a weak smile, the elf took her hand, but his grip quickly tightened until it hurt, and his face contorted in agony. Erin gasped and held him closer to comfort him. Seconds later, he relaxed again and spoke softly but quickly in a language she didn't know.

Erin shook her head. "I don't understand."

When he spoke again in a completely different language, she still couldn't make any sense of his words.

He pointed somewhere off to her side. Following his hand, Erin saw the dagger she had set down near the tree. Then he guided her hand to one of the grayish bruises and pressed her hand against it. The dark trail leading from the bruise was perhaps a finger-width longer now than it had been when she had checked before. She inspected the other bruises and saw the pattern. The lines led toward the center of his chest. A pellet half the size of her smallest fingernail caused a small bump under his skin, not unlike the sidhe's blowgun shots, at the end of each trail.

What was that? There was so much about the fey and the sidhe she didn't understand. Her patient cried out again, clutching his fists so tightly his nails dug into his hands. She held onto him, whispering soft shushing noises and seeking a way to remove the balls that were causing the problem. When the spasm finally passed, he looked up at her with tears in his eyes. His trembling hand wrapped around her freezing fingers.

She let him guide her hand to point first to the knife then to one of the bruises. With his other hand, he traced the path the pellet had made back to her hand. Erin recognized his intentions clearly, but they still had a problem. She looked at the still smoldering corpse of the sidhe, then back to the blade. If she pressed steel against the faerie's bare skin, the knife would burn him as horribly as it had the dark one. Certainly, he wasn't asking her to put him out of his misery, but did her charge really want her to hurt him like that? Hadn't he been through enough?

She took a quick inventory of what she had available. There had to be some way…

Her pitiful cloak might provide an answer. If not, she always had his plan as an option. Erin picked up her knife and wrapped the edge of her cloak around it, hoping the cloth wouldn't hinder the effect of the blade on the pellet. He watched her curiously, then slowly nodded, but she couldn't tell if he meant to acknowledge the gambit would work or if he simply approved of the attempt.

When she pushed the wrapped metal against one of the bruises, he gasped and closed his eyes. The tension in his muscles turned him as rigid as a board. No, this wasn't right. She didn't want to hurt him. As Erin began to lift the covered knife away, his hand snapped up and held hers down with speed she wouldn't have thought him capable of. She watched the pellet follow the path back to the blade. When she heard the muffled ping of the two connecting, he let go of her wrist and she lifted the knife away. The pellet was stuck to the blade like metal filings to a lodestone. Erin used a stick to push the tiny shot off of her wrapped knife.

She continued similarly with the other two bruises, stopping when the painful convulsions wracked the battered body of her patient. When she finally made an end to her work, she set the dagger off to the side again.

"You poor man," she whispered, gently brushing his dark hair with her fingers. "Rest now. I'll watch over you."

He smiled and softly touched the side of her face, then his eyes drifted closed. Erin carefully pulled him closer to the sidhe's fire and wrapped her cloak around them both, giving him the lion's share of it.

Sidhe were more active at night, and the faerie she held in her arms was in no shape to mount a defense if they attacked. She couldn't leave him. Others of the Seelie Court would come looking for him, she hoped.

Looking out through the trees, she saw the sun nearly on the horizon. She'd never prepare dinner in time now. Unless Connor got fed up with waiting for her and returned to the tavern in town, she could count on a beating when she got home. Wishful thinking. He would be home waiting for his supper, and he would be furious. The elf she had helped wouldn't matter to him.

She closed her eyes and felt warm tears on her cheeks. What evil thing had she done to make God punish her with a husband like Connor? She whispered her daily prayer that God would someday have mercy on her.

***

Evening soon passed into night. While she sat holding the fey in her arms, she now and again could have sworn she heard Connor coming. This time she heard his voice. That time, the unmistakable sound of his hard step. If he found her like this, he'd be outraged. He wouldn't care that she was comforting someone who had terrible wounds. All he would see was another man resting in her arms. Thankfully, the things she heard had been solely in her imagination. Connor would never come looking for her. Instead, he would wait for her at home where he could sit by the hearth and drink his ale.

In all this time, the sound of laughing children hadn't left her, but the sign had dimmed some when the elf had fallen asleep. As she looked down at her patient's face, beautiful in spite of his wounds, the laughter grew louder again, but he made no effort to stir.

They had arrived. The fey had arrived. Erin's pulse raced again. Staying might be dangerous. Fey, she'd heard, didn't like to be seen by humans. Erin had to leave and soon. At this point, she didn't even care if she had to leave the cloak behind.

She carefully laid the elf on the ground being extra careful not to let his head hit, but when she rose, an all-consuming fatigue came over her. This had to be fey magic, but she had to stay awake long enough to get away. The faerie she'd helped would be safe now, but she didn't need any complications with shy fey.

Erin struggled to ward off the sleepiness, but she only staggered a few steps before she sank back to the ground and closed her heavy-lidded eyes.

Chapter 2

Luis's tent had never looked so dangerous. Diego stood outside the entrance and took deep breaths to steady his nerves. As uneasy as he felt right now, someone might think he was preparing to confront legions of hell-sent daemons instead of his own brother. With a wry smile, Diego realized the two might very well amount to the same thing. A sniffle drew his attention to the bound, gagged, and blindfolded reason he even considered doing this. He'd helped his brother steal, raid, and even kidnap since, well, further back than he could remember, but this time, Luis was going too far.

Nodding once to the captive lady in a silent promise to save her from the fate Luis had earlier alluded to, Diego turned to the tent's entrance again.

After one last calming breath, which didn't work half as well as he'd hoped, Diego called out, "Luis! It's Diego. Can I speak with you?"

The lady lying at his feet jumped at the sound of his voice and struggled to free herself.

"Shh, *señora*," he whispered. "You'll only hurt yourself."

Tours was so far into the interior of France that he doubted anyone outside the band understood a word of Spanish. Maybe the tone of his voice, at least, would calm her.

"I'm just finishing supper, Diego," Luis replied, his voice muffled by whatever food he was eating. "If you're quick, we can speak now. I have big plans for the evening."

Diego nodded and took one last look at Luis's captive, then stepped into the pavilion. Luis's home away from home could have housed Diego's at least three times over. In sharp contrast to

Diego's spartan quarters, Luis had furnished his own with ornate rugs, beautiful furniture, and elaborate tapestries. Conspicuous shows of wealth were everywhere. As always, Luis's divination table drew his eye.

On a large, beautifully carved table with a blue silk tablecloth, a collection of books with embossed leather covers, dice made of lesser gemstones, and crystals the size of his thumb on beaded gold chains were meticulously laid out. Luis's self-designed system of divination involved peculiar combinations of randomly chosen numbers and a pendulum. Diego had once watched Luis weave his way through his ritual and honestly couldn't figure out how anyone could make sense of it. Once he'd arrived at a plan "given to him by fate," nothing short of divine intervention would cause him to deviate. The books, gold, gems, and crystals on the table alone were more than any five men in the band could pull together among them.

Flaming braziers warded off the chill, reminding Diego of all the nights he'd spent huddled in his cloak shivering. The sweet smell of incense hid the stench of hay and unwashed bodies that Diego had to live with. Magnificent, enameled chests held the fortunes Diego and the rest of the band had acquired for Luis, who did very little more than devise plots and give orders these days. The leader of this band of brigands acted and dressed as a nobleman, while his own brother lived like a pauper.

Just once Diego wanted a shirt that didn't need mending or shoes that not only fit but weren't worn out. Just once he wanted dishes that didn't leak hot broth on his fingers. Just once he wanted something that was not cast off by Luis as inferior. He wanted something that was his.

Luis wiped his mouth with a linen napkin. "Well, what is it?"

Diego reminded himself of the story he'd rehearsed all afternoon. "I know you're busy, so I wanted to volunteer to take the ransom demands to the woman's family."

Luis gave him a perplexed look. "Ransom demands?"

Diego nodded. "I'm a little restless tonight. The walk will do me some good, I think."

Luis smiled. "There will be no ransom demand."

Until that moment, Diego had entertained the notion that his brother might have been joking about his plans for the woman. Diego felt his cheeks flush and cursed his inability to keep his feelings out of his face.

Laughing, Luis tilted his chair back and kicked his feet up on the table. "Oh, you poor boy. Have I offended your delicate sensibilities?"

Diego glared at him. "I just hate seeing you waste your resources."

The humanitarian or moral arguments would fall on deaf ears, but appealing to Luis's greed might do the trick.

"Indeed. How so?" Luis asked.

Diego shrugged and made an effort to act nonchalant. "Look at her clothes. She wears almost as much lace and pearl as you do. Her people must have money. They'll want her back, and we can make them pay for her."

"You do have a mercenary spirit, and here I was afraid you were developing a conscience," Luis said with a nod. "There's more to this than simple wealth, though."

Diego approached and waited for his brother to continue. Luis stood and leaned on the table.

"We're a long way from home, Diego," Luis explained. "I haven't seen my wife in months and neither have the other men. We'll be leaving soon, but in the meantime, morale is low and falling fast. There will be desertions soon, and I'll need them all and the special help I've recruited from the north to succeed in this next campaign. That woman can be the answer to the problem. I'll tire of her in a day or two and give her to the men. If you want, I'll make sure you get her ahead of the others."

Diego spun away to hide his revulsion. He heard Luis's heavy footsteps come toward him.

"I know, I know. I was nervous my first time, too," Luis said, patting his shoulder. "Nature will show you what to do."

Feeling the bile rise up in his throat, Diego swallowed hard. He wanted his first carnal pleasure to be with a wife who wanted him, not with a victim who begged for mercy. Luis preferred to use things, and people, until there was nothing left of them. When Diego knew he had control of himself again, he turned to his brother.

"You're missing the point. That woman we captured is worth more to us if we ransom her. You've dealt with morale problems before without resorting to this."

Luis led the way to a small gold-inlaid table piled with jewelry. Any one of the pieces in this collection would more than sustain Diego's current lifestyle for over a year but would keep Luis in the style he was accustomed to for less than a month. It just wasn't fair. With all the hard work Diego put into pleasing his brother, he deserved so much more than he was getting.

"Look, she has already paid me," Luis said. He carefully picked up a large, heart-shaped ruby in a diamond-encrusted setting suspended on a gold chain. "Look at all this finery she was carrying. Why this heart alone is worth the sacrifice of whatever her people might pay for her."

Diego picked up a much simpler gold band etched with roses. "She belongs to another man. She's not a harlot."

Luis smiled. "All the better. I like a woman who puts up a fight. Once I've taken the spirit out of her, the men can take their turns. When she no longer amuses them—assuming she's still alive—I can still ransom her back to her family. They won't know what's happened until we've been paid. So, I'll solve the morale problem, gain her people's money, and keep all the finery she was carrying. You see, dear boy, I gain even more by keeping her around for a while."

Diego shook his head. Reasoning with Luis had been a long shot, and now that logic had failed, Diego intended to fall back on his other, riskier plan.

"Well, as long as you have it all figured out," he muttered as he made for the tent door.

"Oh, and Diego," Luis called after him.

Diego stopped and looked over his shoulder.

"Bring her to me, will you?" Luis asked.

Diego nodded. He'd take the lady somewhere all right, but it wouldn't be into this viper's nest.

Once outside again, he closed his eyes for a moment and breathed deeply until he felt steady. Dealing with Luis had unnerved him more than usual. When he was better, he looked down at the source of all this trouble.

"Tonight, Diego, if you please," Luis called from inside.

"Just a minute. I-I dropped my knife, and I need to find it," Diego replied.

After glaring at the tent for a moment, Diego knelt on one knee beside the woman. He sat her up and propped her against his leg. She was trembling, probably scared out of her wits as much as cold. With the sunset, the pleasant day had turned into a nippy evening.

"I won't hurt you, *señora*," he said softly as he carefully removed the blindfold.

Her eyes were red from crying. When he drew his knife to cut her loose, she let out a scream muffled by the gag and shook her head. If only he knew more French, maybe he could get her to calm down. His French, though, was terribly limited. The only other language he could try was his broken English learned on the last campaign.

Diego set the knife aside and showed her his empty hands then spoke in English. "I am a friend. I help you."

Recognition sparkled in her eyes.

"What's the holdup out there?" Luis asked.

Diego scowled in his brother's direction. "She fights like a lioness. You'll like her, I think."

"Well, hurry it up."

"Anticipation only makes the victory sweeter," Diego replied.

Turning his attention back to the woman, Diego picked up his knife. This time she didn't panic. At least he'd been able to get that much through to her. Once she was free of the ropes, he removed the gag while she rubbed her wrists and ankles.

She clutched his arm. "Please, you have to—"

"On the other hand," Luis called from inside, "I'll get her myself."

Diego thrust the knife back into its sheath. With his arm around her shoulders, he rose drawing her with him. When she stumbled, Diego tightened his grip on her to keep her up. She'd been trussed up like a goose since mid-afternoon, so he didn't doubt she was stiff. Her limbs might have fallen asleep, but they didn't have a lot of time to be gentle. She'd have much worse than stiff joints if they didn't move quickly.

He half-dragged, half-supported her toward the small clearing where the *burros* and Luis's horse were kept.

"Stop them!" Luis screamed from behind them.

Diego cursed but kept his course. Many of the men who weren't on raids this evening were deep in their cups already, which he'd planned for by waiting until so late in the day. He stole a look back to the camp where he saw a few men still coherent enough to react to Luis's order. They were up and running immediately, though, and closing the distance quickly.

Using his laced fingers as a stirrup, Diego helped the lady mount the horse.

"Go," Diego said, switching to his unsteady English again. "I stop them."

"No, no, they'll—" she began.

He shook his head. "Go!"

To his eternal embarrassment, he didn't know how to ride a horse, and this wasn't the time to learn. Once she was safe, he'd make his own break on foot. He was faster than any of the men approaching him and knew the terrain well, an unexpected benefit of being stuck on patrol duty so often.

"Go!" He slapped her horse on the hindquarters.

Before she could protest further, he turned away and walked toward the approaching men. Diego waited until they couldn't help but see him. On a galloping horse, she'd be well out of range of men on foot by now.

Diego smiled and waved then turned and bolted into the trees at an angle that would take them away from the retreating woman.

"After him!" Luis hollered.

"Oh, yes, follow me, please," Diego muttered.

After he'd spent several boring patrols entertaining himself in this area, he was certain his efforts would catch more than an extra deer or rabbit this time.

Putting as many trees and shrubs between him and his pursuers as he could, Diego wove a path through the forest. He grabbed the spindly branch of a fat shrub and pulled it around as he hid on the back side.

Footsteps came closer. He waited for the first one to pass then released the branch. It swung out toward its original position. The startled cry from one of the men told him he'd been successful, but he darted off in a different direction without waiting to see the result of his effort.

He watched the ground for the sign he'd left marking his next surprise. When he'd spotted the chalk mark on two tree trunks, he zigzagged around the one on the right then put himself back in the line between them. A man following him came straight between the two trees and tripped headlong over the wire, catching himself on his face.

Diego hooked a sharp left and watched for the next chalk marks. This time, he ran between the trees making sure to time his strides to miss another tripwire. The next one following him missed the wire, but the one after that released a makeshift catapult that flung pinecones and rocks.

Two more, then he'd have whittled down enough of them to make a break for it.

He approached a ravine from the least obvious angle and jumped off the edge without breaking stride. At least two of the men following him ran off the edge and found themselves in a tangled mess on the ground.

Diego scrambled up the other side to find Luis there. When Diego turned to the right Rodrigo stood there with a sword and dagger in hand. To the left, Pascual with an arquebus. Behind him, the sound of at least one other man scaling the wall of the ravine. Diego drew his sword and dagger.

Rodrigo, a younger man, rushed on ahead. Matched swords flashed in his hands. Diego had set himself to receive the charge by the time the other man arrived. Immediately, Rodrigo began the attack with a wild, undisciplined thrust. Diego simply sidestepped the blow. Turning to track the once-ally, Diego launched his strike, thrusting at Rodrigo's hip while holding one of his opponent's swords aside with his dagger. The other sword deflected Diego's attack. In the corner of his eye, Pascual aimed the arquebus. Spinning, Diego threw the dagger sidelong at the shooter. The dagger struck a nearby tree pommel-first, but the loud crack made the other man jump and ruin his aim. A deafening boom rang through the trees, but confident the shot had gone harmlessly wide, Diego turned his attention back to Rodrigo.

Too late. A thrust already flew at his face. Diego spun his sword in a circular parry, and by some God-guided miracle, his sword picked up his opponent's. A heartbeat later, the tip of the blade sliced across Diego's thigh.

Staggering back a step, Diego dropped his rapier then fell. The impact with the ground jarred every bone in his body. He rolled onto his side, clutching the new wound. The tip of a sword pushed into his neck. When he looked up, Luis towered over him, ready to open the veins.

Luis glowered. "What have you done?"

"What I had to do," Diego answered. "You still have her wealth. You lost nothing."

When Luis sheathed the sword, Diego knew he was out of danger. His brother would be unhappy about this, but that would pass. They were family, after all, so Luis wouldn't hurt him. Diego accepted that as a fact, just like he accepted the sun rising in the east and setting in the west. Then he saw the error of his foolish notion when his brother's grip on his shirt front roughly jerked him to his feet. Diego cringed with the movement as a burst of pain radiated from his leg.

"You've destroyed everything!" Luis insisted. "She knows where to find us. The militia will be here not long after first light. Maybe sooner."

Diego gritted his teeth against the pain of his injuries. "You said yourself we're leaving soon!"

"In a month, you imbecile. I have great plans in action. Plans that have required me to seek supernatural help. They won't take it kindly if the deal goes sour. Do you have any idea what the sidhe do when they feel they've been double-crossed?"

When Luis threw him back to the ground, Diego groaned loudly. He lay still and struggled to think through the gray fog in his mind.

Luis turned to those near him. "We'll have to be out of here by daybreak. I want three of you to oversee breaking camp. The rest of you will deal with our traitor. Leave him alive, but only just. I want him awake enough to know when the wolves begin gnawing on his bones."

Diego felt his stomach sink. "No, Luis, please. I'm your brother."

By way of an answer, Luis spun on his heel and strode away.

"Luis, please!" Diego pleaded, reaching after his brother. "Luis!"

The only answer he received was a vicious kick to the side of his head.

Chapter 3

Yvret felt something push lightly on his arm.

"Yvret, wake up!" a small voice said.

He knew the speaker somehow, but he couldn't place the voice. Anyway, he didn't want to get up. He ached all over. Couldn't the realm run itself for a little while so he could rest until he felt well enough to deal with his duties? The weariness of his body demanded he sleep.

"Please, Yvret, wake up," the voice begged. "We're not safe here, and I don't want to leave you alone while I go get someone to carry you."

This time, he heard the fear there and the waver of barely contained tears. With something that desperately wrong, he needed to get to work on the matter immediately. His own personal comforts would keep. Forcing his eyes to open, he saw Sarah standing next to his shoulder. The little sprite flexed her glittering wings and smiled.

"Hi!" she exclaimed. "You're okay!"

He sat up, feeling the complaints of muscles insisting on a different course of action. A sidhe Great Prince lay in a heap nearby. Yvret nearly jumped out of his skin as the memories came back to him. After teleporting back to the gate, following a visit with one of his students, Yvret had heard a cry. He had left the ring and walked only a few steps in that direction when a weighted net had dropped out of a tree. While he had struggled to free himself, at least enough to attempt another teleport again, men had come out of hiding and pinned him. One had struck him on the head, leaving him far too dazed to put up a fight. They had given him to a sidhe, that one lying on the ground, and the real torment had begun.

Sarah glanced back at the sidhe. "It's okay. He's dead."

Yvret nodded. "The woman. Where's the woman?"

The sprite pointed. "Right there. I made her sleep so she wouldn't be scared of me."

More likely, the sprite had been afraid of the human, but he let that pass. Semantics really didn't matter in the end. Yvret followed Sarah's hand and found the woman who'd saved his life. As Sarah had promised, she lay sleeping a short distance away.

"How did you compel her to sleep?" he asked. "The prince wove an effect on the whole area to prevent any further energy molding."

Sarah shrugged. "Must've worn off when he keeled over. I've been molding all kinds of effects. I made the human sleep. Then I healed you. And I fixed your clothes. And I cleaned all the blood off of hers."

He nodded and looked himself over. There wasn't even the slightest mark from any of his wounds. "Thank you. You did well."

"Thanks!" She beamed a huge smile.

Grimacing with the stiffness in his limbs, Yvret picked up the cloak piled next to him and rose to check on the human. He tucked her cloak around her. For his sake, she'd given up what little protection from the cold the worn, thin cloth gave her. He remembered somewhat dimly how she'd rushed into the clearing and challenged the Prince, undaunted by the fear Yvret had seen in her eyes. The ridiculous mismatch of opponents would have been funny if his life, and hers for that matter, hadn't been riding on her success.

"Do you think she's gifted?"

Yvret looked over his shoulder at the tiny sprite hovering nearby. "Why do you think she's gifted?"

Like an extra-large butterfly, Sarah fluttered to the sleeping woman near them. "I dunno. Except maybe that she had to be following the signs. How else would she have found you?"

"I—"

He stopped when the words choked in his throat. He'd be sore for days, but Sarah's healing efforts had taken care of his wounds and mended his clothes again. He wished someone could weave an effect to take away his memories of being tortured.

The elflord sighed and looked at the fire. "She probably followed the sound of..." His voice trailed off, and he found that his words had failed him.

Sarah perched on his shoulder. "It hurt you a lot. I can tell from the wounds. You must've screamed, and she followed those sounds. Oh, Yvret, I'm sorry. I should've known something awful had happened when you weren't home on time. I should've gone looking for you sooner. I could've helped you or gotten Kendall or someone else to help you."

Closing his eyes to shut out the pain, Yvret nodded. It took a few moments to drive back his memories of being helplessly bound to the tree while the hideous, dark creature sliced him with its claws and burned him with flaming sticks.

"Don't blame yourself, Sarah. I could've been late for hundreds of perfectly safe reasons. You came as fast as you could. I know that." He looked down at the sleeping woman who'd saved his life. "If she hadn't come along, I'd be dead."

"That's why I think she's gifted," Sarah insisted. "Look at how her hand shakes. Before I transformed, my hand did that too."

Yvret shook his head. "It's cold out here, and that cloak of hers is so worn out I could read a book through it. When I feel stronger, I'll fix it for her."

Sarah set to work braiding the woman's hair. "Now will you start carrying a sword with you when you go out? Kendall can teach you how to use it. He's really good."

He frowned. "Don't start."

"And what if there isn't a brave human around to save you next time?" Sarah asked. "This isn't the first time the sidhe have tried to capture you."

Why did she have to harp on him about this so often? The sprite's job was to advise him on medicine, not security. She knew what he thought about weapons and how much he knew about their use. He'd been a scholar in his previous life and a craftsman, leader, and teacher since his transformation. Weapons felt wrong in his hands.

"Then maybe I've lived long enough and it's time to pass the reign to the next Lord or Lady of the fey." He arched his back and grimaced against the stiffness. "I've been on the throne for over two millennia. There are other elves who can lead the Seelie Court just as well, maybe better, than I can."

"I don't want to lose you!" she cried. Her body heaving with great sobs, Sarah flopped down on a rock and hid her face in her hands.

Yvret shook his head and offered her his hand to step onto. Hesitatingly, she stood on his palm and steadied herself by holding onto his thumb as he brought her up to eye level.

"It's not yet my time, dear. You still think too much in the present. Everything happens for a reason. I believe this human and I will cross paths again. This wasn't a chance occurrence."

Sarah stomped her little foot. "What a wretched way to be introduced!"

Remembering when she wasn't so passionate and delicate brought a smile to his face. Her metamorphosis had changed more than her appearance.

"Isn't it, though?" He glanced around the clearing. "Let's get out of sight, then you can dispel the sleep effect to wake her up. We'll follow her home in case she runs afoul of the sidhe."

His sore muscles protested the movement. Once they were safely behind the trunk of a huge tree, Sarah traced a symbol in the air with her hands. The human opened her eyes and sat up. She looked all around the little clearing and took a couple minutes checking behind and around things.

"She knows we're here," Sarah whispered.

Yvret shook his head. "I doubt it. I was disoriented for a moment, too."

"I still think she's gifted."

Possible, he supposed, but there would be time for speculation later. Right now, he had a chance to learn so much about the woman by observing her. After finding her knife and returning it to its sheath, she put out the sidhe's fire with dirt and the contents of a waterskin from her belt. Then she stirred the mud with a stick and added more dirt for good measure. Yvret was pleased to see her take care to protect the forest. He couldn't count how many forest fires he'd put out over the years because some human had left his campfire to burn itself out.

Any fears he might have had about driving his stiff body to keep up with her vanished as soon as she got moving. Giving the sidhe corpse a wide berth, the woman held her cloak closed around her and walked so slowly that Yvret had to remind himself to stay back to keep her from hearing him.

She walked with her head bowed, which he thought at first was a prudent way to help keep her footing. Then he heard her sniffle and saw her brush her eyes with the edge of her cloak. What was bringing her to tears? If they'd had a language in common, he'd ask, but she didn't speak Greek or fey, and he certainly didn't know English. After his transformation, he'd tried many times to learn new languages without success. Except for muses, fey had a painfully difficult time learning other ways to communicate. He'd given up fifteen hundred years ago. He should've taken advantage of the time when she slept and granted her the ability to speak fey. There was nothing to do about it now, but it saddened him to see his benefactress so distraught. Maybe the stress of the afternoon's ordeal had caught up with her. Facing down a sidhe, a Great Prince at that, was probably not a daily occurrence for her.

At one point, she stopped to gather a bundle of sticks before continuing on. Soon after, she left the forest and made for a small rock cottage some twenty or thirty paces away. She hesitated at the door for a moment before going in.

"You'd think she didn't want to go home or something," Sarah mused.

Yvret looked at her hovering over his shoulder. "That did seem a little strange, but she's had a rough day. I'll come back to check on her in a day or two to make sure she's all right."

Sarah nodded. "Let's get you home. You need to rest and finish healing."

"Yes, doctor." He smiled.

They'd barely gotten a few steps when a loud crash and a deep male voice, yelling, came from the cottage. A female voice responded. Yvret turned to go up to the house. Now may be his turn to defend her from an attacker. Sarah flew in front of him and blocked his path.

"No. You're still hurt," she insisted.

When he stepped aside to dodge around her, she kept getting in his way. "Move, Sarah."

"No! I mean it!" she said more emphatically. "I'll go weave a sleep effect on them. Then it'll be safe."

Gritting his teeth, Yvret considered pushing her out of the way, but stopped himself and shook his head. She was right. Until he'd had a chance to rest, anything useful in a fight would take too much out of him.

"Go," he ordered.

Yvret hid behind the trunk of a tree as Sarah crossed the open space between the forest and the cottage and listened to the voices and crashes coming from inside. Had the woman expected this harsh reception? That would certainly explain why she'd been in no hurry to get home. Her reluctance also meant this sort of thing wasn't foreign to her.

Sarah was nearly to the cottage when the door burst open and slammed against the wall. Yvret gasped, reaching a hand toward his friend as if he could pull her back to safety from where he stood. The tiny sprite fluttered out in the open in direct sight of the door. He might be able to get an invisibility effect made in time. In his current state, the effort would leave him exhausted, but he'd rather not see Sarah hurt.

There wasn't time. A huge man in a kilt stormed out. Yvret watched Sarah dive for the ground and fold her blue and silver butterfly wings closed, angling herself to present them edge on. If she were lucky, she might be mistaken for a stick. Even though Yvret had seen where she went down, he'd lost track of her. That boosted his confidence. If he didn't see her with his keen eyesight, the man in the kilt would never find her.

For his part, Yvret stayed perfectly still as well until the angry human's stomping and growling could no longer be heard. The elflord breathed a sigh of relief when movement near the cottage caught his eye. Sarah's little wings flexed, glinting light off the silver in them, and she took flight. He watched her fly to the little house and look in the window.

"Yvret! Yvret, c'mere!" Sarah called. "She's hurt!"

At least he hadn't sent Sarah home. The healing skills sprites specialized in would be helpful, provided no steel was involved. He made his way to join her as quickly as he could.

Stopping in the doorway, Yvret looked around, wide-eyed. Pieces of what could have been a table and chairs were scattered around the room along with cookpots, shards of pottery, and metal utensils. Blood ran down the woman's face from a cut on her cheek as she struggled to her feet in the far corner of the room.

"Keep an eye out on all those pots," Sarah warned. "We need to find somewhere for her to lie down. After I heal her, she'll have to rest and so will you."

That was going to be difficult, Yvret thought. Too much junk littered the floor in the little one-room shack.

"Bring her to the bed if you can," Sarah suggested.

Yvret nodded and picked a path through the debris, keeping his arms stretched to the sides to improve his balance.

The woman looked up at him, but her eyes didn't seem to focus. She reached a trembling hand toward him, then quickly pulled away again and covered her ear.

"Sarah, you know English, don't you?" Yvret asked.

"A really old kind," she replied. "Do you think she'll understand?"

He nodded. "There's only one way to find out."

The sprite spoke in a language Yvret could make no sense of. When the human responded, her stuttered, slurred speech rendered her words incomprehensible.

Sarah frowned. "I think she understood me, but I can't make anything out of her words."

Yvret slipped when something under his foot shifted. When he put a hand down on the floor to keep himself from sprawling on the debris, he came within an inch of an iron fireplace poker.

"Careful!" Sarah warned, pulling uselessly on the back of his shirt.

She'd never be able to lift his weight, but he appreciated her concern.

After he was back on his feet again, he crossed the remaining distance to the woman. He wrapped his arm around the lady's shoulders to guide her to the bed, thankfully only a few feet away. She fell on the first step, but he managed to catch her. Wincing with the objections of his still-healing body, Yvret picked her up and carried her to the bed.

Sarah joined them. "You're going to hurt yourself again."

He shook his head and covered the woman with a quilt lying in a pile at the foot of the bed. "She's just a little wisp of a creature."

"Uh-huh, and you're still hurt," Sarah scolded.

Sarah landed next to the lady's cheek and spoke to her, but even before Sarah had finished talking, the human's shaking got worse. Her eyes rolled back into her head, and her arms and legs jerked repetitively in coordinated motions. He knew far too much about this worst kind of seizure. Before his transformation, he'd experienced these fits, too.

As Sarah took to the wing to get out of harm's way, Yvret cursed and suppressed his initial instinct to pin the woman down. In all likelihood, he'd hurt them both. The very last time he'd fallen prey to one of these things, someone had restrained him. Only fey skills had properly healed his wrenched shoulder again when the mental storm had passed.

He looked up at the sprite, now perched on the headboard. "Can you put a stop to these things?"

She shook her head. "No, I'm-I'm-I'm sorry. I wish I could."

"It's all right. It'll pass," he said gently. "Mine always did."

"You used to have this kind?" she asked.

"Yes, dear," he replied. "I had them a couple times a week."

Sarah flew over and landed on his shoulder, then pressed against the side of his face in a sprite-hug. "Oh, how terrible! And I thought my hands shaking was bad."

"No seizures are easy to deal with." He glanced up at her. "They all cause their own problems."

The woman's convulsions gradually slowed then stopped altogether. Yvret found a kerchief in a small, overturned chest and used it to wipe the drool off of her face and the blood from her cheek while Sarah drew a glittering healing effect above her patient. The wounds caused by the man in the kilt faded.

Sitting on the pillow, Sarah braided the woman's hair. "Now what?"

"I'm going to stay here until she wakes up in case she has another seizure," Yvret answered.

With her hands on her hips, Sarah flew up and hovered in front of his face. "No. I'll stay. You need to rest. All my hard work will undo itself if you don't, and then what kind of a sorry mess will you be in?"

He frowned. She was right, but he couldn't bring himself to leave. Once morning came and he knew the little human would be safe, then he could go. Until then, he felt somehow responsible for her care. If she hadn't stopped to help him, if Sarah hadn't put her to sleep for a while, the fight that had injured her and the seizure that had followed might not have happened.

"Well, this bed is big enough for two people," he noticed. "I'll sleep here above the covers so no one gets any wrong ideas."

Under Sarah's watchful eye, Yvret climbed into the bed. He grabbed the worn out cloak from a peg near the end of the bed and covered himself with it, then nestled into the pillow. The sprite kissed his cheek.

"I told you she was gifted," she reminded him.

Yvret nodded. "So you did."

"You'll teach her, won't you?"

"If she'll let me."

Sarah fluttered over to the lady and looked down at her face. "What kind of fey do you think she'll transform into?"

Yvret shrugged and closed his eyes. "That depends on her."

***

Ismael sat on a tree branch, watching another beautiful sunset. He never got tired of seeing these. He needed a peaceful evening after a long day of seeing patients and helping humans who wouldn't even know he'd been there. When light from the Seelie gate overhead marred the perfection of the sunset, he looked up to see who it was.

A unicorn slowly floated down to the ground, prancing from hoof to hoof with impatience. As soon as the horned horse touched down, she looked all around.

Trying to make himself even smaller than he already was, Ismael hid behind some leaves. Whatever the matter was, he didn't need to be involved in any unicorn shenanigans today.

When waves of mental energy washed over him, he knew his solitude would be shattered. Eyes he could hide from. Thoughts, especially the strong ones of unicorns, were a whole other matter. Worse, the unicorn ran toward him at a full gallop and skidded to a stop below the tree.

"Hi. I'm Tiffany. You're a sprite, aren't you?" the unicorn's thoughts echoed in his head.

"Either that, or there's a really angry, red and gold butterfly hunting for his wings," Ismael replied.

You took a butterfly's wings?

He sighed. How could they be so stupid? "No, I'm a sprite."

"Oh, good. You have to help me or him or both of us," Tiffany went on. *"There was this woman and a boy. And he made her get on a horse and ride away. But he had to throw a knife. And then it got worse, and he really needs your help!"*

So like unicorns to be totally scatterbrained. How could they find their own stables at night?

"Try that again, more slowly this time," Ismael suggested.

There isn't time! She stamped her hoof. *Just come with me and you'll see when we get there.*

"I don't have time for your games."

The last time he'd honored a request like this from a unicorn, the "help" the mysterious person so desperately needed was someone to play hide and seek.

HE'S HURT! Tiffany thought loud enough to make his head ring.

Ismael's hand went to his temple as he blinked hard. "Ow. Not so loud!"

Sorry, but you have to come with me. He's hurt really bad, and I don't have any healing skills.

Staring hard at the unicorn, he struggled to put all these puzzle pieces together. The rumor mill had it that Yvret was insanely late getting back from some errand in the human world. Sarah had gone off to hunt for him. Was Yvret the "he" Tiffany referred to?

"Who's hurt? What's going on? Slowly, and in complete sentences if you don't mind."

I saw a bunch of mean guys catch her, so I stayed invisible to follow and see what they were going to do. Then later he helped her escape. He made her get on a horse and ride away and made them chase him instead. Someone aimed one of those iron ball shooter things at him, he threw a knife and made the mean guy miss, but then he got hurt on his leg and fell. All the mean guys beat him up because he made her go be safe, Tiffany explained.

That didn't sound much like Yvret, but even in the last century, Ismael could remember the fey lord doing all manner of bizarre things when no other options were left to him. There was only one way to find out.

"Take me there." Ismael flew to the unicorn's head and perched between her ears.

She whinnied and shook her head, and Ismael had to hold on to fistfuls of mane to keep from being dislodged.

"Stop that," he scolded.

But that tickles! she insisted.

Shaking his head, he alighted on the horn. "Better?"

Better.

How anyone put up with unicorns was beyond him. With him clinging for dear life, the creature ran back to the area just below the gate. Slowly, evenly, they rose through the ring of clouds. After a second or two, when Ismael was certain he would suffocate, they appeared in a ring of mushrooms in a dense forest.

Can I just teleport to him? Tiffany asked.

"Please," he replied.

Anything would be better than another wild ride.

The horn glowed brightly, half-blinding him before he got his eyes closed and covered. When the glow faded and he opened them again, he blinked to do away with the afterimages.

There he is. See?

Ismael took to wing and looked around. Lying close to the ravine, he found the cause of all this commotion, and it definitely wasn't Yvret. The injured young man was human. Blood came from several wounds. An arm bent in a completely atypical location gave him the appearance of having an extra joint. An eye too swollen to see through disfigured his face.

Tiffany nudged the human's arm with her muzzle, nearly impaling him on her horn.

"Be careful!" Ismael warned.

See? The mean guys did this to him a lot when he made her go be safe, Tiffany said. *I wanted to be good and help him, but there were too many mean guys, and I was scared.*

"I know," Ismael said. "I wish you'd gone for help faster. You might have spared him a beating. Oh never mind. There's nothing for it now."

Can you fix him?

He nodded. "Unless they used iron on him."

As the human's only working eye drifted closed, Ismael thought he heard the kid say something, but the meaning was lost.

When the sprite wove the best healing effect he had available, the symbol sank into the boy's chest, and Ismael watched the effect do its work with renewed amazement. The broken arm set itself. The horrible-looking bruises faded, and the swelling went down as the damaged eye returned to normal. Even all the cuts went away, except for an ugly one on the leg.

Cursing, Ismael went to check on it. The wound had straight, clean edges. It had certainly come from a blade, and if other humans had done this to him, the knife or sword was almost certainly made from an iron alloy.

You missed one, Tiffany said.

"I can't do anything with that one."

Fire metal made it, huh?

Ismael nodded. "Fire metal, sure."

I knew it! I knew it! I knew it!

"Yeah, congratulations," he said dully.

That wound could be the death of the boy. Faerie skills wouldn't do a thing for it, and even if the human woke up, getting all the way into town with that wound would be impossible, if the blood loss didn't kill him first. Wrapping the wound wouldn't be any good either, even if he had the supplies he needed to do it. More likely than not, the injury would go gangrenous, and that would kill him. One way or another, the boy was dead. Well, annoying as it was, Ismael had done his best, and if he got back to the Seelie Court soon, maybe he could catch the end of that sunset.

Can I stay with him until he's all better? Please? Can I? Tiffany asked.

"If you want to," he answered, just as happy to have a reason to get away from the irksome thing. "If you see any sidhe, you'd better teleport, though, even if you have to leave him here. Understand?"

That's what I always do.

Ismael flew away and was almost out of the clearing when he heard Tiffany's thoughts again.

Hey, it's getting cold. Can I cover him up?

"Um, sure," he replied. "Why not?"

Keeping warm was the least of the human's troubles, but that wouldn't hurt him, either. Then, before the unicorn could ask any more inane questions, Ismael left for the ring as fast as his wings would carry him.

***

Michel shifted in his saddle. Last night, when he'd gotten home and found Corinne gone, he'd assumed the Duchess had kept his wife late for some project. Hours later, he'd gone out to investigate the fast-approaching hoofbeats he'd heard and saw Corinne riding bareback on an unfamiliar horse. Her dress was torn and dirty, and she had scores of scratches and light cuts. Her wrists and ankles were raw from rope burns. Several seconds had passed while his mind assembled what his eyes took in. Then he'd rushed to her side to help her.

In the study, he'd held her in his arms, waiting for the physician and listening to the horrific tale of her afternoon. Bandits, the same ones who had been running amuck in Tours for several months now, had stopped her on the road and forced her to accompany them back to their camp. He didn't need much imagination to figure out what the bandit's leader had intended to do to Corinne.

The thought of his wife's torment had kept him awake as he imagined the screams that would have shattered the still night if those base men had forced their way with her. He should have been there to protect her. Instead, he'd been at home enjoying his pipe and some cognac while his best reason for living lay helplessly bound on the forest floor. Why hadn't he known she needed his help? When he got home and found her gone, he should have mounted a search immediately or at least confirmed she had business with Her Grace. Intellectually, he knew he'd made all the logical choices he should have, but in his heart, he felt personally responsible for the near tragedy.

Corinne had been lucky last night, and Michel didn't dare push luck any further. No longer would he allow Corinne to walk or ride the mile to Tours without an escort. The boy who had given his life to help her escape had Michel's eternal gratitude. He made a mental note to have a Mass said in the boy's honor.

He'd been determined to stop the brigands before, but no longer would he delegate the task to someone else. Michel would personally see to the investigation and neither heaven nor hell would throw him off until he saw every one of those blasted Spaniards hanging from the gallows. As captain of His Grace's guard, he would allocate whatever resources would be needed until he could be certain his wife and all the people of Tours would be safe from those foul thieves and cutthroats.

Now, an hour before dawn, Michel led fifty of his best men to capture the scoundrels who'd planned to do unspeakable things to his wife. Their leader was a shrewd man who kept their base camp too well hidden. None of Michel's patrols had been able to find it, or at least the ones who did were found dead outside the Tours gate the next morning. If anything good had come from Corinne's capture and escape, it was only that she'd left a path of hoof prints and broken twigs Michel could have followed blindfolded.

When the trail ended, Michel found himself in a manufactured clearing of low tree stumps. The trails of trampled ground and obvious patches of bare dirt and dead plants showed where the tents had been. Some of the rings of stones that had once contained fires for cooking and keeping warm still smoldered. Litter dotted the area. The campground had been hastily abandoned in the night. If only he'd been sooner! He still had some vain hope that there would be something here to lead them to the new campground. Hopefully, the thieves had been in too big of a hurry to thoroughly cover their trail this time.

Michel signaled to his men to fan out and look for anything useful. He'd promised Corinne that those responsible for her rough treatment would be found and brought to justice, and he had no intention of letting her down. Something had to be here.

Recalling Corinne's description of the camp, Michel went to look around the place where the bandit leader's tent had stood. Once he'd dismounted, he sought for a useful sign. Nothing. The only things he found were some scraps of red-stained rope near a hole left by a tent stake. Michel's blood ran cold as he remembered the raw, oozing wounds on Corinne's wrists.

"Captain! Captain Gaultier!" Philippe called.

Regaining his composure, Michel turned toward the sound of his lieutenant's voice and found the man some twenty paces from where they'd all entered the clearing. Leading his horse by the reins, Michel walked swiftly to where Philippe waited.

"What is it, Lieutenant?" he called.

Philippe crouched and pointed to trampled plants and recently broken twigs in a direction away from Corinne's path. "Several people ran through here. On foot, it seems."

Michel studied the ground and found a boot print in the dirt. "There. They ran this way."

He let Philippe, the better tracker, take the lead as they followed the signs past a rather robust shrub then a sharp turn. Onward to a couple trees, each with a chalk line, and a thin, but sturdy cord between them.

Philippe glanced back and smiled. "I think your wife's benefactor may have been a bit of a trickster."

Could he have possibly gotten away?

Another couple chalk-marked trees with a cord between them were near a spindly sapling with a lightweight net in the branches.

The trail ended at a ravine.

Hoofbeats pounded the ground on the far side. Michel squinted into the distance. A flash of glitter caught his eye.

"A unicorn?" Michel's hand dropped to his rapier hilt.

"I didn't see anything." Philippe shook his head. "Do you think fey helped Corinne?"

He scowled. "All at once, I'm glad someone helped her, and hope it wasn't fey. They may want something I can't give them in return. Let's see if the trail picks up again over there."

In this area, fey and sidhe activity were both higher than anywhere else in France, which only made his job more interesting. Sidhe were universally violent-tempered and dangerous by all accounts, but fey were a mixed bunch. Some of them almost seemed helpful. Too helpful. No one gave that freely without expecting some payment. Popular lore was littered with dozens of ways to try to curry favor of the fey or at least ward off their potential harms.

Michel crouched on the edge of the ravine then found a foothold halfway down. Philippe jumped and landed at the bottom, but his boot slid and he fell on his butt.

"That's why I didn't jump." Michel smirked. "You all right?"

"Yes, fine." Philippe picked himself up and dusted himself off. "Except maybe my pride."

Michel crossed to the other side and reached for a handhold. He reached the surface and turned to give his lieutenant a hand up.

A rough pile of small tree branches and dead leaves a few feet away were obviously not naturally occurring.

Philippe lifted away one of the small pine branches, revealing the face of a young man. Michel would have placed him at about twenty years old, perhaps younger, and his features exactly matched Corinne's description.

Chapter 4

Michel's breath caught in his throat. They'd found him! This had to be the boy who'd helped Corinne last night. After pulling his glove off, Michel held a hand over the boy's mouth and nose and felt the slow breaths on his palm.

"The fey had pity on him," Michel suggested.

"Then covered him to keep him warm?" Philippe guessed. "It turned out to be a cool night."

Michel nodded. "That or hide him from those who had hurt him."

He and Philippe cleared the debris burying the boy. His clothes were a tattered, stained mess. Blood matted his hair, but when Michel looked for the wound, nothing accounted for it. Other bloody or torn parts of the kid's shirt and pants showed the same lack of corresponding injury. The only thing Michel could find wrong with the boy was a long cut across one thigh. Michel whistled appreciatively.

"Fey," Philippe confirmed. "Had to have been. They must have known the sacrifice he'd made and stopped to help him."

"But at what cost to him?"

"Or perhaps he did them some favor before last night."

"Maybe." Michel pointed to the cut. "Steel stops them every time."

"I'm amazed the bandits left him alive," Philippe said.

"Actually, Corinne says he was the leader's brother. Blood is thicker than water, you know," Michel reminded him.

His lieutenant shook his head. "We're not exactly talking about moral, upstanding citizens here. I mean, I wouldn't let anyone do this to my brother and you know what kind of man he is."

"More likely then, they expected his wounds to kill him, but the unicorn came along before that happened," Michel concluded.

"Or in some perverse sense of amusement, they left him alive on purpose to make him suffer for helping your wife escape," Philippe suggested.

"I suppose it doesn't matter now. I'll get my horse and take him home to have a surgeon tend his leg. Once I've left, continue the search. Those brigands were in too big of a hurry to cover their tracks all that well. I want them found and brought in."

"Yes, Captain."

Michel rose and took a few steps toward the ravine then stopped. "Oh, and Lieutenant."

Philippe looked up. "Yes, sir?"

"Watch yourself," he warned. "This is an awfully slippery bunch we're after, and they know we're coming for them. I don't want to wake up tomorrow and find your body outside the Tours gate."

Frowning, Philippe replied, "They may still be around this area. Maybe you should take a few men with you as escort."

Michel shook his head. "No. I want them all with you. If all goes well and you find their new base camp, you'll need every one of them. I'll be fine."

"Are you sure?" Philippe asked. "I don't want to find your corpse either."

"I'll be fine," he repeated. "If there was an ambush set up between here and home, they would have sprung it on us when we passed the first time."

He headed back toward the remnants of the camp.

***

Erin rested in the twilight between wakefulness and sleep, where she was aware of sounds, but couldn't quite place them. She wanted to vanquish the unnerving sensation so she could go back to her dreams. Her head throbbed and even muscles she had forgotten about ached. What could she have possibly done to feel this bad? If she could just doze off again, everything would be better when she woke up.

Erin rolled over and clutched the blanket closer around her to ward off the slight chill. Someone nearby whispered, but she dismissed the sounds. The voices probably belonged to her husband or her cousin. She didn't feel Connor's weight in the bed with her, and Ian often dropped by to visit. The whispers had to be one of them. More annoying than that, though, was the group of kids outside laughing. Couldn't they play somewhere besides just outside her window?

She'd nearly drifted back to her dreams when something pressed against her chest, and a warm rush flowed through her. Erin's eyes snapped open and dimly saw a figure standing over her. Recoiling, she pushed away the hand touching her.

"Shh, don't panic. You're all right," the man in front of her said softly.

"It's okay. You're safe," a small, almost squeaky voice behind her added. "The man who hurt you, he's not here now. He went away toward town."

Erin spun to see a huge butterfly floating in the air, then scrambled to the foot of the bed where she could keep both intruders in view.

"Who are you?" she demanded. "What are you doing here?" She didn't recognize her own voice, as if she heard herself using words she couldn't possibly know.

"My name is Yvret, and this is Sarah," the man said. "Don't be afraid, my child, we won't hurt you."

After blinking several times to help clear her vision, Erin saw a little sprite she'd mistaken for a butterfly and an elf with piercing violet eyes. Could he be the same one? He had to be. She'd helped him in the forest. Was it yesterday or the day before when all that happened? In any case, he looked much better. Though she had no idea why he should be in her house now, she knew she'd be in no danger from him.

Willing her tense muscles to relax, Erin sat more comfortably on the bed. "How is it I understand you now? Yesterday—it was yesterday, wasn't it?"

"It was," Sarah chimed in.

"We were reduced to a sorry game of charades."

"I used an ability of mine to gift you with the understanding of our language. I'm afraid that's what woke you up." Yvret winced. "I apologize. I thought you were sleeping more soundly. You had a very difficult night. Why don't you lie down again?"

She let him guide her back to bed and tuck her in under the quilt. "I've had a bout with the falling sickness. Haven't I?"

Honestly, she couldn't remember much of last night. Erin remembered waking up in the forest and going home to face the beating she knew she had coming. Her recollection of events afterward became a little fuzzy. Connor had flown into another of his rages, no doubt.

He nodded and gently patted her shoulder. "A bad one, I'm afraid. Sarah healed the cut on your face, and we decided to stay with you until you awoke."

Erin looked away from them and blinked back the tears in her eyes. Why did this have to happen to her? Didn't she have enough other things in her life to deal with?

"You're very kind," she whispered. "It wasn't necessary."

Someday, they'd want some kind of payment for their kindness, and she hoped it wasn't too great a toll. No one she'd ever dealt with had given without demanding something in return.

Sarah hovered above Erin's chest. "No, we didn't have to but after you took such good care of Yvret, I didn't want to leave you alone. I never had the falling sickness that bad, but he tells me it's just awful! And you wake up feeling worse!" She frowned. "Um, how are you feeling?"

"I'll be fine," Erin replied.

She would, but not until later today or maybe even tomorrow. Until then, there was weakness, confusion, dizziness, and a dull headache to contend with. Still, she hadn't lied. She just didn't want to complain about anything. They'd gone out of their way to help her, and she didn't want to do anything to aggravate them. Lamenting her current state would not only show ingratitude but also paint her as a weak person. Maybe she was. Connor always told her so, and Ian often agreed.

"You're very brave." Yvret smiled. "But I know what it's like, and you don't have to pretend to feel better than you do."

She won the battle with her tears and looked up at him. How would he know what it was like to feel his own mind slipping away while his body refused to do even the simplest thing he told it?

"There's a way to make the falling sickness go aw—" Sarah began.

Yvret shook his head. "No, not now. She needs to rest."

Erin scowled. If there was a way to make those debilitating seizures stop, she wanted to hear about it. Anything to avoid another one. "I'd really rather know now if you don't mind."

By way of an answer, he made a strange gesture with his fingers. "Later." He rested his hand lightly on her forehead. "There will be plenty of time later."

Her eyes drifted closed. No! She didn't want to sleep. What had the little fey meant? How could she make the falling sickness stop?

"Rest," Yvret cooed. "I'll still be here when you wake up."

In spite of her best efforts, she soon drifted away.

When she awoke again sometime later, the sunlight streaming through the window told her it was afternoon. A cheerful fire crackled in the fireplace, and whatever was cooking in the pot smelled wonderful. The house was no longer a disaster. Everything had been returned to its proper place, even the metal things. Seated at the now repaired table was Yvret with Sarah sitting on an upside-down teacup, also a former victim of Connor's wrath. All the house's furnishings looked as if nothing had happened.

"There she is!" Sarah exclaimed.

The sprite flew to the bed and hovered above her.

Yvret joined them and smiled. "Hello, Erin. Are you feeling better?"

"Certainly better than earlier," she replied.

The nap really had done wonders, but Erin didn't appreciate being pushed into it. How like a man to take away her choices and control her actions, making decisions as if she were incapable of deciding anything for her own good. If she wanted to stay awake, he should have honored her wishes. What made him think he had the right to make her do what he wanted?

"You'll feel right as rain by tomorrow." Yvret waved her over to the table. "Join us. You should eat something. I've made some soup to help you recover your strength after one of those fits. I'll teach you the recipe later for the next time this happens."

Without even asking what she wanted, his strong arm under her shoulder helped her sit up. She wasn't in the mood to fight him and didn't have the strength for it anyway, so she let herself be led to the table. As weak and sore as her body was, Erin found herself grateful for his steadying arm in spite of her foul mood. The sprite went on ahead of them and sat on the overturned teacup again. After Erin half-fell into a chair, Yvret brought her a steaming bowl of soup and a metal spoon, covered by a heavy linen cloth to protect his hand.

"Careful, it's hot," he warned.

Of course it was hot! It had just come off the fire, and she could see the steam rising from the bowl. Did he want to blow on each spoonful for her? Her brain may not be moving at full speed again, but she wasn't that dense. Erin closed her eyes for a moment.

Stop being such a grouch. They're just trying to be nice. She blinked hard and opened her eyes. "Thank you for fixing it."

He smiled and sat across from her. "I know what it's like. I used to have the falling sickness."

She blew on a spoonful of soup and swallowed it quickly when she found the broth hotter than she'd expected. The odd broth was salty and had a flavor unlike anything else she'd ever had before.

"You used to have it?" Erin loaded the spoon again. "It doesn't bother you now?"

"Nope. Doesn't bug me now, either." Sarah leaned closer. "Not that I ever had the kind you have."

Erin thought back to earlier. "You spoke of a way to stop the sickness altogether. How does it work?"

"Well, ya see, you—" Sarah began.

Yvret held up a hand to stop her. "Do you know where fey and sidhe come from, Erin?"

She shrugged and ate more soup while she thought about it. "No, but I wonder if God didn't make them when He made the rest of the world."

The elf smiled at her the same way an adult sometimes smiled at a child who'd said something cute but wrong.

Erin scowled.

"Well, after a manner of speaking, I suppose that's as true as any other explanation." Yvret shrugged. "God did create the gifted and the normal people."

Maybe it was still an aftereffect of the seizure, but this wasn't making any sense to her at all.

"I don't follow. Be clear if you can. What is this 'gifted?' Who are they?" she asked.

"Fey and sidhe call people with the falling sickness 'gifted.' Like you." Sarah pointed at her.

Erin set her spoon down. "You're pulling my leg."

Yvret shook his head. "Not at all."

She resumed eating. "How can seizures like this be anything short of a horrendous curse?"

Yvret leaned over the table. "My dear child, over 2000 years ago in Greece, I was as you are."

She snorted. "Even if I believed you could be that old, Yvret is hardly a Greek name, now is it? I know my classics. Father saw to that before he died."

Aggravation darkened Yvret's face. "The name I was born with takes over fifty letters in the fey alphabet to spell. Do you have any idea how annoying it is to write so many letters for just your first name? 'Yvret' is the name of the man who helped me with my transformation. When he was murdered by a human, I honored him by taking his name."

Looking into his eyes was impossible. He'd been so kind to her, and she'd repaid him with curt answers and suspicion.

"I'm sorry," she whispered. "I have no call to speak to you as I did. I should be more civil to my guests."

The elflord sighed and shook his head. "I was at least as suspicious as you when my mentor first gave me this news."

An uncomfortable silence followed until Erin couldn't take it anymore. "You spoke of a transformation."

"Yes. How do I explain the gifted clearly?" Yvret looked past her to the corner of the room. "The gifted have innate abilities. Your mind can use them and sometimes it instinctively tries to, but your body doesn't know how to handle the energy. That lack of balance causes the seizures. If you learn to harness those forces, you will transform into some type of faerie, either fey or sidhe. You will be balanced again, and those seizures will no longer plague you."

"Neat, huh?" Sarah twirled midair. "It was the best, and I didn't even have the kind of seizures you two do...uh...did...er...whatever."

"I can teach you," Yvret offered.

Erin shook her head. "I don't think God would be pleased I'm learning magic, no matter what the purpose."

Sarah rolled her eyes. "Magic?" She snorted. "It's not magic. Do you call it magic when birds fly? Or when fish stay underwater for their whole lives? How about when you find an elaborate spider web? Did the spider cast a spell to make that happen? Even what your kind calls 'witchcraft' isn't magic. Not really. Most of the time, people accused of witchcraft just angered the wrong person in power or have something someone else wants. Ask me how I know that?"

Yvret smiled. "Peace, Sarah. I think we all had that same confusion when we first started. I know I did."

"Maybe so, but you know why I got accused of witchcraft, and it's not because I did anything that could be called 'magic'."

Erin leaned forward. "What do you mean? You were falsely accused?"

"By someone who wanted marital privileges without the benefit of marriage first." Sarah rolled her eyes. "I told him to go jump in a snowbank, and the next thing I know, I'm in front of magistrates being accused. A fey in the pond where the 'trial' happened rescued me."

"And all witchcraft accusations are false, then?" Erin asked.

Yvret nodded. "One way or another. When it's not the scenario Sarah found herself in or political, then it's someone pretending to do magic so they can scare their enemies or it's a gifted who revealed their nature to humans."

Erin rubbed her forehead. "Well, if it's not magic, then how is it faeries heal without medicine and hurt without weapons or fix broken furniture or teach someone a language in an instant or—" She ran out of examples to offer and shrugged. "All of that and more?"

"With the right training, you can learn how to feel the energy all around you, and then mold it into the shapes you need to get certain effects." His fingers wove an intricate pattern in the air and formed a ball of light in his palm. "Think of it as if a spider used already existing string to build webs instead of spinning its own."

Sarah leaned closer. "And the best part? When you've learned enough about how to mold energy, you become some sort of fey, or sidhe I suppose, but I sure hope not. I mean who would want to be sidhe? I suppose some people would, but ..." She looked first at Yvret then at Erin. "I'm rambling again, aren't I?"

"Maybe just a little." Yvret mimed, pinching something small.

"Why would it matter?" Erin shrugged. "Aren't fey and sidhe both faeries? Just different kingdoms, or something—"

"Why would it—" Sarah's jaw dropped. "She's serious?"

"Have you been a fey so long you've forgotten all the misconceptions humans have about our kind?" Yvret smiled. "They're more than different kingdoms. Sidhe take the energy they weave into effects from within themselves then replenish their own reserves by stealing it from humans, often leaving the humans dead or nearly so. It's fast. It's effective, and it can be remarkably powerful. Fey, on the other hand, gather the energy they mold from the environment around them. It can be just as powerful and no less effective, but it takes longer to master."

Erin stared at her soup, her thoughts in a fugue. Recovering from the previous night's excitement didn't help at all.

"You need not decide today," Yvret said. "It's not fair of me to ask you to think clearly right now. You should take some time to consider it. Once you start down the road, there's no turning back. Think about it later when your mind's clear, then come to the fey ring in the forest to give me your answer. The ring is about half of a mile east of where I...where you found me yesterday."

Did she really want another man in her life making her decisions?

She'd lost her right to decide her fate when her father had told her whom she'd marry. True, she had come to like, even love, Michel more than she could have expected at her young age, but she'd been given no choice. If her home hadn't been destroyed, she would have married Michel as soon as she'd come of age. Then next came Uncle, who broke that commitment after Father's death when he came and demanded she go back to her mother's home: Scotland. Then Uncle took a turn again when he told her to marry Connor Ross to forge an uneasy peace between the families. Finally, Connor and Ian had put their lot in and issued orders, too. For the moment, Yvret sounded ready to give her time and space to make her own choice, but that couldn't last. Someday down the line, he would take to directing her actions. Why should he be any different than the others?

On the other hand, Erin considered the gift he was offering. Maybe the transformation would be worth giving in to demands he would someday issue. As a fey, her "magic" or "innate abilities" or whatever he called them could protect her from Connor. She could finally be free of his foul temper. Never again could he beat her until she couldn't see straight. Even better, the falling sickness would be a thing of the past. No more confidence-shattering fits. No more days of weakness like today. She would gain so much that spending some time at Yvret's beck and call might not be so bad.

When could she do it, though? Connor's claims on her time were high and failure carried too great a price. Then her cousin had lost his wife last year to consumption, so Erin helped him run his house when she could. Between those two obligations alone, she scarcely had five seconds to herself.

Connor would never approve of her learning some new fey skills, and the last time she'd done something without his permission, he'd beaten her senseless, leaving her bedridden for nearly two months while broken bones mended. Thank God Celia had been there. Erin couldn't risk that again, especially since Ian's wife had gone on to heaven.

Erin shook her head. "No, I can answer you now. I can't do it."

Sarah stood on the table and stalked closer. "Are you insane?"

"Sarah, stop," Yvret warned.

"Don't you realize that once you've transformed, you'll never have another fit again?" Sarah fluttered closer yet.

Yvret scowled. "That's enough, Sarah!"

"Do you just like having the falling sickness?" Sarah demanded.

Yvret blocked her path with his hand. "Sarah!"

The sprite spun toward him. "What?"

"She must decide for herself," Yvret explained.

"But—" Sarah looked at her then back at him.

"It's her decision, not ours."

Sarah flew back to the teacup and sat with her arms crossed, refusing to meet Yvret's or Erin's gaze.

"There are reasons you don't know." Erin glanced toward town. "It truly would be marvelous to be rid of this sickness, but I can't. Not now." She frowned and looked away. "Maybe not ever."

Yvret's hand rested on her arm. "Never is a long time, but I understand. My offer won't go away, so if someday your situation changes, seek me out. I plan to be around for quite a while yet."

Erin nodded. She'd expected him to chastise her and shame her into accepting him as a teacher. Part of her had hoped he would. That would have made her decision so much easier. She could have done what she wanted and blamed the consequences on Yvret, but no. Instead, he was leaving it all up to her. As much as she had always wanted to make her decisions, now that she was required to, Erin felt strangely inadequate for the task. In this critical moment, she wanted Yvret to decide for her, and she knew he would not.

"We should go." Yvret stood. "We've been away too long."

"Yeah, you especially." Sarah fluttered upward.

"Will you be safe here alone?" he asked.

Erin sighed. "Connor will not tolerate being with me when I'm ill. He'll return in a few days, and when he does, he'll be all apologies and promises until the next time."

"See, if you would just let Yv—" Sarah began.

A hard look from the elf silenced her, but only until she growled at him.

"I'm just trying to help," she muttered.

"Yes, and I appreciate it, really." The corners of Erin's eyes burned. "But there are things you just don't know."

Sarah flew to Yvret's shoulder. "Yeah, if you say so." She tapped Yvret's cheek. "Can I at least tell her that I hope she changes her mind?"

Yvret smiled and nodded. "That will do."

Erin shook her head. "I-I-I just don't know."

Exasperating man. Earlier, he had used his spells—or whatever they really called these special energy spiderwebs they drew to make things happen—on her to force her to sleep and learn the fey language. Then he'd made her get out of bed. Why wouldn't he now order her to go with him? Why did he choose now to leave her to her own choices?

Erin rose, leaning on the table for support, and led them to the door. She didn't want to be alone right now, but she had presumed too much on their kindness already, and they should leave before she made a decision she would very likely regret.

Opening the door for them, she said, "Thank you. You're very kind to sit up with me. I know it wasn't what you had in mind for the day."

"You saved my life. I only sat up with a friend who was ill." Yvret laid his hand on her shoulder and smiled. "Take care of yourself. You know where to find me, don't you?"

After thinking for a moment to remember where the fey ring was, she nodded. "Aye."

Standing on the threshold with her arms crossed to fend off the cold, Erin watched them until they disappeared into the trees. She went back inside and felt more alone than she ever had before. With considerable difficulty, she resisted the urge to call after Yvret. If she did, they would only think her a foolish, weak child. He had called her "friend" and pestering him would only cause him to wish he hadn't. God knew she didn't deserve anyone so kind as him, but she needed all the friends she could get. Connor would never approve of her associating with the fey, but maybe Connor didn't need to know this time.

She had just settled back into a chair to finish her soup when the door suddenly opened and slammed against the wall. Erin rose and backed away as a blast of cold wind gave her goose pimples. Her heart quickened. Connor? So soon?

"Sorry, lass, the wind took it." Her cousin moved into the room. His voice carried the cadence that was so common in this area.

No, this was Ian dropping in. That wasn't necessarily better, but for the moment, there wasn't a growl in his voice and his posture was slouched some. She would probably be safe enough for the moment.

Erin released the breath she was holding and let the tension ease out of her muscles. "Ian, you scared—" she stopped when she realized she was still speaking fey and started again. "Ian, you scared me half to death with that. Come in and close the door."

Ian shut out the cold. He sniffed the air and wrinkled his nose. "What is that?"

Erin took a bowl from the cupboard and went to the hearth. "Soup. Want some?"

He shook his head. "Not on your life. What's in that stuff?"

After thinking for a moment, she realized she'd forgotten to get the recipe from Yvret as he'd promised. "Oh, you know. The usual."

"What, old laundry and stinkwort?" he asked.

She shook her head. "They tell me it's good for the falling sickness."

"I don't wonder that it scares the sickness away altogether." Ian wrinkled his nose.

She chuckled. "All the more for me."

Ian smirked. "Aye, and you can have it."

Erin ate a few spoonfuls of now tepid soup, deciding it was better hot. "So, could you smell this stuff all the way across the field or did something else bring you over?"

"I need your help." He flipped the chair around backward and sat.

She set the spoon down and looked at him. This was a new wrinkle. He didn't usually solicit her opinion.

"Don't look at me like that." Ian smirked. "You can still read French, right?"

"Of course. I'd as likely forget my own name as my father's language."

"Good." He fished a small, leather-bound book out of a pocket in the lining of his cloak. "I'm tired of trying to make my way here. I've arranged to leave for Tours by week's end. I'll be taking after your father and making my own fortune on the continent. I need your help to read this."

Her father had been a lieutenant in the duke's guards. Erin had grown up in France. Only after the sidhe had killed her parents had Ian and Uncle fetched her to Mother's homeland. Since then, no day passed that she didn't want to go back. Things there had been so much simpler. She had known where her life was going and understood it all. Now, ten years later in a whole different country, she felt terribly out of place.

"Wish I could go." Erin sighed. "It's been a good long while since I was home."

Ian roughly grabbed her wrist and pulled her closer. "None of that. You have an obligation to Connor. If you can't seem to keep the peace with him, at least you're keeping the peace between our kin, and that'll have to be good enough for you."

Erin pulled against his grip, but he held her fast. "Let me go."

"Things would be so much easier for you if you'd just mind Connor when he tells you to do something. You should remember who the master of this house is."

Since when did a proper marriage involve getting pummeled on a regular basis? Connor had obligations in this marriage, too, and Erin knew they didn't involve sitting around in a tavern getting drunk with a barmaid perched on his knee, just because dinner had come a quarter of an hour later than he wanted. Even Yvret, a complete stranger, treated her with more compassion than her own husband. If it hadn't been for that stupid marriage vow she'd been pushed into, Erin would have walked out the door a long time ago. The day was coming when she would do so anyway and just be damned for it.

When Ian pushed her away, Erin landed hard in her chair and saw stars.

"Get out," she spat.

"Keep your venom for someone else." Ian snorted. "How do you think Connor will like to hear you had a man here, overnight no less."

Erin felt a chill that had nothing to do with the weather. How did Ian know about Yvret and Sarah? Maybe he didn't. Maybe he only grabbed at straws because he had nothing real to hold over her.

"What are you talking about?" she asked.

"Don't play dumb with me, cuz. You had a man here last night." Ian pointed straight down.

"That's ridiculous!"

"Oh? Then who was it I saw leaving here this morning? Don't deny it. He was a tall fellow with dark hair. A butterfly, a big one, flew alongside him." Ian pointed toward the direction Yvret and Sarah would have taken to go toward the faerie gate. "Fess up, woman, who was it? Don't lie to me again."

Oh, God help her. He knew. He actually knew.

Erin glowered at him. "He was an elf. He watched over me while I recovered from one of my fits, and we had a chaperone if you must know!"

"I'll tell Connor differently. Who's he going to believe? Me or you?" Ian said softly.

She gritted her teeth. "Go to hell."

"You'll have a whole new concept of hell if he finds out you have a lover."

"I don't have a lover!"

Ian leaned his chair back on two legs. "I'll tell him you do. And if you think he's angry with you for having his dinner late, what do you think he'll do to you for lying with another man in his own bed no less?"

She slammed her hand into the table. Giving Ian a look that would burn him to cinders if he were more flammable, she went to the window and sought some way out of this sorry mess. It wasn't fair. She'd done nothing wrong. Yvret and Sarah's visit had been completely innocent. He hadn't taken advantage of her in her time of vulnerability, and she had not done anything to urge his baser instincts, if fey still had them after their transformation. Connor would believe none of it, though, especially with Ian egging him on.

Erin heard her cousin slowly come up behind her.

"If you do as I ask, you'll have no worries," he sneered.

Trapped. Again. Just once she wanted to have the upper hand.

She returned to the table. "Fine. What do you want of me?"

"I knew you'd see reason." Ian handed her the little book. "I need to learn the rapier. It wouldn't do to show up in the French Court wielding anything else. The rapier is the thing there. The only manual I could find was this one in French. You'll help me learn it."

She thought he was joking, but only until she flipped through the book and found pictures of men with rapiers and long daggers poised to do each other harm.

"You're daft!" She returned the book to him. "I-I can't read this for you. Women have no call learning weapons."

As she said that, images came to her mind of the sidhe prince lying on the ground, writhing in agony with a steel dagger, her steel dagger, protruding from its back and burning its flesh. The smell was still strong in her mind, and the way the sidhe screamed formed an indelible part of her memory. She'd already used a weapon to kill. How was this any different?

"It's not against the law."

"Maybe not in any formal way, but who in polite society considers it appropriate for a woman to be armed?"

Book in hand, Ian shrugged and took a step closer to the door. "If you'd rather I talk to Connor, suit yourself."

Erin ran to intercept him and yanked the book from his hand. The very next time she had the opportunity to wipe that ridiculous grin off his face, she would.

***

Diego lay awake on a soft bed surrounded by fresh-smelling bedding and covered with a heavy blanket. He hadn't opened his eyes yet and didn't plan to until he knew more about where he was and who had taken him in. Let his caretakers think he still slept. Even if Luis had found some forgiveness in his heart, he had nothing this comfortable in his tent, so he wasn't in his brother's care. A mind trained by years of thieving told him that whoever had rescued him was well off. The sheets were soft and recently laundered. The sweet scent of perfumes filled the air, not the stench of damp, decaying hay.

63

Taking advantage of the time alone, Diego silently went through his morning prayers. For all he knew, night could have fallen hours ago, but since he'd just awakened, morning prayers seemed more appropriate. Once he'd finished all the required ones, he added his own petitions. He thanked God he was still alive and pleaded for the Creator's continued protection and guidance. Luis called him an idiot for trying to be religious, but Diego felt better for his efforts to pray. On those rare occasions when he snuck into town and went to Mass, an inexplicable elation filled him. Someday, when he got up the courage to go to confession, he would be able to take communion, too.

The sound of male voices speaking French—one rich and deep, the other higher and more nasal, and the sound of heavy footsteps approaching brought an abrupt end to his devotions. He strained to hear them and make sense of their words, but they spoke so quickly he got nothing useful from the conversation. As it was, he couldn't even pick out the smattering of words he knew.

When he heard the door open, Diego concentrated on pretending to sleep. He needed to buy time to figure out what they meant for his fate.

The bed curtains were drawn back. The two still spoke in rapid French until Diego heard a chair being drawn across the floor.

"Fortunately, Corinne tells me he speaks just enough English a man might understand him if he were patient," the deep voice said in very precise, thankfully slow English.

"Hm, well, I never cared for English, but if it's all we have to work with, talking in a language the boy doesn't know would be awfully rude. English it is," the nasal voice answered. "What do you think possessed him to turn against his own, not that I'm complaining mind you? Anything to get Corinne out of that place."

"I don't know what he was thinking. Frankly, I don't care."

"The duke will care," the nasal voice said. "When he learns of the boy's association with the bandits, His Grace will have him flogged and hanged as a thief. You may not have done him any favors by bringing him here, you know."

The blankets were pulled aside, taking every faculty Diego had to keep from jumping when chilly air washed over his mostly bare body. He hoped they didn't notice the slight pause in his breathing.

"His Grace only knows what I tell him," the deep voice explained. "Nothing more."

Diego filed that comment away. His benefactor must be someone high up in the ranks of society to have the ear of the duke.

"Michel, it's not like you to tell less than the truth."

Michel? Could that be Michel Gaultier? The captain of the guard? Luis had mentioned him as a definite thorn in the side more than once.

"I simply told him a boy had come to Corinne's aid and took a severe beating on her behalf. I left out his past. That's all. I've ordered the men and advised Corinne to forget what they know of the boy's previous occupation."

A sliver of cold metal slid between his leg and the bandage protecting the wound. Diego steeled himself, and a few muffled clicks later, the pressure around his thigh was gone, causing the pain to lessen a little.

"Don't look at me that way, Fiori," Michel scolded. "He saved my wife's life, and you know full well what payment he received for his efforts. He deserves better than the hangman's noose, and as unforgiving as the duke is, that's the best he could get. His Grace would condemn Christ himself for overturning the money-changers' tables in the temple and call it obstruction of trade. He need not know the boy was once one of the thieves. He certainly won't be rejoining them."

"I don't know, Michel. What if His Grace asks you directly?" Fiori asked. "Will you hide it?"

"No, of course not. I'll lie to no man and certainly not the one who pays my wages, but I'll protect the boy if I can. Being Guard Captain has its advantages."

Good. That was something to remember. Luis had taught Diego to remember those who owed him favors in case he had to recall them later. Having a captain in his pocket could be useful. All the same, now that he had some assurances about his own safety, he wished they would get back to Corinne. Diego was relieved she had reached her safe haven, but he wanted more. Was she hurt? Had the experience left her too paralyzed by fear to return to her previous life?

"It doesn't look as bad as I thought it would," Michel said.

"I'm surprised, too. Could you hand me the bowl? Wounds of that sort usually turn on a man. Remember how much dirt and debris we cleaned out of it three days ago?" Fiori asked.

Diego heard a cloth being rung out.

"Consider it a testament to your skills," Michel answered. "It cannot possibly be the work of the fey."

Fiori snorted. "Careful now. I have a hard time finding decent hats as it is. And, actually, the wound goes more along the surface of his leg than deep into it. That should help it heal faster."

A wet, warm cloth pressed against Diego's injury, causing a stinging pain worse than the venom of a hundred hornets. Before he could check himself, Diego gasped and tensed, grabbing handfuls of the sheet he was lying on and arching his back.

"Oh dear," Michel said.

"That's an unpleasant way to wake up," Fiori commented.

Diego felt a strong hand on his shoulder.

"Easy now," Michel said. "Be easy. It's all right. You're hurt and my surgeon is tending you."

Diego nodded and relaxed, but slowing his breathing down again took much more effort. He opened his eyes, looking up at a French nobleman dressed in black with ornate red and gold embroidery. He wore his brown hair in long curls and sported a mustache and goatee. Michel, he presumed. The other, probably Fiori, had the sharply angled nose, dark hair, and dark skin of Italians. His guesses were confirmed when the men introduced themselves.

"We found you in the forest the morning after you released Corinne." Michel drew a bedsheet over Diego, leaving only the damaged leg uncovered. "I brought you here and had Fiori look after you."

Diego nodded. "Thank you, Lord Gaultier—"

"Michel," he corrected.

"You are...very good to me," Diego finished.

Michel shook his head. "Nonsense. You're a very brave young man. It was the least I could do."

Fiori put the bowl aside. "I'll finish in a little while. We've been calling you 'that boy we found in the forest.' I assume you have a better name?"

That question had never been harder to answer. His mind screamed warnings at him. It was a trick. He should give them a false name. That would buy him time to recover enough to get away.

His heart, though, had different ideas. These men, if they'd meant to harm him, could have killed him as he slept, or, if they didn't want to dirty their hands, they could have simply left him to die in the forest, where he would have surely bled out the last of his life. Michel had promised his protection to Diego. Giving his name would be safe enough.

"I call myself Diego Rodriguez Velazquez."

Tense seconds passed while Diego waited for them to become angry or threaten him or send for the constable or storm away, but he was pleasantly surprised.

"Well met, Diego," Michel replied.

Diego had to shift the focus off himself. "The lady, she is well?"

Michel nodded. "She still jumps at her own shadow sometimes, but she's going to be fine."

Diego felt an immense weight leave his shoulders. She'd made her way home, and she'd be all right. The pain he'd endured had been a worthy trade for her safety.

"The rope they tie her with, it...um..." Diego drew a blank on the word he needed and looked past Michel, as if the one he was looking for were written on the wall behind him. He found another way around. "It hurt her hands."

"The ropes hurt her wrists and ankles, yes," Fiori said.

Diego nodded and cataloged the word he'd been missing.

Fiori shrugged. "It didn't look so bad once we'd cleaned it up."

"A decidedly minor problem compared to what could have happened," Michel added.

Diego sighed. "I try to talk Luis out of his plan for her, but he no hears no one."

Michel leaned against the bedpost. "Corinne was a bit confused on some parts of the ordeal. The stress, I'm sure. I was hoping you could help. Can you tell me what happened?"

Getting two loaded questions inside the same quarter hour had to be a record. Once again, Diego had to trust in Michel's gratitude to offer protection, but was that wise? Familial ties certainly hadn't swayed Luis. More than that, Diego's account of the day could give away his brother's secrets. Did Luis's betrayal make it all right to betray him in turn? Diego didn't think so, but with the other men's eyes staring expectantly at him, he couldn't think. He needed time.

"We are—" He yawned. "Oh, your pardon."

Michel patted his shoulder. "No, no, never mind. I'm being inconsiderate. We'll talk when you've rested."

"I think that would be best." Fiori picked up the bowl again.

"I'll be in to check on you later." Michel stepped away from the bed.

Diego nodded once. "Thank you, *señor*."

"Fiori, join me when you've finished here if you would please," Michel instructed.

"I won't be long." Fiori watched Michel leave then turned to Diego. "I'm afraid I have to finish cleaning that cut."

Diego nodded. He took a deep breath to steady himself. "I am ready."

Chapter 5

Erin grimaced and stretched out her muscles. After nearly four days of helping Ian with his project, the stiffness and soreness were finally fading, but not half as fast as she wanted.

Ian's original idea of having her read from the rapier manual hadn't lasted long. Even before the sun had set that day, Ian had showed a complete inability to follow what she read to him. In a moment of sheer exasperation, Erin had grabbed the rapier from him and demonstrated the move. Even that was a lost cause, and with prayers for patience, she had guided him through it step by step. That had finally worked and had become their standard. She read from the book, showed him, broke it down for him, and slowly built up the pace until he could execute the maneuvers at full combat speeds against her while she defended with the fireplace poker.

Ian flopped onto a hay bale and mopped his brow with the cuff of his shirt sleeve. "How is it...you can still...breathe?" he asked in between gasps.

Erin shrugged and smiled. "Oh, it could be that I spend my evenings doing more than sitting at the fire with an ale."

He snorted. "I'm-I'm in good shape."

"Are you now?" She poked his big belly. "Is that all muscle, all beer, or are you carrying a bairn in there?"

He glared at her as his posture stiffened. So much for his good mood. "Mind your lip, woman."

She turned away from him. "Now that's gratitude, isn't it? Well, come in. We'll eat and maybe after that, you'll be up to a bit more practice."

Leading the way inside, she and hung up her gray cloak, then picked up Ian's from the floor where he'd dropped it and hung that one up as well. After setting the table and serving up dark wine and the stew she had simmering on the fire, she sat and ate.

Ian grumbled and gingerly rubbed his bruised arm.

"You really need to close up that hole in your defense." Erin pointed to his arm.

"You're a vicious taskmaster." Ian stuffed a spoonful of stew in his mouth.

"Do you want to get better at this or not?" She blew across the surface of the spoon.

Rosemary. The stew could use a bit more rosemary. Some garlic wouldn't hurt either.

"You're enjoying this, aren't you?" Ian asked.

"What if I am?" she snapped. "I might as well, seeing as you give me no choice in it."

He glanced at the half-packed bag on the bed. "Well, I won't trouble you with it for much longer. As soon as Connor returns, I'll be going."

With that, any appetite Erin had vanished. She'd only thought about her husband in terms of Ian's demands. That the brute would return had been a dark cloud on the horizon. She found herself dreading his return not only because of his foul disposition but because Ian would leave, taking the rapier manual with him.

He was right, after all. She was enjoying her studies. She had shown skill in something her cousin, a man, struggled with, and she knew she was wrong to want it. The feeling of power she felt when she managed to slip past his defenses was an abomination. Although she shouldn't have anything more to do with it, Erin found herself dreading that loss more than her husband's temper.

"Don't look so glum." Ian pointed at her with his spoon. "If you'd just remember your duties to your husband and work on pleasing him more than you do, he'd not take so hard a hand to you."

Nonsense. She had actually tried that ploy once. No matter how much she bowed to Connor's wishes and waited on him, he always found some reason, no matter how ridiculous, to hit her. The only time he felt good about himself was when she was crying, cowering, or bleeding.

What of those duties, anyway? She was supposed to jump on his command, and he could do anything he wanted in return? It wasn't right. He had also taken a vow to love and honor. She strongly doubted pounding on a person showed either one of those virtues.

"He loves you, and tells me so all the time, but you can drive a man insane, as headstrong as you are." Ian returned to his stew.

"So you say." She pushed her bowl to the center of the table.

Arguing the point with him would only try her patience. She didn't need another one of Ian's unending lists of all her faults.

Once he'd finished eating and Ian had downed the whole bottle of unwatered wine, Erin set the dishes aside in an overflowing bucket and gave him his cloak. The sun, low on the horizon, would give them maybe another hour of usable light before darkness covered them. Erin had just picked up the book and opened to the dog-eared page where they'd stopped when Ian took the book from her.

"Are you going to read it yourself now?" Erin propped her hands on her hips.

He shushed her and nodded toward the path to town. She didn't even have to look to know what the problem was.

"He's back," Ian confirmed. "You mind what we talked about. Make your peace with him and don't vex him any. You bring a lot of it on yourself, you know. And if I was you, I wouldn't tell him about the manual."

Before she could answer him, he gathered his things and went inside. That was the end of it. Her excursion into forbidden knowledge was over, and now she had to return to the hell she lived in. Maybe he was right. Maybe she did deserve it.

Erin looked down at her hands. They were trembling, and it wasn't because of the chill of the air. Back inside their cottage, she flopped into a chair near the fire, chastising herself for not having the courage to take Yvret's offer. Connor would never change, and she prayed to God that He would find some way to free her from this wall-less prison.

The door opened, admitting both a bitter wind and Connor. When she went to take his cloak, he pulled her into a crushing bear hug that threatened to smother her. When he kissed her, she did her best to hide the total revulsion that welled up from the depths of her soul.

"Did you miss me?" he asked.

"What kind of question is that?" She hoped her smile didn't look half as fake as it felt.

He laughed at her weak joke, then suddenly went silent and held her out at arm's length, looking her over intently. After glancing at the rest of the little house's furnishings, he stared at her, making her heart skip a beat. The look of suspicion and hatred she knew so well darkened his face.

"I was joking, Connor." Tension across her forehead threatened a headache. "Of course, I missed you."

"How much of my money did you spend on replacing the furniture?" He pointed at the table he'd shattered before he left.

"None," she replied. "It—"

"So, what, then? You had nothing good for barter."

"It-it was like this when I woke up. It was the fey. It had to have been." She looked in the direction of the faerie ring. "They've done things like that before for other people why not for me, for us."

Connor pointed to the bucket of dirty dishes she'd been too busy to deal with in the last few days. "Stayed with you for dinner, did they?"

"Ian," she explained. "He's leaving for the continent soon. I've been helping him arrange his affairs. He stayed with me in the evening so I wouldn't fear being alone out here."

His grip on her arm tightened, making her wince. "You were alone with another man in my house?"

"Connor, I swear. It wasn't like that! He's my cousin. We did nothing wrong!"

He pushed her down, and Erin hit the floor hard enough to jar her teeth.

"Please, Connor." Her hands shook. "Nothing happened. We ate. We spoke of his trip. He went home. That's all."

"You think I'm stupid enough to believe you?" He stormed over to the stand where his sword rested.

She guessed his intention. He'd always threatened that if she cheated on her marriage vow, he would strike her dead. Erin cast about for something to use in her defense, but nothing was near at hand. She had a clear path to the door, but could she make it across the field to Ian? Would Ian actually help her?

"Now I know why you were so late coming home some nights ago." Connor unsheathed the sword. "You're with him. I should've seen it. Easy for you, isn't it, barren as you are. There's no chance of a baby coming along to show your sins to the world."

Erin bolted out the door and ran across the field. Ian was in front of his house, using the last of the daylight to practice everything they had worked on over the last few days.

"Ian!" she screamed. "Ian!"

He didn't respond. From behind her, Erin heard a loud crack. Stealing a quick look back, she saw the door hanging on one hinge and Connor coming after her, sword in hand. The noise got Ian's attention, and he made his way toward her. When she reached him, he pushed her on past. Erin slowed and watched the confrontation play out. Ian would read her the riot act later, but for now, she could count on her kinsman for help.

"That's far enough, Connor," Ian declared. "No matter what she does to anger you, you've no right drawing steel on a woman."

"Oh, that's right. Defend your whore," Connor replied.

Ian lowered the point of his rapier to the ground. "What?"

"You lost your wife, and now you think you can take mine?"

Ian shook his head "Have you taken leave of your senses, man?"

"I think I found 'em." Connor hefted his sword. "It all makes sense now. Defend yourself, or I'll kill you where you stand."

While Erin watched the two of them circle, she tried by sheer force of will to get Ian to close up the huge gap she saw in his stance. This wasn't a sparring match. Connor would not pull the blow if he got through, but if she called out instructions to her cousin now, Connor would know of the real sin she had committed. Worse, distractions could now be fatal both for Ian and for her.

The fight was over almost as soon as it had started. Connor swung his heavy blade in a wide arc. When Ian backpedaled to get away, he lost his footing and went down on his back, dislodging the rapier from his hand. Laughing, Connor kicked the rapier up to his hand and flung it aside, then stood over Ian.

This couldn't be happening! As unpleasant and demanding as Ian could be, she couldn't bear to see her own cousin impaled. She had to stop Connor. After making the sign of the cross on herself, Erin rose and ran to retrieve the discarded weapon while she begged some guardian angel to help her. Connor taunted Ian, accusing him of adultery and incest, and promising a quicker death than he deserved. The waning sunlight glinted orange into her eyes, leading her to the sword. Now armed, she turned toward Connor.

Her husband had Ian pinned with a foot pressing hard on Ian's chest. Connor stood ready to drive his sword through her cousin's belly while Ian tried desperately to push Connor away.

"Connor!" Erin gripped the rapier, looping a finger over the quillions the way the manual showed. "Leave him!"

"You'll join him soon enough, you ungrateful slut," he snapped.

Erin faced him and assumed the ready stance she'd seen in the woodcuts. "Leave him. Now."

Connor laughed. "What's this? You think you're a man now? Well, we'll see how good you are once I've done away with your lover."

As Connor brought his sword higher, Erin took a deep breath and thrust the point of her blade at his chest, pulling the shot before it could do any real harm. Once freed from Connor, Ian would spring to his feet and take the rapier out of her hand. Connor had to abandon Ian and retreat to avoid her assault as expected, but instead of resuming his rightful place in the fight, Ian rolled onto his side, clutching his ankle.

Recovering from the shock much faster than she had anticipated, Connor circled, then charged at her. Erin simply wheeled to one side and let him run past. He spun toward her again, aggravation tinting the mask of anger. More slowly this time, he approached.

Erin's heart raced just as it had when she had confronted the sidhe prince, and once again someone's life hung in the balance. Like the sidhe, Connor assumed her to be weak. Her unexpected skill would be her advantage. She could take him. She had to because if she didn't, he would kill her and then Ian.

Initiating the next few attacks, Erin thrust for his face, then recoiled and drove for his shoulder, then again for his head. Each time, Connor's parries threatened to dislodge the rapier from her hand.

"Weak. Very weak." He chuckled.

His taunts and insults continued, and she made an extreme effort to ignore him. He would not undermine her confidence. Not again. Instead of his words, she concentrated on his movements, looking for an opening to exploit. A troubling gleam came to Connor's eyes and he smiled. To give herself more time to react to whatever he had planned, Erin backed away from him and tightened her grip on the rapier. This could all be another of his games to distract her and force her to make an error. Toying with her like a demented cat certainly fit with his nature.

Connor let out a mighty yell. He raised his sword overhead and spun it in wide circles as he charged at her. Less than a week ago, she would have been scared witless by such a cry. Now, though, she ducked into a crouch, thrusting upward at his unprotected chest. As Connor drove himself onto the point of her sword, his blade fell from his hand. She rose, pushing the rapier through him all the way to the hilt. Warm blood washed over her hand, filling her with a sense of satisfaction and vengeance. Stepping back, she withdrew the blade and watched him fall heavily in a heap. His ploy to intimidate her had failed. Death served him right for hurting her physically and mentally for all those years.

"What have you done?" Ian demanded.

Erin knelt next to him. "What I had to do, Ian. He'd've killed us both if I hadn't."

"Dammit, lass, you're a woman!"

"Tainted by things I shouldn't know because of you." She glared at him. "What's wrong? Do you not like what you've created?"

She could see the range of confused emotions on his face. Anger, relief, resentment, gratitude, and fear all vied for dominance. Erin felt nothing now. Even what she'd felt when Connor had fallen at her feet had left her, but she suspected that sometime soon, when the crisis had surely passed and she felt safe again, she would play through the whole gamut of emotions herself. For the moment, though, there were other things to occupy her mind.

"You're hurt."

He grimaced. "Turned my ankle as I fell. God help me, but I did a good job of it, too."

"We'll get you inside, and I'll go get someone to help you." She looked around for a stick and leaned aside to grab it.

Erin helped her cousin to the bed in his own small house and made him as comfortable as she could manage. Then she washed the blood from her hands before setting out for the fey ring, without knowing why she did.

There was, of course, the matter of finding help for Ian. If she could prevail upon Sarah again, the sprite could make short work of a sprain, but that was nothing but a handy excuse. A sprained ankle hardly threatened Ian's life. He would heal well enough on his own. Something else, something more elusive drove her on, but her mind was too numb to spend any time on the puzzle now. Every time she gathered her focus, her thoughts drifted away like clouds on the wind. Erin soon arrived at a ring of glittering mushrooms without being any nearer to the answer.

Standing at the edge of the ring, she called, "Yvret! Yvret, I need your help!"

Time passed slowly and she looked around like a deer at the wrong end of an archer's aim.

"Yvret! Please!" she repeated.

A pleasant, diffuse light filled the ring. When the glow faded, the elflord stood there. As soon as she met the gaze of his violet eyes, her own eyes flooded with tears and she fell to her knees at the edge of the ring.

"Erin? Erin, what is it? What's happened?" he asked.

When he sat next to her, she leaned against him and cried into his shoulder. Erin felt his long, thin fingers running through her hair and drew solace from the strength she felt in the arms that enfolded her, reminding her of her father. Even now, there weren't many days that went by when she didn't miss him. Yvret didn't pressure her to answer his questions, and he didn't chastise her for indulging in the tears. He didn't even offer her meaningless reassurances. He only held her until the emotion spent itself and she regained her composure. She felt a little silly for falling apart like that. The whole display must all be a terrible mystery to him. What had made her think she could come here and presume on his friendship like this?

"I'm-I'm sorry," she stuttered. When she pushed away from him, he held her fast. "I—"

He stopped her by laying a finger across her lips. "None of that. Can you tell me what happened?"

She was silent for a while, trying to find the words she would need to tell him about the heinous things she had done since they had last been together. She started with Ian's initial proposal and continued forward from there. All the while, Yvret sat with her and let her speak. He didn't pass judgment or make fun of her. He listened with nothing more than the occasional nod or "umhm" for an answer. When she got used to the idea that he cared too much to condemn her, the words came more easily. Before she was ready, she ran out of story to tell.

"How do you feel?" he asked.

Erin looked away from him to hide the tears in her eyes. "Scared."

"I would be scared, too." He nodded. "I think it would be best for you to come with me now. Connor's kinsmen won't be in a forgiving mood when they discover what happened, but they won't find you in my realm."

"Ian." She looked back toward his house. "He's twisted his leg, and it won't hold him."

"I'll send my people to bring him here," Yvret promised.

She was drawn up with him as he rose. Still leaning into the comforting protection of his arms, she stepped into the ring with him and felt safe for the first time in years.

***

When Yvret heard Erin's breathing slow into the soft rhythm of sleep, he gently tucked the covers around her and tip-toed out of the room. Thinking of Erin as one of the children he'd never have was far too easy. He'd had no children before his transformation, and of course, there'd be none now. The gifted who needed his help and guidance were as close as he would ever get to having children.

By now, the council would be waiting in his study to discuss why he had brought her here of all places. Since he already knew how each one would react, this meeting was nothing but a formality. He had to consult his advisers, though, so that everyone would have a chance to give voice to their concerns, and besides, sometimes someone in the group surprised him.

In the study, he found only three of his four advisers waiting.

"Where's Jared?" Yvret asked once he had greeted the rest of the group. "It's not like him to miss one of these meetings."

Jared, a pixie, was by far one of the most outspoken, and the creative, tactful ways he found for telling someone they were being an idiot always amused Yvret, even when he was the target.

"He's not going to be able to join us this time," Kendall replied, adjusting the lay of his two largest wings.

"Nothing too serious, I hope," Yvret said. After being gone for a day or two, he was still trying to catch up with everyone's obligations and activities.

"Oh, not even close to how you scared us all half to death, no," Terri answered. "It's a territory fracas between some unicorns and pegasi."

"Again?" Sarah asked. "One of these years, we're just going to have to breed our horses to have more intelligence so they can remember where the stupid boundary lines are."

"Or maybe less intelligence, so it won't matter where the lines are," Kendall countered.

Terri smiled. "Well, at least one of them hasn't gotten snared by humans again. That was an ugly affair last time."

"Poor little baby. Did he ever recover?" Sarah asked.

"One wing still doesn't sit quite right, but he's fine otherwise," Yvret answered.

"It holds him well enough when he flies," Kendall added.

"But, I'm glad Jared is simply taking care of some business. Let's get our business out of the way so we can all go to sleep sometime tonight, and I'll get Jared's opinion later."

To buy himself some time to sort his thoughts, Yvret found a seat and gestured for everyone to join him.

"I already know." Sarah settled on the perch set where she could be eye-level with everyone else. "And, Kendall, you're not gonna like this."

"Let me judge for myself, Sarah." The seraph shook his head.

Yvret took a deep breath before he began. "You all know I was rescued from the sidhe by a gifted woman." He paused for a moment while he banished the unwanted images of his torment from his mind. "Earlier this evening, she arrived at the gate calling for help."

Kendall's countenance darkened. "You brought her here."

"Her and her cousin, who isn't gifted, yes."

"Yvret!" Terri exclaimed. "It'll be Deborah and James all over again."

"Deborah and James?" Sarah asked.

Yvret nodded. Sarah had joined them long after the incident. "Two of the gifted who were brought here to be trained. When they transformed, they became sidhe."

Sarah went pale. "But if they were here when they changed, then—"

"Yes, they were unable to escape through the gates," Kendall concluded. "The barrier works both ways."

Terri nodded, turning her hard gaze on Yvret. "And now you've done it again."

He shook his head. "No, she hasn't even begun her training yet. She's a long way from transforming, my dear, and I believe she'll join us, not the sidhe."

"You don't know that." Kendall heaved a terrific sigh. "James wasn't expected to change for a week or two when he made the critical decision, and we were all convinced he would become fey. Deborah likewise was to join us before she maimed someone in a fit of jealousy and transformed the other way. Maybe you could ease our fears if you told us what she's running from that caused you to bring her here?"

"Her husband's family will be hunting her down to get revenge."

"Because," Kendall prompted.

"She killed her husband," Sarah replied.

"What?" Terri bolted to her feet.

Yvret rolled his eyes. "In self-defense."

He wished Sarah would let him do the explaining. Sometimes she could be a little overly fond of the reactions she could get from people and a little insensitive about the feelings behind those reactions. Looking at each of his advisors, he saw Terri had already decided that Erin was bound for the Unseelie Court, and Kendall, unusually diplomatic among the highly protective seraphim, was still undecided. Sarah had previously approved of Erin's presence, but not Ian's.

"Tell me more." Kendall preened a wing feather, a tell Yvret had long ago learned meant apprehension.

Yvret nodded once to his security minister and related the whole story he had gotten from Erin. When he had finished, he waited for everyone to come to terms with the traumatic tale they had heard.

"I want her gone," Terri insisted. "Now."

"She won't transform while she's sleeping," Yvret pointed out. "There's no need to roust her out of bed."

"Erin won't become a sidhe at all." Sarah stomped her foot for emphasis. "She saved Yvret's life, and she didn't have to do that. That counts, doesn't it?"

"She killed someone. Both times." Terri jabbed her finger at Sarah. "That counts, too."

"Reason wouldn't have worked either time," Kendall said. "My last action before my own transformation was to kill with a special ability. I killed someone I once thought of as a friend because he was about to deliberately do something that would have killed hundreds of innocents. The change is based not so much on what you do, but why you do it."

Yvret nodded. "She did try diplomacy both times, after a fashion, to no avail."

"Still." Kendall rubbed his chin. "I won't object to her being here for the moment, but once she learns more than a couple of the most basic skills, she needs to leave."

"That's fair. Terri, what is your opinion?"

"I don't want any more fey killed in their own homes. She goes, then you can teach her all the skills you want." Terri pawed the floor with her hoof.

"I understand."

The centaur who'd taught her all the special skills of their kind had been one of Deborah's first victims. Yvret didn't wonder that Terri was a little nervous.

"You already have my opinion." Sarah shrugged. "She's neat. I like her. She won't go over to the Unseelies."

He looked at each of them to see if they wanted to share any other concerns with him.

"Thank you. Once Jared has his chance to respond, I'll make my final decision," he concluded.

Kendall and Sarah took their leave of him, but Terri stopped halfway to the door. Yvret went to her side and put an arm around her shoulders.

"I miss him." She brushed a tear from her eye.

"So do I," he replied. "Your mentor was one of the best centaurs in our history, and you, my child, were the student who brought him the most pride and joy. He would be pleased to see how you've turned out."

"Don't keep Erin here, Yvret, please." Terri sniffled. "Sarah's cute, but she can't know Erin is safe around us. There's too great of a risk."

"Well, I won't keep her here until she transforms out of respect for your mentor, if nothing else," Yvret promised. "But right now, she knows nothing but pain and fear. That may drive her to the Unseelie Court faster than anything else. Keeping her here, where she feels safe may help her see she has other choices. If I decide to let her stay here for a while, once she has the means to protect herself, I'll send her back to her world until after her metamorphosis. Is that an acceptable compromise?"

Slowly, Terri nodded. "Yes. I can live with that."

Yvret hugged her until Terri was ready to let go a few minutes later, then he walked her home.

***

Diego bolted upright in bed with every sense on alert. Around him, he saw only bed curtains, as he expected. There could be something on the other side. Willing his hand to be steady, Diego pulled the curtain aside but rolled his eyes and let it fall back when he saw nothing unusual. He was being awfully foolish. The room was as empty as it had been all along.

Then he heard it again. A man's voice spoke with the curtness of one accustomed to having his orders obeyed promptly. Even as distant as it was, Diego heard in that tone the threats of vicious reprisals if those instructions were not acted on.

Those were qualities Diego knew full well. Luis often ordered others around just like that. Even the pitch of the voice was the same. Diego felt a hand tighten around his heart. Luis was here? *Madre de Dios*, was it an attack on Michel's household, or was Luis here under false pretenses? Worse yet, Diego wondered if he was to be turned over to his brother.

While he scrambled to make sense of it, he looked around for something to use as a weapon: a sword, a dagger, even a letter-opener, but there was nothing. Even if he had to fight with his bare hands, Diego determined that he'd never go willingly into his brother's care. He could only expect to be beaten again, and this time, Luis would be certain of the outcome. He didn't care for witnesses or survivors.

Worse, there were the ladies of the house to consider. Luis would have enough men with him to overpower Michel, no matter how valiantly he would fight. After that, any menservants would be easy prey. And himself? He couldn't even stand right now, and he'd never been any good at fighting from the ground. Once he was gone, there would be no one to hinder Luis.

Diego concentrated, trying to isolate the voice among the other noises he heard. French? The voice was speaking French? He shook his head and fell back on the pillow. Luis knew many languages, but French was not one of them. That's why the lieutenant he had hired was conversant in the language. There was no way the speaker Diego heard could possibly be his brother.

As he lay there in bed, willing his heart and lungs to return to their usual pace, he listened to get a sense of the conversation, but half of the exchange never reached him and the rest was far too fast.

Instead, he lay in bed listening to the crackle of the fire and considering Michel's earlier request for help. Could Diego help the French guard captain catch Luis? Until now, things had been so much easier. Luis said. Diego did. Now, having to find his own way, he had a real appreciation for the kind of pressure his brother felt making all of the most important decisions for every man in the whole company.

The help Michel had requested of him required a betrayal of a different sort. He certainly didn't know exactly where Luis had gone, but there was the spy network he could tap into. Diego had some good guesses about some places to meet the contacts who could lead him to his brother, even if they didn't know they were doing it.

Luis had to be stopped, certainly, but Diego would do it himself. Once he had Luis in custody, Diego could turn his brother over to Michel for trial and punishment. That would be justice, not betrayal.

Sometime later, Diego heard a large, heavy door close downstairs. The authoritative voice that had shocked him awake before was gone now. Not long after that, he heard a delicate step on the stairs, followed by a slight knock on the door.

"¡*Hola!*" he called, after making sure he was properly covered.

Whoever was trying to come in had trouble getting the door to cooperate, but Diego was powerless to help. He was too far away to reach it; and although he might have hobbled over, he still had no clothes to cover himself with. From the lightness of the step on the stairs, Diego presumed his visitor was a lady, and there was no need to startle her with such immodesty.

Michel's voice called out, and the woman just outside the door answered. Then Diego heard heavy steps running up the stairs.

Finally, the door opened.

"Oh, impossible thing," the woman growled. She spoke French for a moment.

"*Ouí, Madame,*" a man answered.

He recognized the woman's voice. "*Señora* Gaultier?"

Diego pulled aside the curtain just enough to see her and smiled. Aside from the bandages he could see on her wrists and a few thin, red scratches, she looked better than he'd hoped.

The man with her was the servant who'd brought him his meals or escorted the little girl who did. At first, the big man's presence had troubled Diego, but what could he expect? He was a thief, and Michel was a very careful man. The servant ensured that Diego would mind his manners.

"Hello, Diego," she said, setting a covered tray on a small table. "I hope we didn't wake you."

"No," he said a little too quickly. "No, I am awake."

He would just die if she found out how foolishly he'd behaved. Imagine. A man of his years being jolted awake and scared to wit's end by the sound of another man talking.

Keeping her eyes turned from him, Corrine handed him the heavy flannel nightshirt she had draped over her shoulder. "For you. It should fit you well enough and help keep you warm."

Putting on the long shirt was awkward, bedridden as he was, but he managed it well enough. He only ran into trouble when he had to pull it down over his legs while staying seated, but by carefully raising himself with one hand and wrestling the soft fabric into place with the other, he accomplished his feat. The fuzzy material was a little cool at first and sent a shiver through him, but that soon passed.

"Thank you," he said. "You are very kind."

She was still smiling when she tied the bed curtains aside. The servant set a tray next to Diego on the bed. There was a plate of chicken and olives, a large roll, and a cup of wine. The smell of it all reminded him that his last meal had been several hours ago and consisted of bread and cheese nearly thrown at him by a servant girl. Although thankful to get anything, he was glad dinner looked more interesting than lunch had been.

"It looks good. Thank you." He held the plate toward her. "You like some?"

"Oh, no. I've eaten." She held her hand with her palm toward him. "His Grace was here for dinner. It was only when he was leaving that I remembered you hadn't eaten."

"Then it is all the more welcome," he replied.

Trying the chicken first, he found it tasted better than it smelled, if that were possible. After eating a few bites, he used the knife to cut a cross in the bread and spoke a blessing in Latin before breaking it. One of these years he wanted to learn the language of the Church so he could actually understand the words Father had told him to memorize as a boy.

While he ate, Corinne sat in a nearby chair watching. Diego had some sense that she was here for more reasons than to bring his supper to him. Any servant in the household could have done that, just as they had for the last few days. Although he didn't mind her company, the growing silence disturbed him, and he considered some way to start a conversation.

"I feel happy to see you well," he began.

At least he hoped that's what he said. Somehow, the words didn't sound right, but they'd do for now.

She smiled. "It's good to see you. I thought they'd shot you when I heard the gun."

"No. They try, but he...uh..." When the right words evaded him, he rephrased it in his mind. "Shoots very bad."

Of course, Diego's knife hitting the tree just under the musketeer's arm hadn't helped his aim at all, but that felt too much like a boast, so Diego kept the comment to himself.

"What did they do to you?" she asked. "Michel wouldn't tell me."

He found it hard to swallow around the growing lump in his throat. Luis's order returned to haunt Diego again.

He constructed the sentence in his head before speaking it. "They-they teach me to-to listen to Luis. I am a poor student."

Tears sparkled in Corinne's eyes. "I'm sorry."

He looked away for a moment. "No, to see you well makes all things good."

"I'm glad Michel found you. Maybe you can help him capture them." Her smile didn't make it to her eyes.

Diego nearly choked on his food. Once he managed to swallow, he nodded. "I do what I can."

It wasn't a lie. It wasn't. He would do everything he could to stop Luis. He just wouldn't do anything to directly help Michel do it.

"I knew you would." She sniffled. "Someone has to stop him. He'll kidnap others. I just know it. If you hadn't been there..."

Her voice trailed off and Diego reached a hand toward her but pulled it back when the servant stepped between them and growled. Just as well. She was a married woman and Diego had to remember his manners.

"Oh, *señora*, do not have fear." He took a sip of his wine. "You are safe."

"Am I?" She wiped her eyes with the lace kerchief she kept tucked in her sleeve. "I-I-I'm afraid if I leave the house alone, he'll find me. I wake up at night terrified that the noise I imagined is him coming to kill Michel and take me back to his camp. I know he's out there looking for me. I just know it."

Diego sighed. She was right. Although Luis might wait until after the plans he'd alluded to were completed, he would hunt Corinne down again. She'd seen him and escaped his grasp, and he wouldn't rest until she was his. Luis loved the challenges of the hunt and people were his favorite prey.

If Corinne were lucky, Luis would kill her outright. More likely she would be captured and taken back to camp, where he'd follow through on his original designs for her. This time, she'd be so well guarded that nothing short of the whole French army could break her loose. Diego couldn't allow that to happen.

Corinne snorted and shook her head. "You must think me a very silly girl."

Hardly. Not when his own heart echoed the fears she'd confided to him. The difference, though, was that he could take action.

Diego shook his head. "No, not silly. I understand what you feel. I tell you this. When I am good again, I find Luis and I make certain he no hurts you more."

She looked up at him and nodded. "Thank you."

As Diego watched her leave, he wondered if he had promised more than he could deliver. Luis was tricky, and even knowing where to tap into the spy network might not give Diego the information he needed to track his brother down. Worse, Luis would be leaving in some two weeks' time and might delay only shortly to recapture Corinne. He was running out of time and still confined to the bed.

That was the least of his problems. If Luis could be found, how would Diego ever be able to take on not just Luis, but the whole band? Then, what about his brother's supernatural allies in the sidhe. Diego needed help. Even if he had time to raise an army, he didn't have the faintest idea how, and he couldn't go to Michel.

Chapter 6

Luis sat writing a letter to his father to tell him of Diego's death. It seemed the boy had died when he'd volunteered to lead a contingent of men to protect a priest who had needed to travel through Protestant-held lands. The traitors to the Church had ignored a flag of truce and ambushed Diego. He'd been taken prisoner and hung before Luis could organize a rescue. The stories coming out of the Protestant camps insisted Diego had remained true to his faith even when the heathens had tortured him to get him to recant.

Naturally, none of the drama had even the barest inkling of truth, but Father would believe anything. He'd swallow the whole thing and push to have Diego proclaimed a martyr for the faith. Someday, Luis would have to sit down with dear old Dad and give him the real account of not only Diego's death but also what Luis had done all those times when he was "out on campaign to stop the Huguenots." He smiled when he realized the news might well kill the old man. Of all the things Dad could give him, Luis wanted his inheritance the most. The difference between the story and reality, when Luis chose to tell Dad, would break the old man's heart. Literally, with any luck.

The tent flap opened and closed, but Luis kept working. The petitioner could wait. Writing such a heartrending work of fiction took effort, and Luis wanted it to be perfect. Dad needed to despair over the death of his youngest son and rejoice that the death had been so noble. In reality, some pack of wolves had likely had the idiotic boy's bones to gnaw on after dinner.

With one admittedly gutsy move, the shortsighted boy had almost single-handedly ruined months of preparation. Only two things remained before everything fell into place: weapons for the new men and a pact with the sidhe. Then, in a couple weeks, when the duke moved from his winter home to his summer home, Luis would swoop down on him like a falcon. Faerie skills would make short work of His Grace's guard and the baggage train would be ripe for picking.

Diego's interference had nearly brought an unpleasant visit from the militia. Fortunately, their flight over rocky ground and across a stream would be untraceable, so Luis had no fears of detection now.

In an impish moment, Luis had used Diego's blood to darken scraps of rope to leave near the pavilion's former site. The guard captain would mistake the blood for his dear wife's and become enraged. Men who were furious made bad decisions and overlooked information. In part, Luis simply wanted the sheer joy of knowing Gaultier's stomach would turn sour at the sight of something that so brazenly spoke of poor little Corinne's ordeal. Luis only wished he could've seen Gaultier as a look of pure anguish crossed his face, followed by an all-consuming hatred.

After folding and sealing the letter to Dad, Luis turned and regarded Joaquin with a smile. "Glad to see you've returned. What news from the north?"

Joaquin looked away and shuffled his weight from foot to foot. "Mixed, I'm afraid."

This wasn't what Luis wanted to hear.

"Go on," he prompted.

"We had an arrangement with the sidhe prince in Scotland, but-but he was killed," Joaquin explained. "The new sidhe in charge of that region won't deal with me now. They want you or no one."

Impossible. Luis had gone on trips before and left the band in the care of the lieutenant, but if he went on a trip of that magnitude, there would be chaos. He needed to stay here to keep the men in line and remind them of their loyalties. The sidhe's help was imperative, though. Awfully inconvenient.

Everything hinged on the sidhe. Too much had gone into the plans to abort now, and fate had already confirmed the plan. Maybe the time had come for another lesson on what happened to those who failed the tasks they were given.

Luis had a reputation to uphold, so he nodded and reined in his temper while he watched the other man squirm. Slowly, deliberately, Luis crossed to the man and drew his knife. "You failed."

The blood drained from Joaquin's face. "Wait, sir, please. There's good news, also."

"Well?"

"They told me there's another sidhe gate nearby. Here. Near Tours!" the soldier continued. "They told me where to find it. Let me go talk to the local lord, and I swear upon my life they'll join us."

Luis considered that. Joaquin had been hired for his skill in negotiations. No one else was better, but the man needed to think he was expendable. "It will be your life if you fail me again."

"Yes, sir. I'll do it. You'll see. They'll join us."

"Be quick about it. We're running out of time."

He sheathed his knife again and slowly returned to his desk. He'd been seated, pretending to be busy, for a full minute before he heard the tent flap quickly open and close. Luis smiled and chuckled softly, wondering if Joaquin would need to go change his undergarments before he left for the Unseelie gate. Even Joaquin, very new to the band, was aware of the price of failure and betrayal.

Too bad Diego had found out the hard way, but at least his lesson had served to teach others. Fear was a very potent control.

***

Erin finished tracing a symbol in the air. A burst of power surged through her as a glittering shield took form.

She gasped. "I did it!"

Yvret smiled. "Yes, you did, and to think you were certain it would never work. Well done."

Even before he had finished speaking, dozens of tiny pinpricks of light appeared in her eyes and didn't go away when she closed them and covered them with her now shaking hand. The impending loss of her mind wrecked any happiness her success with the shield had brought her. Now she just wanted it all gone: the shield, the seizure, all of it. There was a soft popping noise.

"Lie down." Yvret's arm around her shoulders guided her to the ground. "Walk through the exercise I taught you."

Erin nodded. The whole week had gone the same way. They would work on a skill, and she would practice it, which employed powers her mind could handle and her body couldn't. That would set off the falling sickness, which could be ameliorated by an odd mental imagery technique he had taught her, and then she would rest for a while before he returned from his other duties.

"Can you stop the fit on your own this time?" he asked.

Erin nodded and began. First, she slowed her breathing from the near hyperventilation that tended to occur when the warning signals scared her. After inhaling for four counts, she held her breath for just a moment, then slowly let it out, then repeated the process again and again. At first, her body protested and urged her to breathe faster, but she soon adjusted.

With each breath, she put together parts of an image of a safe place: here, actually, under the shade of a willow on the bank of a stream. One breath. The tree formed in her mind. Another, and the stream took shape. A third and the sound of a chirping bird came in. Still another, and she felt the warmth of the sun, even though the real sun had set some hours ago. Each breath brought the image of her safe place into sharper focus and drove the unwanted fit away.

"Well done," Yvret said.

She opened her eyes and sat up, feeling a little groggy, but not half as bad as she would have if the epilepsy had taken her. "Does it always work?"

He shook his head. "No, you've been very fortunate with the number of successes you've had. Who knows, maybe in your case—"

He stopped and looked past her. She turned to follow his gaze and saw Ian coming toward them like an approaching storm. No need to guess what mood he was in this time.

"Oh, what now?" she muttered.

Ian had done nothing but complain since coming here to the fey realm. She had foolishly thought he would be grateful for their help, but instead, the food wasn't what he would like, and he didn't like sleeping on a pallet of pillows in the huge tree house that made up Yvret's palace. The wine they gave him wasn't as strong as the scotch he preferred, and so it continued with a host of other ungrateful laments. This was hardly a new feature. If someone came along and gave Ian his heart's desire, he would find fault not only with the gift but the giver as well.

Instead of sitting with them, Ian grabbed her arm and yanked her to her feet.

"Now see here!" Yvret exclaimed.

Erin looked back at him and shook her head. "No, no, I have it." Then she twisted free from Ian's grip. Only a second before she spoke did she remember to switch languages. "What is it you want?"

"Good to see you still remember your native tongue." He propped his hands on his hips.

"French, not English, is my native tongue," she reminded him. "And I remember that, too. Well, what is it?"

"Get your things. We're goin'," he ordered.

Oh really? If he thought he could command her like he could a hound, he had gotten the wrong idea in his head.

"I'm not yet ready to go." She glanced back at Yvret. "I have too much to do."

"Did I ask?" he demanded.

"Maybe you should've."

Ian came toe-to-toe with her. He stood a head and a half taller than she did, and she had to look up to see his face. Not too long ago, she would have backed down from a confrontation like this, but now, having proven herself more capable than he was, she easily stood her ground.

"You've forgotten your place, woman." His voice rumbled like distant thunder. "But never you mind. Once we've gone from here and you don't have a fey standing watch over you, I'll be only too happy to remind you of where you belong. Now get your things and tell your friend to see us home."

She glared at him. "If I hadn't done so much practice already today, I'd see to putting a civil tongue in your head."

Before he could say anything more, she turned her back to him. Yvret waited expectantly for the translation, and she shot a quick glare at Ian over her shoulder and gave Yvret an account of what had transpired.

"I can't say I much care for your cousin," Yvret said when she had finished. "Intemperate fellow."

Erin rolled her eyes. "He certainly didn't inherit Uncle's good humor, but I think I can deal with him now."

"Be careful." He gripped her arm. "He's much bigger and stronger than you are."

She shrugged. "But I have faerie skills."

He chuckled. "Oh? I teach you a few simple skills and now you're ready to take on the world!"

That's not what she meant, but maybe he was right. She was too new at her abilities to get cocky.

"I'm only teasing you." He smiled. "I'm glad to see your confidence returning. You're much less pathetic than you were when I left you in that cottage."

It was a little back-handed, but she took it as a compliment. "Thank you."

"Be careful your new confidence doesn't cause you to do something unwise," Yvret cautioned. "You are still merely mortal. Faerie skills are a wonderful equalizer when you go up against a larger, stronger opponent, but to use the focusing moves, you have to have your hands free. Even I fell when my hands were pinned, and I have much more experience than you. There's danger in becoming too fond of the power."

She looked down at her shoes. "I understand."

"Well?" Ian prompted.

"Patience," she spat in English without turning toward him.

"He does have a point." Yvret glanced toward the faerie ring in the clouds. "You should return to your world for a while."

She looked at him wide-eyed. How could he even suggest that? "But I'm not ready! There's still so much to learn. And my transformation—"

"Won't happen for a while yet," he interrupted.

"But—"

"What happened to the incredible confidence I saw in you a moment ago that enabled you to stand up to a man who once had dominion over you? Is that gone so soon?"

"Why? Why do I have to go?" Tears burned in the corner of her eyes. "You can at least tell me why."

"That's fair." He gripped her shoulders. "You are a visitor, and according to some of my people, not a very welcome one."

She let herself be drawn toward him. "I don't understand. Weren't they all like me before they transformed?"

"Of course, they were." He smiled. "Some of them have forgotten and others, well, they have a reason to fear you right now."

"Fear me? But I'd never hurt a one of them," she insisted.

"You're at a very dangerous time where every decision you make when you use faerie skill, no matter how trivial, may determine if you transform to a sidhe or a fey," he explained. "There will be one choice that decides everything. Some feel you showed what choice you'd make when you killed Connor."

Erin pulled away. "What was I supposed to do? He had Ian pinned!"

He held his palm toward her. "I know. I know. You made the only decision at the time that would have made any sense, and I think they're wrong. You haven't yet made the critical choice."

Ian tapped her shoulder, but she shrugged him off and glared at him before returning to her conversation with Yvret.

"I want to stay," she insisted.

Yvret sighed. "You can't. It's not allowed."

"Are you the leader of your people or aren't you?" she asked.

Were they going to give her a glimpse of paradise only to shut her out? How was that fair? How did that even make any sense? She felt a shiver throughout her soul. Now that she'd found somewhere she wanted to be, the people already there wanted her gone. Would she never have a home?

"It's not that easy, and they have reason to be afraid," Yvret said plainly.

She studied him for a moment and read the real pain in his eyes, which he hid by looking away from her. "Others who transformed while they were here, they became sidhe and hurt your people. Didn't they?"

He sighed heavily. "Yes. Two thousand years ago, when I faced this troubled time, the law required I stay outside of the Seelie Court until after my transformation, then they happily welcomed me. Some decades later, some human killed my mentor because the lesson he gave another gifted was misunderstood to be an attack. The Seelie Court chose me to succeed him as ruler, and I decreed that any gifted who were being taught should be trained here, where we would all be safe. For many years no problems arose until the worst happened."

"Someone made the wrong choice and became sidhe," she guessed.

He nodded.

Erin remembered how she had come across Yvret that cold afternoon. The thought made her shudder.

"After that first time, we enacted safeguards where the gifted student was never to be left alone, and that only led to the guard being the first victim of the new sidhe the second time," Yvret continued. "After that, I reset the rules to the way they were when I went through the training. There are still times when mentors are endangered in their efforts to teach the gifted, but the risk is not as great as it was when the student came here."

"If a student becomes a sidhe, then only the teacher is in danger," Erin said. "Else it was your whole realm."

She looked up at him and saw the haunted expression fading from his eyes. He had been so kind to her while everyone else in her life had bossed her around with threats and insults. She dreaded returning to her own world, but now she understood and vowed to be as little a burden as possible on Yvret. She would prove herself to the others who already believed she was a lost cause.

"I understand. Then how do I do this? How do I make sure I transform into a fey?"

"I'll guide you through it," Yvret promised. "Just consider what I tell you carefully."

She sighed. "I don't want to be a bother to you now."

"You're not a bother, my child, but even I have to follow the rules." He looked past her to Ian for a moment. "What do you fear about going back?"

Erin looked down and shook her head. "I don't feel safe in my own world."

"Me either." He lifted her chin. "But you'll do fine. You have a means to protect yourself from harm and one to put someone to sleep, which is helpful for all kinds of things, and even one to use for an attack. And I've watched you training Ian with our practice swords. I know little about things of that sort, but you're very strong in that skill."

She blushed. She shouldn't be strong in that skill. It wasn't right.

"Stop that," he scolded sharply. "Stop thinking like a human. You are a faerie, or will be someday at any rate. Such archaic notions are beyond us. You may never be as strong as a man, but your woman's build gives you better balance and your small frame makes for better speed. Take advantage of the abilities your mind and your body offer you and stop shunting away the power you have. You aren't as weak as you let people convince you that you are sometimes."

She looked away, unable to meet his gaze. Erin felt like she was in the bucket of a well. At one instant she could stand her ground and take all challengers, and the next she felt too meek to be much good against a flea.

Yvret sighed and shook his head, then continued more gently. "If you stop limiting yourself, anyone who intends to do you harm will find themselves an unexpected force to reckon with. You'll be fine. Just be careful not to overdo the practicing when you can or you'll drive yourself to a seizure."

"I'm waitin'," Ian snarled.

Erin ignored him. He'd just have to keep waiting.

"Will I still be able to see you and talk to you?" she asked.

"I have a gate near Tours," Yvret explained. "I'll meet you there in the mornings and work with you."

Good. If she could turn to him when she needed help, she could still face whatever challenges she needed to.

"Thank you." She looked down.

"You'll do fine," he replied.

Erin turned to face Ian. "We leave in the morning."

"Not good enough." Ian started to reach for her but abruptly stopped and crossed his arms over his chest. "We're going. Now. Make the arrangements."

Erin looked up at the ring of wispy clouds sparkling in the moonlight overhead. They marked this side of the fey gate. "Well, you go right ahead, cousin, but tell me, how do you propose to get to the ring? Even with all the things Yvret has taught me, I don't know how to fly, and at last check, I didn't see wings on your back."

"Tell your friend to take us to the ring," Ian barked. "Immediately. I'll not waste any more time here. I need to get to the continent."

"You'll just have to be disappointed." Her hands clenched at her sides. "Yvret says we leave at first light, so we leave at first light and that's the end of it, unless you'd like to go up against the lord of the entire fey realm."

She could see the fire burning in his eyes as he glared at Yvret. For his part, Yvret gave Ian the smile a small child might receive for stamping his little foot and declaring he would hold his breath until he got his way. A wave of satisfaction filled Erin's heart when she saw that Ian, for all of his bluster and all of his threats, would not get his way this time.

"Let's go back to the palace." Yvret led her by the hand. "After we've eaten, you should rest and recover your strength. Tomorrow is a big day."

Erin nodded and followed him up the path, leaving Ian to stay or follow as he wished.

***

Yvret led Erin into the convocation chamber near his rooms. Here, he met with his advisors and kept an eye on his gifted students, particularly the ones who gave him cause to worry.

Today, he was going to use the plight of one of the students to teach another one the need for caution.

He conducted Erin to the best place to watch the viewing wall. "Right this way."

Steve, a muse who often stayed here recording important events, acknowledged them with a nod. "The trial hasn't started yet, but Avril is already in place and waiting for the opportune time."

"Good. Thank you." He turned to the viewing wall.

A group of people were gathered around the edge of a murky pond. A small dock had been built from one side out toward the center. A pair of men in dented and scuffed up plate armor held a blindfolded and bound woman by the arms at the end of the pier.

"What's this?" Erin asked.

Yvret pointed to the wall. "Witchcraft trial happening near Madrid right now."

Erin's eyes grew wide. "Right now? Shouldn't we be doing something to help her instead of watching like some perverse voyeur?"

"Something is being done. One of my nixies has laid a claim to that pond. The worst that will happen is a bit of a fright."

"Then we're watching for morbid curiosity?" Erin looked at him out of the corner of her eye.

Yvret shook his head. "There's a lesson in this. She is gifted, like you, but she wasn't very careful about showing her new skills. In fact, in spite of her mentor's warnings to the contrary, she was bragging and putting on a bit of a show. Then came the witchcraft accusations, and she could hardly deny it when most of her village saw her."

"But Sarah said all witchcraft accusations were false." Erin's brow furrowed.

"Yes, they are, but humans have so many superstitions. Anything they don't rightly comprehend gets labeled witchcraft, and there's no lack of people in power who would accuse someone of witchcraft for revenge or some manner of personal gain."

Erin blew out a breath. "So best to hide all fey mag—fey skills."

"Exactly, I don't have nearly enough nixies to watch all the ponds used for these trials. This young lady is fortunate this pond is claimed."

The two armored men shoved the woman off the edge of the pier.

Erin gasped and took a step back.

Steve raised his hand as if tossing a ball straight up. The image scrolled as the view shifted to show the hazy image of what was happening underwater.

"Well, that's useless." Steve scowled. "She really should do something with that."

"It's fine, Steve. I think the point was made."

Half hidden by the suspended silt in the water, a woman with flowing fins swam past.

"But even if your nixie frees the woman, won't she just find herself in the same mess or worse?" Erin squinted at the viewing wall.

"We won't leave her there. Avril will teleport her to a new location far removed from this town. Hopefully, she'll heed her mentor this time." Yvret guided Erin away from viewing wall. "Just remember to keep your developing skills hidden. We've seen so many betrayals and baseless accusations that the risk is too great."

Erin nodded. "I'll remember."

With her recent history of abusive relationships, she'd better. Perhaps, he should have Steve watch her a little more closely. He wouldn't be surprised if her cousin tried to make a name for himself at her expense.

***

When Erin awoke, soft dappled light streamed through the windows and the sounds of children laughing in the distance serenaded her as it had from the time she had first arrived in the Seelie Court. She lay awake listening to the chirping birds for a while before getting up and going out to the balcony near the crown of a tall tree. From her height, she could see across a massive expanse of Yvret's territory. Below, other platforms were arranged in expanding tiers. Above her were the leafy tree branches that rained tiny white blossoms on her head when the wind blew. The only tier above her own housed Yvret's rooms and the grand audience chamber where he received his visitors.

Thinking of him as royalty proved harder than she had expected, even though he commanded more than she could see. Human nobility was often aloof and self-absorbed. In stark contrast, Yvret spent much of his time with his people.

He was teacher, craftsman, counselor, student, and sometimes even servant as well as the ruler; and she marveled he found time to do it all. That made her value the time he had spent with her lately so much more.

Erin pushed those thoughts away and admired the sunrise through the leaves. She could stay here forever, if only they would allow her to. The feelings of peace that permeated her faded as the door burst open and someone came in. She stole a glance over her shoulder. Ian, of course. His furrowed brow and narrowed eyes suggested he was in one of his worse moods today. If she could defuse his temper by not paying it any mind, this might not go so horribly, but she had a pretty good guess about why her cousin was here at this hour.

"It's daybreak." He stopped well away from her.

"Aye, cousin, it is, just as it is every morning." She waved for him to join her. "Come out to the balcony. It's beautiful out here."

"We need to be going."

Her jaw clenched. So much for not letting Ian annoy her. She dreaded leaving her temporary home but, as usual, she had been given no choice in the matter. Ian and Yvret had, for very different reasons, already decided she should be going. Her time here was ending. Every time her world seemed to settle down, someone came along and stirred things up again.

"Get Yvret," Ian insisted.

"I can't just order the Lord of the Seelie Court around, Ian." She looked out at the sunrise again, determined to make the most of this last time she'd see it in, well, who knew how long.

"Did he tell you when he'd be by?" Ian joined her at the rail.

"He doesn't clear his schedule through me." She rolled her eyes. "He's a busy man. He'll get to us when he can."

Ian slapped the rail with his hand and went back into the room, muttering.

He flopped onto the pillow pile she'd slept on last night, while she turned her full attention back to the new light of morning until the sun was well past the horizon. Periodically, she heard her cousin grump about the delays, but she ignored him.

The events of the last several days came back into her mind, showing her how much things could change in a short time. Just last week, she had a normal life, such as it was. She woke, did her chores, took care of her husband, and went to bed only to wake up again the next day and start all over again. So her part in the human world had continued on its tedious way.

Human world? There was a change in itself. Before recently, there had been nothing but that human world. Oh, she had known the Seelie and Unseelie Courts existed, but they were much more legend than real to her. Since the first encounter with Yvret and the sidhe prince, everything had snowballed. The normal life she'd had a mere week ago could never be reclaimed. Now the arts of the faeries drove her to do more and take control of her life. Her coming transformation filled her with excitement. Yvret had spoken of when, not if, she became a faerie.

Her life would never be the same, but wasn't that what she had wanted? Erin smiled and looked heavenward, whispering prayers of thanksgiving. As unpleasant and frightening as her days and nights had been two weeks ago, God had answered her prayer. Free of Connor's tyranny, her future lay within her grasp.

The sound of laughing children became suddenly louder. She closed her eyes and focused on the sound until she sensed the fey only a few feet behind her, showing as a gentle white light in her mind's perception. She could thank Yvret for teaching her how to make sense of the sensations she felt when fey or sidhe were around. When his long, thin-fingered hands rested on her shoulders, she didn't even jump.

"Good, you knew I was there."

She nodded and looked back at him, covering his hand with her own. "I heard you. Does that go away when I transform?"

"Yes, and as you get nearer your transformation, you'll learn to turn it on and off," he replied.

"You seemed to just appear," she said.

He leaned on the rail next to her. "Teleportation. You'll learn it when you're ready, if you become a sort of faerie who can handle that skill."

"Ian is antsy to leave." She pointed back over her shoulder.

"You'll be leaving soon enough." He leaned on the rail. "A few more minutes won't hurt either of you. He can wait."

A few more eons wouldn't hurt her at all. The human world held nothing for her but more pain and aggravation.

"I don't want to go." She leaned her elbow on the rail and her chin on her hand.

Yvret shrugged. "We all have to do things we don't like."

Erin scowled at him. "Is that supposed to help?"

"Until you've transformed, you don't belong here." He put his arm around her shoulders. "I wish the rules could be different."

She nodded, recalling the story he'd told her last night and her promise to do her part to relieve the stress his duties put on him. "True enough. Where do I go from here?"

"You can't stay in Scotland. That's for certain. After what you did, you'll have to flee the country and hope Connor's family doesn't follow. I had assumed you would go to France with your cousin."

She'd been away from there for so long, well, ten years at least. At the tender age of ten her father had arranged her marriage with Michel, a sergeant of the guards her father belonged to. They had only been waiting for her to come of age. She still had fond memories of him as the kind, young man who would go on long walks with her and their chaperone. He had sent her little presents and letters promising his eternal devotion if she remained true to him.

She wondered how much he'd changed over the years. He would now be in his thirties, so if time had been gracious to him, his brown hair wouldn't show the gray of age yet. More than likely, he had married another after Uncle had come for her and paid out her part of the contract. Hopefully, his marriage had been cordial at least. She would love to see him again just to reminisce about better times.

She smiled. "France? Really? I can go to Tours with Ian?"

Yvret chuckled. "Yes, my child, if that's what you'd like. What's to prevent you?"

"How will I stay in touch with you?" she asked.

"I told you I have a gate near Tours," he replied.

She must not have been paying attention, because she didn't remember that part of the conversation. Maybe she'd been close to a fit. That sometimes jumbled her memory.

"It's in the forest. I'll take you out by that gate so you'll know where it is, and we can meet there now and again."

Ian's snoring, which could wake the dead in Tours, reminded Erin of the other half of the problem.

Seeing her plans go up in smoke, Erin frowned. "Ian won't be happy about it. He will not let me go with him no matter how much I ask."

"Why do you need his approval?" Yvret looked at her from the corner of his eye.

"Well—because—it's just that—I have no idea."

He nodded. "You're an adult, aren't you?"

"Well, yes, but—"

"And you know how to make your own intelligent decisions, right?"

"Aye, I like to think so."

"Sometimes, people have power over you because you allow them to." He turned toward her. "I understand that allowing Connor to have control was better than getting pounded on for the evil infraction of, say, breathing, but that's not an issue anymore. Ian is just a man. Stop giving him the power to decide the course of your life. If you wish to go to Tours, go to Tours. I'll take you there. If you want to go somewhere else, I have other gates. If Ian doesn't like it, that's not your problem. You're the one with friends there. It's familiar ground to you. If he were a wise man, he would be glad to have you there as a guide and translator if nothing else."

Erin's face flushed with embarrassment. His words sounded so ridiculously logical she should have come up with them on her own. Why had she needed to hear him say it?

"It's hard to leave the past behind." Yvret shook his head. "You'll learn to. It only took me a few hundred years."

She smiled in spite of herself and gestured to Ian with a nod of her head. "We should see to waking Ian."

Anything to get the attention off of her for a few moments while she digested all the new ideas he'd given her.

He gestured for her to lead the way. "After you."

After standing over Ian for a few moments and wondering how in the world he could snore that loudly without waking himself, Erin gently shook his shoulder. "Ian, wake up. It's time to go."

Ian inhaled sharply and opened his eyes. "About time."

She stepped back. "Get up. We have a long way to go."

"We? You think you're coming with me, then?" He sat up and rubbed his eyes.

"How's your French these days?" She smirked. "Or do you think they all speak English there? You could count on one or two men in the guards who will understand even one word you say, and just maybe a merchant who has business in the islands, but that's about it. How fast can you learn your French?"

He only glared at her.

"And your letter of introduction to the guard captain? Where's that now?"

Ian's eyes threatened to burn her to cinders where she stood. Erin hoped he liked feeling so helpless. He'd done it to her so often. For once, she had the upper hand.

"Is there a problem?" Yvret stepped up behind her.

She looked over her shoulder at him for a moment. "He's not so happy to hear I'm going with him."

"Well, if you're going in any case. His approval is unnecessary." Yvret shrugged.

Ian stood up and fixed his eyes on Yvret while he spoke to her. "Let's go. We'll talk about this later when you haven't got your pet elf to watch over you."

"Really? Shall I translate that for him?" she asked.

The look of complete hatred he gave her answered for him.

"Where to?" Yvret asked.

"Tours," Erin answered. "Ian may go where he will from there."

Yvret smiled. "Good. I'll take us to the gate on this side then bring you through it."

Erin watched him closely as his fingers traced the path through the focusing move, more intricate than the ones she'd been taught. She'd have to see it a few more times before she could duplicate it. Soundlessly, her treehouse room faded away and reformed as a rocky hill.

When Ian staggered, Erin steadied him with her hand on his arm. "Are you well, cousin?"

"Of course I am." He jerked away from her, nearly tossing himself to the ground.

Erin turned to Yvret. "What's wrong with him?"

"Teleporting has that effect on those who can't grasp the energy involved," Yvret explained. "The dizziness will pass." He pointed skyward. "There's the gate."

She followed his finger. A ring of clouds marked this gate, but it looked different from the other somehow.

"No two are alike," he said, answering before she could even ask. "That helps us keep them all straight. You'll get used to the differences after a while. It only took me about fifty years."

Erin smiled. She wasn't yet half that old. "Is that all?"

He traced an entirely different symbol, but did this one so slowly she was certain she could imitate it herself. Feeling an odd tingling sensation rush through her, she lifted off of the ground, floating up in the air like a dandelion seed. Ian's iron grip on her arm reminded her of just how much he hated heights. When they were kids, he'd once been too scared to come down from a tree until she went up after him.

Yvret wouldn't drop them. Didn't he realize the rare opportunity he was getting? For as long as she could remember, Erin had watched the birds, butterflies, and even the most common bugs, envying them for their ability to leave the ground behind and ride on the winds. From this height, people looked like dust motes in a breeze. Yvret's huge tree palace took on the appearance of a stunted shrub. She loved every second of her time in the domain of the birds.

The experience lasted too long for Ian, if the nervous darting of his eyes could be trusted, but for Erin their flight ended far too soon. They reached the gate less than a minute after leaving the tree. As they passed through the clouds, Erin felt the same suffocating constriction on her mortal body that she had on her first trip through, but this time she didn't panic.

The clouds on one side of the ring gave way to a circle of mushrooms on the other side. Once they were standing on the ground again, the tingling sensation faded, and she heard Ian panting to catch his breath. He muttered curses, but Erin just let him rant. Yvret led them outside the gate.

"Yes." Yvret chuckled. "You do get used to the feeling you get coming through the rings."

She shuddered. "You'd have to."

They were standing in a dense forest very different from her mother's country, which she'd left for the last time. Leaving that unwelcome land for good almost made up for leaving the realm she wanted to live in forever. Tours, her old home, would have to do for the time being. She used to go on hikes in the forests with Father or Michel, but she had a tough time getting her bearings now that she'd returned.

"The city is that way." Yvret pointed. "I'll meet you here every morning, at about dawn, hm? Practice what you've learned."

As Erin watched him step away, fear roiled in her gut. Maybe Ian had a point. Having Yvret there to watch over her gave her strength.

Yvret came back to her. "And Erin, I know I told you to stop thinking like a human, but as you change, at least pretend to think like one. I didn't and I had an amazing amount of trouble for my efforts."

Erin nodded, certain she'd have trouble remembering to pretend to think like humans.

Yvret took both of her hands in his. "You'll do fine, my child. Before you know it, the time will come for you to join the faeries permanently." His look hardened. "And I saw the way you were watching me. Don't try to duplicate anything you see me do until it's time. Some facets of the falling sickness can do you real harm if you're not careful, and you're not ready for those power levels yet. Do you understand?"

Erin felt her face flush. Nothing got past him, did it? "Aye, I won't try them. Promise. I'll see you in the morning."

She watched as he entered the ring and then turned to face her.

"Things may have changed, even in only ten years," he warned.

Before she could ask what he'd meant, he had disappeared again.

Ian spun her toward him. "It's high time I was going. Just point me in the right direction."

"I'll take you." She gestured.

"No matter what your pretty little elf says, I don't need you." Ian pushed her back. "You'll only slow me down."

He turned his back to her and walked away.

"Good luck finding enough people who speak English," she called after him. "And ones who can make sense of your accent, too."

He stopped. "I'll manage. You'll only be a problem for me."

"Why? Do you plan on telling the world a wee slip of a woman saved your skin in a fight because you couldn't keep your feet under you? Maybe they'll laugh you right back to Scotland."

Ian returned to her. "Now understand this and make no mistake. I saved your life. Not the other way around." He grabbed her arm. "And if you have any daft ideas of telling what really happened, just you remember no one will believe a woman is skilled with a sword. They'll believe me, just because I won't sound like a raving madman."

Erin quickly traced a pattern with the fingers of her free hand down at her side and felt a surge of power race through her. She focused on keeping the effect small. Ian yelped. When he retracted his hand, she grabbed his arm and watched his face contort with pain. Finally satisfied he'd learned his lesson, she released him with a generous shove.

"What in God's name." He rubbed his arm and flexed his fingers.

"Just one of my new skills, and mind I kept it as contained as I could. Keep your hands off me, or next time I'll blast you back home with it."

To keep Ian from noticing one hand was shaking just a little, Erin walked past him to lead the way to Tours. She smiled with some satisfaction when she heard Ian following along behind her.

As she walked, she recognized more of her surroundings: a huge boulder in the clearing where she and Dad had watched the stars, the babble of a nearby stream she and Michel had followed many long afternoons, the pond where Michel had taught her to skip rocks.

How would her one-time fiancé react when he saw her again? Would he welcome her as a wayward friend or send her away to avoid an awkward situation with his wife? Would he even recognize her? Her appearance had greatly changed in ten years.

Where would she stay if he didn't give her a place? She had no money, and as she counted back through the days, she figured the date. On a Sunday, she wouldn't be able to get any quick work to earn a few sous for a room and a pauper's meal. If the old convent still operated north of town, she might prevail upon the sisters for help, but where would that leave Ian?

He'd just have to find his own way. Her cousin had insisted he could handle this alone. Maybe she should let him. She would try to find a place for him, but if she couldn't, his accommodations were his concern.

When she saw a tree on which Michel had carved their initials in the middle of a heart, she knew she would soon reach his manor, and her thoughts returned to him. In her mind's eyes, she could still see his handsome face clearly. She'd always been drawn to his dark brown eyes, which radiated gentleness and compassion. Some nights she would see him in her dreams and hear his deep, rich voice.

Of all the wonderful qualities he had to recommend him, Erin remembered his generosity the most. An honest man or woman unafraid of doing legitimate work might prevail upon him for a place to stay or at least a decent meal. He only required them to work for it. Other men in his company had chided him for his charity, and she recalled times when someone had taken advantage of him, but he had continued his pious work unabated. No, she wouldn't have to fear being put out. At worst, she might have to earn the roof over her head and the food on her plate, but Michel would not turn her away.

Her realization did nothing to cage the butterflies in her stomach. When she reached the gate of the manor, she stopped. Michel would not send her out onto the streets with no money or even a decent prospect of work. She knew that, but could she risk a cold reception? Would she be able to handle his rejection?

Erin had no grand delusions that Michel would gather her in his arms and whisper kind words in her ear, nor did she think she wanted that. She would join the fey soon, so the last thing she needed was a love in this world to break her heart when the time came for her to leave.

They came through the last of the trees to a road facing a modest manor, which was still grander than anything Ian had been in. A tree-height wall surrounded the property. Roof peaks were only just visible over the crenelations.

"This is it?" Ian asked.

Erin frowned. Ian needed to be considered. Even if Ian could afford an inn, he didn't have enough of the local language to find a bed to rest on. She'd offered her help and couldn't back down now. She would have to risk proving her fears true.

Chapter 7

Michel walked into the kitchen for breakfast and found Diego seated at the table. The stable hand assigned to watch him stood nearby. The Spaniard may have helped Corinne, but he had grown up stealing, and oak trees never spontaneously sprouted pine needles. When Diego made a move to rise, Michel waved him off.

"No, no, don't bother." He sat across from Diego.

As much as Michel appreciated the respect the boy was trying to show him, his wounds were still mending.

"It's good to see you up," Michel said.

Diego smiled. "Yes. The—uh—stick?" he asked, holding up the black cane Michel had loaned him.

"Cane."

"Cane. It helps. Thank you."

"I picked it up a few years ago when I twisted my knee and haven't needed it since, thankfully. I'm glad it's useful to you." Michel absently rubbed the side of his leg.

The injury wouldn't have been so embarrassing if he hadn't gotten it for something so silly. The next time one of the cats got behind his desk, he was of a mind to leave it there.

"The clothes you give to me are yours once?" Diego asked.

Michel looked him over and nodded. "I was much younger and smaller when I wore those. They won't fit me now. They're yours. How's the leg?"

"It hurts me, but it gets better." Diego glanced at the cane. "The doctor says I no need the stick—uh—cane soon."

"Good, good. Have you given any thought to giving me the information I need to track down the band of thieves?" Michel asked.

Diego shook his head. "No."

"No, you have not considered it, or no, you will not help me?"

"I no can help you," he replied.

Michel frowned. So he had saved the boy's life, and now Diego couldn't see his way clear to help catch the criminals?

Michel nodded. "I see."

"I no think you do," Diego insisted.

"Oh, I do. What makes you think you'll be able to return to them?"

Diego leaned forward. "You no understand. Luis is my brother."

"Yes, and he already ordered you killed once."

"So, he betrays me, and I can betray him?" Diego asked.

Michel studied the boy. The argument carried a certain logic.

He stroked his beard. "Bringing a criminal to justice is not betrayal, even if it is your brother."

Diego set his jaw and shook his head. "I find Luis. I deal with him. It is a fight between brothers. This no is betrayal."

That was all very reasonable in theory, but Michel suspected some deeper motive drove the Spaniard's convictions. Michel had some pretty good guesses at what those might be.

"I suppose I can see that," Michel said with a shrug. "If my brother, well, any man really, did to me what he did to you, I'd want to be the one to wring his neck. Personally."

Diego's eyes went wide. "What? Maybe I hear you wrong."

"Revenge is completely understandable." Michel brushed the idea away with a sweep of his hand. "You do want him to pay for what he did to you, don't you?"

"Yes. I mean, no! It is different than what you say."

Michel smiled. The boy's gut instinct had spoken before intellect had tempered the response. Faulting Diego for it, though, would have made Michel the worst sort of hypocrite. Even with age and experience to teach him better, Michel couldn't say for certain he wouldn't want vengeance. He had to admit paying the bandits back for their rough treatment of his wife drove him on. Revenge wasn't the only thing leading the boy, though.

"It must have been difficult for you to see your brother's wealth and have nothing of your own," Michel continued.

Diego nodded and frowned. "*Sí*, I work very hard, and still I live almost as a beggar, but Luis has all. He is warm. He is dry. He eats good food. He has good things. I freeze. I have only things he uses until they break or are bad. My tent leaks and is too small for me almost. Much of my food turns soon. Anyway, it is this way for many years."

At least he was honest about that much. He admitted greed was one of his reasons to pursue his brother. Understandable greed, certainly, but greed all the same. Even more impressive, he freely owned it. Others might have hid it or become incensed that the matter had even been brought up. More points in the boy's favor.

"You won't be able to keep the wealth, even if you find it all," Michel warned. "As much as possible will need to be returned to the original owners."

Diego's countenance darkened, but when he spoke, he didn't become irate. "You think I am only a thief."

"No, no, not at all."

"I promise Corinne to make her safe again. I no wish to see her have fear." Diego's brow furrowed. "I keep my promise. You see. I steal before, but not now."

Michel raised his hand to stop the boy. "Of course, Diego. If you were so poor in character, you would never have put yourself in danger to free Corinne. In fact, you would have applauded Luis's plans. You're a good man, but I was once your age, full of ideals and ready to solve the problems of the world on my own. I couldn't, and neither can you."

"No, but I solve one problem. Luis."

"That sounds good except for one small thing." Michel mimed, pinching something between his thumb and finger. "How will you take on all your brother's men to be able to reach him? You are one man. If the campsite was any indication, they're about fifty, maybe even seventy-five if they were a little cozy."

"Yes, about so many, but Luis is not always with his men," Diego explained. "Once I have him, the rest, they are easy."

Michel had his doubts. Focusing on revenge and greed would get in Diego's way and could lead him to make bad decisions. Youthful idealism could cloud his judgement. Pushing him, though, forcing him to reveal what he knew, might make the young man disappear. Then the only decent lead Michel had would be gone.

On a more personal level, Diego had his faults, but he was a good kid. This plan of his might get him killed. Going after a band of brigands was as sure a way to die as any. Michel had certainly lost enough of his guardsmen to the bandits already, and all they had done was patrol the area around the city walls. Fortunately, there was a way to give the boy what he wanted and still protect him from his own exuberance.

"You'll need weapons, I assume," Michel suggested.

Diego nodded. "*Sí, señor.*"

"I'll have Philippe issue you something from the armory," he promised. "I trust you to do this, and let me know if you change your mind about accepting help."

"Thank you," Diego replied.

Even as Michel smiled and nodded his acknowledgment, he made a mental note to have a duty rotation established to have men keep an eye on Diego and monitor his travels. Diego could lead them to his brother without even realizing it.

***

Diego thanked Michel again, but the accusations kept coming back to him. Revenge and greed. The suggestion had been that he wanted revenge and he might be considered normal enough to want to get back at the brother who had hurt him so much. Maybe that was true, but what of it? Luis had to pay for what he had done. He had been cruel and perverse. Such men needed to get the justice they deserved.

Further, Michel could have the luxury of calling proper ambition by greed's name. The guard captain had a huge house, well-made clothes, plenty of food, and a beautiful wife. He was important. He had power.

Diego had nothing. He lived on charity now without any prospects. According to everything right and natural, he should strive to improve himself. To do otherwise would be sloth, a deadly sin. If he could acquire even a small amount of Luis's wealth, Diego would have something to build on at least. He should have much more than that. If Michel wanted to call those things greed and revenge, let him. Diego wanted only justice.

When Corinne joined them, Michel reached across the table to clasp her hand. The cook served a breakfast of bread, jam, eggs, and bacon. Not too long ago, half the food dished onto his plate would have been his whole day's fare, not just his breakfast.

Aside from some pleasantries about his health and continuing recovery, the conversation stayed away from him, thankfully. He had been scrutinized enough for one day. Lord and Lady Gaultier spoke of their day's work and plans for the evening. When Diego didn't hear himself mentioned anywhere in there, he hid his frown. Just as well. He had plenty to do. Finding a link in the spy network would take all day if he could find one at all.

They were just finishing when the housekeeper rushed in and spoke too fast for Diego to pick out even a few words. Understanding conversations was hard enough when they remembered to talk at a rate he could make decent use of. Whatever the matter was brought a puzzled look to Corinne's face. Michel's eyes sparkled and his usually stern look softened into a kind smile.

"What is it?" Diego asked.

"Probably just some lost travelers." Corinne pushed back from the table. "Like as not, they're on a pilgrimage or something and got here only to run out of money, so now they're looking for charity. I'll have Giselle make up the guest rooms." She leaned over Michel and kissed his cheek.

With such a generous heart, Diego had to wonder how they kept what wealth they had.

Michel rose and nodded. "With any luck, they'll be staying with us for a while."

Using the cane and the table for support, Diego pushed himself up to his feet and followed them toward the entryway. Now would be a good time to try to find an informant to help him locate Luis. He didn't have the promised sword yet, but all he wanted to do was ask questions. Defending himself shouldn't be necessary.

In the small reception room just off the foyer, the couple was waiting. The man, lounging in a chair, wore a red and black plaid kilt. His dark hair was windblown, and his shirt was half tucked into his kilt and half out. He looked for all the world like he had been traveling at a dead run since the day before.

The woman's appearance was similar enough to be kin. Small white flowers dusted the woman's dark hair, as if she had just come in through a shower of the little blooms. The season was still too early for flowers, but there they were anyway. Instead of Corinne's almost skeletal thinness, this woman had some size to her. She wasn't obese by anyone's standards, but she looked more natural. She stood as they entered.

"Erin?" Michel studied the woman. "Is that you?"

Looking up at his host, Diego saw more than recognition there. Michel cared, or had once cared, very deeply about Erin.

"Have I changed so much?" The woman smiled.

Her voice had a pleasant but challenging lilt, requiring some concentration on his part.

Michel kissed the back of Erin's hand. "Well, I recognized your cousin immediately, but what happened to the ungainly ten-year-old I said goodbye to all those years ago?"

"I grew," she said.

Introductions were made all the way around. From the way Ian grunted and groaned as he stood to greet everyone, Diego thought the big man had been wounded.

As Diego bowed to make his acquaintance of Erin, his cane slipped on the polished wood floor, but before he fell too far, a firm grip on his shirt collar brought him up short and choked him. A second later, Erin caught him across the chest, relieving the pressure on his throat. He hadn't anticipated such strength in a woman, and he felt goofy now for his clumsiness. As graceful and elegant as she was, she would see him as an oaf.

"Are you well?" Erin asked.

"Yes, thank you," Diego said as he righted himself again with her and Michel's help.

"You'll have to excuse him," Michel said. "He recently found out just how sharp a sword could be."

"To prevent me from finding out," Corinne added.

Michel pulled her into a one-armed embrace as Corinne leaned into him.

At that, Ian covered his face with his hand and coughed in a way that was clearly intentional. Diego thought he saw the man's cheeks color a little.

"So what brings you back this way?" Michel gestured to the squashy chair behind Erin then sat in another one.

"Well, Ian was hoping to take after Father, and I have nothing else to keep me in Scotland, so I came along." Erin leaned forward. "And the truth of it is, I'm a wee bit homesick."

"How long can you stay in Tours?" Corinne asked.

"For Ian, a long while, we're hoping. For myself, I'm not so sure," Erin replied.

"Well, you must stay here with us."

"I wouldn't want to be a bother." Erin shook her head.

"Nonsense. You're staying here. I won't hear of anything else. I'll have two of the guest rooms made up." Corinne waved over one of the maids.

Erin nodded once. "Thank you."

"Does your husband not travel with you?" Michel laced his fingers across his chest. "I assume you married after you left here."

Erin bit her lip. "Yes, I was married until recently."

The pain Diego saw in her eyes wrenched at his heart. Nothing short of a tragedy widowed a lady at such a young age.

"Connor drew steel on her. When he wouldn't hear reason, I had to take him," Ian explained.

His voice had a much more severe version of Erin's lilt and so many of the words were clipped short that Diego had to fight to get the meaning of each one.

"Oh, Erin, I'm so terribly sorry." Corinne clasped Erin's hand. "Oh, you poor dear. You're shaking!"

"That's, um, natural for her, dear," Michel said softly.

"I have the falling sickness," Erin explained.

Diego nodded. About a year ago, Luis had recruited a man with that problem. The fits he'd experienced would drive him to bed for days, but for alerting them to the presence of fey and sidhe, no one could do better.

Then Juan had been apprenticed to a sidhe, and the skills he had learned had come in handy. Until he vanished one night, killed by the sidhe they found sleeping in his tent Diego guessed, Juan had shown remarkable skill as a one-man raiding party. He had even taken on a whole garrison and laid waste to it.

Was Erin also a faerie apprentice like Juan had been? If she possessed the same abilities, he might be able to recruit her help against Luis. Normally, he would never have even entertained the idea of a woman filling that role, but if Erin studied with the fey, she might consent to helping him repair his wealth and stop Luis's cruelty. Could he even trust her? Without more information about who she was and the content of her character, keeping his own counsel would be safer for now.

"Have you eaten?" Corinne asked.

"Nay, we just left our last place a wee bit ago even afore breakfast was served." Ian smirked. "Erin was in such a hurry to get here. She was excited about seeing you again."

The tension in Erin's face, brief though it was, called Ian a liar.

Diego excused himself from the rest of the conversation and left for town. He'd watch Erin as closely as he could in the coming days. Before he made his plans known to her, he wanted to be certain she could do what he hoped.

In the meantime, there were people he could talk to.

The walk into town took longer than he'd expected, and his injured leg protested the activity loudly. Diego leaned a little heavier on the cane and made his way to the tavern a short distance inside the main gates. This was a common hang out for men who had fallen out of Luis's favor badly enough to get ousted from the band. He tolerated no failures, even if the man could not have prevented the mistake. A flip of a coin or a roll of the dice or a random selection of a card decided a man's fate more often than any sort of rational thought.

The severe reaction had deprived the band of skilled men and created a surplus of bitterness and resentment.

The tavern was populated with tables and chairs that appeared to be made from old barn wood. The patrons wore clothing that was more patches than intact material except for a conspicuous, better dressed group in the corner, the very group of men he'd hoped to find.

Hernando, a muscular mountain of a man driven from the group when a sudden rainstorm had put an end to a planned night of thievery, stood and rested his hand on the pommel of a short sword as Diego approached. The other four men at the table twisted around and scowled.

Diego held his hand palm out and spoke in their common language. "Peace. I'm not here to cause you trouble."

"What do you want, then?" Hernando's eyes narrowed.

"The same thing you do." Diego stopped outside of the reach of a blade.

Alonso, the antithesis of Hernando in nearly all respects, snorted. "Do you? I want your brother's head on a pike."

"Is that all? Luis ordered my death then left me for dead."

"His own little brother? For what crime would he do that to you?"

"Does it matter? He demands unwavering loyalty from his men but never shows the same in return." Diego took a step closer and lowered his voice. "But I have a way to use our own skills against him to weaken his plans so at the end of the month, the law itself will get our revenge."

"Why should we believe you?" Hernando asked.

Diego shrugged. "Don't then. Let Luis gain more and more wealth and power while you have nothing. I just thought you might like to increase the contents of your purse while making Luis understand what he lost by driving us out." He turned away. "Suit yourselves."

"Wait, wait. I for one want to hear what he has to say," Jaime, dismissed for missing his night's quota by a single *peseta,* said.

"All right, we'll hear your plan." Hernando pulled a chair over from another table nearby.

Diego returned to them and eased himself down into the chair. "At month's end, Luis has a grand raid in the works. If he loses enough men before then, he cannot possibly succeed against the opposition. The law will capture him, and his punishment avenges us all."

Jaime rolled his eyes. "It'll never work. He'll just abort the plan."

Hernando tapped his finger on the table. "Maybe. Has he consulted his divination yet?"

"He did." Diego nodded. "A pendulum selected the book. A die roll told the page number. A random card chose a sentence."

"Figures." Hernando shook his head at Jaime. "No, he won't change it. He might recruit more help, but no amount of counsel or reason will convince him to abort now. 'Fate has spoken.'"

Alonso nodded. "And if it fails, it'll be because one of his men betrayed him. It could never be that he was wrong, no never that."

"So, details. What's your plan?" Jaime asked.

"Do anything you can to pick off his men." Diego numbered off ideas on his fingers. "They're more vulnerable alone, so catch them out on patrols or intercept them when they've come into the city for a little pickpocketing or slip past the patrol at night and eliminate a few at the edge of the camp or any other situation where you can find someone alone. Then when the end of the month comes, Luis will be short-handed."

"That all sounds easy enough." Alonso smirked. "And what are you doing while all this is happening?"

"The night before Luis enacts his plans, I enact my own."

Hernando struck the table. "Details!"

"No. I keep my own counsel. Otherwise, the word gets back to Luis, and he prepares for it. I don't want to know the details of your plans, either. Reduce Luis's numbers however you like."

"And if we go along, how do we get paid?" Jaime asked.

"We meet and divide the spoils. How else?" Diego looked around the table at all five men, pausing at Gabriel and Bonito, the two who hadn't spoken. "What do you say? Do we get our revenge and gain the wealth Luis collects at the expense of men he cares nothing for? Or do we allow him to continue as he does?"

The five exchanged a look before Hernando sat back in his chair. "All right, we're with you if for no reason other than anything that causes Luis trouble is fine by me."

Diego smiled and nodded once. "Fine. Then we meet here two days after the next new moon."

As he rose, Hernando stood. "Don't betray us. You're a much easier target than Luis."

"Trust me, *amigo*. I want to see Luis's fall no less than you."

He hobbled out of the tavern without another look back and smiled. Now, to find a contact who could lead him to the camp.

***

When her image of the willow tree by the brook showed all the detail she could give it, Erin opened her eyes and held up her hand. The tremor had only lessened slightly, but her mind had lost the numbing fog. Her time practicing faerie skills had improved her sleep effect, but she would wisely make an end of her studies for the day.

She heaved a sigh. As much as she'd rather keep going, she had to be sane about learning to control her new abilities. If she didn't stop now, she'd be too groggy to remember more than her name for a day or two. Crippling fatigue would help neither her studies nor her sword practice.

Rising from her bed, she went to the dresser where she had hidden the rapier manual under two old chemises Corinne had said once belonged to her mother. The cloth had yellowed some with age and use, but both were serviceable. Erin had gratefully accepted the gift.

Her fingers had brushed past the leather book when a knock on the door made her jump. She quickly replaced her manual and covered it. A blush rose to her face. If Michel ever found out what she did in the privacy of her room, he would demand uncomfortable explanations from her. As stern as he could be about the mores of polite society, he might even turn her out.

"Yes?" Erin called.

Corinne peeked in. "I'm going into town for some errands. Henri's going with me, but he's not much on conversation if horses aren't your fancy. Would you like to keep me company?"

Erin considered the offer. Yvret had suggested she continue learning to use the rapier, but a trip into town piqued her curiosity. How much had Tours changed over the years? Oh, major features like the palace and the cathedral should be the same, but what of the rest of the city? Would she even recognize it?

"I'd love to," Erin replied.

Practicing with a sword could keep until her return. Grabbing her cloak, Erin followed Corinne downstairs where they met a man who reeked of the stables.

On the way to the city, an awkward silence hung in the air between her and Corinne. Erin had to get the conversation started somehow to keep from going mad.

"Um...how long have you and Michel been married?" she asked.

"Eight years," Corinne replied.

Erin waited for her to say more, but the quiet reigned. Corinne's eyes darted around searching the trees for a threat. Faeries worked and played freely in the area as Erin recalled. Maybe Corinne worried sidhe were hiding just out of sight.

Erin leaned closer. "There are no faeries of either sort about."

Corinne looked at her. "What?"

"The falling sickness lets me know when faeries are around." She made a wide gesture with her hands to encompass the whole area. "Right now, I don't have any of the signs I would if they were close."

Corinne stopped. "It's not that. I-I-I shouldn't have come. I should've stayed home and let someone else go."

"I don't understand. What's wrong?"

Michel's wife leaned closer and spoke softly. "There are bandits in these woods. Diego used to be one of them until they beat him for helping me escape."

Taking on a group of bandits to rescue someone? Let no one doubt his bravery.

Erin's eyes widened. "You were their prisoner, then?"

"Yes," Corinne whispered.

"We'll be fine. Henri is with us," Erin assured her.

Corinne shuddered. "I-I don't know. Would you think me terribly silly if we went back?"

"Nay, but what if you give me your list?" Erin suggested. "Henri can take you home and I'll go on to town and see to running your errands."

Henri cleared his throat. "Begging your pardon, *Madame*, but his Lordship insisted I not allow Lady Gaultier to walk alone. When you got here this morning, he made his order go for you, as well."

Erin scowled. Touching, but unnecessary. She could handle a few cutthroats. She had her faerie training, but then again, what if that weren't enough? Already, she'd harnessed the energies that powered faerie effects today. Even one more might drive her over the edge. Her visit to Tours would have to wait.

"Please, Erin, come back with me. Don't go on alone." Corinne clasped both of Erin's hands.

Seeing the tears in the other woman's eyes, Erin hugged her. "We'll take you home again, then maybe Henri would agree to take me to the city with your list. I'm sure you have plenty to do at the house."

She felt Corinne nod.

"*Señora? Señora* Gaultier, are you well?" a voice called.

Erin looked over her shoulder and saw the Spanish boy. Diego wasn't it? He hobbled over, leaning hard on his cane. When he went to put a comforting hand on Corinne's shoulder, Henri cleared his throat loudly.

Diego pulled back. "What is it? Why do you cry?"

"We went to run the errands, but something's spooked her a wee bit." Erin rubbed Corinne's back. "She'll be fine."

Corinne dried her eyes and fished her list from a small, ornately embroidered pouch. "Diego, could you take this to town to get the things I need for dinner tomorrow?"

He took the pouch but replied, "I am happy to help you, *señora*, but I find out today how little I speak here. No one understands me."

"I'll go with you," Erin suggested. "I can translate."

Corinne turned to Erin. "There's enough money there to get everything on the list. Thank you."

Erin smiled. "Won't be a problem. Take care of yourself. We'll be home later."

As she watched Henri follow Corinne away, Erin's mind flooded with second thoughts. She knew nothing of Diego's character. If he'd been a brigand before, how could she be certain he'd had a change of heart? What if he led her into a trap? The one chivalrous act she knew about might have been a fluke or motivated by personal gain.

She looked at him. Leaning so heavily on his cane, he clearly posed little threat. She might not be able to engage her new training, but she could run. Corinne clearly trusted him. If he'd protected her escape at his own expense, Erin ought to be able to rely on him to behave himself. She gestured for Diego to lead the way.

***

Alone with Erin now, he considered taking advantage of their solitude to ask her about faerie training. Taking her into the actual fight would be unacceptable, but maybe she could do something from a safer distance. Every time he screwed enough courage together to say something, he stopped himself. There were too many mysteries surrounding Erin. Until he could be certain she wouldn't run to Michel, he would continue to watch for clues about who she was and what she knew.

Maybe talking to her would help him feel more natural.

"I have fear Corinne never recovers," Diego said.

Erin shook her head. "She'll be fine. She's a strong lass who's had a bit of a scare. How long ago did it happen?"

"Two weeks."

"Well, then, that's not so long. These things take time."

Diego nodded, hoping the confidence he heard in her voice meant she understood Corinne better than he did.

"What happened to her?" Erin asked.

"She runs into the men of my brother," Diego explained.

He described the events of that day two weeks ago, and his efforts to secure Corinne's release by promising a noblewoman's ransom would be significant.

"Luis no hears me. He says this one necklace, a heart of sacrifice, is more than any ransom we could get." Diego continued, ending with what payment he received for helping her get away.

Erin looked up at him with pity in her eyes. "I don't understand how people can turn on their own relatives."

He heard a familiar pain in her voice and recalled her cousin's comment about her husband taking arms against her. While he sought for something helpful to say, they continued down the path in silence.

Erin drew a deep breath. "Are you looking for your brother and his men?"

Should he risk telling her his plans? If he kept the explanation general enough, there should be no harm. He'd keep the specifics for himself. No sense in tipping his hand too far.

"*Sí*." He nodded. "I know a few things to try."

"Those had to do with the errands you had a tough time dealing with today, hm?" she asked.

"I find it is difficult to understand and speak to people. No one speaks Spanish and English. My French?" He groaned.

She shrugged. "Well, we can take care of questioning people today."

Diego shook his head. She could take the information she heard and go to Michel. "That no is a good idea."

"Don't be daft." She glanced at him. "When else would you do it?"

"It is too dangerous."

She gave him an incredulous look. "Translating between you and another is hardly life-threatening."

He snorted. "So you say, but Michel kills me if I bring you into this."

"I'll handle Michel."

"I no think so, *señora*," he replied.

"Suit yourself, then." She numbered off points on her fingers. "But, I'll tell you now, Corinne is too scared to come this way to be any help and will be for some time. Servants of the household have enough to do without running your errands. If you wait for Michel to have a free moment or two for this, we'll all be gray when you start your inquiries. Take my word for it. My father was a lieutenant, and he barely had time to breathe."

Erin had an excellent point. He needed help, but could he trust Erin to keep the information from the captain? Head spinning wildly with his worries, all Diego could think to do was stall.

"I must think. I answer you later."

She shrugged. "As you will."

Her words expressed disinterest, but she rolled her eyes and turned away from him. He didn't need good English to know what that meant. The ensuing silence was heavier than the chests full of gold and silver in Luis's tent. Didn't she see he only meant to protect them both?

"You no understand," he insisted. "I look for my brother, and—"

She held up a hand to stop him then took a deep breath and blew it out, deflating the rigidity in her posture. "I understand, Diego. You fear what happened to Corinne will happen to me, too. What you don't realize is that I know what terror that poor lady feels. I lived with it for far too long. There was no one to help me escape it, so I want to help Corinne just as much as you do. I should not engage in the real fighting, of course, but I can talk, can't I?"

Diego nodded. The logic sounded solid enough, and he really did need someone to help him deal with the locals. However, getting a woman involved still felt wrong, especially one who had such close ties to the city guards.

As they came around the bend in the path, the Tours gate came into view. Without knowing if any of the guards spoke English, Diego couldn't risk them overhearing this particular conversation.

"We talk later?" he asked.

***

Erin thanked the innkeeper and turned to Diego. After a few more disagreements, he had finally decided to let her help him, under a stern warning that Michel had left the investigation in his hands. She didn't know whether or not to believe his claim, but time would tell. At least she had an excuse to not tell her former fiancé about her involvement in what would be considered a "man's business."

"He no helps us?" Diego guessed, indicating the tavern's proprietor with a nod.

She shook her head. "I'm afraid not. I hope you have other places to check because we've hit a dead end here."

He hung his head. "No. This is it. We try all the places I know."

"We'll think of something."

"I no have your…um…" He stopped and looked at the wall beyond her.

"Confidence?"

He nodded. "Confidence."

She picked up the basket containing their day's purchases. "You're not giving up, are you?"

"No," he answered, "but I need to think more about this. There are so many spies. I believe this is the easy way to find them, but I no am right."

As Erin followed Diego out, she said, "If you still need a translator, I'll be around for a little while."

"You go somewhere?" he asked.

"Home." And none too soon for her liking. That brief time in Yvret's realm had spoiled her for anything else.

Diego frowned.

"What is it?" she asked.

He forced a smile. "Nothing, *señora*."

"I don't believe that, either. The afternoon may have been disappointing, but we're not finished yet. You'll find them. I don't imagine your brother has gone too far away. We'll go home and try again tomorrow."

Erin admired his courage and the persistence he needed to hobble through the streets of Tours for the last several hours. She would've been laid up in bed with a wound like the one he'd described. He hadn't even complained once. For his benefit, she'd asked to stop a few times during the day to give him a chance to rest. During their breaks, she'd found him an engaging conversationalist, even if he did have problems picking the right words. After a short adjustment period, she'd even gotten used to his accent.

"Someone follows us," Diego whispered.

She stole a look back. The two men were easy to see in the nearly empty streets. They weren't even trying to hide themselves.

"The contacts we've been looking for?" Erin asked.

He shook his head. "They are from the camp. Bandits, like I am once."

Erin felt her blood run cold. "What do we do? You're in no shape for a fight, and I—"

She stopped herself just short of saying she shouldn't be using her new talents now. Although she felt much better than earlier and could manage something if she kept the effect small, Erin knew better than to use anything Diego might classify as "magic." The witch trial Yvret had shown her argued loudly for caution.

"The office of Michel...um...the guards. Where do we find them?" He glanced down a side street. "The men who follow no are so stupid as to go there."

"The garrison is this way," she replied.

Turning down the next street, Erin struggled to remember a path. The shops along the way had been repainted or new ones had replaced the ones she'd once known. Then she saw the church spire. Unless her memory had failed her, she'd find the garrison within a block of the cathedral. She made for that and remembered another landmark.

Her nanny used to take her to a bakery to get a sweet roll. Then they would take a shortcut through an alley to the garrison to see Father and Michel. She could make use of that alley.

When she saw the tailor's shop, now with bright red and yellow paint, Erin knew this street also had the old bakery.

"They get closer." Diego's voice was barely louder than the cane clicking on the stone street. "How far?"

"If I can just find the baker." Erin spotted her goal, looking much more dilapidated than she remembered but definitely the place where she and her nanny used to stop. "There! Now we can go through the alley next to it, and we'll be at the garrison."

She directed Diego into the alley and stopped as her breath caught in her throat. Diego muttered something in Spanish that probably wasn't fit for polite company.

"That wall wasn't there. We just went straight through here two, three times a week." Erin spun back toward the open end of the alley.

"Never mind. Go back. We find a different way."

The humorless smiles on the faces of the two men blocking the alley's only exit tensed her shoulders. What did they want? After she set the basket down, Erin's hand dropped to the knife at her belt as the two brigands exchanged words in Spanish with Diego. She understood too little to get their meaning, but their tones told her this wasn't a happy reunion.

"Behind me." Diego stepped past her.

"Like you're in any condition to fight." She gripped the hilt of her knife. "You're not even armed."

He swung his arm back and pushed her. "Behind me!"

Tripping over her skirt, Erin fell back on the cobblestones with a loud groan.

As the two men came closer, both drew knives of their own. Using his cane, Diego struck one on the hand, making him yowl as he dropped the blade. The other charged at Diego and knocked him down. The first sprang back to his feet and went after Erin. She scrambled to stand up in time to meet the attack and drew her dagger. Bringing her blade up, she felt the steel point sliding between ribs. When she pulled her knife back toward her, it caught on something, so she let go. Leaving him, she turned to help Diego and found him reaching for his cane just beyond his fingertips while holding his assailant's wrist to keep the knife away.

After looking around for the knife her attacker had dropped and failing to find it, Erin turned to her fey abilities. The lightning one would burn both Diego and the brigand. Shield wouldn't help. She'd have to use sleep and hope she could confine the effect to the thief. Quickly weaving the symbol in the air, Erin approached and grabbed the back of the man's neck.

Her mind swam in a deepening haze, and she didn't even know for certain if the trick had worked. She fell to her knees and fought to think clearly enough to start the control exercise Yvret had taught her. Lights flickered in her teary eyes, and she knew the seizure was coming.

Chapter 8

The pressure on Diego's arm evaporated as Pedro's eyes rolled back in his head a moment before the bandit collapsed. What had taken the fight out of him so suddenly?

The sound of a woman crying rose above Diego's confusion. Erin! Was she hurt? Ignoring the pain lancing through his leg, Diego rolled the weight off of him and saw Erin on her knees only a few feet away. She looked at her violently shaking hands as if they were possessed.

He crawled over to her and put a comforting hand on her shoulder. "Are you well, *señora*? How are you hurt?"

She shook her head but didn't speak.

"What do I do?"

Although he couldn't say what he'd expected for an answer, she surprised him by simply sitting down and leaning her forehead on her fingers.

"I am here, Erin. I no leave you."

She slowly nodded.

He watched her for a few minutes, but she made no further moves. Gradually, the crying stopped, replaced only by occasional sniffles. The tremor in her hands slowed. Even after she seemed calmer, she still sat there in the alley.

When a loud snore broke the silence, Erin chuckled softly. Diego twisted around to Pedro. The man slept? How could that be? What sane person fell asleep in the middle of a fight, especially one he was winning?

A spell! Was faerie magic at work here? No other explanation made sense. He thought back to the sidhe apprentice Luis had once hired. Casting spells had eventually driven Juan into one of those fits. Erin's seizure had started just after Pedro had fallen asleep. The two had to be related. Erin, like Juan, had to be a faerie apprentice. His theory would even explain why she had been ready to help in the fight. In a darkening alley off of a fairly deserted street, she would need to fear little if she revealed her abilities.

A loud voice from the alley's entrance barked an order in French. Diego spun toward the voice and waved over the guard who stood there. Erin slowly looked up as the man squatted next to her. While the two of them talked, Diego watched the Frenchman's hard look soften. His own name, hers, and Michel's came up more than once, but Diego got little else out of the conversation.

At some length, the guard turned to check on the two bandits.

Erin turned to Diego and spoke slowly and deliberately. "I told him how the fight started and about your efforts to protect me. You killed that one over there." She indicated the dead one with a nod. "We're not sure why the other collapsed, but I heard the sign of fey nearby."

Diego nodded, filing away their story in case they were questioned separately later. He saw his ideas about her go up in smoke. "You hear fey?"

A faerie in the area could have cast the spell as well as Erin could have even if she were a fey apprentice. Had the stress of the fight brought on the fit, or was she hiding her own abilities?

"How else do you explain his sudden nap?" she asked.

Before he could ask her if she had really been the caster, the guard came back to them, bringing the cane and all three knives. Using the cane to support himself, Diego grimaced and stood up.

Erin had only just risen when her hand went to her head. The guard caught her one-handed as she fell.

"Erin?" Diego asked.

"Dizzy," she replied. "Not uncommon after a seizure. Even a little one."

When the guard held out the knives, Diego put them in the basket and picked it up. The Frenchman swept Erin up in his arms and led the way to the garrison. As they passed through the gate, Diego's stomach turned flips like a trained acrobat, and he had to remind himself he had come as a guest, not a prisoner.

They entered a small building where he found the surgeon Fiori treating a man with an ugly gash on his palm. Quickly finishing with his patient, the doctor led them into a smaller room with a single bed. After setting Erin down, the guard left. Diego stayed at Erin's side and wrestled with the puzzle of her as a caster of faerie spells.

***

Michel set his quill in the inkwell and rubbed his eyes. Making the guard corps run on the pitiful budget His Grace allocated would give anyone nightmares. Going over the accountant's ledgers to reassign funds would drive him to the brink of insanity if he didn't stop soon. Having Erin back in Tours didn't help his concentration.

Although he certainly didn't mind her visiting, thoughts of her had distracted him all afternoon with fond remembrances of their time together. Not long after her arrival, duty had called him away, but he'd promised his curiosity he'd spend tonight talking with his lost love. He could, he hoped, rekindle their friendship.

He looked forward to the evening of recounting their lives since fate had taken her from him, but he found himself dreading what he might hear. Time had formed her into a beautiful lady, but he'd caught a glimpse of bitter pain in her eyes when Ian had mentioned the death of her husband.

No matter how much Michel wanted to, he couldn't take Erin in his arms and comfort her like he had when they had returned from their very last walk. Instead of finding her father waiting in the yard, her home had been razed, and everyone in the household had been slain in ways too horrific for a ten-year-old to see. Even at twenty years old, he hadn't been prepared to find her father's dismembered corpse either. When he thought of that wretched day, he could still hear Erin's terrified scream, the last sound she'd made for almost a week.

When her uncle had come to get her, Michel had taken some comfort in the hope that Scotland would be far enough from France to let her forget the anguish of that experience. Now, he wondered if she'd left one painful place for another. Imagine a man drawing a weapon on his own wife! If Ian hadn't already dispatched Erin's brute of a husband, Michel would have taken a sabbatical to Scotland to teach the fool a lesson himself.

A knock on the door disturbed his thoughts.

"Enter!"

DuBois came in and bowed. "Captain, while I was following the Spaniard and a lady, I was distracted by a man who wanted to report a theft. When I caught up with them again, I found them in the alley by the bakery."

"Wait," Michel interrupted. "Who's the lady?"

"Said her name was Erin Ross."

Michel's heart skipped a beat. Ross must have been her married name. "Go on."

"They'd been attacked by a pair of bandits."

"Were they hurt?" Michel asked, taking every ounce of his training to force down a wave of panic.

"I didn't see a mark on either one of them," DuBois replied. "One attacker, though, was dead by the boy's hand. The other slept like a baby."

Michel leaned forward. "I beg your pardon."

"I know it sounds weird, sir, but Erin—"

"Lady Ross," Michel corrected.

DuBois nodded. "Yes, sir. Sorry, sir. Lady Ross says she heard fey in the area. Thinks one helped them."

Michel nodded, recalling times when Erin had heard or felt signs of nearby faeries while walking in the forest. But again, probable fey involvement in a matter involving Diego. What possible bargain could the boy have made with fey to get their help not once, but twice? He'd better be careful. No one did so many favors without demanding a price in the end.

"I left Lady Ross and the boy with Fiori before coming to make my report."

"You said they were uninjured."

"Yes, sir, but Lady Ross couldn't walk. She seemed pretty unsteady. I think the whole incident scared her. She shook like a leaf."

Michel stood and put on his hat. A seizure. Maybe he wouldn't be able to sit with her tonight after all. "Thank you. You're dismissed."

DuBois bowed and left.

As Michel made his way to Fiori's surgery, he worked out the logistics of how to stay with Erin while sending for the carriage. The most straightforward way would be to send Diego, but the city gates would be barred by the time he got back. Either Michel would have to leave her with Fiori and return tomorrow or retrieve the carriage himself to use his authority to reopen the gates on his return.

Such logistics would have to wait. If one of those bandits slept, he wanted to see about questioning the man. Since Diego wouldn't help track down the brigands, Michel would have to use his own methods. He saw a long night ahead of him.

When he walked into the infirmary, Fiori met him at the door and pulled him aside.

"She's all right," the doctor said before Michel could ask. "She told me she never lost consciousness during the seizure because she has some way to divert them if she has the time."

"Really?" Michel looked past him toward the room beyond. "She never used to do that before."

"I've never heard of it, but she's the first epileptic I've actually treated," Fiori admitted. "Diego confirms her story. He said that when the attack was over—you know about that, right?"

Michel nodded.

"Good. Well, Diego says Erin was shaking but she sat still with her eyes closed and the tremors slowed to where it is now. At the moment, she's coherent, and I'm having a tough time keeping her in bed. She insists she's fine."

Michel nodded, recalling how she'd always stumbled out of bed earlier than the physician liked. "Typical."

"*Señora*, please," Diego scolded from the next room. "Fiori says you sleep now."

"What does he know?" Erin asked.

"He is a doctor."

"Who's never had a seizure, I'll wager. I'll sleep better in my own bed anyway."

Michel smiled. That was the Erin he knew and loved. Once loved. He was very married and happy about his life with Corinne. He and Erin could be friends now, but nothing more.

Fiori sighed. "See what I mean?"

"I'll take her off your hands," Michel offered. "Before I can do that, though, I need to take care of another piece of business."

"What do I do with her?" he asked.

"I'll talk to her." He went into the smaller room and sat on the edge of Erin's bed. "I hear you had a scare."

She nodded. "Aye, but I'm fine now."

He looked at her trembling hands. "Shaking of that magnitude isn't normal even for you."

"You know how much I enjoy the company of doctors." She crossed her arms over her chest.

He remembered some of the painful treatments other physicians had suggested then glanced back at Fiori. "Fiori just wants you to rest for a little while, which you and I both know you need. He'll make sure you're not disturbed."

"I'm well enough to go home, and I'll sleep there."

"I need Diego to help me with something first. When we come back, we'll take you home. In the meantime, see if you can make this stop." He picked up her hand by the wrist to show her how bad the tremor was.

Erin glared at him then flopped back on the pillow. "Oh, all right."

"We won't be long." He stood and turned to Diego. "Show me where the attack happened." When they were safely out of Erin's hearing, Michel turned to the Spaniard. "What happened in the alley?"

Michel visualized the events as Diego reported them all the way to finding a dead end where Erin had remembered a shortcut to the garrison. He knew just the place. The new printing press had gone in about two years ago.

"We turn and they are there." Diego mimed taking a weapon by the hilt. "I use her knife to kill one, then the other hits me, then he sleeps. I no understand until later when Erin says there is a faerie near. I look for her, and she is on her knees. I think she prays until I see her hands. Then I know it is bad. Then your guard comes.”

“You seem to have faeries watching over you,” Michel said.

“Maybe they are friends of San Judas.”

“St. Jude, the patron saint of lost causes?” Michel chuckled. “Oh, I wouldn’t call you a lost cause.”

When they reached the alley next to the bakery, Diego gasped. Michel stepped past him and scowled when he saw the bodies lying on the cobblestones. He’d hoped to interrogate the sleeping bandit, but neither man would be answering questions in this world. Although one was dead from an obvious knife thrust to the chest just like Diego and DuBois had described, something unnatural had killed the other. A huge, torn hole in his gut made him look like he had swallowed a loaded musket, then fired it. Michel had seen that sort of wound before. Ten years had passed since he’d found the cook of Erin’s house. Only one kind of fiend could do so much damage to a man in so little time.

“He is not like this when we leave him.” Diego took a few steps closer. “What does this to a man?”

“Sidhe,” Michel replied.

Diego paled. “They can do this?”

Michel nodded. “Yes, but they haven’t come into the city in some years. I’ll send a guard to keep people out of this alley until the undertaker arrives.”

As they returned to the garrison, Michel made a mental note to increase patrols of the city. With His Grace’s impending move to his summer home and the bandits’ continuing attacks, Michel’s forces were already spread too thin. He did not need the sidhe to become more active, too.

***

Rodrigo walked into camp. Excitement and fear fought for control over his mind. After his part in bringing Diego down, Rodrigo had enjoyed the favor of the captain, but all that might change tonight. Diego wasn't dead. Just this morning in the city, Rodrigo had seen him.

At first, he hadn't believed his eyes. The traitor had been left beaten and bleeding out his life on the forest floor. Yet, there he was, walking with a limp and a cane, but otherwise unharmed. There were no bruises or cuts Rodrigo could see and even the broken arm worked better than it should have. Fey had to be involved. Without faerie magic, no man should have survived the treatment they'd given Diego.

Luis would know the answer to that mystery, but news of Diego's survival wouldn't sit well. For his part, Rodrigo had secured a considerable collection of coins and gems from a merchant too busy with wealthy customers and from some customers who weren't minding their purses well enough. He hoped that would stop any threats headed his way.

When he reached the tent, Rodrigo joined the line of men waiting to see Luis. To keep from thinking about what would happen once Luis heard the news, Rodrigo listened as closely as he could to the other discussions going on inside to gauge Luis's mood. As always, the leader's feelings were too well hidden. One man received hearty thanks and appreciation while the next was sternly dressed down. Never once did Luis raise his voice, but men who received his scolding left the tent in fear for their lives.

Finally, Rodrigo's turn came. He entered the pavilion and saw Luis in his finery sipping wine. A deck of cards and a set of amethyst dice sat on a nearby table, ready to decide the fate of anyone who displeased him. Looking in awe at the ornate furnishings, Rodrigo knew one day he would impress Luis enough to become an officer. He even dreamed the captain would someday train him to take over the band. Then all the wealth would be his.

"What news for me today?" Luis asked.

Rodrigo felt the blood drain from his face as all his dreams went up in smoke. He would die here today if Luis didn't like the news. Tension across his shoulders unsteadied his hands.

"You look like you've seen a ghost." Luis twisted in his seat to check behind him.

He drew a deep breath then spit out the words as quick as he could. "I've seen Diego."

Rage, amusement, even joy were things Rodrigo had expected, but all Luis said was, "I see. Where?"

"In Tours. Early this morning. I was looking for a good target when I saw him," Rodrigo explained.

"And, how is he?"

Was this concern for his brother or was Luis after tactical information? The difference might affect how Rodrigo colored his report, but he couldn't tell one way or the other. With no queues to go on, he went for a strictly factual delivery.

"Except for leaning hard on a cane, he seems all right."

"No sign of his other wounds?"

"No, sir."

Luis nodded and thoughtfully sipped his wine.

"I followed him for a while to see what he was up to."

"Fey. I knew I should've killed him then and there. The fey healed him, except for that rapier wound." Luis shook his head. "Sorry. Thinking out loud. I missed that last part."

"I followed him. He stopped at several of our meeting places but stayed only long enough to take a look around and leave again. A couple times he talked to someone, but he couldn't make himself understood. I left off trailing him when he left the city at about mid-morning."

"That's fair." He went silent and refilled his goblet. "What are you up to, Diego? Why are you looking for me?"

"Maybe he wants to rejoin," Rodrigo suggested.

Luis shook his head. "No, he knows better. Revenge is more likely, although with his newfound conscience, he may instead be helping Gaultier search for me. We'll have to try to watch for him again. Did he see you?"

"No, sir." Rodrigo shook his head. "I kept my distance and hid my face from him."

"Well done. He won't know he's been discovered. That works to my advantage. Did you find your targets or did your task keep you too busy?"

The tension bled away. At least Luis wasn't going to stage an immediate execution. "Yes. I found several targets actually. They now have much less gold to keep track of."

He brought the bags to Luis and stayed nearby while the captain checked the contents.

"Jewelry, coins, a considerable amount, what with your extra errand."

Beaming, Rodrigo said, "Yes, sir."

"Well, the others could learn from your example." Luis fished out four sous for Rodrigo's wage.

Turning them over in his hand, Rodrigo smiled. The usual payment for a day's hard and dangerous work amounted to two sous. Tomorrow, maybe he could afford an egg or two with his bread and cheese. "Thank you, sir."

Luis shrugged and set the rest aside. "A worker deserves his wages. Just keep it up and you'll do fine."

As Rodrigo left the pavilion, he dreamed of the day when Luis would make him lieutenant.

***

Diego's restless sleep wasn't doing him any good, so just as dawn began to lighten the eastern horizon, he gave up on it and rose to dress. As he did each time he changed his clothes, Diego inspected the wound to his leg just like the doctor had taught him. He looked for the edges to turn a flaming red, and made sure it wasn't draining pus, then he gingerly felt along the edges to see if it hurt worse in one place than another. The wound was healing well now, and Diego thought he might even be able to walk without a cane, although he would keep it handy just in case his hopes were a little ambitious. Once finished with his task, he bound the injury again and cast the old bandage into the waning fire.

When he'd made himself presentable, Diego belted on the simple, utilitarian rapier and dagger Michel had given him and left his room. He heard two people arguing softly in French at the foot of the stairs. When he reached the landing, he saw Erin and Michel having a quiet but animated discussion.

Diego continued on his way down but averted his eyes to show he wasn't eavesdropping, not that he could understand a word they were saying anyway. In his peripheral vision, he saw Erin try to leave more than once, only to have Michel block the way.

Michel looked up at him. "Diego, talk some sense into her fool head. I get up early to see to business and find her ready to go for a stroll in the forest. You've been out there. You know what it's like."

"I have an appointment with a friend." She spaced each word. "I am expected."

"At this hour?" Michel asked.

"Yes. The time was set for me."

"Then you'll just have to be late." Michel checked his pocket watch. "It will be an hour until I can arrange an escort for you."

She frowned. "I do not need an escort!"

He showed her the key to the door, then dropped it into his belt pouch. "And yet the door will remain locked until you have one."

As he turned away, Erin's hands came up, just as Juan's used to when he prepared a spell. If she were a fey apprentice as Diego suspected, Erin intended to leave one way or another.

"I walk with her," Diego said quickly to save Michel from whatever Erin had planned.

First her willingness to fight in the alley, then the seizure after Pedro had collapsed, and now this. She had to be a faerie's student, and he had to convince her to help him against Luis. With her magic to support him, they could make sure Corinne and all the other ladies of the area were safe.

If he helped Erin now, she would owe him a favor, and he might have an easier time convincing her to work with him. At the moment, though, her icy gaze outdid the most intense blizzard he'd ever seen.

With doubt playing across his features, Michel turned.

"I feel much better today," Diego added. "I bring her to her friend and bring her back again."

After considering the plan, their host nodded. While Diego made his way down the stairs to them, Michel unlocked the door and stayed in Erin's way as she stared hard enough to drill a hole through the head of the man she'd once loved.

He placed his hands on her shoulders. "I'm only trying to protect you."

She shrugged away from him. "I don't need your protection. I can take care of myself."

"That's what Corinne thought, too, and you can ask Diego to tell you what happened to her. Just humor an old friend, will you?"

She sighed then closed her eyes for a moment. "I realize your intentions, but—it's just—you don't know what it's been like for the last ten years."

"Maybe later, when you get back, we can have that talk we meant to have last night."

"If you're half as busy as Father was, you don't have time in your day to hear me gripe."

"When did I not find time for you?" he asked.

She forced a smile.

"You'd better go before you're late for your appointment."

As Diego followed her out, he considered ways to ask her about magic. Time worked against him. The end of the month would arrive soon, and the plans needing sidhe help would go into action. All of Tours could be in danger. Diego had to know if Erin was a faerie apprentice. If she were, would she help him? If she wasn't magical or wouldn't help him, he'd have to consider two unimpressive options: watch people get hurt when he failed to find Luis or betray his family.

With everything that had happened in the last two days, Diego thought he might be able to pass off his question as simple curiosity, but he feared asking her directly might make her go on the defensive. On the other hand, the fight with Michel had upset her. She might tell him more than she would otherwise because her anger distracted her.

"Who do you go see?" He walked alongside her.

"A friend," she replied.

"Do you know him from when you are a child?"

She shook her head. "We've only recently met."

"So you meet him when you come here?"

"Look, Diego, I'm really not up for an interrogation."

He had to keep her talking. "You are sad."

"Something like that. I know you're trying to be polite, but I've a lot on my mind."

"About your studies?" He made the comment sound offhand.

"Yes." A second after she said it, she cringed and muttered darkly in French. He had her. She'd admitted to studying what she shouldn't. That had to be magic. "I mean." She stuttered a few useless syllables. "What do you mean?"

"Do not fear me, Erin. I no give you to the Inquisition."

She cleared her throat and looked at him. "Since when do women get turned over to the Holy Office for knowing how to use a sword?" She shook her head. "Knowledge of arms is hardly ladylike but it's a long way from sorcery or matters of heresy, now isn't it?"

Diego frowned, doubting himself again. He'd guessed wrong. Maybe a fey had been there to protect them yesterday. Her confidence in the fight could have come from an unnatural understanding of weapons.

"What did you think I was studying?" she asked.

"Magic."

She stared at him. "Witchcraft?"

He shook his head. "No, no. My brother once hires a man who has falling sickness as you do, but he studies magic with a sidhe."

"And you thought I did, too."

He blushed. "*Sí.* With Luis hiring sidhe from the north, I thought you might help me with your magic."

"You're a silly man. I would never study anything with the sidhe."

As Diego watched his aspirations die, he caught a glimpse of an odd glitter at the edge of his vision. When Erin lightly touched his shoulder, his knees buckled and his heavy eyes closed.

Chapter 9

The light level in the room woke Yvret. He rolled onto his other side and drew the covers over his head. One of these nights he would actually get a decent amount of sleep. If only his schedule allowed Erin to meet him at a more normal hour, but he had people to meet with, disputes to settle, projects to work on, crises to solve, and students to teach. Erin was only one of three right now, but she worried him the most. She had the soul of a protector, but she had been abused and betrayed by those who should have cared for her. Although not a foregone conclusion, she could become a sidhe if she became too enamored of her new sudden strength. He vowed he would never lose another student to the dark lure of evil.

Groaning, he rolled out of bed. He had promised to meet her at the Tours gate, and her continued development wouldn't be helped by his tardiness. When he reached the human side of that gate, he found Erin already there pacing.

"I'm late." He stepped clear of the ring. "I'm sorry."

"You're late?" She sighed. "I didn't think I'd be able to make it at all."

He gestured for her to sit on a fallen tree near the mushroom ring. "Oh? Trouble?"

"He wouldn't let me leave!" Her muscles tensed.

Yvret listened as she described the confrontation with her friend and nodded. As much as he wanted to do differently, he kept himself from encouraging her to be calm. Looking at the situation from the outside, he didn't see what all the fuss was about, but with her history, she would see nothing more than someone else who wanted to control her. She had tunnel vision, which needed to be corrected.

"Sounds like your friend is concerned about keeping you safe. Did you ask him why he's so worried?"

She blew out a breath and relaxed. "There's a band of thieves operating in the area. Michel's wife was captured by them. Diego helped her get away."

Yvret nodded. "Then it sounds like Michel had good reason to protect you."

She sighed. "Yes, I know. I know, but somehow that doesn't help." She picked up an old leaf and studied the veins. "So you think I should have let him have his way and just been an hour or two late? You have too much to do to have to wait on me."

That was hopeful. He'd worried she had been eager to continue her quest for power to thwart those who controlled her. Instead, she thought more of an imposition on someone else. Such indications of her true nature gave him confidence she would have no problem becoming fey.

"Better that than what the bandits would have done to you." He leaned closer. "I'm busy, but not so busy you should put yourself in harm's way to see me."

She didn't answer, and Yvret let the silence remain for a while, allowing her to consider his suggestion more carefully.

"Diego was one of the thieves not so long ago." She tossed one leaf aside and picked up a different one. "He told me the leader's name is Luis. I think some of the men in the group were the same ones who captured you. The sidhe prince mentioned someone named Luis, and Diego told me he's worried his brother is recruiting sidhe."

As images of his capture flooded his mind, Yvret felt all the terror and pain of his captivity.

Erin touched his arm. "You're as white as a sheet."

He nodded but couldn't speak again until he had banished the images. "That's why my scouts never found those men in Scotland. They're here." He patted her hand. "I'm all right, my child. Thank you."

The suspicion in her eyes revealed her doubt.

"I'm sure you are." After gripping his arm more tightly for a moment, she released him.

"We won't meet in the forest anymore. I'll teleport to you. This place isn't safe for any of us. Not until those men are gone."

"Diego wants me to help him defeat the bandits," Erin mentioned. "Should I?"

"Just the two of you?"

She nodded.

With a shrug, he replied. "I'm not going to be able to answer that for you."

"I thought you said you'd tell me what to do until I transformed."

Yvret shook his head. "That's not what I said. I said I'd guide you. It's not the same thing."

He'd seen such mixed emotions before. People who wanted to regain control in their lives still looked to others to make their decisions. He wasn't too surprised. Decision-making was a skill like anything else, and she had been given very little practice at it.

With the sudden snap of her wrist, Erin threw the leaf to the ground. "Fine. What would you do if Diego asked you to help him track down a large group of very dangerous men who'd captured and tortured the most powerful person you knew?"

"Well, I'm not much of a fighter." He smiled. "I prefer to leave combat to people who are good at it and are willing to do it."

"So, I should tell him no?"

"No, *I* would tell him no." Yvret pointed to his own chest. "You aren't me. There isn't one right answer. Consider the same two points I mentioned before."

She tilted her head to one side. "Two points?"

"First, are you able to do what he asked?" Yvret suggested. "Is the request reasonable?"

"I don't know."

"Consider what you've done lately."

"How do you mean?"

"Even without fey training, you stopped both a sidhe prince and Connor from doing more harm to someone. Neither of those accomplishments is something to scoff at. You've impressed a fair number of people."

She nodded. "Does that mean I can do this?"

He was not going to let her off the hook that easily.

"I don't know. You have to decide." He paused for a moment. "The other matter is more difficult. Are you willing to put yourself in danger? What he's asking of you could leave you injured, perhaps permanently, or even dead. Are you prepared to face that possibility?"

While she considered that for a good, long time, he watched her stir the leaf litter with a twig. A few times, she opened her mouth as if to speak then stopped and went back to the leaves. He often needed someone to use as a sounding board, so maybe he could be one for her.

"Tell me what you're thinking," he suggested.

"They hurt you. They hurt Corinne." She stuck the twig in the soft dirt. "Someone has to stop them, but Michel—"

"Why?" he interrupted.

"Huh?"

"Why does someone have to stop them?" he asked.

"They'll keep hurting people." She looked at him from the corner of her eye. "Fey and humans are going to die if they run free."

He nodded. "All right. What else?"

She took a moment to regain her train of thought. "Michel can't even find them. Diego will probably be able to track them down again, but he feels honor bound to protect the information. He sure won't be able to capture his brother by himself."

"And that's your problem because," he prompted.

"He asked me, and I know some faerie skills, which might help against the sidhe especially if there are just the two of us involved."

"So, what's the problem?" he asked.

"Doing this will take away from my study time," she finished. "Won't it?"

"Yes, and no," he replied. "It will certainly give you fewer long blocks of time to sit and practice, but sometimes working in an isolated, predictable setting slows your improvement. Experience, real experience in real situations, is often a much better teacher. There's much to be learned from using your skills in a real encounter. On the other hand, this is a big job you're considering. You have to decide if you would be taking on too much at once."

She frowned. "I don't need any more fits of falling sickness."

"That's fair." Even so many centuries later, he remembered how anxious he'd been to leave all that behind. "It's up to you. Is the risk worth the rewards?"

She looked up at the canopy for a few minutes, but he let her consider the conundrum as long as she needed. Acquiring new skills often took time.

"As long as they're out there, they can still hurt you or Sarah or someone else. If I can stop them, I should at least try."

She had exhibited the same compassion when she'd taken care of him in the forest, knowing full well what her husband would do if she arrived home late. The protector's instinct ran strong in her. He only hoped she didn't get herself killed on such a dangerous endeavor.

"It sounds like you've made a decision," he said, reminding her that she had done the work. He hadn't imposed this on her.

Yvret took a turn staring at the leaf debris. He had to go back a few centuries to find a student as perplexing as Erin. She had the most amazing temper, which drove her right to the edge of making a bad decision. Each time, she had managed to rein the anger back in, but the day might come when she used the wrong skills and went into a rage. He could lose her if that happened. She liked her new power too much.

But she could be compassionate. She had taken care of him and repeatedly endangered herself for another person. Selflessness like that should have all but guaranteed her metamorphosis into a fey.

The last time he'd had a student with such a convoluted path, he had helped turn his apprentice down the right road by assigning something else to focus on. With any luck, a new task could help Erin stay focused on the final goal. If all went well, she would lose her power lust.

"I think you're ready," he said.

"Ready? For what?" she asked.

"Your quest." Although he made it sound as common as dishwater, the truth was, very few needed one. Most developed the appropriate nature without so specific an assignment. "With the stronger version of the skills I'll teach you today, you'll be able to complete your quest, and as you continue practicing, you'll build your strength even more. To help you transform into a fey, you'll need to find something very important. Without it, you'll become a sidhe when you transform."

She leaned forward. "Is this one of those things where I'll find I've had it all along?"

He shook his head. "No, you definitely don't have it now."

"What is it?"

"To become fey, you'll need to find the heart of sacrifice," he replied.

Yvret saw a brief spark of recognition in her eyes before she looked away for a second or two then shook her head. What was that about?

"What does this thing look like?" Erin asked.

"You'll know when you find it."

"Well, can you tell me where to find it?"

Yvret shrugged. "I don't know, but I can tell you it's nearby. You'll find it at the darkest time."

Erin sighed. "So, I'm supposed to find something when I don't know where it is or even what it looks like. All I know is that I'll find it in the dark."

The task sounded impossible, but he could say little else. He hoped she wouldn't give up before she got started.

"You can do it," he assured her.

"And you can give me no clues?" she asked.

Yvret shook his head. "I wish I could, but for each person it differs in its manifestation and location."

He had to be able to tell her something more, but what?

"But it's always in the dark."

"It has always been found during the seeker's darkest time," he corrected.

"Where did you find it?" she asked.

He scrambled for a way to give his answer that would make sense within the parameters he had set up. "In the marketplace."

He'd made his critical decision there.

"I'll never be rid of these seizures," she muttered. "This is impossible."

"Oh, you'll do fine." He hoped he sounded more certain than he felt. "Now, after we review your skills and improve upon them, we should consider teaching you how to use them across distances. That will help you stay safer whether you help Diego or not."

Erin dropped the leaf she was fiddling with. As he began the lesson, Yvret felt much better about his student.

***

Erin sat staring at the faerie ring long after Yvret had left. She had to be insane to commit to helping Diego take on an entire bandit camp probably reinforced by the sidhe.

Yvret, though, seemed to think the experience would make her strong, and she was going to need real power to do well in her new life. She couldn't back out now. She'd given her word, and after her mentor had given her plenty of rope, she'd hung herself rather handily. He certainly hadn't given his own opinions, even after she had decided. Whatever else she thought about that, Erin had to trust he wouldn't let her do something too dangerous. He didn't seem to want to be rid of her. Before he'd left, he'd told her, though, to be sure of her choice. Yvret would understand if she backed out, wouldn't he?

One thing could decide this for good. Yvret's quest had her looking for some kind of heart, and she could have sworn Diego had mentioned a piece of jewelry with a similar-sounding name yesterday. Did Diego know about the object of her quest? If he did, she'd have to help him to get his assistance in locating the artifact.

Erin returned to Diego, hidden just beyond the clearing's edge, and jostled his shoulder. He groaned and inhaled sharply, then opened his eyes. Erin hid her quivering hand in the folds of her skirt.

"Oh, what happens?" He sat up and leaned back on one hand. "I no think I am so tired."

Erin looked down. "You weren't. My mentor would not have appreciated company for our lesson."

"Your teacher is fey?" he asked. "This is why you want to go alone?"

She wouldn't be ready to answer his question until she knew beyond doubt she would be working with him.

"Diego, yesterday you said your brother had a piece of jewelry he said made up for the ransom." She sat next to him on the ground. "He called it something. What was that name?"

"I no am certain he means it for a name, but he calls it a heart of sacrifice or something like that."

That was it! Yvret had told her to seek a heart of sacrifice! They had to be one and the same. They just had to be! Going after the necklace Diego had described would mean confronting the whole band of brigands. Life meant taking risks, but this could be suicide. Without the heart, however, she would become a sidhe. When she thought of the vicious creature she'd killed and the pained, worried look that came over Yvret's face each time his captivity came up, she knew she couldn't bring herself to hurt him more by becoming what he feared and hated. Death would be better than that.

"*Señora*?" Diego asked.

Erin shook her head quickly to clear it.

"Your friend, he is still here?"

"No." She cast the twig in her hand to the ground. "No, he left a while ago. Diego, I—"

Erin stopped. Fear stole the words from her mouth. She had to help Diego. By furthering his goals, he would lead her to hers.

"What is it?" Diego asked.

She took a deep breath, which didn't steady her nerves like she'd hoped. "I lied to you earlier. Yvret is teaching me to be a fey. I will transform soon, just as your brother's man changed to a sidhe."

"I know it!"

"There's more. I talked to Yvret about someone helping you with Luis. He seems to think—" She paused to gather her courage and went on. "He seems to think I can do it without putting an end to my studies."

His eyes lit up. "You help me?"

She nodded, further proof of her complete insanity. "Aye, but I think you're daft to not go to Michel with this."

"I no can do that," he replied.

"He's better able to help you. The duke's whole guard is at his command, and any one of them would be better to mind your back in a fight than I would be. Be certain of that."

"You have magic," Diego said as if fey skills solved all their problems.

"Not magic. Fey abilities are no more magical than fish breathing underwater. And your brother has numbers and sidhe with more training than I have, I might remind you."

He shook his head. "I no betray my brother."

She snorted. "Instead, you'd rather go into a fight with no one but a woman at your side. You risk getting us both killed, and then Luis would get away, and Michel would have nothing to go on to find him again. You don't think it's better to go into the fight with enough men at your back to know without a doubt that Luis couldn't possibly escape?"

"If I go to Michel, then I do to Luis what he does to me. Luis dies because I say so."

Convoluted, but she could almost see his point.

"So what do you plan to do if you catch him?"

"I try to convince him to turn himself in," he replied.

"You really think that will work?" she asked.

He slowly shook his head. "No. I think he and I fight, and I must let him go or one of us dies."

"And how is that different from telling Michel?"

"The *problema* stays in the family."

"By involving me, you're taking it out of your family."

"It no is the same. Please, *señora*, you no can change my mind."

"Men, I can't understand a single one of them," Erin muttered. "Are you certain you're not into this for the revenge? With Michel's men alongside of you, one of them might do the killing blow."

He only scowled, fuming while he put words together.

"Or maybe this is about the money. I suppose you had to leave it all behind when you helped Corinne, if he even let you have any in the first place."

"So, you tell me you no learn magic because you hate men?" he asked through clenched teeth.

"It's not magic. You don't even understand what you're saying," she answered in a low voice.

He didn't understand. How could he? People who didn't have epilepsy could never comprehend how terrifying the falling sickness could be.

"I learn fey skills to stop the seizures," she insisted.

"A nice gift, yes, but it does not hurt that you have power," he answered. "You hate men. The magic gives you power over them."

"It's. Not. Magic. I don't hate all men, just the ones who hurt me," she said.

"Or protect you, like Michel. You plan to use your magic, whatever you say it is, over him this morning when he blocks you. I see it, and I know," he added. "You hate men who cross your path."

"Or ones who don't know to keep their mouths shut!" she yelled.

She didn't need to sit here and take this. Without another word, she got up and headed for Michel's house again. Lucky for Diego she was too tired to do any sort of fey skills.

***

Instead of trying to call after her, Diego just followed along behind. Maybe he shouldn't have pushed her like that, but she had left him no choice. Who did she think she was, anyway? Just like Michel, she didn't understand. This wasn't about revenge and greed, but justice. Luis had to pay for all the evils he'd done, and his future plans had to be stopped. Whatever he had going on with the sidhe couldn't be good.

But there was the equality Diego deserved. Ever since he was old enough to shimmy through small windows, he'd worked for Luis. Instead of getting a fair share of the profits for his hard work, Diego had been cheated out of wealth, power, and even comfort. Luis refused to make good on what he owed, so Diego would just have to take his fair share by force. A person should be paid for his work. Diego figured his back wages would amount to a very tidy sum by now.

When he realized Erin's pace was much greater than his, he sighed. If she got too much further ahead, there would be no point to him being there as an escort.

"Erin?" Diego called. "Erin, wait!"

Although Erin stopped, she didn't turn back toward him. When he reached her, she started walking again without so much as a look his way. She sniffled.

"Are you well?" he asked.

She didn't answer him. He had upset her. Now that he had found an ally in his mission, he had sabotaged the arrangement with ill-chosen words. She would go her own way for certain now, and where would that leave him? He needed her help. Only her magic, or non-magic as she insisted, would give him the power to overcome the whole band and the sidhe. Why should he have to make the apologies, though? She had started the fight. Still, if he didn't offer peace, she wouldn't help him.

"Erin, I feel bad. I—"

"No." She shook her head. "You shouldn't feel sorry for something I started. You have your own purposes and I have mine, and we each have our own reasons for working toward them. If we can follow the same path for a time, maybe it'll be a wee bit less lonely."

Diego nodded. That was probably as close as he would get to an apology from her. "Peace?"

"Aye. I won't question your motives if you don't question mine."

"Yes, I agree," he said.

"Where do you suppose we should start looking your brother?" she asked, casting a quick glance up at him. Tears reddened her eyes, but she pushed her feelings aside with a not-quite-sincere smile.

"I think I find the spies," Diego explained. "Luis has many. It is how he finds his ideas to start."

"They won't know you?" she asked.

He shook his head. "I know the names. I see Luis's list, but I no meet any of them before."

"Even if you never were a contact for them, they'll pick up on your accent, just like that." Erin snapped her fingers for emphasis. "It's well-nigh as bad as mine."

Diego frowned. That hadn't occurred to him. He hoped he hadn't revealed himself yesterday when he went on a tour of the most common meeting places. If he had tipped his hand too soon, Luis would be ready for him. Surely, he was still safe. The men who had confronted him were dead. Without a doubt, he would have seen someone following him.

"Maybe we watch for a messenger and follow him back to camp."

"If there are more than two places to look, we could very well miss the meeting altogether," Erin pointed out.

When she stopped in her tracks, Diego felt her fingertips brush his arm as she reached for him.

"What is it?"

"Shh!" She placed her finger across her lips. "Sidhe."

"She who?" he whispered.

"No, not a woman. Sidhe. You know, evil ..."

"... faeries," they said together.

Looking all around for some sign of them turned up nothing. "Where?"

She closed her eyes slightly. "Ahead, and to my left."

As quietly as he could manage, Diego drew his sword, grimacing at the faint sound the steel made as it slipped past the sheath. At the same time, Erin pulled out a long, thin dagger.

"How is it you use steel?" he asked.

She nodded. "Until I transform, iron remains harmless."

He shrugged and let her lead, trusting her perceptions to keep them from harm.

"Give me the other knife," she suggested.

"You need your hands to—" If magic wasn't the right idea, what was? "—to cast, yes?"

She shook her head. "I've used too many skills today, and besides, dropping a dagger is easy enough and how would you use it and your cane as well? Better maybe you should hand over the sword."

Not a chance, unless maybe she studying both magic and swordplay. Though he would never relinquish the sword, the dagger was useless to him right now. He could actually use the cane as a defensive weapon if he needed to.

"Take the dagger," he said.

When she nodded and turned toward him, he let her get the other blade and smiled when he saw her loop her finger over the quillions. She knew exactly what to do. Clearly, she had familiarity with weapons, but where had she learned? Certainly not from that clumsy cousin of hers.

Erin half-closed her eyes for a moment and scowled. "Now where have they got off to?"

She gasped. Her fist and the pommel of one dagger struck his shoulder. The blow stung a bit, and knocked him off balance, throwing him to the ground hard enough to feel the impact rattle his bones. Something hot flew over his head and exploded onto a nearby tree. Diego shook his head to clear it, then rolled onto his back.

Nearby, Erin regained her feet and interposed herself between him and a hideous, skeletally thin dragon standing only half her height. Both daggers were aimed at the evil creature—one held high and the other low—and the two combatants spoke the language he had once heard Juan use with his teacher. The dragon eyed the steel in Erin's hands and stayed well back. As Diego rose again, leaning hard on the cane, other voices reached him. He strained to hear them and caught their language in a lull of Erin's conversation.

Spanish! The voices he heard spoke Spanish! It had to be some of Luis's men. If he could find them, he could follow them back to the new camp. He looked back at Erin. She had steel. She had her skills, but could she handle the little dragon? While he stood here debating, the voices were getting fainter by the moment. If he wanted to catch up with them, he had to do it now. Erin could handle the sidhe just fine without him, but Diego might never get another chance like this.

With a quick prayer for her safety, he left to find the owners of the voices. He walked as quickly as he could, ignoring the protests of his almost-healed leg. Periodically, he paused to get a new fix on his target and re-orient himself. At each stop, the voices were softer, until finally, he didn't hear them at all.

Diego swore and spent several minutes looking for a trail they might have left. All he found was his own path. They had gotten away from him. If only he hadn't been injured, he could have run to catch them. At least he had a vague direction to look in now. What other reason could they possibly have for being around here? They certainly weren't out for a nice stroll. Still grumbling about his failure, Diego turned and followed his path back to Erin. By now, she probably had the sidhe under control.

***

Erin dove for the ground as another searing blast of fire rumbled through the air above her. If she could just get close enough to that wiry, little dragon, she might be able to run it through, which incidentally was the same plan she had in mind for Diego when he returned, if he ever returned. Had she known part

174

of the deal would involve fighting sidhe alone while he ran for it, she never would have agreed to joining him.

She had sensed two faeries earlier, and although only one had shown itself, the other had to be around here somewhere. A chill ran down her spine when she realized the other sidhe might have caught Diego while her back was turned. As injured as he was, he would be no match for an agile sidhe. If she could get rid of the one she fought, she could go find him and help him. Erin only hoped she wasn't too late.

Odd though it may have sounded, she actually hoped the sidhe were more interested in tormenting him than killing him outright. The foul treatment might be horribly unpleasant, but it would give her more time to reach him. If the sidhe killed him, there was nothing she could do.

As she rolled to one side and quickly came up to her knees, the dragon landed heavily where she'd been lying moments before. Before she could strike at it, it flew out of range.

"Hold still!" the dragon screamed.

"I thought you'd be amused by the game," she retorted.

She had just gotten back to her feet when the feeling of oppressive heat and the red cast to her vision, which signaled the sidhe's presence, became worse. Something grabbed her right wrist, putting pressure on the base of her thumb. As pain shot through her arm, she cringed and dropped the dagger. Her assailant twisted her arm behind her so hard she cried out. Two muscular arms came across her chest, pinning her other arm to her side, but leaving her hand free. A huge hand clamped tightly over her mouth. The other faerie had arrived. Did that mean Diego was dead?

"That's better," the dragon purred. "Forgot we teleport?"

Erin couldn't answer, but she had indeed forgotten. If she survived this, she would make that simple fact as ingrained in her mind as breathing.

She struggled to free herself, but the one holding her was too strong. If she could change her grip on the dagger in her hand, she might be able to stab the one behind her. When she tried it, her hand slipped and she lost the blade entirely.

"Feisty!" The dragon laughed. "It won't do you any good."

The beast reared up on its hind legs and approached her, almost pressing its stinking, scaly body against her. If only both sidhe touched her at once, she would risk using the skill she had zapped Ian with on their arrival. She could've used the long-distance version, but even the smaller one would very likely bring on the falling sickness. Even that wouldn't be as bad as the treatment Yvret had received from the Unseelie Court's prince.

The huge lizard smelled like raw sewage was an integral part of the sidhe diet. To keep from catching some foul disease carried by such an odor, she breathed as lightly and quickly as she could.

Using its talons, the dragon traced the tendons on the side of her neck. As it rested one in the hollow of her throat, tiny pinpoints of light marred her vision. That was the first of the two warning signals before the falling sickness took over. No! Not now! She couldn't deal with this now. The dragon's sharp talon pressed painfully into her neck as it murmured malevolently in her ear.

With her hand hidden in the folds of her skirt, Erin focused on the lightning skill. Power coursed through her, but neither sidhe made a sound. The dragon collapsed in a quivering mass, and the one holding her loosened its grip then toppled over backward dragging her with it.

Scrambling to her feet, she grabbed both of the daggers she had dropped, trying to ignore the loud ringing in her ears: the second sign. The gray fog of confusion was already consuming her mind. Seconds separated her from the falling sickness now.

She drove one through the chest of the dragon and slashed across the throat of the other one before dizziness threw her to the ground. She was out of time.

Chapter 10

Diego felt sick to his stomach as he quickened his pace. He was awfully close to the clearing where he had left Erin to face down the faerie. Battle sounds of some sort should have reached him by now, but all he heard was silence.

His mind conjured images of what he would find, and most of them involved Erin gruesomely slain. He should never have left her. How would he ever explain her death to Michel? How could he ever admit he had gone off without her on some foolhardy, useless quest to track down men he hadn't even seen? She was dead because of him, and now he had no one to help him find Luis.

When he found her, the first thing to catch Diego's eye was the huge, four-armed, jet-black sidhe on the ground. Its throat was slit, and the wound's edges smoked as if the knife had been on fire. The dragon, nearly half his own height, also lay nearby, pinned to the ground with a dagger through its scrawny, seething chest.

Between the two lay Erin, her whole body wracked with violent spasms timed to a rhythm he couldn't hear. Sitting beside her, he cradled her in his arms, holding her tightly in some hope his sheer strength could make the fit stop. As near as he could tell, his effort did nothing, and the force of the twitches surprised him.

In time, the spasms lessened until she rested quietly in his arms. Her clothes weren't torn, and the only wounds he could see were some scratches on her cheek and a small spot of congealed blood between her collarbones. Rest, it seemed, was all she needed.

As he surveyed the area, he wondered where the second sidhe had come from and how she had managed to take them both.

The daggers had obviously caused the fatal wounds, but the dragon's position suggested it had been down already when she'd killed it, and he could see no other wounds. She must have used her newfound skills. Nothing else made sense. The rest of the details could wait.

One thing was certain: he would never underestimate her again. Her skill to mix swords and fey magic impressed him. He swore never to leave her to fight alone. She'd saved him by giving him a bruise to the shoulder to keep him from being burnt to a crisp. He had repaid her shamefully. Never again.

Unable to carry her, go for help, or send for help, Diego had no choice but to wait out the aftermath of the seizure. He had no idea how long he sat there holding her in his arms, but at last, she moaned softly and weakly raised her hand to her head.

"Erin?" he asked softly.

Her eyes opened slightly and slowly blinked as the recognition set in. "Diego?"

He had to strain to hear her barely whispered answer. "Yes, I am here."

She frowned. "You left me. Why? I needed you. There were two of them. One had me pinned against its chest. Why? Why did you leave me?"

Meeting the pain and fear in her eyes was too hard. He had to look away. "I hear voices. My brother's men try to come up behind us. I go to stop them, but it takes longer than I think. There are few, but they lead me away, and I no see that at first. I come back as quickly as I can."

Nothing but bald-faced lies, but he couldn't bring himself to give her the truth. She would hate him, and then he would be on his own again.

"I thought the other sidhe had killed you."

Her real worry had only deepened his shame. She should have been furious with him, but instead, she had been concerned.

"I am here. They no injure me." He helped Erin sit up and kept his arm across her shoulders to steady her.

"They'll come." She twisted around, checking every direction. "The other sidhe. They'll come for their dead. We shouldn't be here."

"You sleep a long time," he said. "I no see them."

"Yvret says they always come."

If there was any chance that were true, they had to leave immediately. Neither one of them would be any good against sidhe at the moment.

"You walk now?"

She nodded. "If you'll help me."

After what he had done to her, that was the least he could do. Once on his feet, he helped her up and held onto her until certain she was steady. Diego retrieved both daggers and offered Erin his arm.

Supporting himself with his cane and Erin with his other arm, they slowly made their way back to Tours. All things considered, he was lucky the day hadn't gone worse.

***

Joaquin entered the clearing containing a ring of six stones. Each one had blood red markings on them that didn't seem to sit still. The marks slowly changed as if they were alive. Being here made his skin crawl, so he hoped the sidhe would come quickly. The sooner he concluded this sorry business, the better.

"That's the gate?"

Looking over his shoulder at Gustavo, Joaquin smiled. "That's the gate."

181

Gustavo had been told to come along to help Joaquin with their prisoner, but how much did Gustavo know about his real purpose for being at this meeting? Luis had been terribly nonplussed to find the man drinking while on patrol. Joaquin had been told to remember that sidhe could be unpredictable and extra bargaining power might be needed. The tacit message couldn't have been clearer. Joaquin would be the only one expected to return to camp.

The sharp pull on the rope in his hand brought a scowl to his face. He jerked the rope hard and sent the man tied to the other end of it sprawling.

"Don't be an idiot," Joaquin said in French.

The man was Luis's gift to the sidhe, too. This time, instead of having to capture his own, Joaquin had been given a nobleman's son, caught while strolling through the woods with his sweetheart and her nurse. After his family had refused to pay the demanded ransom for a fifth son, he had become expendable. Neither gift was as impressive as the fey lord Joaquin had captured in Scotland, but he didn't have time to lay another trap, so he had to make do with what they had.

"What now?" Gustavo asked.

Joaquin squatted to look at the ring's stones and marvel at whatever it was that flowed across the surface of the rock, making first one shape then another. "We wait."

"How long?"

"Until they show." He looked back at the man. "Last time, it was only a few minutes before they sent someone up to find out why we were loitering around their gate." He gave Gustavo their captive's tether. Best to make his "partner" think he'd come along for a reason. "Hold onto him or it's our hides."

Gustavo nodded. "He's not going anywhere."

They didn't have to wait long. The marks on the stones glowed, bathing the area in red light. When it faded, a woman stood in the ring. She would've looked human except for her red eyes. Joaquin stood speechless as he admired her beauty, enhanced by a dress that clung to her every curve and left nothing for his imagination to figure out.

"My king wishes to know why you sit here?" she asked in French.

He blinked a few times and shook his head to clear it. He would do well to keep his mind solidly locked on his task. Beauty in sidhe, he reminded himself, was a façade.

"I represent—" He stopped when his voice came out as a high-pitched squeak. Clearing his throat, he started again. "I represent Luis Rodriguez Velazquez. He wishes to arrange some business with your people."

"Why isn't he here himself?" She slinked toward him.

Focus. He had to stay focused. With some effort, he made himself look only at her face. Those red eyes should make him remember what he was dealing with.

Joaquin smiled. "Why isn't your king here?"

"He's busy. I'm his negotiator."

"Likewise."

The sidhe laughed, and Joaquin had trouble figuring out if it was a more humorous or diabolical sound.

"I'm Bella."

"Joaquin."

"And your friends?"

He indicated them with a nod. "Their purpose will be clear shortly."

She shrugged. "Fine. So, what does Luis want?"

Against all rational sense, he took a step toward the sidhe. If the thing knew he feared it, he would lose influence. "A trade. He is planning a military action soon and would benefit from your people's assistance. In return, any survivors of that attack would be turned over to your king to dispose of as he wished."

"Tell me more," Bella insisted.

"I'm afraid that would be unwise until we have your agreement," he replied. In reality, Luis hadn't let him in on the whole plan. All he knew was that the goal, generally, was to launch a massive attack on the Duke of Tours. "I can tell you the payment for your people would be considerable."

"That's too vague," Bella said. "I need something to convince me of your good intentions."

Joaquin handed her the rope attached to the nobleman's son. The lad tried desperately to pull away, but with a simple gesture of the sidhe's hand, the young man fell and stayed still.

"This is all? This squirmy little human goes to the king, and what do I get?" Bella asked.

"For you, I have payment for your troubles."

Bella's eyes appreciatively looked Gustavo up and down. "Does he know that?"

Joaquin chuckled. Sidhe, like everyone else, could be motivated by the promise of personal gain. They simply wanted a different kind of payment. "No, he's unaware of his real purpose here, else why would he be waiting so patiently?"

"I like this Luis," Bella purred. "Tell him I'll come by later to finalize our role in his plan."

As Bella walked slowly toward Gustavo, Joaquin turned to leave. The other man started to call after him, but the sentence was never completed. Luis, he hoped, would be pleased with the result of this meeting.

***

Ian snored so loudly in the next room that Erin wondered how anyone could possibly sleep around here. Although still exhausted from the morning's fit, the noise wouldn't let her rest. After concluding that hiding her head under the covers had gotten her nowhere, Erin sighed and shoved the covers and the bed curtains aside. Glaring at the common wall between her room and Ian's, she left the warmth of the bed.

Erin wrapped her cloak around her shoulders to serve as a makeshift robe and left her room. Hopefully, she could go somewhere in this house and not hear Ian snore.

The bare wood floor in the hallway leading to the great stairs was even colder than the ornate area rugs in her room, and the chill sent a shiver through her. She kept going, though.

When she arrived at the top the stairs, Erin carefully reached out for the handrail, which didn't seem to be where she remembered it. Once she found the carved banister, she made her way down. The last step wasn't where she expected, and she stumbled. A table near the door stopped her fall and made a loud scraping sound.

"Hush. You'll wake the house," she whispered to the table.

Not wanting to risk any further collisions with inconsiderate furniture, Erin went to the large foyer window near the door and looked out at the yard. If she had thought to dress in something more appropriate than a nightgown and cloak, she would have gone to the bench near the tree to study the stars. As it was, the mildly annoying, cold floor was working on being totally uncomfortable now. At least down here she didn't hear Ian's attempts to start an avalanche in the nearest mountains.

As she thought back through her day, she realized just how little of it she really remembered. That came as no great revelation to her. Much of the morning had been ruled by a seizure and that had required her to rest for most of the afternoon.

Surprisingly, the part that bothered her the most was not how close she had come to dying, but that Diego had counted on her to help against the sidhe; and in their first encounter, she had lost track of one of them. He was lucky the sidhe hadn't caught up with him. Maybe he shouldn't rely on her so much. She had strengths to draw on, just as Yvret had said, but she felt hopelessly inadequate for what Diego wanted her to do. She would only let him down. When he really needed her help, she knew she'd fail, just like she had failed at things all her life.

"Stop that," she scolded herself to end the duet Connor and Ian had sung in her ears for so long.

She had saved Yvret, taught Ian, stopped Connor, learned fey skills, and most recently killed two sidhe even as her mind and body were warring with each other. With so many successes lately, she shouldn't be concentrating on perceived failures of the past. Because of her persistence against the falling sickness today, Diego was very much alive, and so was she. When Diego really needed her help, she would do what she had to do. She would succeed.

Hearing someone on the stairs, Erin looked over her shoulder and saw Michel coming down with a candle in his hand. Being around him again wasn't quite what she had expected. Although she still enjoyed his company, the affection that she remembered feeling for him wasn't there anymore. Perhaps her memories had turned him into a perfect man over time, but she couldn't explain the exact changes she perceived. Maybe the weight of his duties had changed him.

She still cared for him, but the spark they had kindled a decade ago had died out. Erin felt more of a sisterly closeness rather than a romantic one. That was just as well. He had a wife who spoke of two charming sons away at school. Anything more intense than friendship would necessitate an extra visit to a confessional. His marriage made him happy, and she rejoiced that he had found someone who matched him so well.

"Did I wake you?" Erin asked when Michel joined her at the window.

"No. If I can sleep through Ian's snoring, I can sleep through anything." He scowled toward the stairs. "My wife, on the other hand, still sees bandits in the woodwork. When she hears things in the night, I dutifully go check for her."

"Poor lady. I can imagine what she went through." She looked up at him. "Probably not so easy for you either."

"Oh, she'll be all right, and until then, I'll be patient with her, because that's what a good husband does, and I love her too much to do anything different. It will be a great load off of my chest when those thieves are in prison or dead."

Erin nodded. "I don't doubt it will."

With a quick tilt of his head, he motioned for her to follow then led her to the study where the rough rug was a welcome relief to her cold feet. Erin sat in a chair nearest the waning fire while he stoked it back to life.

Michel sat across from her. "In that vein, has Diego told you anything?"

"About what?"

"You know what about: his hunt for Luis."

"I'm not a spy for you, but no. We were on our way to talk to some people when the falling sickness started."

He frowned. "'We?' Again? Are you letting him tangle you up in this?"

"Is that really your concern?"

"You are involved." He shook his head. "You're part of his plans."

"He needed a translator to help him with his inquiries, Michel. Who else could he turn to? You're awfully busy right now, and Corinne isn't a good choice."

"As long as you don't get roped into more than simple translation."

"That's not your problem now, is it?" She glared at him.

He held up his open hands. "Let's not get started down that road again. He speaks a lot about justice and wanting to protect the people of Tours from a scheme his brother is cooking up, but I'm serious, Erin. There's more to it than that. I'm getting a definite undercurrent of revenge in his motives. His brother lives in opulence and treated him like a beggar, so it's only natural he'd want his due one way or another. Problem is, he's just one very young man against a band of experienced men. He's going to get himself killed, and I don't want to see you get dragged down with him."

Abandoning the quest now would be so easy. This might be her very last chance to get out of helping Diego find Luis. She could blame Michel. He was older, more experienced. Everyone knew how much she respected him. Based on his suggestion, she could go back to Diego and Yvret both and explain she was not going to get involved in the manhunt.

Erin sighed. She could do it, but it wouldn't be right. Luis had scared Corinne with threats of heinous violence, and no matter how hard she tried, she couldn't get the sight of Yvret's ordeal out of her head. Then, she had her own search to deal with, too. Luis had the heart of sacrifice she needed to transform to a fey. Helping Diego was within her power. She should not abdicate responsibility for the decision to someone else who didn't have all the facts. Michel still thought of her as the little girl he had been betrothed to. He knew nothing of her fey skills or her ability with a sword.

Those things evened out such confrontations in a way he couldn't fully understand.

"How is Ian's petition progressing?" she asked, changing the subject before he could get her to change her mind.

"Philippe and I will make our decision in the morning," Michel replied. "I promised Ian he'd know by midday. The language barrier is a significant problem, though. You and I won't always be there to help him understand what's going on, and none of my other men know English beyond 'Can I have a beer?' or 'How much for one of these?'"

Erin nodded. That made perfect sense. She had to be off to the Seelie Court soon, and a captain's duties would rarely keep him near enough to help Ian talk to people. More to the point, commands and information were all given in French. Ian's reluctance to even attempt to learn the language since coming here didn't help opinions about him. To an outsider, it seemed as though he expected everyone to learn English for him.

"And I find it hard to believe he killed Connor as he said. The story he told me doesn't work." Michel shook his head. "Dishonesty is something I cannot tolerate."

"Well, maybe he exaggerated a little," Erin admitted.

He leaned forward. "Erin, I wouldn't be at all surprised if he made the whole thing up."

Erin laughed with genuine mirth. Even though he'd been so mean to her, she didn't want to see Ian hit rock bottom, but she found a poetic justice in seeing his own plans coming back to get him.

"Maybe you can shed some light on this," he said.

Erin listened as Michel related Ian's version of events, painting him as her savior and her as a helpless victim.

She grimaced. "Well, the most significant points were true. Connor did draw a weapon against me. I did run to Ian for help, and he did take up his rapier to defend me."

That had lasted about as long as she took to pray an Our Father, but he actually had done those things.

Erin yawned mightily, in part because she really was tired, and in part because she needed an excuse to end this discussion before she revealed the truth. If she were supposed to pretend to think like a human, telling Michel exactly how Connor had died wouldn't help.

"Oh, excuse me," she said.

Michel stood and offered her his hand. "Let's get you back to bed."

"You think I can sleep through Ian's snoring?" she asked.

"I'll wake him up and see if that helps, at least for a little while."

She nodded and accepted his help up the stairs.

***

No sooner did Yvret exit the Seelie gate near Tours than he concentrated on Erin and teleported. Around him, scenery changed from the forest near his gate to Erin's room in her friend's house.

He had expected to find her already practicing molding energy or reading from the rapier manual or even pacing impatiently. Instead, she sat half-reclined in a chair, sleeping with her forehead resting on her fingertips. Where was all the enthusiasm he had come to expect in her? Had something happened yesterday after she'd left the ring with her young friend?

Yvret debated leaving and letting her rest, but the curiosity would kill him. If necessary, he'd leave her to sleep more after he'd heard the news. Going down on one knee by her chair, Yvret saw

190

reddish scratches on her cheek and a small cut between her collarbones. The injuries weren't major, but where had they come from?

If someone had been abusive to her again, he would personally make sure the cretin would never be able to lay a hard hand on her. Her emotional state wouldn't take too many more blows before she would be driven to the sidhe.

He lightly touched her shoulder. "Erin."

With a gasp, she opened her eyes and shrank away from him.

"Shh. It's all right, my child. It's just me."

She threw her arms around him and hugged him as if she were afraid he would vanish again.

"I'm glad to see you, too, but what's all this? Is everything all right?"

"Oh, Yvret, it was terrible." The words spilled out like a flood. "We didn't get back here until afternoon. We weren't even out of the forest when we ran into them."

"Them who? Sidhe? Bandits?"

"Both."

"Both?"

She had lived through that? Yesterday, when they spoke of Diego's mission, he had expected the problem to take a while to fully surface. That would have given her more time to develop her powers. Had he known she would encounter the enemy so soon, he wouldn't have spent so much time on actual energy weaving. He supposed she had still been too weak to build even the simplest of effects after their lesson.

"Tell me what happened." He perched on the side of the chair, keeping an arm around her to comfort her.

"I sensed two sidhe, and they teleported."

She gave him the series of events in a surprising level of detail considering she'd ultimately fallen to a seizure.

Yvret whistled appreciatively when he was certain Erin had finished relating the previous morning's adventure. "And you defeated both of them by yourself?"

She nodded. "Yes, but they nearly had me."

"But you did it, and that's impressive. And your friend, Diego, he wasn't hurt, was he?"

"No, he's all right. His brother's men led him on a merry chase, but he's fine."

"How about you? Are you well?"

"I have some bruises on my arms," she said. "And, I'm a little fuzzy-headed, but I'll be fine. I slept all afternoon yesterday. It could have been much worse."

It certainly could have. Based on what little description she could give him of the sidhe who had attacked her, they weren't lightweights. She was lucky she wasn't dead. Although he still couldn't tell if she was destined to join the Seelie or Unseelie Court, he would have mourned her loss. She had saved his life, and even if he lost her to the sidhe, he would never forget that.

"Well, if your mind is still fogged, we don't want to practice more skills today," he suggested. "Your body is already too weak from expending so much energy. It's not safe this morning. If I have time this afternoon, I'll come back and we can work then."

Erin frowned and nodded. "I understand."

"I didn't say we were finished. We'll just take a break on specific skills." He stood and offered his hand. "We still have things to do."

Erin's eyes brightened. "What can we do?"

Her enthusiasm was contagious. Seeing this kind of reaction was exactly why he enjoyed teaching. New apprentices who came to this project with all the anticipation of a child rejuvenated him.

Yvret pulled her up. "Let's start by considering what happened yesterday morning. When you used the energy to stun the sidhe, did you mold the effect once or twice?"

She looked away while she considered that.

"Do you remember?" he asked. "Sometimes it's hard to recall things that close to the seizures."

"Once," she said. "I had to wait until both of them were touching me."

"Didn't we work on using effects over a distance?" he asked. "Do we need to review that?"

Shaking her head, Erin replied, "No. I felt unstable enough already. I didn't want to risk it."

"That's fair. Even after your transformation, strength conservation is very helpful. Oftentimes, there's a temptation to go for showy abilities to impress your enemies or allies. Your enemies don't care past how much damage they'll get if they don't avoid the attack. Your friends will be happy enough with something that works. Always use the lowest level skill that will get the job done."

She nodded. "I'll—I'll remember that."

"Good, it's a useful tool, even at my age. Now, for today, we should see about recording what you know."

"Notes?" she asked.

He smiled. "You know three basic skills and their more advanced counterparts. While I've no doubt you'll remember that easily enough, as you progress, you'll need the notes to help refresh your memory. Depending on what sort of fey you become, there might be a lot to remember."

After looking around the room and finding no other chair, Yvret gestured for her to join him on the floor. The morning's task wouldn't take long. When they finished, he would let her rest and recover her strength. He had a feeling today would be at least as exciting as yesterday had been.

***

Bella walked into the human camp, reveling in the catcalls and awestruck stares she received. Humans were too easy. She could still remember a time when she was mercilessly ridiculed for her ugliness. After she started learning skills from a fey, one she had later murdered in his sleep, Bella had used her abilities to kill a man who made fun of her appearance. The attempt had driven her to a seizure, and when she'd awakened, she had been delighted to find she had become a succubus. Now, men who would've scarcely given her a second look before couldn't take their eyes off of her. Better yet, at her slightest whim, she could touch a man and drain his life to renew her beauty.

Consequently, she didn't mind walking into this brigand's camp alone. In fact, she hoped someone made a move against her. Draining the life of Joaquin's present had only awakened her thirst for more. Later, after completing this part of the negotiations, she would look for another victim.

The leader of this camp had to be in the biggest tent, so Bella made her way to it. On the way, she acknowledged the looks she was getting with a smile, which she hoped would cause strife and division in the band. Each soldier would swear he had gotten a favorable response from her, and then men being men, they would fight over her affection, which none would ever get.

As silently as she could, Bella slipped into the leader's tent. Luis sat at a desk writing. When he didn't look up at her, she softly padded up behind him and peered over his shoulder.

"'My dearest Isadora,'" she read. "'Every second without you feels like an eternity.'"

Luis didn't even jump. Only the brief pause of his pen signaled he had even heard her speak.

Bella groaned. "How can you write this stuff?" she asked, speaking Spanish like a native, like Gustavo in fact.

Absorbing another's life energy was often very enlightening. In addition to the power of the soul itself, which kept up her beauty, all the knowledge of the donor became hers as well. In times past, the trivia of a man's life would annoy her, but now she enjoyed watching all the pain and suffering a human life held. Her victim's horrified memory of his last hour or two on this Earth as she slowly sucked the life force away was an exhilaration that remained with her long after the man's body was a lifeless, gray husk.

"A letter full of sap like this one will spare me troubles galore when I return home," Luis replied absently. "I'll be with you shortly. Sit and be comfortable."

Although her body, still energized by her recent meal, pleaded for another infusion of life force, Bella kept her power in check as she lightly stroked Luis's face. Extra energy could delay her eventual decay, but she wouldn't really need another soul for at least a few days.

"I can keep myself amused."

Luis didn't even flinch. He reached under the desk and brought out a finely decorated steel dagger and set it on the table. A bitter chill raced down Bella's spine.

"Sit. I'm nearly finished here, and then I can give you my full attention." He kept his eyes on his work.

Bella snorted in disgust and did what she was told. He had better be careful, or next time she touched him, she would forget to shut off her powers. Her orders were to form the alliance, but there were always accidents, and she was still somewhat new to her powers.

"Business before pleasure," Luis added.

She didn't answer him but looked around the tent. For a camping expedition, the furnishings of his tent were impractically ornate, but everything she saw showed unusual wear at the joints. Apparently, it could all be broken down into more manageable pieces. Having all this custom designed must have cost him a small fortune. She was still admiring the plush cushions and gold-inlaid wood when Luis blotted the paper and sealed it before announcing he was finished.

"I expected you two hours ago." Luis turned his chair to face her.

"Well, I was in the middle of my supper." She licked her top lip. "It's never much good once it's gone cold."

He leaned back and gestured to the door. "If that's the way of your timeliness, then we can skip all the formalities and you may be on your way. I don't need allies who can't be punctual."

"Oh, come now." She snorted. "All we have to do is come to an agreement. Two hours one way or the other causes no harm to either of us. When the real attack comes, we will, of course, be available to you at the time you set. Now then, the king is interested in your proposal. What are you expecting of us, and what will you provide as your payment?"

Luis nodded once. Turning back to his desk for a moment, he picked up a paper and handed her a legal contract. She smiled and looked it over, amused that he thought sidhe could be bound by such a document. If they "failed" to hold up their end of it, what did he plan to do? Sue them in court? Bella had, herself, broken every single contract she had signed and had no intention of honoring this one if she didn't feel like it. Humans were so gullible. She scanned through the document to get an idea of what he wanted.

"I will need your assistance in three matters," Luis began, quoting the contract almost word by word. "First, our weapons supplier may need a little incentive to get the promised work completed at the promised time. Second, one of my former soldiers—"

"Your brother if I recall your name properly." She pointed to the name on the paper.

"Yes, but that's irrelevant." He dismissed the interruption with the wave of his hand. "He's trying to find me, very likely to help the duke's guards find me."

"You should have killed him outright instead of hoping for him to suffer and die on his own." She recalled Gustavo's recollection of the second-hand information related to that incident.

Luis shrugged. "Yes, well. What's done is done. Our peoples will work together to lure him here where I will personally destroy him."

Bella looked up from the contract. "Some professional advice: make sure he's dead this time. I'd only be too happy to help, of course."

"An option I'll consider. He must be taught the price of going against me, which he failed to learn the first time. Once I'm certain he understands, perhaps I can be persuaded to let you have him, if he's still alive."

She smiled, anticipating this Diego's slow, tortured death as she absorbed everything that made him human.

"Finally," he continued before she was ready to give up her fantasy, "the day after the new moon, my spies have informed me of the duke's move from his winter palace to his summer one. We will together attack that convoy."

Nodding, Bella considered the lopsided offer. "And what do we get in return? Taking Diego's life will please me, but what of my king?"

"Any survivors of the convoy attack will go to the sidhe to do with as they please," Luis explained. "The duke's party will include His Grace's family, his guard corps, and no small number of servants."

That could be considerable. Just her share alone could sustain her for months.

"I would advise you, Bella, to keep your people's involvement to a minimum. Each sidhe's portion of the reward would be much greater."

"And you would also have fewer of us to keep your eye on." She glanced at him over the top of the paper.

He smiled and nodded once. "We understand each other, then."

"We will provide what forces are necessary for the tasks," she agreed.

Just to appease him, she signed the contract and wondered if Luis realized he was signing his own death certificate. If he didn't die in the fighting, he would himself be a survivor of the coming battles.

***

Erin sat on a bench under the huge tree in Michel's front yard. The pleasant weather should have refreshed her mind and body, but she wasn't enjoying it much. Despair gnawed at her wits. Yvret's assignment to find this "heart of sacrifice" troubled her. Maybe she was yet confused from yesterday's fit, but Erin didn't understand how to do what he wanted of her. Clearly, Luis had what she needed, but how would she find him? If she could locate him, how could she and Diego take on the entire band?

Where was Diego anyway? He had asked her to meet him here so they could go continue their hunt for Luis. Morning would soon pass to afternoon, and they had too much to do. Her patience came up short today, but she closed her eyes to try to make herself relax.

When the manor's door squeaked open, she looked up, hoping to see her partner, but frowned. Ian's quick, agitated stride warned her more than the scowl on his face that a confrontation was at hand.

"Get your things. We're goin'," Ian announced without even the courtesy of a greeting.

Erin forced a smile. "I'm fine this morning. How about yourself?"

He grabbed her by the wrist and pulled her up. "I don't have time for your games, woman."

She pulled away from him and sat down again. "And what's gotten into you? What about your plans to follow after my father?"

"Gone. All of it." He jabbed his hand toward the manor. "My petition to join the guards was turned down. I'm not good enough with a rapier or musket."

"Sorry to hear it, but you can't blame them. It's important business being in the guards. I can ask Michel to help you find a good situation while you continue to improve your skills, and I'm certain he'll let you stay on here until you find a place to stay."

"Oh, he helped me, all right." Ian clenched his fist. "I can work with a blacksmith. He's the only one hereabouts who speaks any English."

"And what's wrong with that? It's honest enough work. Plenty of people would jump for joy at that opportunity."

"It's beneath my station!"

"It's better than starving. Isn't it?"

Movement behind Ian caught her eye, and a quick glance showed Diego and Michel approaching.

"This is all your fault." Ian stomped closer to her.

Erin rose to face him more directly. "Mine? How do you reckon that?"

"You're a woman."

"Aye, all my life, and?"

"You're the one who taught me the rapier!" he screamed.

Erin winced. Without a doubt, Michel had to have heard that. Polite society had little regard for women who wielded weapons. The practice was too manly.

"I never should've learned from a woman." He stepped well within arm's reach. "It isn't even proper for you to handle a sword!"

Well, that was gratitude. She had only done it in the first place because he had threatened to tell Connor a pack of lies. How could this now be her fault?

With her hands on her hips, she got as near to him as she could. "You thought it was proper enough when it saved your life!"

She never saw it coming, but the slap to her face sent her sprawling on the ground.

"*Señora*!" Diego called. She could hear the note of worry in his voice.

"Ian! Stop right where you are!" Michel demanded with a tone that left no room for disobedience.

Erin lay still for a moment, too stunned to move. The last time Ian had laid a hand on her, she had given him a warning with a minor shock. That should have stopped this from ever happening again. It hadn't worked. Any normal man would have seen the power at her command and respected her. Ian didn't.

Her cheek stung where he had hit her, and she could taste blood where her teeth had cut her cheek. There was only one way to make sure he could never hurt her again.

Erin rose quickly and wove her attack skill for distance. Even if he ran from her, she could still hit him. A rush of energy filled her, and blue sparks arced between her fingers. One last gesture was all she needed, then it would be over. Never again would she worry he would come after her.

Ian backed away. "Erin, I'm sorry. I didn't mean to hit you, but you know better than to push me like that."

"That's no excuse." She followed after him to keep the distance separating them constant. "You're supposed to be my kinsman. Complete strangers treat me better!"

"It won't happen again." He held both palms toward her.

"You're right," she agreed. "You'll never do it again. I mean to be certain of that."

The fear she saw in his eyes as she raised her hand brought her a feeling of power and control she had never felt before. He deserved to suffer for all the times he had threatened her and hurt her.

Ian tripped over the leg of the bench and fell flat on his back. In a second, she was on top of him. Her knee across his gut and her free hand, pushing on his chest, held him down, but he was too stunned to fight back. When she saw his eyes darting back and forth between her face and the sparks dancing across her hand, she smiled. He was getting a taste of his own medicine, and Erin hoped he enjoyed it.

"Erin, stop!" Diego called.

"I have to do this," she said.

"No, please," he begged. "Michel is the law. He sees everything. He sees Ian hit you. Let the law punish Ian."

She had tried going to the law once when Connor had beaten her. They had told her he had every right to strike her and she must have done something to bring the punishment on. They had blamed her for being beaten. No, the law wouldn't help her.

All of her feelings of power dissolved with that recollection, and she felt bitter tears welling up in her eyes. When she blinked, streams ran down her face.

"The law—is—the law is no help," she said. "This is the only way—the only way to be sure he won't hurt me again."

Her mind flooded with memories of all the times she had been threatened or hit. Since Connor's death had stopped his abuse, only Ian's death would stop his.

"Erin, listen to me." Michel stopped just outside of reach. "Let me help you. I'll do everything I can to ensure he'll never harm you again, but you have to let him go."

She shook her head. "No, this is the only way. I'm tired of being the target of his anger. It's not my fault!"

"If you kill him, it will be," Michel warned. "If you strike a man who's already down, you'll leave me no choice but to bring you in, too. I don't want to do that. You were the victim of that attack. Don't become the aggressor."

Diego drew nearer and crouched next to her. Erin looked up at him and saw the worry in his face.

"Please. I need you to help me," he pleaded so softly that Michel couldn't possibly hear it. "If we no stop Luis, many more people are hurt. I know what it is to be hurt by a member of my family. Do not have the blood of your family on your hands. Please, Erin, let Ian go. Let Michel help you."

It wouldn't work. Despite all the promises and assurances, if she let Ian go, Erin knew he would be back. On the other hand, she had defeated him, and she could best him again. Maybe next time there would be no witnesses to be appalled when she did what she had to do to protect herself.

"Next time, Ian," she promised.

With a gesture, she sent the blast of lightning into the ground several feet away, not even flinching when the thunderclap rumbled through the air.

"*Mon Dieu!*" Michel exclaimed as he took a few steps back from her.

Diego instinctively shielded his face with his arms but didn't move from her side.

Under her, she felt Ian tense and heard him gasp. Good. Maybe now he would understand she had power, and she wasn't afraid to use it. Perhaps he would respect her. If not, and if Michel couldn't make good on his promise, she had the ability to make sure Ian never threatened her again.

Erin let Diego pull her up and guide her away from Ian, who lay still where he had fallen, too scared to move. He watched her with the wariness of a mouse that had miraculously escaped the cat. So he should.

Michel roughly pulled Ian to his feet and led him away with a firm hand on his arm. Only when she heard the front gate close did Erin relax. She sighed, shaking her head. Unbelievable. She'd had the opportunity to stop one of her abusers and let herself be talked out of it.

Diego helped her to the bench. Tears freely ran down her cheeks. When Diego tried to pull her closer, she resisted. It was improper for a widow to rest in the arms of another man, and she certainly didn't need him thinking he was more than a friend. Just having him there, she was safe again, for the moment, and that was enough.

He patted her back. "He is gone. Michel keeps it that way. I am certain."

She snorted. "The law never helped me before, Diego. I've no grand hopes that it will help me now."

"But, if you give Ian what he deserves, then you suffer for hurting him. You are a victim again. It no is right."

Erin nodded. "No, but it's my fault, of course. It always is."

"This time Michel is the law, and Michel cares for you. He no lets Ian return here, and anyway, soon you are fey, and then you no need to fear Ian."

Oh, how little he knew! Yvret had been a fey for two millenia, and still mortal men armed with nothing more incredible than a net had taken him captive, then given him over to the sidhe for their perverse amusement. Being fey was no protection, but Diego was sweet to try comforting her.

Erin wiped her eyes. Michel would be back later to demand explanations for what he had witnessed, but for now she could sit with Diego and pretend that everything would be okay.

Chapter 11

For all Michel knew, his eyes had deceived him. He had absolutely seen Ian hit Erin, but after that, he could believe nothing else. Erin could not have pinned a man of Ian's size to the ground, and he refused to believe that any mortal, man or woman, could throw lightning.

Thankfully, he hadn't been required to arrest Erin. Whatever Diego had whispered to her had convinced her to show mercy to her cousin. If he hadn't been seeing things and if she could repeat that lightning bolt at will, could any cell in his or any other prison possibly hold her? He would have to express his gratitude to the boy later.

By the time he reached the garrison, confusion still muddled Michel's mind. He took Ian to the office and roughly planted him in a chair before sitting down on the other side of the desk. Where could he even begin with this interrogation?

"Care to explain what happened?" he asked.

Ian snorted. "You didn't see it for yourself?"

Now safely away from Erin, all the fear had left his eyes, and he had returned to his usual gruff self.

Michel leaned forward on the desk. "Make no mistake, MacAllen. Cross me, and I'll imprison you and forget where the key is. The locksmith? He's awfully busy these days. What with all the robberies lately, locks for things are in high demand. Once again. Refresh my memory about what just happencd in my front yard."

Ian glowered. Michel gave him a mental five-count before he intended to make good on the threat and just missed getting to five when Ian spoke.

"I went to tell Erin I was leaving, and she came after me. She pushed me and—"

Michel shook his head. "Do not take me for an idiot. She's not the sort to initiate an attack. Begin again, without any creative embellishments to the truth. I'm very short on patience, MacAllen."

"But—"

He slammed his palms on the desk. "The truth, Ian."

"It is true," Ian replied. "I said I was leaving and told her to go pack her things. We argued, and she pushed and pushed. She's very headstrong, you know. Finally, to make her stop, I hit her. I didn't mean to do it. She just doesn't know when to quit."

"That's no excuse to strike her hard enough to throw her to the ground," Michel said.

"I tried to apologize to her, but she wouldn't have it, and then the way she gestured, lightning sparks came to her hand. Next thing I know I'm flat on my back, and she's on me like a she-daemon."

"What was that argument about?" Michel asked. "What was 'proper enough when it saved your life?'"

Ian took so long to answer that Michel wondered if he was trying to come up with the answer from scratch.

"She has some mad notion that she saved me from Connor instead of the other way around. Ever heard anything so daft in all your life?"

Actually, given the way he had seen her handle Ian, Michel didn't find the proposition so hard to believe. It was definitely more plausible than Ian's tale of impossible stunts with a sword.

Ian looked around as if he needed to make sure they were truly alone. "I would've said something sooner, but if she found out what I'm about to tell you, she'd have my hide. The friend she sees so much, I'm certain he's teaching her witchcraft."

Michel scowled. Very possibly, even very likely, Ian said that to save his own skin. He wouldn't be the first to blame another to get himself out of trouble, and he wouldn't be the last. With all the things Ian had done to call his honesty into question, Michel thought for certain he would have to go check outside a window if Ian suggested the sky was blue.

On the other hand, what else could explain the lightning? Faeries could do things like that, but Erin was as human as he was. Witchcraft was the only other logical explanation for what he had seen earlier.

The matter would bear some investigation, but if he found more evidence of witchcraft, he would have to arrest Erin and deal with her in accordance with the law. Watching her burn to death would break his heart, but what else could he do? Even he had to obey the law.

In the meantime, he had to do something with Ian. No matter what else had happened, Erin had been born into nobility just like Michel had. Ian's family wasn't even landed if he recalled correctly from better than ten years ago. Violence across class lines against someone of a higher station had stiff penalties. There was also the matter of his promise to Erin. He had given his word that Ian would do her no further harm. At least until Michel had more answers than questions, Ian would have to be confined. If Ian were falsely imprisoned, amends could be made later.

***

Long after the tears had stopped, Diego sat with her, no chaperone in sight, rules of civil society be damned. Better for them both, though, if they left before Michel returned. The guard captain would have endless questions that would likely annoy and embarrass Erin.

Reluctantly, Diego stood. "We leave before Michel returns."

Slowly, she nodded. "Aye, else we'll never be able to get out of here."

"*Sí*," he replied. "I see his face when everything happens. He no understands."

"I should be more surprised than I am."

He offered a hand up and felt the quiver in her hand. The sickness wasn't so far away from her now.

"Maybe it is better if you stay here," he said. "Michel no disturbs you if he thinks you rest now."

She held up her shaking hands. "No, this is annoying, but it won't get worse unless I do something foolish. I haven't even gotten one of the warning signals yet."

He smiled and nodded, glad to have her company. Hopefully, she wasn't pushing herself too hard. "We find nothing in the city, so we go to the city gate. Any messengers of my brother must go through there, and perhaps sidhe no come so close to the city in the day."

"Aye, we can watch for them, but what if they see you?" she asked.

Having her around was awfully helpful. There wouldn't be anywhere to hide since all the brush and trees had been cleared from around the city wall to hinder an attacking army. Any of the men Luis would trust to be errand runners would recognize him, even from the back, so if he let Erin be his eyes, they would still know him. If Luis found out he was being hunted, this mission would become much more deadly.

"My cloak," Erin said. "The hood will hide your face well enough."

"Your cloak fits me?" he asked.

She looked him up and down. "It won't cover your knees, but other than that, I think you'll be fine."

Following her back inside, he waited at the foot of the stairs while she ran up to get what they needed. When she returned some minutes later, she carried a faded, drab, gray-brown cloth over her arm. Diego inspected the material. The cloth was so thin, he thought he could fold it into a thin strip, blindfold himself, and still successfully navigate a crowded room without help. Even his cloak, a mended hand-me-down from Luis, had been better than this.

"This is your cloak?" he asked.

She smiled. "Impressive, isn't it?"

He slung it around his shoulders and fastened the pitiful garment with the cracked button at the collar. "Hm, this works for today."

At least he wouldn't bake in this one. The day was shaping up to be on the somewhat warm side of comfortable. Leading Erin back outside, he felt a terrible sense of urgency. If they had remained on the bench for too long, Michel might return and catch them before they could get away.

The feeling resembled the tension of robbing a house or a store and hearing the owner stirring. When he was alone against the house's occupant, this fear was something to live for, because a successful escape brought on an indescribable elation. Now, with Erin to protect, the fear of detection held no promise of satisfaction later.

Michel's questions for them both would only delay their departure, and there had already been too many setbacks. As they quickly made their way to the gate, Diego imagined running into Michel when they were mere steps from the safety of the city crowds. The long hike, from the manor's gate down the private path to the public road leading to the city gates, took an eternity.

"Relax," Erin said.

He scowled. "How? At any time, there is Michel."

"So we'll tell him you're taking me to see Yvret."

Diego shook his head. "Michel has questions. They take very long to answer because he does not like what he hears. I know this. I remember how he watches you."

She shrugged. "We'll tell him we have to be there soon. Maybe we can say we're running a wee bit late so Michel will have to wait. Hopefully, he'll forget by the time we get home."

Diego looked at her and shook his head.

"No, I don't believe it either." She frowned.

Despite his apprehension, they arrived at the city gate without a problem. There were a handful of guards and a collection of merchants who'd set up pavilions to display their wares. A few people were there browsing or haggling the purchase price. With the wild gesticulations they were making, Diego supposed the negotiation was more difficult than they would have liked.

After exchanging a look with Erin, Diego brought her to the merchants' tables. Making the circuit as slowly as he could without drawing unwanted attention, he kept an eye on the gate and on the road leading into town and watched for someone he recognized. They had made the rounds twice when Erin leaned nearer to him.

"We're being watched," she whispered.

"Sidhe?" he asked.

He was never more relieved than when she shook her head. "No, one of the guards at the gate. Every time I look his way, he quickly looks somewhere else."

Diego smiled. "I no blame Michel for trying anyway."

"What do you mean?"

"I no tell him where we go, so he sends his man to see what we do and be his eyes and ears."

He had done that job before. Tracking someone took more effort than it might seem, especially since a good amount of the task meant sitting around waiting for something important to happen. Boredom could be fatal.

"You're not upset?" she asked.

"No. Michel helps us, and I no betray Luis to get the help." He pretended to admire a plain metal cup.

She smiled and nodded. "I see."

After a few more passes through the different merchants, whose looks said they were none too happy about repeat customers who weren't buying, Diego recognized two men. They stopped at a weaponsmith's table and began a conversation. With constant reminders to move slowly, he waved for Erin to follow and led her to the adjacent pavilion as casually as he could. Tipping off the messengers wouldn't help. Diego turned his back toward them and picked up an ugly silver candlestick to pretend to admire. His quarry spoke Spanish clearly enough and loudly enough that Diego had no trouble understanding them.

"Listen, Carlos, that's the best I could do," the merchant insisted. "Luis wants too much in too little time."

"Then maybe some of our allies can convince you to work faster," Carlos said.

Diego knew what kind of "allies" he meant. Having sidhe breathing down his neck would certainly speed him along. On the other hand, the resulting sloppy work would please Luis as much as waiting for the promised goods.

"I have every apprentice and journeyman in my shop on it. My other customers are getting upset because I haven't been working on their orders."

"Would you prefer upset customers or a dead family?" Carlos threatened.

"You want the impossible."

"We want what you agreed to. You're holding us up, and if we miss our opportunity, you'll regret it for the rest of your short life."

"I need more time."

"A mile up the road, at midnight tonight, bring everything you have," Carlos said. "Pray I'm impressed by what you have to offer me."

Turning his head slowly, Diego looked through the nearly transparent cloak and saw his brother's messenger leading his companion away. Once they had gotten a reasonable distance, Diego put the candlestick down and followed them while he gave Erin the short version of the conversation. They were out of sight of the city guards when Carlos left the road for the forest.

Diego felt Erin's firm grip on his arm and turned toward her. She studied the trees carefully.

"What is it?" he asked.

"Sidhe," Erin answered. "Not far inside the trees. We need to go back."

"I no can lose them now," he said. "Carlos will lead us straight to Luis."

"Aye, and the sidhe will end that excursion in a hurry," she replied, holding her unsteady hand up for him to see. "I need to rest before I can use any fey abilities again, or do you suppose you can take on two men and three sidhe alone? If I had a sword, I could help you, but this dagger of mine is pretty well useless, as I found out last time."

Diego scowled. He was so close! Following Carlos back to the camp would be an easy matter, but if they ran into sidhe, Erin would have to protect them. She would do it, he knew, but that would drive her into one of those seizures, and he'd have to stay with her until she recovered enough to get her home. By then, Carlos's trail would have gone cold. Even if he could enlist Michel's spy to watch over her, he couldn't very well take on the whole camp without her to support him.

"I'll rest this afternoon," she said. "Then we'll just have to make it to their rendezvous tonight maybe a wee bit early."

Sighing, he looked at her. Although he liked the way she thought, letting this opportunity pass annoyed him beyond all human comprehension. She was right. This trip hadn't been fruitless. They would be here at midnight to wait for Carlos.

Diego nodded and turned back toward the city. "We go home. You have another seizure so you sleep. This keeps Michel away from you."

"He'll just give all his attention to you, then."

"No, I run errands and things to prepare," Diego replied.

If Erin could use a sword, he should see about getting one for her. That, and some other things.

"Shouldn't I be with you to translate?"

He smiled and debated telling her, but he would rather it be a surprise. "No, I do this myself. You need to sleep."

With a gentle push on her shoulder, he guided her back toward the manor.

***

Diego entered the city, his mind still reeling with the missed opportunity to follow Carlos back to the camp. He should have sent Erin back on her own and tried trailing them on his own. He knew how to be stealthy. It could have worked.

But then what would have happened to Erin if she run into trouble—supernatural or otherwise—on the way back to the manor.

213

As much as he hated to admit it, she was right. They would make tonight work.

A tall, imposing figure moved up in his peripheral vision. The size and slight weave in the gait suggested Hernando. Diego used the reflection in a conveniently angled store window to confirm his guess and slowed his pace to allow the other man to catch up.

"How goes your efforts?" Diego asked.

"Fine. A couple more plans in the work before the new moon, but Luis has a half-dozen men fewer than when we last spoke." Hernando snorted. "Two took our hint and deserted. The rest? Well, they're no use to Luis anymore."

"That's excellent. We make our move the night of the new moon."

"Good. Remember, we all get our share, or you will also be of no use. To anyone."

Diego dismissed Hernando's concerns with the wave of his hand. "*Cálmate.* Unlike Luis, I believe a worker deserves pay equal to his task. I will not forget you."

"Best you don't." Hernando turned a sharp right down the next street.

He blew out a breath. Yes, Hernando and the others had cause to be concerned after how Luis treated them, but Diego couldn't wait to be rid of his brother's shadow.

***

Michel held the gate open for Philippe, then followed his lieutenant into the yard. Thoughts still spinning with Ian's accusation, Michel could not believe any of the story. He remembered Erin as a young child, which made any thought of her as a possible follower of Satan ludicrous. Ian had to be lying. Erin could not be a witch, but where had the lightning come from? If there were any other logical explanation for the bolt that had flared from her fingertips, Michel would have leapt for joy, but nothing at all came to mind. Now, with Philippe here as much for moral support as anything else, he would try to dig up evidence to support Ian's claims. Given his choice, Michel would have preferred to ride into battle horribly outnumbered and outclassed.

"I don't like this." Michel walked into his house.

Philippe shook his head. "You're making it too personal. A woman was accused of witchcraft. That charge is too serious to ignore."

"Ian was just as likely as not trying to save his own hide. Why should we believe him? He has put together very elaborate lies for our benefit before."

"Then she'll be quickly exonerated."

Michel led the way up the stairs and stopped in front of Erin's door.

"Would you rather I do the looking?" Philippe offered.

Michel sighed. "No. This is my house and she's my guest, so I'll do what I have to do. I'm required to do my job, liking my duty is optional."

With one last reminder that he was here to clear Erin, not condemn her, Michel opened the door and stepped into the room. From inside the closed bed curtains, Erin moaned softly and rolled over. Michel cringed and stayed frozen in place while he came up with a more logical, less embarrassing reason to be in her bedroom in case she woke up and demanded that explanation. He had heard she was ill and had come to check on her. That sounded better than "I heard you were a witch and came to find out if the story were true."

After a tense moment, he concluded she would stay asleep, provided he be as quiet as church mice during Mass. Michel left the door open so Philippe could watch and provide witness that nothing inappropriate went on. Michel would never molest a woman, but people often looked for improprieties to bandy about without first engaging their brains, and rumors were hard to put a stop to once they found tongues to wag. Philippe could vouch for his honor and integrity if need be.

Draped on the chair near the bed were some of the old clothes Corinne had given Erin. On the floor was the knife Erin usually carried. Although women didn't typically carry one all the time, Michel remembered Erin's mother doing the same thing. Mary had claimed she needed the knife to scare off the sidhe and cut herbs while in the woods. Even after marrying into nobility, she still insisted on doing some of that work herself. The dagger was nothing more sinister than a leftover quirk from Erin's time in the islands.

A more thorough search might have to wait until she was no longer in the room, but nothing turned up under the bed, in the nightstand, on the desk, or in the wardrobe. While digging through the dresser, though, Michel came across two books. Holding his breath in hopes he'd found something silly like a diary, Michel pulled the books out. When he saw the title, he scowled: *Giacomo Digrassi and his True Arte of Defense.*

What was a woman doing with a book on rapier combat? For a moment, he suspected the manual might be a simple gift for a man she knew, but when he flipped through the pages, he found notes in the margins written in a light, feminine hand. English, French, and an unrecognizable language filled the empty margins.

There in the white space of the book, she had written notes about specific maneuvers or possible modifications to account for long skirts and having only a dagger to use. Judging by the amount of information recorded there, she had been very busy. The quality of the notes impressed him, too. She had made some very interesting conclusions and observations. Had the topic been appropriate, he would have enjoyed the opportunity to sit down with her and discuss her thoughts on Digrassi's work. Michel bit his lip. Even thinking about that seriously was wrong, and he knew better. Although the law didn't care one way or the other, God did not intend for women to be skilled with arms, so he should do nothing to encourage her.

The second book was little more than folded papers. Writing in the third language he'd found in the rapier manual practically leapt off the pages. He could read none of the words, but the pictures showed hand motions and on one page, he saw lightning flare from a person's fingers.

For once, Ian had told the truth. Erin had turned to Satan to gain the power of witchcraft. Michel's heart broke. Why? Why would she do this? He would have protected her from harm. He would have seen that she lacked for nothing.

What else could it be? Faeries, he supposed, could also cast spells, but was that really any better? Sidhe were universally brutal, and fey had their own fickle ways. They still used magic, which was illegal and subject to trial and execution.

Sadly shaking his head, Michel rejoined Philippe in the hall and gave him the books.

"The writing is hers," he whispered as Philippe flipped through the book on sword combat. "It doesn't prove witchcraft. The second one might. I want to give her a chance to explain."

"Captain, Michel, I know you care about this woman, but you have a duty to perform," Philippe insisted. "If you won't fulfill the role His Grace gave you because of your familiarity with her, I will."

Michel scowled. "I'm aware of my duty, Lieutenant, and if her testimony doesn't free her from suspicion, I'll order her locked away like I would any other criminal."

Without giving Philippe a chance to say more, Michel left him at the door and quickly strode down the hall to his study. Confronting her here at the house might mean dragging her through town back to the garrison. He wouldn't inflict that kind of embarrassment on her even if she were guilty. If he could lure her to his office, that would make questioning her easier to deal with. Michel wrote a deliberately cryptic note to Erin. To learn the meaning, she would have to come find him. That should do what he needed.

Back in her room, Michel hid the note where the books had been. On the way out, he looked at the knife again. She may not discover the book for a while, but the missing knife would get her attention as soon as she woke up and dressed.

With her knife in hand, he left her room and quietly pulled the door closed. He prayed Erin's explanation of her activities would alleviate all of his doubts, but he couldn't imagine any words that could satisfy the demands of the law.

***

Erin awoke and stretched. She still felt sleepy, but it was more the weariness of a person who had slept too long than one who hadn't slept long enough. Her hands were still shaking a little, but the morning's mental haze had lifted. Pulling aside the bed curtains, she looked out the window and found long shadows crossing the yard. She should roust her miserable butt, dress, and spend some time studying the rapier manual in preparation for tonight's inevitable fight.

With a groan, she rolled out of bed and put on her darkest skirt and bodice. That would help her stay hidden tonight while they waited in the shadows. As she got up and moved around, the weariness left her.

Now, where had she left her knife? It wasn't where she usually kept it. Looking all around the floor nearby, she found nothing. Thinking she might have put it elsewhere, she looked in every reasonable place, then expanded her search to most of the unreasonable ones, too. Where had she left the stupid thing?

Dimly, she recalled coming halfway out of sleep at the sound of someone coming in. She had dismissed the intrusion out of hand earlier as the remnant of a dream, but she had the sinking feeling someone had been in her room and had gone through her things.

The books! If someone had taken her knife, they might have found the books, too. Rushing over to the dresser, Erin pulled open the drawer. The chemises she had neatly folded there were not so neat now. Pulling them aside, she confirmed they were missing. In their place was a folded paper. She snatched the paper out of the drawer and read the contents.

"I need to speak with you.—Michel."

She ripped the note in half and threw it to the floor, then left, slamming the door behind her. When she found Michel, she would give him a piece of her mind and get her property back.

Still fuming when she reached the study, Erin knocked loudly. She might be mad enough to spit nails, but she wouldn't be as rude as he had been. Imagine the audacity of going into a lady's room while she slept and rummaging around through her underwear drawer! She had thought he was a gentleman.

"If you're looking for Michel, he's still at work," Corinne called from the foot of the stairs.

Erin took a deep breath to make sure she could answer calmly. "When is he expected back?"

"He mentioned working late tonight to prepare for the duke's move to his summer home tomorrow."

Erin frowned. "Thank you."

She wouldn't wait that long. Things needed to be done tonight, and while she could make do without the books, the knife was the only weapon she had. If she had to go to see Michel at his office, she would. One way or another, she would have her explanation and her things.

The trip into town didn't take nearly as long as she expected. Along the way, she rehearsed exactly what she would say to her "friend" and imagined how he would at first protest his innocence then agree that he had indeed behaved inappropriately.

Upon reaching the compound, she gave her name to the guard who escorted her to the building. He led her through the maze of halls to a door with the captain's crest painted on it.

Erin knocked loudly and waited for him to open the door. When Philippe looked out to invite her in, all of her plans evaporated. Philippe hadn't been around to see the fight against Ian. The lieutenant wouldn't understand, and he would think she had gone over the edge.

Philippe, however, didn't speak English. She could still give Michel the tongue-lashing he deserved, but no. Talking in a language someone in the room didn't know would be rude. She could speak French fluently, so she should, just to be polite. She would not have Philippe thinking she was as ill-mannered as her cousin was. For now, she would have to contain her anger, but later Michel would not like to hear what she had to say about this.

"Come in, Erin." Philippe opened the door wider.

Not yet trusting her voice to be civil, she only nodded to accept the invitation.

"Ah, Erin, we were hoping you'd join us." Michel gestured to the chair.

The books and her knife were on the desk in front of Michel, out of her reach unless she either went around or jumped onto the desk.

She gestured to her property. "You went through my things. What gives you the right?"

As upset as she was, she surprised even herself by keeping her voice fairly level.

"That is my house," he answered. "And after this morning, I wanted to give you the opportunity to explain yourself. More appropriate to do that here than there, and I knew you'd come looking for your knife at least."

She cast a quick glance at Philippe. "This is between us. I would prefer less of an audience."

"We don't always get what we want."

"You fear me that much?" She snorted. "I should be surprised to see our friendship means so little to you?"

"You aren't the same person I knew a decade ago, and caution is not the same as fear. Ian was not terribly tight-lipped after I arrested him."

"You gave your word you would make certain he wouldn't be able to hurt me again!" She leaned forward and jabbed her finger at him. "And now I'm here because of something he said? Is this what your word is worth?"

"He suggested you might be a witch," Michel continued. "That's too severe of a charge to let pass unnoticed. Now, before I have you burned at the stake, I wanted to give you a chance to defend yourself. Think of this chance as a courtesy to an old friend, but don't think for a moment I will hesitate to do my duty."

Erin rose and paced halfway across the room before turning back to Michel and Philippe. "One word from a dishonest peasant like Ian will get me burned at the stake? This is what French justice has become under your leadership? In Father's time, nobility meant something."

Michel stood, fuming at her accusation. "Are you engaged in witchcraft or not?"

"Witchcraft? Are you mad? I'm no follower of Ol' Nick. Connor never let me go to Mass properly, but I still believe in the one true God."

Yvret's warning about telling people what she was becoming made perfectly logical sense, especially in light of the images she'd seen on the viewing wall in his palace, but she just might have to tell these people to get out of this alive.

"I'd like to believe that." Philippe turned to face her. "But Michel tells me he saw lightning come from your fingertips, and you subdued a man twice your size. That's not something a lady can do. And they say the falling sickness is caused by daemons."

"You have had a lot of those fits lately," Michel pointed out.

"Old wives' tales. Even the Church doesn't officially condemn those with falling sickness. Do you know more than His Holiness on those matters?" Flopping in the chair again, Erin leaned her forehead on her fingertips. "You've already made up your mind, haven't you? Will anything I say actually make a difference?"

The answer was so plain on their faces that they didn't have to respond at all. She had already been condemned. What could she do? If they intended to arrest her, she would be tried for a witch and killed in one of their trials or burned at the stake. Although she couldn't allow that, she was still unwilling to harm her friend. She would very happily fry her cousin and even Philippe if he pushed her to it, but not Michel. Was it too much to hope one of Yvret's fey laid claim to the pond where witch trials happened? She couldn't count on that.

Only one way to escape remained. She would have to put them all to sleep and run for it, but where could she go? Until she transformed, the Seelie Court wouldn't take her. Without money, she couldn't get a room at an inn. Her last option was to take up residence in the woods and deal with the risks of the sidhe and bandits. None of those sounded promising, especially since a seizure would leave her helpless for a day or more. She would have to try to convince them she was not a witch.

"Let's start with something easy." Michel held up the rapier manual. "Why do you have a rapier manual?"

Erin took a deep breath and prayed to God for help "Ian wanted to learn the rapier so he could impress you and join the guards to make his fortune. He doesn't know his letters. I'm literate in both English and French. He bought the French translation of that book then used threats to force me to read it to him, but it didn't work. I could go over the same passage with him fifty times and he still wouldn't be able to grasp the meaning. The only way he understood was following me as I led him through it. He probably doesn't even know I still have the book. I'm certain he believes it was lost when we fled the area."

She watched their faces, but both men still had the same stern looks. Did they believe her or not?

"After watching Ian with a rapier, I don't believe he could have killed Connor unless your husband was asleep," Philippe said. "You did it. Didn't you?"

Looking away from them, she considered telling them the truth. Officially, being a woman and wielding a sword was no crime, but society accepted such things were an abomination. Loose women were almost better regarded. Yvret's words came back to her. She was to think as fey think.

She nodded and looked directly in Philippe's eyes. "Yes, but not how you might think. He drew on me. I ran to Ian for help, and when Ian fell and Connor was ready to kill him, I picked up the rapier to get Connor away so Ian could get back up. When my cousin wouldn't rise, Connor charged at me, and I killed him with the sword."

Erin could still see the whole thing, now almost three weeks later, playing through her head. She could see the fear in her cousin's face and hear her husband's cruel laughter. What was she supposed to have done? Watch Ian die, then just stand there while Connor killed her, too? From the looks on her audience's faces, apparently so.

"You didn't think there was something wrong with that?" Philippe asked.

"I did what I had to do." She glared at him. "Knowledge of weapons may not be preferred in human women, but that doesn't make me a witch. If Ian wasn't such a clumsy oaf, he wouldn't have tripped over his own feet, and I wouldn't have needed to do anything."

Michel frowned and made some notes on the paper in front of him. While he wrote, Erin reminded herself of the finger positions she'd need for sleep. She might need to use it before all was said and done.

"Well, at least that matches what I heard this morning. Now, the lightning and this book," Michel prompted, tapping her notes with the quill.

Those were the real reasons she'd been tricked into coming, and she knew it.

Erin shook her head. "What's the use? You won't believe me."

"Maybe not, but if you don't give me some sort of response, I'll have no choice but to arrest you and inform the courts you're a witch," Michel warned. "You'd do best to tell me the truth."

"Fine."

He could try to arrest her. See how far he got before he fell over snoring. If he meant to burn her, they would have to catch her. Closing her eyes for a moment, she collected her thoughts. She would tell them, all right, and if they believed her, all would be well. If not, then she had her other plan.

"Someday, soon I hope, I will transform to a fey," she began.

Erin went all the way back to the time when she first met Yvret and continued from there, telling them everything. When she reached Yvret's explanation of the falling sickness, she took extra care to be as clear as she could. Then she went on to tell about her time in the Seelie Court and her continuing studies. Not magic. Fish could swim. Birds could fly. Faeries could mold energies. It was as natural as breathing. Michel leaned forward studying her carefully. Erin wondered if he wanted to look for horns or pointed ears or wings or other signs she was fey already. More likely, he searched for signs she had lied, but she didn't care.

As she spoke, she gained confidence. She hadn't realized until now how far she had come since this had all begun. The men interrogating her, though, had their hands full trying to keep their real emotions out of their faces. Several times their stark stoicism had given way to glimpses of fear and awe. They were quickly realizing she could not to be trifled with, and that suited her fine.

"And once I find this heart of sacrifice, I'll transform," she concluded.

"Hmph. We've had it all backward. Those with the falling sickness aren't possessed by daemons, they become daemons."

"Or elves, or sprites, or dragons, or a host of other things," Erin corrected.

Hadn't they been paying attention? Hopefully they had heard more than the parts they wanted to hear.

"And what does this Yvret fellow say about you using swords and helping Diego on that fool's errand of his?" Philippe asked.

"He encourages me. If I have a skill, I should use it, and I should help Diego because I can and I'm willing to."

An awkward silence followed. Even if he informed her she was indeed a witch, Erin wished Michel would say something. Anything would be better than his fatal silence.

When she couldn't take it anymore, Erin leaned forward. "Well?"

He didn't answer and refused to meet her eyes. Her heart sank. Her long-time friend thought she had sold her soul for magic. Erin stood and went for the door before they arrested her and locked her up like a criminal in an iron cage.

"Guards!" Philippe called.

The door opened and four guards entered. If this situation had been less dangerous, she would have been flattered they thought so highly of her skills. For now, she was more interested in getting out. Erin started the focusing movements for sleep. If she took care to create it as a wide-area effect, she could take all six men down at once, then make her escape. It wouldn't hurt them in the least.

"She's casting!" Michel exclaimed. "Don't let her complete the spell!"

While two of the guards drew swords, the other two rushed forward and grabbed her hands.

"Put the swords away," Michel ordered.

As the men obeyed the command, Erin fought to get loose from the two holding her, but they had her too firmly.

"Stop, Erin, you'll only hurt yourself," Michel suggested. "They're accustomed to dealing with full grown men twice your size."

"What? Spare myself some bruises now so I can burn to death at dawn?" she asked bitterly.

"You will be tried as a witch and be burned at the stake only if you prove to be one," he corrected.

"So you'll hold me underwater for an hour, and if I drown, I pass, and if by some God-given miracle I come up breathing, then I'll be burned as a witch. Some choice that is. Either way I'm dead."

"At least the first way, you'll go on to heaven."

"I see what our friendship means to you," she snapped.

"Erin," he said. "You don't understand."

"Oh, I understand just fine. You're prepared to take the word of Ian, a common man who has proven himself a liar, over the word of a lady born into nobility, even though I have never, not even once, done anything to harm you. I am the apprentice of a fey, not a witch!"

"I have a job to do," he insisted. "My personal feelings in the matter do not count."

How convenient for him to be able to hide behind his job! It relieved him of the need to think.

When tiny pinpoints of light marred her vision, Erin stopped fighting and willed herself to breathe more slowly and evenly. Her fear and her too-fast breathing would drive her to a seizure, and that wouldn't help anyone. Maybe she should let the fit happen anyway. Then she would hardly be coherent while they killed her.

Chapter 12

Yvret crouched next to the sprite perched near the shoulder of a very recently transformed fey. A dryad had brought him here when he'd collapsed in her wood. The poor man, a dryad himself now, had rushed into a forest fire to combine his developing skills with the dryad of the area to contain the blaze and protect a shrine that was sacred to the local people. He had succeeded, but the cost might have been too high.

"How is he, Ismael?" Yvret asked.

"Well, I healed all the burns, but he breathed in a lot of smoke, even after the fire was out." The sprite winced. "I'm afraid he's not out of danger yet."

"And the other dryad, Gerta?"

"She's fine. She protected herself much better, but she never thought he would need help to do the same."

Yvret nodded. Dryads were like that. They meticulously cared for the places they protected, and sometimes forgot the people in them.

He turned to the pixie who had been the new dryad's mentor. "Is there anything you need, dear?"

She shook her head. "No. I'll sit with him until he recovers from that fool stunt. Thank you, though."

After patting her on the back, Yvret left. He hadn't gotten ten feet down the hallway when he heard someone running toward him.

"Yvret! Sir!" his scribe called.

When Yvret turned to Steve, the look on the muse's face worried him.

"What is it?" Yvret asked.

"Come quickly," Steve replied.

Yvret frowned and followed his scribe down the corridor. Sometimes getting information from a muse was like pulling teeth with a sledgehammer. He waited expectantly for the rest of the answer.

"She's in trouble," the muse continued.

"Erin?"

"Yes, sir. I've been watching her while you were gone, like you asked."

"And?" Yvret prompted.

"Sir?"

"What happened?" Yvret asked, promising himself he would not lose his temper.

"She's been arrested," Steve replied.

He waited a count of five to give Steve a chance to continue. "Because of what?"

"They think she's a witch."

"Why?"

"She hurled lightning this morning," the muse answered.

He had been afraid of this. Since before his time, humans had trouble accepting what they couldn't, or more often wouldn't, understand. Faeries and the gifted ranked very high on the list of things generally considered incomprehensible.

When he reached the viewing wall, Yvret picked up the book Steve used to compile notes and scanned through the day's events to get a picture of how things had gone. One mistake had been compounded by another worse than the first. For exactly this reason, he'd shown her the trial and warned her against revealing what she was.

If only she had been more careful, none of this would have happened. To be fair, though, he had made his share of blunders before his own metamorphosis. He supposed he should let that temper his opinions of her actions.

Yvret looked at the image on the wall and saw Erin being chained in a cell. Looking on was her friend Michel, doing nothing to help her. His stoic face hid any hint of emotion. Erin looked far too stunned to really react. Another betrayal by someone she cared about was not what Erin needed.

"Should I get him?" Steve asked.

Yvret gritted his teeth and reminded himself that muses couldn't help themselves. "Get whom?"

"Kendall, who else? Maybe one of the other seraphim?"

After considering that for a moment, Yvret shook his head. "I'm not sending Kendall, or anyone else for that matter, into such a large group of well-armed men to get into and out of a cell made partly of iron bars."

"Someone else, then?" Steve said.

Who was left? Certainly not Ian or Michel. Both men had made their opinions known through their actions. Ian had falsely accused her to justify his own crimes, and Michel had believed the horrible fiction despite her assurances and empirical evidence that her cousin was a most foul liar. That left only Diego. Leaving Erin's rescue in the hands of an injured boy filled Yvret with more dread than hope.

In case Diego failed, though, Yvret would be prepared to rescue her during the trial. The humans used the pond outside the city wall for the farce they called witchcraft trials. One of his nixies claimed that pond, so one way or another, Erin would not die at human hands. He owed her at least that much for saving him.

***

231

Before leaving the patch of open ground near the stream, Diego looked once more at the pile of sticks and leaves hiding all the things he had collected for Erin today and the little crockery bombs he'd made for tonight. They would be fine there. After all, he was only going home to get Erin and promptly return. Passing the equipment off as his own would be easy enough, but explaining why he needed a new rapier and gloves would be much more challenging. More importantly, he and Erin needed a place to practice far away from eyes that would be faster to condemn than to understand.

Satisfied his cache would be safe, he set out for Michel's house. When he heard Michel's spy unsuccessfully try to follow without being detected, Diego had to smile. His host really had to find the time to train his men to trail someone quietly. Even on the worst day, Diego could do better. He thought about stopping and giving the man a few pointers, but there was far too much to do tonight. Maybe some other time he would.

Diego's extra shadow left him at the gate to Michel's land. Although this was the only official way in or out of the property, the surrounding walls were certainly low enough to climb with a minimum of trouble. Losing the guardsman would be an easy matter if he found a need to do so.

Once in the manor, Diego looked for Erin but didn't find her in the kitchen or in any sitting room. Could she really be sleeping still? Maybe she only pretended to rest to avoid Michel's harangue. Corinne, who should be in the kitchen overseeing dinner, would know for certain.

"Erin still sleeps?" he asked after greeting the lady of the house.

"Oh, heavens, no," Corinne replied. "She's in the city. Michel needed to see her in his office. Odd, though, she wasn't entirely happy about going."

The news filled Diego's guts with lead. Although there could be a perfectly innocent reason behind the summons, the whole thing had the feel of a trap. Maybe paranoia had him looking for problems that weren't there, but there was some safety in being so remote from the prisons. Michel could have talked to her about anything he wanted. He'd asked her to join him for a reason, and Diego couldn't shake the feeling that a pleasant little chat didn't figure in as part of the plan. He had hoped Michel's concern for Erin would protect her from the usual blame-the-victim routine, but Michel was the law first and Erin's friend second.

"When do they return?" he asked.

"Michel won't be back until very late tonight. There's just so much to do yet for His Grace's move tomorrow afternoon."

The duke was on the move tomorrow? Conveniently, the timing matched up to Luis's plans, the ones that were so involved that he needed sidhe help. Of course. The bulk of the guard corps would be involved along with whatever household staff and protection attended the duke directly. That would be more than Luis's little band could manage, especially with Diego's other allies whittling down the numbers.

Corinne looked toward the city. "Oh, I do hope he can spare a man to escort Erin home when their business is done. She'd be dreadfully bored waiting around all night."

Her prolonged visit would ruin their opportunity to track Carlos at midnight, too. Maybe Michel had called her there to keep her from helping in the hunt for Luis. Corinne had given him the perfect solution.

"I go to bring her home," Diego offered.

"Well, thank you, Diego." She picked up a covered basket. "Would you be a dear and bring Michel his supper?"

That would lend credibility to his reason to be there, so Diego took the basket from her. "We return soon."

Since leaving the spy here would be best, Diego went out the kitchen door and headed directly toward the city. The stones making up the perimeter wall were stacked and mortared unevenly. Visually appealing, but there were so many handholds and footholds, scaling the wall marking the boundary of Michel's land was ridiculously easy. Erin could manage, long skirts and all.

Once certain the guard assigned to watch him wouldn't see him, Diego returned to the road. He did not want to climb the city wall. The last time he had tried on a dare, he'd nearly broken his fool neck when his boot slipped on a tiny foothold.

When the guard's compound was in sight, Diego stopped. He had to be insane to go in there again. He would be alone this time, surrounded by the duke's men and every one of them well armed and trained to work together.

Surely Michel wouldn't do anything to hurt Erin. Being stuck there until the ungodly hours of the night would actually be safer for her than what they had planned for themselves. He really didn't need Erin to track Carlos to Luis's camp. After tonight he would know where to find the camp, and tomorrow, while most men were out thieving or gathering information, Diego could take Erin to confront Luis.

Diego looked at the basket he carried and growled. He had promised Corinne he would deliver Michel's dinner, and he had to stay true to his word.

When he reached the gate, he held up the basket for the guard to see. "Michel Gaultier."

The guard started rattling off directions in French, but when Diego shook his head, the man stopped mid-sentence and just pointed to one of the buildings. After going through that process a few more times, Diego found himself at a closed door and knocked loudly. The answer from within, in French of course, could only be "enter" or something to that effect, so Diego walked in.

"Hello, Diego," Michel said, looking up from some papers he was studying.

"¡*Hola*! Corinne asks me to bring you dinner and to bring Erin home."

Michel sighed heavily and looked down at his desk. "I can't release Erin to you."

"Why?"

"I had to arrest her. Ian said she—"

"You say to her 'I protect you from Ian' and this is how you do this?" Diego slammed the basket on the desk.

"She may be a witch!" Michel exclaimed.

Oh, that was rich. Erin? Into witchcraft? Someone must have done something funny to Michel's tobacco.

"Because the ones who follow the way of evil are so kind and so helpful?" Diego rolled his eyes "You no understand what you say."

"You saw her this morning. How many normal people do you know who can shoot lightning out of their hands?"

Diego never thought he would see fear in the guard captain's eyes, but he saw terror there now. The Spaniard considered telling Michel about Erin's secret. She would understand the breach of trust, and revealing her studies might be the only way to save her from being drowned or burned in the morning. His argument depended heavily on how much Michel understood the nature of the fey. Since he wasn't even seriously entertaining the idea that faeries were involved, he likely had the usual opinions.

"Faeries also use what we say is magic," Diego said. "Her teacher is fey. I see him once. A very powerful fey, too. You risk angering the fey if you kill one of them. Your whole house is dead for this one error because you kill a fey. Already, you put one in prison for the word of a man who lies as often as he breathes. You no think the fey take their revenge? Do you know what angry faeries can do?"

"Erin is no faerie," Michel replied.

"She is soon. Her teacher shows her what to do."

"Then she will pass the test when I try her in the morning."

"You mean you will kill her tomorrow morning." Diego leaned on Michel's desk. "If she passes or no, she dies and you wear the blood of an honest woman when God sees you, and you have the anger of the fey to get you to God so much sooner. What of Corinne? What of your boys? What of your servants? You kill them, too. So much honest blood you wear."

Michel stood and went to the window. "I must do my duty. She was accused of witchcraft."

"By a liar!" Diego pushed off from the desk. "How many times does Ian lie to you this week? You believe him now?"

"She must be tried!" Michel continued over him. "I must do my duty, even if I'll hate myself for it."

This was hopeless. Michel wouldn't even follow his own convictions about Erin's innocence.

Duty was such an easy thing to hide behind. Diego had seen uncountable men in the band perform the most horrendous crimes, then justify their actions with, "I was only following orders." Well, if Michel wanted to bind his own hands with duty's manacles, Diego would have to save Erin himself. "I see Erin now," Diego insisted.

"No," Michel said without turning. "If there is any chance she really is a witch, it's too dangerous. No one is going in there until morning."

"You deny her confession?" Diego demanded.

"The priest will absolve her tomorrow if she allows it."

"Oh, so when Christ says 'visit people in prison,' you think he also says, 'but no Erin?' I hear you or no?"

Michel sighed and hung his head but didn't answer.

"I pray with Erin tonight and ask God to forgive her. And you, also."

If that didn't do the trick, Diego might have to resort to some other means of finding her. Captain Gaultier took a long time to answer him.

Michel motioned for Diego to join him. "Do you see the red brick building with the clay roof there by the garrison wall?"

Diego nodded. "Yes."

"She's there." He turned back to his desk and wrote on a paper, then used wax and his signet ring to mark it officially. "Here is the pass the guard will need to admit you."

With the authorization in hand, Diego turned away.

"And Diego?"

He turned as he opened the door.

"Tell her I wish things could be different," Michel said.

"She is a good woman," Diego replied, as one final twist of the guilt knife. "She knows this."

As Diego walked toward the prison Michel had indicated, he noticed most of the men were going into a large, flat structure in the middle of the compound. The city clock struck the Angelus hour. Time for prayer and supper. If Erin could scale the wall, they had it made. He had never seen a woman climb that well, but then he hadn't seen any other women use swords or mold faerie energy, either. Ever since they had met, she had surprised him again and again. Now she would have another opportunity.

***

237

Erin sat in the cell, wishing she could hug herself. Sitting on the stone floor and leaning on the brick wall was just chilly enough to be uncomfortable. With her hands chained, she couldn't even scratch her nose without some odd contortions.

Once again, Yvret had been right. Things had indeed changed. Michel had once been her friend, but he currently thought of her as one possessed. Before this afternoon, she had wondered if she could leave the world behind and join the fey, but as more and more people turned their backs on her, she saw few other options. Only one betrayal remained: Diego. Even though he had looked after her when she was ill and had come to her defense, Erin knew his concern for her wouldn't last. Just like everyone else, he would turn on her, too, probably as soon as he had Luis. When she outlived her usefulness to him, he would hurt her like everyone else had.

Once they had her in chains, she had sworn to herself she wouldn't cry, but the tears had come anyway. Since then, she had spent all her tears and given up on trying to call for Michel. Worse, Diego wouldn't know where to find her, and Yvret couldn't get to her through the iron barred cell even if he somehow knew she needed him. No one would come to help her, and tomorrow, she would drown, because even if she could get her hands free, none of her skills would do her any good. At least in death, she would finally be free from those who hurt her, but that comfort was even colder than the stones around her.

Her last hope was that Yvret would find out in time to have one of his nixies in the pond, but he had warned her that there were too many ponds used for witchcraft trials and not nearly enough nixies to go around.

The door squeaked open, and she looked up to see if Michel had come to free her, after having come to his senses, or maybe the priest had arrived to hear her last confession. Could she rely on

238

him to help her? Surely the good Father would take the side of someone falsely accused.

Erin bit her lip when she saw her visitor to keep from calling out to him until she knew what he was up to.

Diego set a piece of paper on the floor by the cell's door and fumbled with the keys, looking for the right one to open her cell. "Why do they post a guard? They think you escape after they lock you in here and chain you to a wall?" he muttered.

"Diego!" she said. "How did you know where to find me?"

He smiled. "Corinne tells me you are upset when you speak to Michel here. I think this is bad, so I come talk to Michel."

She squinted up at him. "And he just let you come in here, keys in hand?"

"I make him feel bad about what he does to you. He gives me a paper because I say, 'Christ says to see people in prison and pray.'"

She smiled. "Clever."

"He wants me to tell you he wishes things are different," he continued.

Erin didn't believe that. If Michel wanted things to be different, he could have made them different. He had promised to help her against Ian then turned around and took Ian's side against her when her cousin had obviously lied to save himself. Whatever respect she had for Michel was gone now, never to be reclaimed. Although she wouldn't go out of her way to hurt him, she would think twice about trusting him again.

Once Diego had released her from the chains, Erin rose and rubbed her arms to try to restore the blood flow. Diego wrapped his doublet around her shoulders.

"They hurt you?" he asked.

"No." She leaned on him for support. "I knew fighting them was useless, so I didn't try after the first wee bit."

He glanced around the cell. "We find a way to get you out of here."

"What about your paper?" she asked. "What permissions does it give you exactly?"

"I no read it." He led her out of the cell. "Michel writes it in French."

She took the paper from him and smiled as she read it. Just to make sure she hadn't misunderstood, she read the pass through a few more times. "Either he doesn't realize what he's done, or you've made him feel worse than you thought."

"What does he write?"

"'Diego Rodriguez has my permission to see to the rights of Erin Ross as provided by the Church. He has my complete confidence.' Then he signed it and put his seal."

She saw Diego's eyes light up.

"No, I think he knows exactly what he does." Diego looked over her arm at the paper. "He thinks, 'I know Erin is good, so I give Diego a way to help her.'"

"Unlikely." She sighed. "But, anyway, it doesn't matter now."

"We use this even if Michel does it by mistake. Quickly, before he changes his mind or Philippe hears what happens. How do you say it, 'I take her to confession,' in French?"

Erin saw where he was going and quickly gave him the words he needed, then had him repeat it back to her, correcting him until his words were nearly right. She intentionally left his pronunciation a little off to keep the guard from suspecting anything or trying to strike up a conversation.

"We are ready." Diego took his doublet back. "Remember, you no want to do this. You no do nothing wrong so you no need to confess nothing."

She nodded. "I understand."

After she helped him put his doublet back on, she followed him. With a firm grip on her arm, he opened the door and pulled her outside. When the guard barred their way, Diego showed him the pass from Michel.

"I—um—I take her to—to confess," Diego said in even more broken French than he had practiced.

Did he have a royal case of nerves or was this part of the act, too?

Erin pulled against his hold just hard enough to look convincing. "You can't make me confess to something I didn't do."

"Good luck with this one," the guard said.

Diego only smiled.

All the way to the gate, Erin's mind conjured up every conceivable way the plan could completely, catastrophically fail. They might run into Philippe, or the gate guard may insist they all go talk to Michel, or the guard wouldn't even wait to hear where they were going and sound the alarm for a jail break. The guard might even demand a bribe.

"I don't know about this." She looked down at the ground.

"Trust me." Diego adjusted his grip on her arm. "It is well."

All her worries were for nothing. At the gate, all Diego had to do was flash the paper to the guard, who was too deeply engrossed in a discussion with his friend to really care.

Once safely around the corner, Diego let her go, and she released the breath she hadn't realized she was holding.

Diego blew out a breath. "I wish everything is so easy tonight."

"Had you been there earlier, you wouldn't think it was easy," Erin replied. "What now?"

"You wait for me outside the property Michel owns. I go over the wall and tell Corinne all is well, then come out the gate to meet you."

"Over the wall?" She raised an eyebrow. "Need your exercise today?"

He shrugged. "It is easy. I no want the man following me to see me go in to see Michel and come out with you, so I make him think I go in the house then I leave a different way. Now I must make him see me come out or he knows something is not right."

Erin nodded. She would leave all those machinations for him to fret over.

As they neared the last bend before Michel's gate, Diego disappeared into the woods before continuing to their meeting place. To avoid unwanted attention, she also took to the trees and hid about a stone-throw off the path.

The sound of laughing children reached her: fey, but she didn't bother trying to figure out where.

"Can I join you?" Yvret asked.

Erin looked over her shoulder and saw him standing by the tree. "Please, but Diego will be here soon and there's another man nearby. They might see you."

"We'll have to be quiet, then, but I need to talk to you for a minute or two." He sat next to her. "I saw what happened. First this morning and then this afternoon."

She stood up and spun toward him. "You've been spying on me, too?"

"No, Erin," he said calmly. "I'm not spying on you. Please, sit down."

Sitting across from him again, Erin brushed her eyes with the back of her hand, then stared at the fluid on her knuckles. "Well? What then?"

"After you told me about the sidhe attack, I've been watching over you," he explained.

She had judged too quickly, but with everything that had happened today, who could really blame her. He had so many things to do. Why would he waste his time watching her?

"Have you been so bored that watching me go through my day is your only amusement?"

"No, not bored. Much more worried, I'm afraid." He leaned forward and clasped her hands in his. "I don't want to lose you. I might be able to help if the sidhe attack you again, but only you can keep you from turning into one of them."

Erin leaned forward. Surely, she hadn't heard that correctly. No one had ever even asked her what she wanted to become.

"What do you mean? I-I don't want to become a sidhe! I want to be with you. Don't I have a choice? I thought you said I could choose."

He nodded. "Of course you can, but some of your choices lately are troubling."

"How do you mean?"

"Take the matter with Ian this morning."

"What of it?" she asked.

"You nearly killed him."

"He hit me!" she hissed. Had he been watching, he would've seen that. "I didn't strike him once!"

"Why not? You had him pinned. You had the lightning ready. You could have dispatched him easily and freed yourself from the worry that he'd come after you again. Why didn't you?" Yvret asked.

"Michel would have arrested me," she replied. "Diego talked me into letting Ian go."

He scowled and looked away for a moment. "That's what I was afraid of. Right decision. Wrong reason."

Why was he hounding her on this? She hadn't harmed Ian in the least. All she had done was scare him, so what was the big deal?

He had certainly done much worse than that to her within the last week.

"What, do fey not get mad?" she asked.

"Oh, they do. Trust me on that one." Some real doozies came to mind. "You haven't seen angry until you've seen Sarah on a rant. Heaven help us all."

Erin smiled at the thought of the tiny, butterfly-winged faerie in a fit of temper.

"Fey do get mad," Yvret continued. "They even mold energies when they're mad, but they never use the skills against someone who's powerless. Once Ian was no longer a threat to you, you should have released him."

She closed her eyes tightly and felt a tear roll down her cheek. "It's the only way I can make him stop hurting me."

Yvret pulled her into an embrace. "Michel imprisoned him for unprovoked threats and attacks on a member of the landed class. By the time he's released, you'll be in your new incarnation. You need not fear him. All things considered, he may not even recognize you anymore."

She could only hope that was true. After pulling away, Erin dried her eyes. "What about this afternoon? Did I do the wrong thing again?"

"That depends on why you didn't put them to sleep," he replied.

"I didn't have the chance to, but I started to," she said. "I would have put them all to sleep if they hadn't stopped me and put me in chains." She sniffled. "Is that wrong?"

"Tell me what you think," he suggested.

Things used to be so clear, but now that he had warned her, fear of becoming a sidhe made it virtually impossible for her to tell if even walking across the road would be acceptable.

"I don't know. No? I guess not."

"No. You did the right thing there for the right reason," he said. "Had you put them to sleep, you could have escaped without harming them. Then when Diego freed you, you decided correctly again. You could have used your power to get vengeance on them, but instead you escaped with the least amount of damage to anyone."

"Is it too late?" she asked. "Do I have to become a sidhe now?"

He shook his head. "No, it's not too late, my child, but you're going to turn all my hair gray if you keep doing like you've been doing."

"Then when I killed the two sidhe yesterday on the way back from the ring," she began. "They were down when I killed them. That was wrong?"

He shook his head. "They were still a threat to you and to Diego. You'd only stunned them with your bolt. If they'd come around while you were in the grip of the seizure you knew was coming, they could have killed you and ambushed Diego when he returned."

Erin frowned. "It's so hard to tell. How do I know if I'm doing the right thing?"

"Watch why you do things and how. Use your skills to attack your enemy and defend yourself and your friends, but once the enemy is no longer a threat, use none of the faerie skills. That's probably the safest course for now. Once you've transformed, others of your kind can teach you better ways to discern these things. There are nuances unique to each type of fey."

The difference still seemed unclear to her, but she couldn't come up with a question to ask to find out what she didn't understand.

"I have to go," he said. "You're about to have more company."

"Wait, what do I do about Michel?" she asked. "I can't go back to his house. I can't go to an inn. I can't go with you. Living in the woods would be too dangerous. Where should I go?"

"I think Diego has an idea about that. If not, come to the gate, and I'll take you somewhere safe to rest." Yvret rose and took a few steps away before turning back toward her. "It's not too late for you, and I have every confidence you can make the decisions you need to. Good night."

There was too much left up in the air, too many questions she needed answers to. Clearly, he couldn't stay long enough to even hear what they were and give her the direction she needed. She would have to find her own solutions and pray they were the correct ones.

"Good night, Yvret, and thank you."

He took a few more steps away before he disappeared, leaving her alone in the stillness of the night. The loss of his company made her feel even more lonely than before, and she no longer welcomed the solitude.

Leaning back against a tree, Erin looked up at the sky through the loose canopy of the woods. The trees were still skeletal, but there were tiny leaves and buds marring the sleek outline of the branches. In another week or two, full-blown leaves would block her view of the stars and the moon. There must have been a new moon tonight, and that would make the evening's plans with Diego easier in some ways and harder in others.

Without the light of a full moon, hiding from Carlos would be easier. On the other hand, if they had to track a trail, the darkness would make it so much harder, and they couldn't exactly carry a torch with them while they went. There was no sense in advertising their presence unnecessarily. Since she had no frame of reference to this line of work, she wasn't sure which was the lesser of evils. Diego had experience in that arena. She would rely on him for guidance.

"Hello, Erin," Diego said from just over her shoulder.

She jumped halfway to the stars and turned to face him. "Diego! You scared me half to death!"

He smiled. "Sorry."

She wasn't buying that. His smile said he'd scared her on purpose. Had she been in a better humor, she might have found his antics amusing. As it was, wringing his neck for that heart-stopping scare was much more likely.

"How long were you there?" she asked.

He sat next to her. "I just see your teacher leave as I come up. I no see him well, but he disappears."

"I didn't hear anything. How do you do that?"

"Very carefully," he replied.

Erin rolled her eyes.

"I no scare you again," he promised. "But we go somewhere else before I show you what I get today. We need to do things those people no wish to understand. There is a place I go sometimes to be away from the band."

As she followed him, she realized Diego walked with a bit of a limp, but he wasn't using the cane. For that matter, he hadn't had the cane when he came to free her from prison either. Why hadn't she seen that before?

He saw her staring. "I no need the cane now. My leg is well enough."

"That's excellent, Diego."

Smiling at her, he led her down the road. Once away from Michel's land, Erin felt more relaxed. She walked with Diego in a comfortable silence. Only her anticipation of finding out what he had picked up ruined her calm. He led her by the arm into the forest, but away from all the places where they had encountered sidhe or bandits. Without his help, she certainly would have fallen over ground clutter at least a dozen times, but he expertly navigated her around fallen trees, rocks, and uneven ground. Did he have owl's eyes? They stopped next to a babbling brook and sat on new grass at the edge of the water.

"If we talk quietly, the water hides our voices," he whispered.

"How do you find your way so well in the dark?" she asked.

He smiled. "When your job is at night, your eyes learn to do this." He dug a bundle wrapped in her cloak out of a somewhat conspicuous pile of tree branches and leaves. "I get these things for you."

She carefully unwrapped her cloak. Inside she found a very simple rapier and dagger and a pair of dark gloves.

"I find pretty ones, but the blades are very bad on them," he explained. "This no is pretty, but it serves you better."

Carefully, almost reverently, she picked up first the rapier, then the dagger and admired how the steel shined in the starlight.

"The gloves protect you if you change when the weapons are still in your hands," he continued.

Setting the weapons down, Erin tried on the gloves. They were both a little loose, but they would do just fine. The gloves flared at the end to cover most of her forearm.

"Diego, this is wonderful. Thank you very much," she said. "How did you get all this?"

"I trade," he said.

She glanced up at him. "Authorized trades, I hope."

He nodded. "I still have what is left of the money Corinne gives us to go to the market. She no takes it when I try to give it to her that day. Michel gives me a cane I no need now. So, I run some errands for the man with the sword this afternoon and trade my work, the cane, and the money of Corinne for these things because

I think, 'Erin knows how to use the sword. I get her one.' But I have fear because you only know what a book knows. Many real fights no read books."

She understood. He wanted to teach her to use the rapier. No guilt clouded her mind this time. She had the skill to use a sword, and she should. Wasting the skill would be a pity. When Diego pulled cork balls out of his pocket to cover the points of their weapons, she nodded. The book had shown men practicing with bated blades to keep from injuring each other. Her work with shadows and mirrors was all well and good, but a live sparring partner could teach her so much more.

Chapter 13

Erin's sword slipped away from Diego's dagger. As he retreated to get out of range, she pursued him until the cork ball touched the middle of his chest. Amazing! No matter how fast he moved, she still got him at least as often as not. The way she could switch directions on a coin and leave change was mortifying. Only his greater strength gave him an advantage over her, but she had to allow herself to be lured into a contest of muscle. After he had gotten her several times that way, she had stopped trying to match strength with strength. Either Erin had natural skill, or her studies with the book had done more than he could have expected.

"Good," he said, panting. "Enough. Rest. We try more later."

As they sat on the bank of the stream to catch their breath, he noticed Erin's hand shaking again. Earlier, when they had squared off to start the bout, he had noticed the point of her blade wobbling back and forth across a space the width of his hand, but she had shrugged it off. Did physical exertion bring on the falling sickness? Both the tremors and her willingness to push herself past sane limits worried him.

"*Señora.*" He nodded toward her quivering hand.

When she didn't respond, he tapped her shoulder, making her jump a little.

"Sorry," she said. "What did you say?"

"Are you well?" he asked. "Your hand."

She looked at her hand for a moment, like she might become cross with it for being uncooperative, then sighed. "Did we have dinner tonight?"

"No."

"Then I haven't eaten since lunch," she concluded. "And Yvret's assignment was so confusing that I missed breakfast."

"And then I teach you the rapier and that also takes much strength." He frowned.

He wrapped up her blades in the cloak again, then rose and pulled Erin to her feet.

"We eat food, then we come back and practice more," he insisted. "We do not fight well tonight if you no keep up your strength."

She looked at him a little sheepishly and nodded.

Diego guided her back to the main road, helping her avoid obstacles her eyes weren't trained to see.

When they reached Michel's gate, Diego left her hidden in the brush with their weapons while he went on alone. If he did this right, no one would know they were even here.

He quietly entered the kitchen, keeping one eye covered to preserve his night vision as he worked by the light of the fire in the hearth. Into a small basket, Diego put some bread and cheese. Anything else would be too sloppy and the stream would give them all the water they needed. It was a pauper's dinner, but such simple fare would do better for them than the heavy meals Michel's household indulged in. His conscience chastised him for stealing, but he silenced those recriminations with a reminder that if not for their other activities tonight, they would be dining as guests. He was simply preparing their meal for travel.

Once in the obscuring darkness again, Diego uncovered his eye and made his way back to Erin. There, he traded the bundle of swords Erin had picked up for the basket he had before setting out for the stream again. On the way, he heard the clock in town toll nine. In two hours, they would go set up their ambush at the camp. When they returned to their earlier camp, they sat and ate.

"What is the plan?" Erin tore off a piece of bread and popped it into her mouth.

"We meet Carlos. Carlos leads us to Luis, and you have the heart of sacrifice. There is enough time."

"And if Carlos won't cooperate? Then what?" she asked.

He grimaced and looked away for a moment. "Then we have six or seven hours to daylight, and we know where Luis is not."

"Fine, but what do we do when we find the camp?"

"I find men Luis sends away, and they agree to help us. Luis has fewer men now. I have a way to create much confusion in the camp. We use the confusion to help us."

Erin nodded but seemed less than convinced. He could get her mind off the problem. They still had time to practice, and her anxieties would only interfere with her concentration. He didn't know much about fey skills, but he believed distractions would ruin her efforts. As soon as they finished eating, he helped her up and suggested adding a new parry to her skills.

***

"Erin."

Diego's whisper barely registered, but the light touch on her hand woke her instantly. She had fallen asleep? All she had intended to do was rest her eyes for a bit.

Leaning on his arm for support, Erin sat up and brushed the sleep from her eyes. "Diego, why did you let me sleep? We have too much to do."

"You need the rest," he replied.

"What's the time?"

"I just hear the city clock. The hour is eleven. We go now."

After splashing cold stream water on her face to chase away the last vestiges of her nap, Erin accepted his offered hand. Then,

253

under the watchful eye of her partner, she belted on her weapons: sword at the left, dagger at the right, just as the book had shown.

Once she had Diego's approval, she took his hand to let him guide her through the forest to the road. She could see better now, but still didn't completely trust herself.

When they had left the safety of their little clearing, Erin felt a nagging fear that someone watched them. Since there was no oppressive heat and no distorted red cast to the night, sidhe weren't trailing them. There was no sound of laughter in her ears, so fey weren't involved, either; but still, something was there.

Either that or she was being awfully silly. More likely than not, she simply had a wretched case of nerves, and with good reason, too. They were going to find a bandit camp and deliberately pick a fight with them. She didn't commonly do this as part of her daily routine.

All the same, the feeling would not leave her. When they got to the road, Erin stole a look back the way they had come but saw nothing. She had to be imagining it, because Diego didn't look perturbed at all.

What if only she could sense their visitor, like the way she knew faeries were about? Maybe he didn't seem to notice because only the gifted could pick up on what she sensed. If she ignored her feelings, then they might walk into a trap. Erin had to tell him, even if he scolded her for being silly.

Erin tapped his arm. "Diego?" she whispered. "There's something back there."

"I know," he replied. "It is the man Michel sends. This one is worse than the last. He makes too much noise."

"What do we do about him?"

Diego shrugged. "We meet Carlos and hope the man no ruins our chance."

"We hope?" She turned him to face her. "There's too much depending on this to just hope he doesn't interfere. We can't lose Carlos tonight or I lose my chance and you lose Luis in the bargain."

After considering her for a few moments, he nodded. When they came around the next curve in the road, Erin followed him a short distance into the brush. Without the sound of her own footfalls to obscure the noise, she heard the other man clearly.

"You talk to him; I get his attention," Diego whispered.

Erin nodded.

A man wearing the duke's colors came around the bend. As soon as he walked past them, Diego stepped out and tapped the man's shoulder. He spun, drawing his sword.

"Wait!" Erin called in French as she stepped into the open. "There's no need for that. We won't hurt you."

When recognition set in, he sheathed his sword. "How did you know I was there?"

"Never mind that." She turned to Diego and spoke English again. "Go on ahead. I'll convince him to stop following us and catch up with you."

Her partner smiled and nodded then continued up the road. When Diego was out of sight, Erin returned her attention to the guard. He was maybe her age, but heavyset.

"I don't want you following us." She spoke French. "You make enough noise to wake the dead all the way in Paris."

"I have my orders."

"And I'm giving you new ones. Tell Captain Gaultier I'll leave a trail for him to follow starting about a mile up the road from the city gate."

He took a step back and put a hand on his hip. "I do not take orders from a woman. Do you know who I am?"

She didn't know, and she really didn't care, as long as he went away. Erin nodded. "Yes. You're the man who'll get us all killed if you keep making so much racket. Now be on your way."

Much to her annoyance, the standoff continued. This wasted time she didn't have. If they didn't reach the rendezvous site at the appointed hour, Carlos would escape them. Erin didn't have Diego's confidence they could find the camp without a guide. This needed to end, and it needed to end now. Was Michel's man enough of a threat to justify use a sleep effect on him? Maybe, but while he slept, he would be out here at the mercy of whoever or whatever came along.

"Let me put it to you another way. I command the faerie energy. We can't have you following us because you'll alert our quarry a quarter of an hour before your arrival. You can leave on your own and deliver the message to Michel, or I'll force you to obey me. I'll let you choose which you'd rather."

The guard went pale but stayed his ground.

Erin shrugged. "Suit yourself."

Raising her hand, she made some useless gestures to try to scare the man. No sense in really sapping strength she would need for later. He went for his sword but fumbled with it. Erin drew first, but left her dagger in its scabbard, in case she needed her left hand to form a real skill.

"I wouldn't if I were you," she cautioned as she settled into her fighting stance. "I need only one more gesture, and you're finished. I do not wish to hurt you, but if you force my hand, I will."

Slowly the guard backed away from her, regarding her warily.

"Now go. I'm out of patience," she growled through clenched teeth, trying to sound angrier than she really felt.

When the guard turned and left, Erin smiled. She'd done it. She'd stood up to a man and hadn't let herself be bullied.

***

Diego stood as Erin came over the rise.

She looked back over her shoulder. "Intemperate man. I sent him on his way."

"I think you scare him," he replied.

"Good."

"Michel is unhappy about this," he added.

Erin sighed. "And what if he is? After tonight, I'll be fey, and what he thinks won't matter. Besides, he'll be unhappy enough with the both of us for escaping his prison."

What a change from earlier. Just this evening, she had been thoroughly distraught about her confrontation with the guard captain. With her goal in reach, she no longer feared him and what he could do to her. Diego liked the confidence he saw in her. Now, if she didn't get cocky, they would be in business.

As they neared the site where Carlos would meet his contact, Diego slowed their approach. Every sense went on alert for some sign of another person. He neither heard nor saw anyone, but that didn't necessarily mean much. Most of the men in Luis's band were at least as skilled as Diego was when it came to hiding from prying eyes.

They needed to get off this open road before they were spotted. He led Erin by the hand into the brush at the edge of the forest and continued parallel to the road.

Erin's grip on his hand tightened. "Sidhe. Over there." She pointed further up the road.

"How far?" he whispered.

After closing her eyes for a few moments, she nodded. "A quarter mile maybe?"

He went on just far enough to find a place where they could be shielded from the sidhe by a small tree and from the road at their side by a low shrub. The plants weren't the best protection in the world, but they would have to do.

In the distance, the Tours clock chimed midnight. Carlos, trailed by a sidhe nearly half again the size of a normal man, came out into the road.

"Are we going to have to fight that thing?" Erin whispered.

Diego held his finger to his lips and shook his head. He didn't intend to fight until they reached Luis's camp, and then only if Erin couldn't use some effect to take care of all the inhabitants. If things went perfectly, he wouldn't even draw his sword this evening.

From his vantage, Diego could see Carlos and the sidhe talking, but he couldn't hear them. He couldn't even begin to guess what one discussed with an eight-foot tall, bat-winged daemon.

An eternity seemed to pass before he heard the weaponsmith and a few others coming down the road, weapons clanking as they walked. Moments later, the huge man from the marketplace came into view followed by three men only slightly older than Diego. Each of them carried large sacks with sword-points sticking out of the top.

When the two groups met, Diego watched the negotiations. The meeting became heated almost immediately with the weaponsmith on the defensive. Although Diego listened carefully, he only picked up bits and pieces of the conversation. The smith's lateness was an obvious problem, and there seemed to be an issue with the quality or quantity of the blades. Diego wished he could get more information to satisfy his curiosity, but satisfaction wasn't worth the risk of getting any closer.

Then the whole encounter turned deadly. The sidhe struck the weaponsmith with its huge, clawed hand, lifting the man off the ground and shaking him. The others panicked, but some unseen force held them in place. Putting his back to the tree, Diego drew Erin to him to protect her from seeing such atrocities. He closed his eyes and wished he could shut out the screams as well. As she clung to him for security, he felt Erin jerk with every terrified cry. Explosions and thunderclaps joined the cries, and then all fell silent. He continued to hold Erin in his arms, afraid that if they so much as moved, the sidhe would add them to its list of targets.

***

With her eyes still tightly closed, Erin leaned heavily on Diego's shoulder. She shook, not so much from the falling sickness as from the fear that the daemon would somehow feel her presence.

Minutes passed after the cries ended. Not daring to look with her eyes, Erin reached out with her mind and sensed the sidhe's location, like a deep black void, darker than the nothingness that surrounded it.

Even concentrating on the sidhe in her mind's eye didn't do away with the images of the smith's death. She could still see the daemon lift that man, that poor man, with its clawed hand. She could still hear the screams, and she had done nothing to help.

"I-I should've helped him," she whispered.

"Impossible from here," Diego replied.

"No, I should've created a shield." She sniffled.

"And then the sidhe knows you are here."

"How can I protect you if I couldn't protect them?" She brushed her eyes with her hand. "I can't do this."

With a solid grip on her shoulders, Diego pushed her back so they could see each other. "Listen. We do this. The smith no prepares for a fight. He thinks he meets Carlos for business. Carlos surprises him. They no surprise us. We prepare for them, but they no prepare for us. You hear me?"

He was right. Erin knew to expect trouble and was as ready as she could be. Diego would be with her, too, and she couldn't believe that Yvret would let her go on a suicide mission. Since he hadn't stopped her, he had to think they could come out alive.

Erin swallowed hard and nodded.

"I also fear tonight. I never fight sidhe before. You have the advantage of me."

The void in her mind moved.

"They're leaving."

"You see them that well?" he asked.

She shook her head. "Only the sidhe."

When Diego looked around the side of the tree, Erin leaned aside, but he held her back. She pushed past him and regretted her morbid curiosity as soon as she saw what was left of the corpses that had once been humans. She turned away as soon as she could but not fast enough. Even when she closed her eyes, she could still see the bodies lying in the middle of the road.

Diego sat down again. "How far away do you see it?"

Erin shrugged. "I don't know. About as far as we are from it now?"

He nodded. "Good. We are more safe if you see them. I have to follow closer."

She followed him as he led her deeper into the forest. Their path angled away from the road, which suited her fine. Anything that put distance between her and the massacre couldn't be too bad.

As they went, she kept the sidhe's location in her mind's eye. If she lost them or overtook them, she would lead Diego to his death. She needn't have worried. After Diego stopped to look at a small, broken branch, they turned and took the same path Carlos and his vicious companion had used. A few feet down the path, she stumbled, finding the ground more uneven than she had anticipated. Diego caught her and steadied her.

"I'm all right," she assured him. "The ground wasn't where I thought."

He knelt to inspect the ground, then nodded and smiled.

"What did you find?" she asked.

"The sidhe is heavy, and the ground is soft," he answered.

"Leaving footprints, is it?"

She squatted next to him to look at it. The foot-shaped depression was almost two fingers deep. She was lucky she hadn't twisted her ankle.

"That makes it easier for us to follow," he said. "And you no have to make the path you promise the man Michel sends."

"How did you know about that?"

He shrugged. "How else you make him go away?"

"I can't pull anything on you, can I?" she asked.

He gave her a smile full of mischief and offered her his hand.

Following the trail a little further, she stopped when he did to look at more broken twigs and large footprints.

"We stop here and wait," Diego suggested. "We no need to be discovered."

Erin turned him to her. "Are you mad? We'll lose them!"

"Not with this trail," he said.

"And if they cross rocky ground or leave the forest, then what?" she asked.

After a few seconds, he nodded. "*Sí*. Watch where you step."

They continued on the trail.

***

Diego reached back to take Erin's hand to help her over a fallen tree. The trail they followed was just as obvious now as before. Since they had encountered no rocky ground or streams, he again doubted the wisdom of continuing along the path so close to Carlos and the sidhe. With so many footprints and broken twigs to follow, he would be much more comfortable waiting for a while before continuing on to the camp. He wanted to give his brother's men time to go off to sleep. Although Erin's point was well-taken, coming across the camp when everyone was awake would be deadly.

He stopped and sat down, gesturing for Erin to do the same.

"We stop here and wait," Diego informed her.

He expected her to be angry with him, and she didn't disappoint him. The disbelief and anger in her eyes weighed heavily on his shoulders.

"Diego, we've gone over this. If we lose their trail—"

"Then there is another new moon in twenty-eight days," he concluded. "We still go after Luis. You have the heart then, certainly."

"And if we find them tonight, then I won't have to live with seizures for another month," she insisted, pacing up and down the path with a hand on her hip.

"*Sí*, but that is better than getting to the camp when everyone is awake," he said.

"So we'll follow them to the camp then go away for a wee bit and return when they're all sleeping," Erin suggested.

"We cross the patrols three times?" he asked. "I no trust my luck so well."

"Your mission is the only one that matters, isn't it?" she demanded.

He winced, fearing she was right, but no. Their objectives were too intertwined. The necklace she needed to complete her quest was with the man he needed to find. If they reached one goal, they reached them both.

Erin stopped pacing and closed her eyes for a few moments, then sighed heavily. "It doesn't matter now. While we were arguing, I lost track of them. We've nothing to go on now besides the trail anyway."

He motioned for her to join him. Reluctantly, she did.

"There is time, Erin. We find the heart for you. I wish to attack soon, also, but I no want to see you die or worse."

"I don't want any more seizures, Diego," she said softly. "You don't know what it's like."

He remembered finding her in the forest after she had single-handedly dealt with two sidhe. Thoughts of that one event still brought an overwhelming shame to his heart. Never again, he promised himself anew.

He had found her after the seizure had a hold on her, but he had only witnessed the onset of the lesser fits. Never had he seen the start of the more severe episodes. Even with his vivid imagination, he supposed he could never fully grasp being at war with his own mind and body.

Diego shook his head. "No, I no understand as you do. I see how they affect you, and I no wish to see you so weak again. The new moon lasts all the night. We only wait an hour. Maybe we wait two. When the sun comes up, all is well. You see."

"I'll hold you to your word," she promised.

"Good. Someone keeps me honest."

Erin gasped.

"What?" Diego asked.

"You two would be such a cute couple if you were to survive the night," a woman's voice said.

Even before the voice had faded, Diego was on his feet with sword and dagger drawn. Erin followed suit within moments.

"How many?" Diego asked.

"Four? Five? They're all around us," she replied.

"Run, Erin! I hold them here," he ordered.

"Have you totally lost your mind?" she demanded.

"Go. Do not worry for me," he insisted.

"I won't leave you here," she replied. "We both go, or neither of us."

If he could get her to run, some of the sidhe would stand guard on him and rest would pursue her. Maybe she could escape or fight off the smaller number. Then she could go to Michel and lead men down this trail to the camp. Although he wouldn't have a hand in Luis's capture, the brigands would still be stopped. Erin could still find the heart of sacrifice and transform. Both of their goals would be accomplished even if he didn't live to see the plans come to fruition.

"Please, Erin, do go," the unseen sidhe said. "I love a good hunt. We'd have you back here with Diego before too long, certainly by morning. Just to make it a sporting challenge, I'll even give you a head start."

"I won't play your games," she replied.

"A pity, really. I do so enjoy games." The sidhe laughed. "Now be good little humans and drop your weapons."

Erin threw hers down immediately. For a moment, Diego thought the sidhe had somehow taken control of her mind, but she raised her hands and started drawing a rune in front of her. Whatever she was doing, he hoped her plan would work.

Chapter 14

Bella had them right where she wanted them. All five of her people were well-hidden, but in positions good for blocking any escape attempts. If Erin had run as Diego wanted, she wouldn't have gotten very far unless Bella had allowed the woman to escape. She hoped Erin would try to make a break. Hunting humans could be almost as much fun as feeling them quiver under her hand while she drained their life's energy.

When Erin cast her weapons aside, Bella thought her wish had been granted, but then the gifted woman raised her hands to mold a sleep effect. Bella laughed out loud as soon as she recognized what the woman had formed. Didn't she realize that such a pathetically low effort would do nothing to sidhe? Apparently not.

Bella signaled one of the others in her group, and Dafyd leapt out of his place, striking Erin with the front two of his eight spider legs. The blow knocked her against a tree too far from her friend to benefit from his protection. Erin struck the trunk with a loud groan and sank to the ground with a hand pressed to her chest.

"Erin!" Diego cried as he turned to deal with Dafyd.

The huge spider rapidly scuttled over to Erin, wrapping her hands in sticky spider silk to prevent any other forays into faerie skills that might prove more effective. While watching Diego carefully in his peripheral vision, Dafyd transformed into his more human-looking incarnation. Hc drew a bronze dagger and held it against the woman's throat.

"Get away from her!" Diego screamed.

Bella stepped into the open. "I advise you to stop where you are and put down your weapons, unless you want Dafyd to encase her entirely in spider silk. She could become his guest of honor tonight for dinner."

"Tell him to let her go." Diego lowered the weapons but kept them in hand. "I-I stay with you. Just let her go."

Bella laughed. "You're already my prisoner, so I gain nothing from your proposed trade. No, no, she is for our amusement. You, dear boy, are for your brother's. Then, when he's finished with you, you will be ours, too, if there's anything left."

"Luis?" he asked. "Luis sends you?"

"Oh, yes, he knows all about you," Bella explained. "Rodrigo reported seeing you in Tours some time ago, and your brother is very anxious to be reunited with you again."

"We walk into a trap!" Diego exclaimed. "The footprints and broken branches, all part of his plan?"

"Well, no. The real site was about a half-mile further up the path, but when I saw you stop, we decided to come to you," Bella explained. "What do you say, Diego? Will you yield or would you rather see your darling Erin drained to a lifeless shell by a rather large spider? Or maybe if you do yield, Luis will want you to witness what he has in mind for Erin back at the camp."

Bella imagined she could see the gears in Diego's mind grinding to a halt as he considered his options.

Erin looked up at Diego. "There is time."

Whatever she meant by that, her cryptic message finalized his decision. Slowly, Diego nodded and lowered his blades, then dropped them at his side.

Bella smiled. Using a kerchief, she picked up the four blades and tossed them into the brush where they couldn't harm her people. By the time Bella had finished with her task, Diego's hands were also bound with spider silk.

Dafyd held up a net wrapped around some small crockery jars. Each had a small wick poking out of the top. "What do you suppose this is?"

"Light one and find out." Diego smirked.

Bella eyed the human as the other sidhe in her party came out of their hiding places. Something tricky was in the works. Her curiosity might gnaw at her later, but for now, she didn't trust the human half enough to find out.

"Toss it. We don't need the extra excitement."

When Dafyd pitched the net sidelong, Diego cringed. The jars hit the ground and shattered, but nothing more exciting than that happened. How totally anticlimactic, but then Dafyd hadn't lit one before throwing them.

Now all they had to do was wait for Rodrigo and his men to catch up. Then they would all take a trip to the Unseelie Court.

***

Toppling his chair as he rose, Yvret left his viewing wall and walked over to the window. Erin and her friend had been captured. Things had been going so well for them. He should have seen this coming. The path through the forest had been far too obvious, now that he considered the sheer number of footprints and broken branches. He should have recognized a trap for what it was and warned them. Two thousand years of experience had taught him many things, and he had still been blindsided.

"Erin's a little rattled, but at least they're not hurt." Sarah fluttered nearby.

"I should've known," Yvret mumbled.

"We all missed it, but that won't be changed now," Kendall said. "The only thing you can do at this point is react to what has happened."

Yvret turned to his defense minister, a tall seraph with gray and brown bird wings sprouting from his shoulders, the base of his neck, and his ankles. "Well, Kendall, what do you suggest?"

"We could rescue them," Sarah offered.

Yvret shook his head. "She has the potential to make her final choice very soon. We would do best to avoid all interference. If we rescue her, we limit her chances to decide and transform."

"And if the sidhe kill her, that pretty well ends her chances altogether," Kendall added. "She doesn't have the power to take on five sidhe. At her level, sleep won't do much at all, and she would have to use the others too many times in rapid succession."

Yvret thought back through her training. "You might be surprised. She's made a lot of progress in the last couple weeks. If she uses the skill strategically, she could cut the repetitions significantly."

"Maybe, but she can't do much of anything with her hands bound."

The seraph had a point. Even with her hands free, quite a few things would have to go right. She needed confidence. Knowing a friend was at hand would help.

Yvret turned to Kendall. "Stay hidden, and go be with them. Only take action if Erin is in true mortal danger, and even then, do as little as you can and delay as long as you can."

"And if Erin and Diego are separated?" Kendall asked.

He could send two protectors and assign one to each, but in the grand scheme of things, only Erin truly mattered. Diego was important by virtue of being Erin's friend, but Yvret wouldn't risk a second seraph, not when there were so few already.

"Stay with Erin," Yvret said. "Protect Diego if you can, but her safety is the most critical."

"She'll sense him around and tell her friend," Terri pointed out. "If Bella hears that, Kendall's cover will be ruined."

Yvret turned to the centaur. "We have to take that risk."

"On a woman you still think may become a sidhe?" Terri asked. "I know you've predicted that she'll become a seraph if she makes the right choices, but are you sure you want to risk losing even one seraph in the hope that you might gain another?"

Kendall shook his head. "There are so few of us because we have dangerous jobs, and we can't do them by waiting in the wings. I want to help her if I can."

Sarah laughed so hard she almost rolled onto her back in the air. "Seraphim waiting in the wings. Good one." When all eyes turned to her, Sarah blushed. "Sorry. Guess it was just funny to me."

"Look, I just don't think a human woman is important enough," Terri insisted.

Yvret blew out a breath. "She's not just a human woman. She's the gifted human woman who took on a sidhe prince to save my life, and all she had when she came to my aid was a silly little dagger."

"Yeah, and she helped him even though she knew she'd get beat up when she got home." Sarah hovered in front of Terri with her hands on her hips.

"I'll be careful, and I won't take any unnecessary risks, but I will be there." Kendall flexed all three pairs of wings.

"Thank you." Yvret pointed to the viewing wall. "I'll continue to watch from here."

Sarah flew over to Kendall and kissed his cheek. "Come back quick, okay?"

"Wait." Yvret hustled to the shelf behind his worktable and picked up a mind sensor. "Take this. It will let us communicate as long as I can see you on the viewing wall." He pinned it to Kendall's tunic.

Kendall patted it. "Thank you." He walked to the balcony.

Before returning to the wall, Yvret watched him fly away and hoped he would see the seraph again.

***

When Dafyd had his back to her again, Erin tugged to get her hand out of the glove, but no matter how hard she twisted, contorted and pulled either hand, the silk threads binding her were too tight. If she kept at this, she would only end up doing herself some mischief. There would be another way to escape.

"Struggle, struggle, little fly." Dafyd looked over his shoulder and grinned. "If you're lucky, I'll use my venom to paralyze you first, but probably not."

Erin's stomach turned as her mind conjured vivid images of what he meant to do to her. What choice had he made to transform into something so disgusting?

Looking across the clearing, she found Diego bound just as she was. The sidhe leader spoke to him in Spanish. Erin understood none of their conversation, but from the angry look to his eyes, she supposed his conversation with their captors was much like her own.

She blinked back tears. There had to be a way out of this mess.

Faint in comparison to the overwhelming sensation of five sidhe in close proximity, Erin heard the unmistakable sound of children laughing. A fey waited nearby, probably only one of them. Yvret must still be watching over her from his court. With a massive effort, Erin forced herself to not look around to find the faerie. She didn't even reach out with her mind to find the image of the newcomer. The sidhe might notice her attempts. If there was just a single fey she was picking up, he would have to bide his time until the conditions were just right, and now she would have to make sure she didn't do something to reveal him too soon.

If only there were some way to tell Diego, he might take some comfort in knowing Yvret had sent someone to help them. Regrettably, any way she could think of that would get the point across to him would tip their hand to their captors. Diego would have to remain in the dark.

***

When Bella turned his head to look at her again, Diego jerked it away, wincing when her fingernail raked across his chin. She had done nothing but taunt and threaten him since he had surrendered, and he didn't want to hear any more about what he would be forced to watch them do to Erin before they gave him to Luis or killed him.

Whatever Erin had planned, he hoped she acted soon. Did she really have a plan, though? What if he had misunderstood what she had been trying to say? She might have simply been unwilling to see him die or maybe she could have been unwilling to die herself. If he had misunderstood and she had no plan to fall back on, better for them to have continued the fight and died quickly.

"Is that any way to treat a lady?" Bella asked.

"You are many things, but you are definitely not a lady." Diego spat.

Bella laughed and took a few steps further down the path.

When he heard men approaching, Diego looked up. For a tense moment, he thought the sounds might herald Michel coming in response to the spy's news of the path being left for them. Diego wanted to shout warnings to the guard captain about what he was walking into, but when he heard someone talking in Spanish, he gave up that notion. It wasn't Michel. Unless Diego missed his

271

guess, the voice he heard belonged to Rodrigo. Seconds later, Rodrigo led a half dozen of Luis's men into the area and confirmed that guess.

"Why didn't you wait for us?" Rodrigo demanded. "This was supposed to be a joint effort."

The young man wasn't even Diego's age, and only looked more ridiculous standing toe-to-toe with the succubus. Bella could kill him on a whim, but he didn't seem to realize his peril.

"You were too slow." She took in her whole band with a wave of her hand. "And, see? We didn't really need your help anyway. They were easy. Too easy. I don't even know why Luis thought you would need our help to catch them."

"They must be awfully incompetent." Dafyd sneered.

Bella nodded. "Well, obviously, but to be fair, Rodrigo, would you like the opportunity to come with us to the Unseelie Court? You could file a complaint with the king."

Rodrigo backed off and went several shades paler.

"I didn't think so," she said.

"Just give us Diego, and we'll be on our way," Rodrigo ordered. "Luis will contact you when we need you for the last part of your agreement."

"I'm sure he will, but Diego's not going with you," she replied. "We have plans for him first."

"Luis's orders were to capture them once Carlos and your daemon passed us then return with Diego. The woman is yours, but he comes with us."

Diego saw movement at the edge of his sight, then Rodrigo and the men with him collapsed. Dafyd came forward to bind their hands with spider silk while the other sidhe either stood guard or disarmed the bandits. A firm, clawed hand on his shoulder reminded Diego that escape was still impossible. Another sidhe stood near Erin to give her the same reminder.

At least this time, the other party doing business with the sidhe didn't end up in gruesome pieces. At least, not yet anyway.

Remembering that Rodrigo had been the one who cut his leg in their last encounter, Diego almost smiled with satisfaction at seeing the other man get what was coming to him. Seeing Rodrigo dead might be the only consolation Diego would receive.

With a gesture from the sidhe standing not quite behind Diego, Rodrigo and his men moaned and opened their eyes. All of them cried out in alarm and shouted epithets at finding their hands tied and their weapons gone.

"What is this?" Rodrigo tugged uselessly at the spider silk binding his hands.

"Well, you see, Rodrigo, in any fight there are casualties," Bella explained. "You unwisely rushed headlong into the fight without our support. And since Diego's little friend is a fey apprentice, she mortally wounded most of you. You, dear boy, were slain by Diego who wanted to get revenge because you cut him. Tragic, really, because we were able to catch them ourselves just moments later. Once Diego sees poor Erin die, we'll send him on to Luis just like we promised. Unfortunately, you won't be around by then."

Rodrigo cowered. "I'll give you anything you want. Just let me go."

"The only thing I want from you is your life." She blew him a kiss.

Even though Rodrigo bawled like the child he was, Diego felt no sympathy for his brother's henchman. He had taken part in every one of Luis's schemes without even a second thought.

A rough grip pulled Diego to his feet and pushed him along a new path. The Unseelie gate couldn't be too far away, he assumed.

***

Kendall resisted the urge to swoop down into the midst of the sidhe, grab Erin, and fly away. Tempting idea, but he knew better than to try such a difficult maneuver. Not only would he be violating Yvret's orders, but flying through forests this dense was impossible with a wingspan of more than twelve feet. Even his smaller eagle incarnation with half that would have a wicked time flying around in these trees. Then there were the sidhe to consider. Alone against five, and one of them a princess, guaranteed death as surely as falling on his own silver sword. So far neither of his charges were in any danger of immediate death. Scared, worried, and angry, certainly, but who wouldn't be in that situation. No matter how impatient he felt, Kendall could afford to wait for a while yet.

Erin impressed him. She had to know about his presence, but after a brief spark of recognition had crossed her face, she had given no other signs that she was aware of him. Kendall wondered if he could have been so passive if he were in Erin's predicament with her level of training. He hoped her fear hadn't paralyzed her. That would be completely understandable, but he might need her to take some sort of action when he made his move.

When the sidhe got everyone moving, Kendall had a sinking feeling in his gut. They weren't headed toward the bandit camp, but to the Unseelie gate. With his invisibility skill still in place, he followed along quietly. Although he hung far enough back to avoid detection, he stayed close enough to help Erin if he needed to. With her at the back of the group, he had no problems keeping her in view.

Before long, the troupe reached the ring of stones marking the gate to the Unseelie Court. There, any hope he had of following Erin farther died. The gate wouldn't let him through any more than the Seelie gates would let sidhe through. Once beyond the gate, Erin and Diego would be on their own again. Even Yvret's viewing wall would be unable to track them.

For tense seconds, Kendall watched the sidhe herd the humans into the ring. If he was going to do something, he would have to act now.

"No." Yvret's voice rang in his head when Kendall had his sword drawn a few inches from the scabbard.

"If I don't do something now, it'll be too late," Kendall looked down at Yvret's artifact pinned to his tunic. *"If she transforms while on the other side of that gate, she'll be trapped."*

"I know, but the danger to you is too great. We could lose you both."

"The risk is mine, and I'm willing to take it."

Red light came from the gate. When the glow faded, only the succubus remained. The window of opportunity was past, and he clenched his jaw to keep from swearing. The last sidhe set out for the human camp.

"Now what?" Kendall asked.

"Wait. They'll come back through."

"Not with Erin." He sighed. *"You heard their plans. They will kill her."*

"We've no other choice now, my friend. Be careful and watch for Bella to return."

Kendall shook his head and knelt. He prayed God would help Erin find a way to save herself and her friend. The matter was no longer in fey hands.

***

Luis finished dressing and checked himself in the mirror. After fixing the lay of a piece of lace on his collar, he poured

275

himself a glass of wine and sat, waiting for Rodrigo to bring Diego to him. Carlos's earlier report of the traitor's capture could not have been better news. Since then, Luis had contemplated ways to pay Diego back for this second betrayal. The first lesson obviously hadn't done any good. The next one would.

The best Luis had come up with was waiting until Corinne's recapture. Diego could see that his earlier sacrifice had been in vain. What Luis wanted, Luis got, and the sooner everyone in this camp knew that the better. After properly convincing Diego, Luis would start in on his brother and reduce him to begging just to deny the mercy Diego pleaded for.

The tent flap opened, and Luis stood in anticipation of seeing the look on Diego's face. Would he be terrified or distraught or furious? Defiance was probably the most likely. When Bella stepped in alone, Luis frowned. He sat down and gestured to a nearby chair for the sidhe to sit in. Instead, Bella sat in his lap and planted a kiss on his lips.

"Miss me?" she asked.

"Oh, I'd say my life is simply not the same when you're not at my side," Luis replied.

He wanted nothing more at the moment than to get the sidhe away from him, but angering her wouldn't be prudent. For now, he would tolerate her proximity, but if she tried anything, the steel signet ring on his right thumb could be used to good effect.

"Hm, I'll bet not," she said. "How do you put up with the boredom?"

He smirked. "I have my amusements."

She looked around at the room then smiled. "I'm sure you do."

Thankfully, she left his lap and poured herself some wine then sat in the chair he'd originally indicated.

"I understand you and Rodrigo caught my brother," he said.

"Yes, well, a tragic turn of events, really."

"Oh? How so?"

"Rodrigo was far too young to command. He rushed into battle counting on his numbers to take Diego and his lady friend," Bella replied.

He shifted in his seat. "He failed, I take it."

She nodded. "As I said, it was a tragedy. The woman is a fey apprentice. A few well-placed bolts and most of the men were dead or dying. Rodrigo himself died on the end of Diego's sword. The pair were no match for five sidhe, of course."

"Of course."

She must have thought him an idiot. More than likely, she had taken Rodrigo and the other men as part of her payment. For precisely that reason, he hadn't sent his best men.

"If such unfortunate occurrences continue, I may need more sidhe help than I originally thought," he explained. "That would mean less profit for each of you, regrettably."

She frowned. "Well, we'll work more closely with yours in the future, but do tell them not to go off half-cocked."

Satisfied she understood him, he returned his attention to the more critical matter.

"Where is Diego?"

"He's currently a guest of the Unseelie Court," she replied.

He scowled. "That wasn't part of the agreement we outlined. You were to return him to me here where I can deal with him myself."

"And I promised him he could watch his little fey apprentice die." Bella leaned back and smiled. "If you want him destroyed, that will certainly help."

Luis smiled. "Enamored of her, is he?"

"Oh, I don't think I'd go that far, but all that chivalry nonsense gave me a stomachache." She rolled her eyes. "When she made him aware of our presence, he was ready to die in some vain hope we'd let her escape."

Taking a sip of his wine, Luis considered what that meant. "Indeed. How fascinating. I wouldn't have thought the boy had it in him. Well, could she be brought here as well?"

Bella shook her head. "Not unless you're willing to pay a great deal for her. As I said, she's one of the gifted. I think she may even be apprenticed to the king of the fey. I can promise you, though, Diego will witness her death, and her demise won't be pleasant."

"Well, that will do nicely then."

Erin's death followed by Corinne's recapture would devastate the boy by proving the point that he was helpless to protect others.

"So, about the attack on the duke tomorrow. I need details to put together my part of the group," Bella said.

"Even with some recent attrition, I have half the manpower I need," Luis explained. "You'll need to provide enough of yours to eliminate at least half of the duke's men."

Bella chuckled. "Is that all? I thought you said this would be tough. I can do that myself."

"Then we can split the spoils between us. You take the survivors, and I'll take their wealth," he replied.

"I like it." Bella finished her wine. "When and where?"

"My sources tell me the move is planned for tomorrow afternoon," Luis explained. "Meet me here before midday, and we'll leave to set up our ambush together."

She set the wine glass aside. "I'll be here, and I'll have Diego with me, still mourning for his loss, I'm afraid."

"That will be such a pity," Luis agreed. "Well, goodnight, Bella."

"I'll see you tomorrow at midday."

She slinked out of the tent. Luis refreshed his wine goblet and smiled.

***

Diego leaned against the copper bars of the cell and looked out at the cave around them. An unnatural, sourceless red light lit everything he could see. Fifty feet from the cell was the edge of a cliff, and below that, just barely out of sight, was the ring of fire marking this side of the gate. The sidhe had to have purposely set this inescapable prison so close to the gate that would lead to freedom. The cell didn't even have a door with a lock he could try to pick. The sidhe simply teleported in, grabbed whomever they wanted, and teleported out again with their prey in hand, kicking and screaming.

When he heard a sniffle, Diego looked at Erin. He needn't have worried. Erin was still pacing a hole in the floor. Rodrigo on the other hand still cried and desperately worked at removing the webbing from his hands. One of the other men sat nearby praying a rosary on a set of beads he had managed to wriggle out of his pocket. Diego had spent some time in prayer with Erin, too, but the screams coming from further inside the bowels of this place had made concentration on anything but his not-too-distant fate virtually impossible.

Only the four of them remained. The rest of Rodrigo's men had been taken away by sidhe a long time ago. Without stars, sun, or moon to help him, Diego had no idea how long they had been imprisoned. Soon, the sidhe would return for more victims, and Diego had no interest in seeing himself or Erin added to the sidhe's body count. Unfortunately, neither one of them had come up with any way to free themselves.

They couldn't even find anything sharp enough to cut the spider silk off. The rock walls and floor were too smooth and the room was bare. Diego's fingers still smarted from trying to tear the sticky web off of Erin, and her hands, bound tightly inside the ill-fitting gloves, couldn't get enough purchase on his bonds to try.

Diego looked at Rodrigo cowering in the corner. "Are you ready to talk to me about getting out of here? If we work at this together, we just might come up with something."

"Leave me alone!" Rodrigo shrieked.

"Look, if I can trust you, you can trust me at least long enough to get out of this place. Once we're out of here, we can settle our differences."

"There is no way out of here. Don't you see that?" Rodrigo asked.

"I'm not giving up yet," Diego replied.

"Then you're an idiot."

Diego rolled his eyes. He'd been called worse, but as long as he was still alive, he wouldn't give up hope.

"He still won't hear reason I take it?" Erin asked.

After taking a moment to switch languages to English again, Diego replied, "No. We no count on him."

"Maybe we can rescue him in spite of himself," she suggested.

Diego snorted. "We are lucky to help us."

Maybe Ibrahim would do better. Earlier Diego had decided to wait until the other man had finished praying his rosary before talking to him about their flight from this daemon pit, but looking at the beads in his fingers, Diego saw that Ibrahim had restarted again. This was his fourth time. Clearly, he didn't intend to stop soon, and they were quickly running out of time. When Diego squatted in front of the kneeling man, Ibrahim wouldn't look up at him.

"Ibrahim," Diego whispered.

"...full of grace. The Lord..."

He shook the man's shoulder. "Ibrahim."

"...is with thee. Blessed art thou..." he continued more loudly.

"Ibrahim!" he said urgently. "I know you can hear me."

"...among women and blessed is..."

"We could use your help to get out of here," Diego said, but as he got louder, Ibrahim did, too.

"Looks like it's just the pair of us, then." Erin stayed still for a moment while she spoke before returning to her restless motion.

"I feel better if we have more."

"Well, no one can say you didn't try, and we can't force anyone."

Sitting with his back to the wall, he motioned for Erin to join him. Her constant movement was about to drive him insane. Erin shook her head.

"Please. I no can watch you anymore." Diego waved her over.

She sighed and nodded, but had only taken a single step toward him when a sidhe appeared behind her.

"Erin!" he cried as he reached toward her.

His warning came too late. The bat-winged sidhe pulled Erin back against its massive chest and wrapped a muscular arm around her throat. Visions of the dying weaponsmith and his journeymen flooded his mind. As Diego scrambled to his feet, Bella appeared.

"I wouldn't suggest you make another move," she sang in Spanish. "Luis wants you in one piece so he can deal with you himself, but poor Erin. She doesn't have that protection."

Diego froze in place, worried that if he so much as breathed too loudly the sidhe holding Erin would break her neck.

"Now, which one of you do I want?" Bella asked.

Fuming, he watched Erin try to relieve the pressure on her windpipe by pulling at the sidhe's arm. Even Ibrahim looked up from his prayers, but when he stood and stepped toward the sidhe, Erin winced as the daemon tightened its hold on her.

"No!" Diego called. "Ibrahim, stop, please!"

"Ah, a volunteer. Just what I needed," Bella said.

The succubus gestured, and her prey was pulled to her as if she had grabbed the man's arm from halfway across the cell. Just before they all disappeared again, Diego saw Ibrahim's glazed eyes and wondered if he would even know what Bella would do to him before it was too late.

Without the beast to hold her up, Erin fell back and hit the floor hard enough to bounce. As Diego rushed to her, she rolled onto her side and struggled to regain her breath. He put a hand on her shoulder, wishing he could instead hold her in his arms.

"Erin?" he asked. "Erin, are you well?"

"Aye, I'm—I'm as well as could be expected," she said after a few bursts of coughing.

After what seemed like far too long, her breathing evened out. He helped her sit up as well as he could and kept a steadying hand on her arm.

"I am sorry," he said.

She shook her head. "There's nothing you could've done."

That didn't make him feel any better. He was a man. He was supposed to protect her.

She looked past him, squinting. "What's that?"

Following her gaze, he saw nothing unusual. "I no see nothing."

As she reached past him, he followed her hands and saw the dull metal of Ibrahim's rosary beads just as her hand touched them. He must have dropped the necklace when Bella had claimed him. They inspected the beads formed in the shape of rose buds as well as they could in the dim light, and Diego saw reddish-brown specks on the gray metal. If that was rust, then the base metal had to be something they desperately needed in this place.

"Iron," Diego concluded, closing her fingers around the beads. "Keep it. Maybe it helps you."

"No," Erin replied. "I want you to have it."

He shook his head. "I have Luis's protection."

What cruel irony that the man who wanted him dead gave him the reason he was safe here.

"Which will only last as long as the sidhe are amused, and I wouldn't count on that to be much longer." Erin looked around. "I can't even think of one way to get out of this forsaken place."

"We must wait until they take us from this—this room," he said, drawing a complete blank on how to say "prison cell" in English. "Then maybe there is a way."

She nodded but didn't speak right away. Moments later, she opened her mouth as if she would say something but shook her head and remained silent.

"What is it?" he asked.

She shook her head.

"Please, tell me."

After a painfully long silence, she spoke.

"Promise me something," she said softly.

"Anything I can."

She took a shuddering breath before continuing. "If-if I transform while we're in the Unseelie Court, promise me—" She stopped and looked away, then began again. "Promise me you'll kill me. Quickly."

He stammered and stuttered for several seconds while trying to find his voice. Was she serious? Kill her?

"I no can do this!"

"Please, Diego," she pleaded.

He got up and turned away from her. "Why?" he demanded. "If you change, you have your powers and then—"

"Then I'll be a sidhe." She stood. "I don't have the artifact."

He'd forgotten about that.

"I don't want to be one of them," she concluded.

"I promise," he said, unable to look in her eyes. "If you become a sidhe, I will do what you ask, if I can."

She slowly nodded. "Thank you."

"We no need to fear that," he assured her. "We get away from here before you change."

"You're an incurable optimist," she said.

"A what?"

Somewhere between her accent and his vocabulary, the meaning was lost to him.

"You, well, never mind," she replied.

He shrugged.

Then, with a final heartrending scream from somewhere nearby, everything went silent. Diego stood and went to the bars again, straining to see or hear something, but except for the sniffling coming from the corner, he and Erin could have been completely alone in the whole Unseelie Court.

Chapter 15

Erin joined Diego at the bars. "I don't like it."

She never would have thought she would prefer to hear someone screaming with such consuming pain and terror, but after hearing nothing else for at least the last hour, this fatal silence was worse. Minutes ticked by while nothing changed.

The boy cowering in the corner asked something in Spanish, and Diego snapped back an answer, then everything was still again. Erin wanted to go comfort the boy, but when she had tried earlier, he had pushed her away. After that, she'd decided he would have to find his own counsel.

"You see anything?" Diego whispered.

Erin scowled. Since coming here, her mind had instinctively shut out all the sidhe's voids from her perceptions. She would make her critical decision soon, if she understood Yvret's warning correctly. In the meantime, the block wasn't perfect, but she could keep her sanity. She closed her eyes and reached out with her mind. A heavy weight descended on her, making even breathing difficult. Sidhe voids were everywhere around them, crowding in on her. Before they could crush her, she shut them out again.

"There are too many of them," she lamented.

"Any come to us?"

She sighed. Maybe she could look for that. That information could help them figure out what was going on. "I'll try again."

Erin closed her eyes and took a deep breath. Ever so slightly, she opened her mind to her perceptions of the faeries. Once again, the oppressive heat and the almost tangible weight of so many sidhe pressed in on her, but with her mind better guarded, the intrusion didn't seem so bad. Carefully, she focused on each void to find its direction of travel until she found what she sought after, then shut it all out again.

"Three," she said. "Heading this way in a wee bit of a hurry."

"Why do they no teleport?" he asked.

"Not all sidhe can." She frowned. "Or, maybe they have something else in mind."

Diego looked ready to ask another question when the three she had sensed came around a corner. A tall, almost stately-looking one was flanked by two that were larger and stronger, like the one who had half-strangled her earlier. Erin looked down at her hands to confirm the rosary beads were not visible. For fear she would lose them, she clutched them even tighter until she could feel the edges of the crucifix through her glove.

"Is this our chance?" she whispered.

"No," Diego replied.

"We may not get another."

"There are too many, and we no have weapons. There is another chance."

"There had better be."

No more time was left for their debate. Their jailers stood just outside the cell.

"You're very lucky, Erin," the stately one said in faerie. He smiled, revealing the pointed teeth of a vampire. He gestured, and the bars creaked loudly as they bent to form an opening. "Dafyd is so disappointed, but His Majesty wants you for himself. You should feel honored."

"And yet somehow I don't." She shook her head.

"Now come on out of there and behave yourselves, or the guards just might get out of hand. They do that sometimes."

"What does he say?" Diego asked.

Erin quickly translated for him and saw his brow furrow with concern. She could see him weighing their chances against all three. They were outnumbered with neither fey skills nor weapons to rely on. Maybe if they could have counted on Rodrigo, but no. Fighting now would only make the situation worse.

"No, you were right. This isn't the time."

She stepped through the opening in the bars. When Erin turned to help Diego, one of the guards grabbed her by the arm and yanked her away. The other guard took Diego. Rodrigo jumped up and ran for the opening, but by the time he arrived, the herald had closed the bars again.

"Not yet, dear boy. Your time is coming," the herald said. "Dafyd will be by for you soon enough."

While Rodrigo called after them, the vampire led them around the corner and into a large, open hall. Perched on the high dais at the other end of the room was a huge snake with a man's head and torso. Erin exchanged a look with Diego as they were brought forward. They should've taken their chance when they had it. The only one way in or out of this room would be well guarded.

"Excellent," the king said. "Leave her at the steps. Bind him to the stake where he can see everything. Then leave us. I want no interference."

"But, Your Majesty, they're—" the vampire protested.

"I said leave us!" the king bellowed. "Do you think I need your help to control two pathetic little humans?"

"No, Your Majesty, of course not."

Looking back and forth between the huge snake-bodied sidhe coming down the ramp and the guard pushing Diego away, Erin took a deep breath to quell the insects eating away at her guts. If she hadn't been wearing gloves, the crucifix would have cut into her hand. With a conscious effort, she relaxed her grip.

When she reached the foot of the dais, Erin felt something strike the back of her knees. She broke her fall as well as she could but almost lost her hold on the beads when she hit. Diego's guard took him to a wooden pole standing near the foot of the dais. A leather thong already secured there was slipped around the silk tying his wrists and knotted. Then the herald and the guards left. The loud thud of the doors made Erin jump.

"Scared?" the king asked.

Erin nodded. Lying wouldn't do any good. "Yes."

"You should be. After I'm done with you, you will die here."

Swallowing hard, Erin made herself breathe more slowly. Although she had gotten neither of the warning signs, her hands were already shaking, and she didn't need that problem to escalate.

"Do you know why I wanted to deal with you myself?" He slithered closer.

"It's been a dull night?"

"Oh hardly. Those others, they were most amusing. You heard them, didn't you?"

Erin clenched her jaw tightly. How could she have heard anything else? Although they were all certainly dead now, she could still swear their screams echoed in the halls.

"You did, of course," he said. "I have a special reason to deal with you. Don't you know what it is?"

"Nothing comes to mind."

When he reached her, he grabbed the front of her chemise and hauled her to her feet. "You killed my heir! Stabbed him in the back with a steel blade like a coward."

"He was torturing a fey!" Erin exclaimed, remembering the look on Yvret's face when their eyes first met. "I asked him to stop, but he wouldn't."

"Who are you to give a prince orders?" he demanded. "It's past time Yvret should die. Finally, after centuries, we had him in our grasp, and then you come along and destroy everything."

He pushed her away and Erin stumbled back a few steps but managed to keep her feet. As he slithered around behind her, he drew a thin, bronze knife from a sheath on his forearm. Erin closed her eyes, expecting to feel the blade slide into her back. Instead, she felt him wrap halfway around her, and then the knife slipped between her hands. A second later, the pressure on her wrists was gone. Erin opened her eyes and looked at the sidhe king. What was this? He couldn't possibly be letting her go.

"Oh, no. No easy death for you. First, you'll try to help your friend. I don't care about what Luis wants, so don't think for a moment I won't really hurt him. We'll keep right on doing that until you transform. Then, I'll take an iron blade and drive it through your back, and you will die the same way my heir did."

"I won't do it," Erin said. "I will not weave any effects."

"Then you will watch your friend die by inches, knowing that with your hands free, you could have saved him." He returned the knife to its sheath. "And it won't stop there. I'll bring others here, and you will see them die one by one until you cooperate with my plan."

With his hands a blur of motion, red sparks danced on his fingers. Erin raised her hand to form a shield to protect Diego but stopped. If she didn't try to weave effects from energy, she wouldn't transform. There had to be another way to save him without resorting to molding energy.

The sidhe laughed as he slithered in front of her and turned to face Diego. "For his sake, I hope you change your mind before he's too disfigured to recognize."

"Erin?" Diego asked. "Erin, what is it?"

She looked away, unable to face the fear in his eyes.

"If you're one to pray, pray now that she changes her mind about saving your life," the sidhe said in English.

She clutched her hands tighter and felt a dull pain in her palm. The rosary! Erin turned to the sidhe king and pressed the beads into his bare forearm. Screeching in pain, he pushed her down and threw his prepared effect at her. Rolling to one side, Erin felt the heat of the blast burn the ground where she had been. Before she could rise to her feet again, he was on top of her.

His snake tail wrapped around her legs. To get him off, she held the rosary against his scaled hide. Her ploy didn't have the effect she wanted. The scales protected him. Erin grimaced as the coils tightened instead of releasing her. With his hand pressing down on her shoulder, he pinned her to the floor. Drawing nearer to her face, he hissed and his long fangs folded open and snapped into place.

Erin reached around his back and shoved the rosary beads down his shirt. Over the anguished gasp that escaped him, Erin heard his flesh sizzling from contact with the metal. Now more worried for himself than for making her pay, he unwrapped himself from her while he tried desperately to get at the beads.

She didn't wait to see any more. Getting to her feet as quickly as she could manage, Erin ran to Diego. Taking off her gloves and holding them with her teeth, she untied the leather strap. Then, after looking at the sidhe writhing on the floor to make sure it was completely preoccupied, Erin led the way back to the huge doors while she pulled on her gloves again. Two guards rushed into the room. Grabbing a torch from a sconce, she struck one guard on the head before the monster could draw its weapons. When the sidhe fell, clutching its burned face, she turned to the other only to find the huge sidhe running to help the king. As they ran back to the gate, she kept a hand on Diego's arm to steady him.

Loud horns sounded, and by the time they reached the passage leading to the cell and the gate beyond it, footfalls and flapping wings echoed off the rock walls. She stopped to look back over her shoulder to catch a glimpse of their pursuers.

"This way." Diego pointed.

Ready to catch him if he stumbled, she followed him. When they neared the prison, she slowed down. They should see about helping Rodrigo.

"No time, Erin. Come this way!" Diego yelled as he came toward her.

They were too late to help the kid, anyway. No one remained in the cell.

As they ran to the edge of the cliff, Erin heard something bouncing off the rock walls around them and floors behind them. Blowguns. They were shooting blowguns like the ones the sidhe prince had used on Yvret. If either she or Diego got hit by one of those pellets, they were dead. The rosary, the only iron they had found since coming here, was currently burning the sidhe king's back.

Erin looked over the cliff and saw the fiery ring of the gate. Below that, the cliff face went down hundreds of feet.

"We jump," Diego said.

Erin closed her eyes and looked away, having no desire to see her dinner again. "No. I can't do it."

"They kill us if you no do this. I am with you."

Pellets pinged off the rock around them and one whizzed past Erin's shoulder. She saw another bounce off Diego's heavy doublet.

"I count three, then we go," he said.

Erin looked over her shoulder. The sidhe were almost to the cell. They would be recaptured if they didn't go now.

She nodded.

"One, two, three!" Diego called.

He jumped and disappeared through the ring, but Erin still stood rooted to the edge of the cliff. She would never make it. She couldn't make herself step off into empty air. Rising up from the ground was a different matter altogether, but jumping from here? If she could only fly, this would be an easy matter.

Turning, she saw the sidhe so close she could almost feel their hot breath. Something struck the side of her neck. Erin cried out as much from surprise as from pain. As she spun away from the attack, her foot slipped, and she fell over the edge.

***

When the red light faded, Diego stepped out of the ring. Where was Erin? He looked all around but didn't see her anywhere.

"Erin? Erin!"

No answer came to him.

He swore. She hadn't jumped when he had. In spite of the vow he had taken to never leave her to fight sidhe alone again, he had done exactly that. He should've known better. If only he had made sure she was safely through, then he could have followed after her.

Red light flared from the ring. Diego squinted and looked into it, hoping to see Erin appear. When the light faded, she lay in the center of the ring with her hand pressed against the side of her neck.

"Erin! Erin, leave the ring," he said urgently.

The sidhe couldn't be far behind her. She got up more slowly than he would have liked and stumbled toward him.

"What is it? What is wrong? You are hurt?" he asked.

"We have to find something with iron in it," she answered.

He pulled her hand away from her neck and saw an odd grayish bruise just below her ear.

"I was shot," she explained.

How iron was supposed to help or even how she could be shot in the head and still be alive, he couldn't guess, but he'd trust the expert. He checked himself over for anything that would work but found nothing useful. Their weapons and scabbards were back at the trail where the sidhe had ambushed them earlier. The rosary was gone. The belt buckle Michel had given him was silver, not steel.

Erin cried in pain and fell against him. Diego reached for her to break her fall, but with his wrists still wrapped in spider threads, the attempt was in vain and she dropped like a rock. As he knelt beside her, red light poured out of the Unseelie gate. A huge dragon took shape in the center. With no weapons and Erin too tense with pain to even look up at him, they were as good as dead. The dragon turned toward them and reared back, ready to strike with its huge, clawed forefoot. Diego huddled over Erin to protect her.

A glittering silver dome formed over the gate, trapping the dragon within. In her current condition, how in the world could she do that? He hadn't even seen her draw the symbol. He could figure that out later.

Seconds passed while he helplessly watched her writhing on the forest floor and listened to the dragon roar in rage and pound on the walls of its cage.

When she finally relaxed again, Diego helped her sit up. The bruise he had seen before now had a deep red trail coming from it about the length of his last thumb joint.

Between breaths, Erin said, "We have to find something iron."

"We have nothing," he replied.

"Weapons."

"Back at the path, but I no leave you here."

"I'll be all right," she insisted.

"No. Too many sidhe. You can walk that far?"

"If I have to."

He stood and helped her up. She held onto his arm now more to support herself than to guide him. After making sure the dragon was staying put, Diego led Erin toward the path they had followed earlier that night.

"How did you make the shield that holds the sidhe?" he asked.

She shook her head. "Later. I can't tell you now."

He could understand that. Plenty of other things were taking up her concentration.

By the time they reached the path, Erin had collapsed, gripped by intolerable pain, four more times. After each of the episodes, the dark trail leading from the bruise had grown.

Leaving her by the base of a tree, he went foraging for a weapon and quickly found a few. Diego grabbed a dagger, not caring if it was his, hers, or one of the bandits' as long as it was made of the right metal.

Another devastating cry from Erin urged him to greater speed. The end of the dark line had nearly gone below the neckline of her chemise. Although he didn't absolutely know what the final outcome would be, he assumed she would die if he didn't get that thing out of her.

"Do you have it?" she asked after catching her breath again.

He nodded. "What do I do?"

"Press the metal on the bruise. It'll draw the pellet back."

To avoid accidentally slitting her throat, Diego pressed the pommel of the dagger on the bruise. He winced in sympathetic pain when her jaw and eyes both closed tightly. Her hand locked painfully around his arm, but that discomfort couldn't be anything to what she felt. Soon, he saw the little bullet coming back up along the path left on the first pass.

When he heard a muffled ping and felt a slight vibration in the dagger, Diego carefully lifted it away. The pellet clung to the dagger, like an extra decoration on the pommel.

"And to think I pulled three of those out of Yvret." She squeezed her eyes closed and then opened them again.

Diego looked at the pommel, then back at her. If just one had laid Erin low like that, he didn't want to think what three would have done. He looked up at the sky through the skeletal canopy. There were maybe three or four hours left until dawn, as nearly as he could tell.

"Rest," he said.

She nodded. "Not too long. We're losing the night."

"Just for a few minutes, then. After dealing with the dragon, you need rest."

"Dragon?"

"At the gate. I still no understand how it is you do this."

She motioned for him to come closer and whispered in his ear. "That wasn't me. Yvret sent a fey to help us. He stayed hidden, but I felt him there."

That explanation made more sense.

"Here, let me help you," she said, pointing to his hands.

He handed her the dagger, carefully avoiding the pellet. With gloved hands, she removed the shot and threw it away. After he pulled his hands apart as much as he could to help her keep from slicing open his wrist, she freed him.

Erin yawned. "Maybe we should get moving again. If we rest, I'll fall asleep."

He nodded and stifled a yawn of his own. "Stop that. You make me yawn, too." Diego stood, pulling her up with him. "You see? I tell you I no have to kill you."

Once they were armed again, he led the way down the path.

***

Michel rubbed his eyes as he walked into the garrison. He should be in bed, and he intended to head that way as soon as he checked in to make sure nothing else needed his attention. He would have thought that after moving the duke's entire household twice a year for ten years this would all be old hat. It never failed, though. His Grace could make a grand production out of anything.

The guard on duty sitting behind the front desk acknowledged him with a nod, but dutifully stayed at his post. Looking over the roster, Michel checked for the men still working at this hour. He would excuse them tomorrow for the grand move. Guards who were dead on their feet were no good to anyone. When he added the name of the guard assigned to trail Diego tonight, Michel whistled appreciatively. The man hadn't returned.

"Chevalier is still out? What is Diego doing at this hour?" he mused.

The Spaniard should be well on his way out of the country with Erin by now, if he had any intelligence. Surely Chevalier wouldn't trail him that far.

The guard cleared his throat. "Begging the captain's pardon, sir, but Sergeant Chevalier is here. He returned just as I came on duty."

"Really? Did he go back out?"

"No, sir. You're the only one to go in or out of that door after he came in."

Michel had no reason to doubt the man's honesty, but if that were true, Chevalier had fallen down on the job. The guardsman had been given orders to personally report on Diego's activities before turning in for the evening. When Michel gave orders, he meant for them to be followed, but maybe this meant Diego had fled the area after all. The Spaniard would see to Erin's safety and forget this quest to go after Luis, wouldn't he?

"I see. Thank you." Michel headed down the hall.

Candle in hand, he checked each room's occupant list until he found the one he needed. He opened the door and stood there, watching his men sit up, groaning and rubbing their eyes.

"I'm looking for Robert Chevalier," Michel announced.

"What do you want? I'm trying to sleep," someone complained.

"Shut up, you idiot. That's the captain," another man scolded.

"The captain?" he whined.

"Sergeant Chevalier, if you would step out into the hall with me, please?" Michel let the ire creating the tension in the back of his neck echo out in his voice.

He went back into the hall. While he waited, Michel listened to the men speculate on why their comrade was being summoned at this ungodly hour. Once the man joined him, Michel indicated the door with a nod.

"Close the door."

Squinting, Chevalier did as ordered.

"What was your assignment tonight?" In all fairness, he should give the man plenty of rope to hang himself.

"Follow that Spaniard, Diego something something de la something."

"And then what?"

"I did it. I followed him until about eleven or so and came back," Chevalier insisted.

"What are you supposed to do immediately upon your return?"

Chevalier cursed. "Sorry, Captain. I forgot to sign in, didn't I?"

"You also forgot to report your findings to me," Michel pointed out.

"He's going to meet someone at midnight."

Michel scowled. Diego hadn't gotten Erin away, then. "You left your assignment before it was finished?"

"I had to, sir," Chevalier replied, looking everywhere but at Michel. "There's a witch-woman with him or a fey or maybe even a sidhe. I don't know what she is, but she threatened to put a spell on me, and sir, she was armed like a man, and it looked like she knew what she was doing."

Gritting his teeth, Michel shook his head. Erin was free now and should have been on her way toward Spain or some other country. If she wasn't, he would have to delay looking for her until well after the move, and all the other related but terminally annoying details were dealt with. Maybe this time the tedious parts would just take a little longer than usual. He had to give them time to get away.

"Oh, and I forgot," Chevalier continued. "I was so mad it must have slipped my mind."

More likely, he had been too embarrassed to report that a woman who weighed maybe a hundred and thirty pounds fully clothed and soaking wet had scared him off with a simple threat.

"She said she'd leave a path for you to follow, starting a mile or so up the road from the gate," Chevalier continued. "From what I overheard them saying, I think they might have a lead on the bandit camp."

Michel pushed past him and ran back to the front desk. The tongue-lashing and other appropriate fines and consequences for Chevalier would keep.

"Sound the alarm," Michel ordered.

She should hate the air he breathed, but Erin was leading him to the brigands, and if he hurried, he might still catch them before they broke camp and moved on again. As the guard ran out and rang the huge bell in the courtyard, Michel hoped he wouldn't get there to find the campsite had been struck already. Hopefully, Erin and Diego weren't counting on him to bring troops to reinforce their efforts. If they were and the sergeant's cowardice had gotten Diego and Erin killed, Michel would never forgive himself or Chevalier.

***

There was light up ahead, and the pop and crackle of small campfires left to burn through the night made for a familiar backdrop. The lack of voices provided a measure of reassurance. By this hour, everyone should be in their beds or too drunk to cause much trouble.

Leading Erin by the hand, he went closer and took advantage of the trees and brush for cover. At the edge of a huge artificial clearing, Diego hid behind a bush and carefully surveyed the area. The camp's arrangement was typical. Luis's huge pavilion stood off to one side. Near that Diego found the collection of officers' tents, then scattered around the rest of the clearing were the tents of the common soldiers, significantly fewer than expected. The rejected men he'd recruited in the tavern had certainly done their job. Desertions of one sort or another had reduced Luis's men to a little over half.

Diego looked next for the sentry's post, really not more than an elevated platform. When he found it, he had to smile. Fortune favored them tonight. The man on guard duty slept with drool running down his chin. If Luis found out, he would have the man's head.

There were patrols to consider, too. Before getting this close, Diego had hidden and waited until he saw the patrol pass, so they had maybe ten minutes before the next one came. He didn't count on having nearly that long, though. They needed to start their attack well before then. Another concern was the number of sidhe. That one unknown made this whole endeavor so much more dangerous. There could be several like the one who had accompanied Carlos and killed the men in the road. Worse Bella could have beaten them here.

"What's your plan?" Erin asked softly.

"Plan?" His mind was still focused on the sidhe problem.

"Aye, plan, or were you thinking of just walking in and nicely asking Luis to come back with us?"

"No, of course not," he answered.

Unfortunately, Dafyd had destroyed all the little bombs Diego had made. He'd meant to light the fuses and use a tree to launch them from the net into the camp. Whether the bombs themselves took out bandits or just generated confusion, they could've used that to gain an advantage. Now, he was going to have to improvise.

"Is your fey friend still here?"

"Not since we left the ring."

"Well, then, you have your own skills."

"Who am I using it on? I don't see a soul stirring."

"The camp," he said, indicating the whole clearing with a sweep of his hand.

"The whole thing?" she asked, a little more loudly than he would have liked.

"How else do two people take on so many? Can you make them all stay asleep?"

She sighed and shook her head. "I might be able to expand the effect that much. It won't last as long, and those larger tents may be too far away, but I'll try."

"Quickly, the patrols come around again," he said.

She took a deep breath then stepped past him and made weird motions with her hands. A symbol made of light formed in the empty air. When she finished, she gestured toward the camp with an all-encompassing sweep of her arms. The symbol floated away from her, expanding and tilting downward until all the tents and even half of Luis's pavilion were covered. The symbol sank and disappeared when it reached the ground.

When Erin staggered, Diego rushed forward and caught her. Every muscle trembled. Cursing himself, he helped her sit down and held her. He hadn't meant to bring on a seizure. She closed her eyes and breathed deeply for a couple of minutes.

"I ask too much," he said.

"No, no, I might have missed Luis if he was in the wrong part of that tent, but I think I did it. They'll all sleep, but not for long, so we'll have to move fast," she replied. "I'll be fine, but I'm done with any energy molding for the night."

"Let's go, before the guards come." Diego stood and pulled her up.

The shaking had lessened some even with that brief rest. As they slowly walked into the camp, he kept ahold of her arm and watched carefully for another sign of the falling sickness. He should never have suggested such a large task. Luckily, he hadn't lost her entirely right there.

"I'm all right," she insisted. "Just don't count on me doing anything else of that sort."

"I think you rest now," he suggested.

Erin shook her head. "I don't need a mother hen, Diego, I told you I'm—"

"You there! Stop where you are!"

Diego froze and pulled Erin to a stop in case she didn't understand the Spanish. The voice had come from behind them. Lost in his concern for Erin, he had forgotten to watch for the patrol.

"Go." Erin nodded toward the largest tent. "Stop Luis. I'll deal with the guard."

"I no leave you again," he insisted.

"Go on, Diego. I can take him."

"Diego?" the guard asked. "You look good for a dead man."

He recognized the voice now. Carlos was good with a gun, but slow with a sword. With her speed, Erin could do this on her own while he took care of Luis. Maybe Diego would even be able to find the heart of sacrifice for her.

Diego looked over his shoulder. "I run well, too."

With that, he took off for Luis's tent. As he did, he heard swords being drawn. Erin could handle the fight, he reminded himself. She had greater speed, and Carlos would underestimate her because he only saw a woman. He wouldn't expect her to be skilled at all, and that would give her another advantage.

As he neared the pavilion, the door flap slipped open and Luis came out, half dressed and carrying his sheathed weapons in his hand. Diego slowed to a walk and drew his sword and dagger.

"Diego?" Luis asked.

"Surprised?" Diego replied.

"To see you alive? Yes, actually, I was certain the sidhe would dispose of you regardless of our agreement. I'm even more surprised to see you here. What do you hope to gain? You have no army, and I don't see any of Gaultier's men."

The hairs on the back of his neck prickled. "I came to bring you in. Yield or I will have to kill you."

Luis laughed. "Kill me? I taught you everything you know, boy."

"No, you taught me everything you know." Diego took a step closer. "I had other teachers besides you."

"It didn't do you any good last time."

"Last time you had your men do your dirty work, and I had a lady to protect." When images of the previous fight came to mind, he forcefully shoved them away. "This time your men won't wake up. You are not the only one to seek alliances with faeries."

"And what of your lady friend? Aren't you afraid Carlos will have her?"

"She doesn't need my protection." Diego rested his hand on his hilt. "It's just you and me this time."

Luis nodded. "If you're so eager to die, I'll oblige you."

Diego ignored the threat calculated to shatter his will and settled into his stance to wait for his brother's attack.

***

Erin pivoted, throwing her back foot in an arc toward her dagger hand. Carlos's sword passed harmlessly by her as the move carried her out of the way. While he recovered from his lunge, she launched attacks of her own.

He easily parried the first two thrusts she threw at his face. Striking his sword with hers, she held his blade aside with her dagger as she stepped in to cut him. He stepped back and kicked her in the stomach hard enough to knock her onto her back.

Before he could take advantage of her vulnerable position, she scrambled back to her feet again and circled him while trying to regain her breath. He spoke to her, but all she could make out was the tone of a challenge or maybe a taunt. His Spanish could have been gibberish for all she cared, and it was probably better that way. He couldn't shake her confidence with a well-aimed jibe.

As she came around him, Erin stole a quick glance to Diego. He fought a taller, larger man, Luis she assumed. Her friend seemed to be holding his own so far.

Movement at the edge of her vision brought her back to her own battle. Carlos was quickly closing with her. While taking a step back, she tried a wild parry and felt her blade connect with his and push it off to one side. Erin flinched as the rapier passed within an inch of her ear. As fast as she could, she retreated out of his range and swore to herself that she would not be distracted again. Diego would be fine. He definitely had more skill with a sword than she did.

Carlos laughed and came at her again, but this time she was ready. Waiting for him to lunge at her, she parried the shot aside with her sword and replaced the rapier with the dagger. His awkward, fully extended position actually served to protect her as she stepped in past the point of his blade. Bringing her own blade up, she drew her arm back and slashed his throat, ending in a perfect position to stab him in the chest.

Erin withdrew her sword and watched him fall. He didn't move. Dropping to her knees, she took a few well-earned seconds to catch her breath. Before she was ready, a red haze came over her vision and a stifling, unnatural heat made breathing uncomfortable.

"Oh, God help us, not the sidhe," she mumbled.

There had been more than enough sidhe in her life for one night. Her legs still ached from where the king had wrapped his tail around her.

With her eyes closed, she reached out with her mind and found the void that marked the evil faerie's presence. Unless she was mistaken, the beast had drawn awfully close to Diego.

Her eyes snapped open, and she rose to her feet. She found Diego still embroiled in the fight with his brother. The sidhe, the enormous daemon they had seen earlier on the road, slowly crept up behind him.

"Diego! Diego!" she called as she ran toward him. "Diego! Behind you!"

No response came back, and there was no sign from him that he had heard her above the clash of swords.

"Diego!"

The daemon, on the other hand, heard her just fine. Turning toward her, it smiled, baring jagged, sharp teeth. She hoped it would abandon Diego and come for her, but it resumed its approach toward her friend's unprotected back.

Images of what that thing had done to the weaponsmith and his apprentices flooded into her mind. Even at her fastest run, she would never make it to him in time. If a gun had been somewhere in reach, she might have tried shooting the faerie, but she had only her own weapons and her skills.

She could still mold energy. Especially over that kind of distance, any effort would certainly bring on a fit, but if she could protect Diego, she didn't care, and she knew just the one she would need.

Erin drew a deep breath and threw her rapier aside. She quickly traced the shield symbol in the air and gestured to Diego. Painfully bright specks of light obscured her vision, but she saw the glittering shield enclose Diego just as the daemon's claw descended. When the high-pitched note sounded in her ears even before the spots had faded, Erin fell to her knees. Before the seizure took her, the sidhe turned toward her. Diego would be safe now. Whatever happened to her next mattered less than that.

Chapter 16

An instant after the sparkling blue energy surrounded him like it had the dragon, Diego heard a loud bang behind him. Flinching, he turned and stared wide-eyed at the daemon. He moved back to keep Luis and the sidhe in view and found that the energy barrier moved with him. The barrier wasn't a cell but a shield. Erin must've done this. She must've seen the sidhe coming up on him and made the shield to help him, but how? She had said earlier she wouldn't be able to do anything faerie-related again tonight.

"I want him for my prisoner. Dissolve the shield and capture him!" Luis ordered.

"Can't do it." The daemon's voice sounded like crunching rocks. "He has to will it away or his little fey-apprentice has to die."

"Then kill her and bring him with you to the place we discussed!"

The sidhe bared its fangs. "Gladly."

Luis turned on his heel and stalked away. Diego looked for Erin and found her kneeling halfway across the camp. Even as far away as he was, he could see her whole body tremble. As the daemon walked toward her, she fell.

Diego looked back at his brother. If Luis got away now, Diego might never find him again, but if he chased after his brother, the daemon would kill Erin while the falling sickness had her. Luis had to be stopped or he would keep stealing, raping, and murdering. Diego wanted his brother to pay for all his crimes, but especially for treating him so poorly for all those years and for betraying his own family. Erin knew what such a betrayal felt like. She would understand.

After only a few steps toward Luis, Diego stopped. No, he would not leave Erin to die. She had protected him with the last of her strength, and he had already seen what that monstrosity drawing ever nearer to her could do to human flesh. Diego had left her before and had promised himself to never do it again. If he couldn't be true to his word, he was nothing. Someone else would have to bring Luis to justice.

Turning, Diego found the daemon still closing in on Erin. He ignored the dull pain in his leg and ran to catch up with the beast then interposed himself between Erin and the evil faerie.

The sidhe flailed at him, but every attack splashed harmlessly off the shield Erin had given him. When his attacker dodged aside to get around him, Diego kept himself in the way. Raising his own weapons, he thrust at his opponent only to have the blade rebound off the inside of the shield. He felt the force of that impact all the way to his shoulder. Oh, perfect. His protection hindered his attacks, too. What good was that?

Although he couldn't attack with the energy barrier in place, he left it there to keep himself safe. As long as Erin was alive, the sidhe could do nothing to him. Hopefully, the daemon would lose interest in the game and leave. If not, Diego would just have to watch over his friend until she recovered enough strength to deal with the sidhe herself. After what she had given him, he could do that much at least.

Diego saw movement somewhere near the edge of the trees but didn't dare take his eyes off the sidhe. Michel's clear, deep voice shouted some French command. Musket shots boomed behind him, and Diego dove for the ground, hearing some of the bullets ping off the shield. Most struck the beast in front of him. The smell of burning flesh filled the air as the iron tore into the creature's body. Smoke issued from the wounds as the sidhe screamed with the sound of rending metal. It fell, writhing in agony and clawing uselessly at its own wounds, only tearing its body with its efforts. Within seconds, it lay still.

From behind Diego, a fierce, bright light blinded him. He tightly closed his eyes and covered them with his arm until the glow faded. Blinking several times to clear away the afterimages, he looked around for any other signs of attackers. He found only Michel on horseback leading dozens of men.

Given the ultimatum and threats the guard captain had levied on Erin earlier, Diego couldn't be entirely certain Michel was friendly. He certainly wouldn't be pleased with how Erin had handled the man sent to follow them. Erin had to be protected. Diego would take her out of here as quickly as he could, if he could get this now unnecessary shield to go away.

Even as the thought came to him, the barrier vanished with a soft pop, then he turned to Erin and marveled at what he saw. She had transformed into a fey with broad wings like a hawk's coming from her shoulders. Smaller wings above those were extended to hide her face.

How could this happen? She couldn't have possibly had the time to locate the heart of sacrifice in Luis's pavilion. Hadn't she said that she wouldn't change until she had found it?

Those details didn't matter. She was here, she was fey, and she wasn't moving. God help him, was he too late? While he had been distracted with Luis, did the sidhe have time to kill Erin, or had she been wounded in her earlier fight and succumbed to her injuries after creating the shield for him?

Diego dropped his sword and dagger then quickly removed his sword belts. After checking himself over for anything else that could hurt her, he knelt at her side.

Very carefully, he eased the dagger out of her left hand and threw it aside to join the rapier she had apparently tossed away herself. Thankfully, the gloves he had given her had protected her from the steel. Her dress was torn where the wings came through, but he couldn't tell if she was hurt. Being as gentle as he could, he folded both of the larger wings.

When he rolled her onto her back, his heart stopped. Blood stained her dress, but a quick inspection proved it to be someone else's, Carlos's probably. With a sigh of relief, he cradled Erin in his arms and leaned over to see if he could feel her breath on his cheek. She was alive. Thank God, she was alive.

He heard a horse trot up behind him.

"Diego, where's Erin?" Michel asked.

"You care?" He held Erin tightly to him to block her face from the guard captain's eye. Anyone who wanted to burn her at the stake for witchcraft would have to do it over his corpse. "Earlier tonight, you threaten to burn her as a witch because she draws steel and uses faerie energy. I no let you hurt her."

"On my word, I won't," Michel promised.

He considered answering that. Michel's word was given, but would that be enough? The number of times Michel had shown concern was nearly equaled by the number of times he hadn't.

"You give your word before and then put her in prison on the word of a man who proves himself a liar." He glared. "Your word is nothing."

Michel scowled but didn't protest the accusation. "Where is she?"

"I no tell you this. You want to drown her or burn her at the stake, you go through me."

When Michel dismounted, Diego looked for his weapons. They were nearby, but to get to them, he would have to leave Erin's side. Instead of drawing his sword, though, Michel unbelted the sword and dagger and cast aside the pistol. Then he knelt in the grass.

"With God as my witness, I will allow no harm to come to her if I am at all capable of preventing it," Michel said.

Michel wouldn't fake an oath to God. He would be forever damned to hell if he went back on his word to his Lord. If Erin couldn't avenge herself, God certainly would.

"She is here." Diego prayed he wouldn't regret the revelation.

"Where here? What more do you want from me? I swear to you before God I won't hurt her. Where is she?"

The desperation in the guard captain's voice sent all doubts away.

"I know this." He loosened his hold on her enough to let Michel see her face. "I tell you. Erin is here. This is Erin."

"God above," Michel whispered. "Then it was true. She's no witch. She's fey."

"She tells you as much and so do I, but you no hear her. All you care about is the words of a dishonest man and a book that is not what you think. You forget who she is and arrest her for doing no wrong."

Diego glared at Michel, daring him to respond to that and protest innocence. Instead, the embarrassment colored his cheeks.

"I know. What happened to her?" Michel ran a hand along the smaller wings at her face.

"She puts the camp to sleep but misses Luis and a patrol. Then she creates a shield to protect me from that." He nodded to the sidhe corpse. "And then I see her fall as the sidhe comes to kill her. Now this. She changes. I no understand. She never finds the heart of sacrifice her teacher sends her for."

Michel smiled and nodded. "She did, actually. She had to know that by protecting you, she would probably die in that thing's attack. She was ready to give her life for yours."

"Then she never needs the necklace?" he asked.

"Probably not, or maybe she's close enough to it now if it's in Luis' tent. Who knows?" Michel answered. "Let's get her home. Philippe will take care of the rest of the camp."

Diego nodded. He'd traded Luis's escape in return for Erin's life. It was a fair trade, more than fair.

***

Diego awoke and sat up. He had meant to stay awake and watch over Erin, but he must have dozed off in his chair. Judging from the burnt-out candle on the nightstand, several hours had passed. When he and Michel had brought Erin home, Corinne and one of the female servants had come in to undress Erin and put her in a nightgown, slit down the back part way to accommodate her wings and pinned at the collar to hold it on. He had waited outside the door until they had admitted him again. Since then, he hadn't left her side for any reason.

More than once, he had jostled her shoulder to awaken her to see if maybe she only slept from exhaustion, but she hadn't yet responded. Afraid of something far worse, each time he had held his hand in front of her face to make sure he still felt her breath. Managing a smile, Diego softly ran his hand along one of her smaller wings, folded now against the back of her head.

When the door slowly opened, Diego looked up to see Michel come in. Diego stood as a show of respect for the guard captain.

"No change?" Michel whispered.

Diego shook his head. "I no understand what to do, but she no wakes up."

Michel gripped his shoulder firmly. "Just stay with her. I have to leave, but I'll return home tomorrow night after His Grace is situated. Corinne is at the market, and she'll be back later in case you need anything. If—" He stopped for a moment. "When she wakes up, tell her I'm sorry for what I did. I should have trusted her, and I didn't. I'll understand if she never wants to see me or speak to me again, but please, just let her know how sorry I am."

"I tell her," Diego promised. "When you return, I tell you how she is."

Michel nodded. He softly kissed Erin's cheek, then turned away and left.

Diego sat again and resumed his vigil. Maybe he'd judged Michel too harshly. He seemed to have forgotten all of his threats.

Moments after hearing the front door close, someone appeared at his side. In a single, fluid move, he stood and picked up his rapier leaning in the corner of the room just behind him. A pointed-eared faerie with violet eyes and dark hair stood there. If Diego hadn't seen so many attractive sidhe lately, he would have assumed the visitor was fey, but he just couldn't tell anymore.

"Stay back," Diego warned. "I no let you hurt her."

Since some faeries had spoken to him in Spanish as well as English recently, he repeated his words in his native tongue. The visitor looked perplexed for a moment then shook his head. He made an odd motion with his hand, which glowed with diffuse red light, like the sidhe king had done earlier this morning.

Diego scowled and settled into his stance. "Go away."

The faerie backed up a step, showing his empty hands and speaking in words that sounded at once familiar and foreign. That voice. Diego knew that voice. He had heard it outside Michel's gate just last night. Could this be Erin's teacher?

"Yvret?" he asked.

The faerie nodded. "Diego."

He lowered his blade into a less threatening position but kept it in hand, in case this was a trap. Sidhe could be awfully tricky. This one could have gotten his name and the name of Erin's teacher from all sorts of places.

Tentatively, the faerie calling himself Yvret reached his glowing hand toward Diego. This didn't feel like an attack, but Diego still couldn't completely trust the man. Tightening his grip on the sword, Diego held out his open hand. The faerie touched him, then quickly backed out of range again.

Diego gasped, but not because the red glow racing up his arm hurt him. It radiated a soothing warmth throughout his body before fading away.

"You should understand me now," the faerie said. "I hope."

Although he absolutely knew he shouldn't be able to understand the weird words, he did.

"Yes," he replied in words that couldn't really be his. "I understand. You're Erin's teacher."

"Yvret, yes. Erin's lucky to have such a diligent protector. I wish all new fey had one. So many are hurt after their metamorphosis by those who don't understand or even those who mean well enough."

Diego smiled and sheathed his sword, then returned it to its place. "She's my friend." He looked down at Erin, oblivious to the whole confrontation that had just taken place. "Why won't she wake up?"

Yvret's hand rested on his shoulder. "Transformations with that much physical change are horribly taxing on the mind and the body. To make matters worse, she had one last seizure just before the change occurred, and you two had an unbelievably trying night. She is simply exhausted, but she'll be fine."

"Does she know I'm here?" Diego asked.

"Hmm, well, that's hard to say, but probably so," he answered. "I knew my mentor was watching over me, and many of the others report the same kind of thing. Just keep doing what you're doing, and when she's ready to wake up, she will."

Diego nodded and gestured for Yvret to sit in the chair.

"You gave up a lot when you went back for Erin." Yvret took the indicated seat.

"The sidhe would have killed her," he explained, sitting on the bed where he could still be near her. "I couldn't let that happen."

"But Luis got away," the elf continued. "What about all the people he'll hurt if you don't catch him?"

Sighing, Diego closed his eyes for a moment. He had been so close, and now he didn't know if he would ever have the chance again.

"I know, but she is more important. Someone else will have to deal with Luis. He won't stay around now. He may even forget about Corinne for the moment to save himself. I'll never find him again."

"Well, I don't know about that. I can help you find your brother again," Yvret offered.

"How? Do you know where his new camp is? Can you show me?" Diego asked, excitement making his voice louder than he would have preferred. He looked down at Erin again to remind himself that she still slept.

Yvret shook his head. "Nothing like that."

Diego frowned.

"It'll take me a week to make the artifact, but I can give you something that will always give you the direction to go to find Luis."

"Thank you!"

"The least I can do, young man."

Diego nodded. "You sent someone to hold the dragon away from us at the gate."

"Yes, I did," he admitted. "Kendall, another seraph like Erin. Once you were taken through the Unseelie gate, we couldn't see you anymore. Will you tell me what happened?"

Diego took a deep breath. It was hard to believe the whole thing had happened just this morning before dawn. After taking a few moments to collect his thoughts, he began.

***

Erin felt stiffer and more sore than she thought possible, especially across her shoulders, at her ankles, and at the base of her neck. She lay face down on a bed, covered with a soft but heavy blanket. Thinking back, she couldn't remember how she'd gotten here. The last thing she recalled was weaving a shield over Diego, then seeing the sidhe come toward her as the falling sickness had claimed her. Odd, though, missing was the mental fog that usually marred her mind after one of those fits. How long had she slept?

Opening her eyes, she looked out through the drawn bed curtains and saw Yvret sitting by the bed. Diego stood nearby.

"Yvret? Diego? What are you doing here?" she asked.

"Oh, watching you sleep. Worrying that you'd never wake up. Michel was by for a while, too, but duty called. He wanted you to know that he was sorry for all the threats he made against you," Yvret explained.

Erin frowned and tried to think through the sleepiness.

"How do you feel this morning, my beautiful little seraph?" Yvret asked.

"Seraph?" she asked. "What do you mean? And why didn't I hear the sign that you were here?"

"You're not human anymore," Diego explained in perfect faerie.

Erin looked up at him. "Y-you speak fey now?"

"Yvret taught me how to talk to him and to you."

"When I saw how he cared for you before and after your metamorphosis, I thought he could be trusted." Yvret smiled.

"Wait, I'm…I've transformed?" she asked.

Diego stepped closer. "You can't tell?"

"But I never found the heart of sacrifice, the necklace."

Yvret looked over his shoulder at Diego as if she hadn't spoken. "Didn't occur to me either when I woke up."

"But you didn't have three sets of wings," Diego replied.

"Wings?" Erin exclaimed.

With that, all the fog of sleep left her mind.

"There's a mirror over here," Diego suggested.

"Yes, that's what it took for me," the elf said. "We'll have to help her, lad. Until I teach her how to walk with the changes in her body, she'll be horribly off-balance."

"I can walk," Erin insisted. "My mind's not fuzzy at all. Not anymore."

She slipped out from under the bedcovers and stood, but immediately wobbled and fell. She threw her arms out to the sides to help regain her stability and catch the posts at the corners of the bed. At the same time, the tension in her shoulders, neck, and ankles increased dramatically as she heard and felt three pairs of bird-like wings extend. The middle set was almost twice her height from tip to tip and both ends hit the walls, but the others were much smaller, no longer than her forearm.

Erin gasped in amazement while Diego and Yvret steadied her.

"I was surprised, too." Diego nodded.

They guided her to the mirror where she saw her new brown wings, the same dark color as her hair.

"What have I become?" she asked, staring in disbelief at a reflection that couldn't possibly be her own.

"A seraph. They're our protectors," Yvret replied.

"Protectors? Of what?"

"People. Dryads protect places. Seraphim protect people. You can choose which ones to give your attention to, of course."

Slowly, she reached up and touched the extra wings, just to make sure they were really there. "I thought I would become an elf. Like you."

Yvret shook his head. "Elves are leaders and teachers. You probably could lead, and I'm sure you can teach, but this suits you better."

"You always made your strongest decisions when you were protecting someone or yourself," Diego reminded her.

"Now you have to relearn your balance, and I'll have to teach you to radiate light and shapechange to your other two forms. Someone will have to teach you to fly, too."

"Shapechange?" she asked.

Her mentor nodded and straightened out an errant feather. "Yes, to an eagle and a lioness. And, too, you'll have to learn how to care for all these wonderful feathers."

Diego frowned. "Sounds like you'll be very busy for a while."

"Well, come to the ring and visit before you go after Luis again," Yvret suggested. "I'll have something for you."

"Luis got away?" Erin asked.

Diego nodded.

"I know how important that was to you. I'm so sorry."

"I'm not. I had to let him go to keep the sidhe from killing you. Yvret said he could make an artifact for me to track Luis. I'll get him yet."

In the distance, the front door opened and closed. Her heart raced. When had she come to fear being seen?

"We have a lot to do, Erin." Yvret offered his hand. "Are you ready to go to your new home?"

Erin looked up at Diego, then away again when she feared she might cry, but she wasn't losing her friend. She just had to go to her new home. "Yes, I guess so."

Diego stepped back. "I'll come see you soon."

She smiled and blinked back the tears, knowing she would miss him terribly. "I'll look forward to that."

As Yvret molded the energy to teleport them, Erin looked at her image in the mirror. Having three sets of wings sprouting from her body would take some getting used to.

***

One of the longest weeks of his life had passed since Diego had seen Erin disappear with Yvret. All the wealth Luis had stockpiled had been returned to the rightful owners as much as possible. Diego had laid claim to the rest, which Michel disapproved of. Undaunted, Diego had taken his case to the duke, boldly claiming he deserved a reward for leading to the arrest of all but one of the bandits. The duke had kept half of the money for charity, probably the charity of his own pockets, and had given the remainder, less the Church's tithe, of course, to Diego on the condition that Luis would be brought to Tours within one year. Diego had no grand delusions His Grace wouldn't hold onto the Church's tithe, too, for "safe keeping," naturally.

The meeting with the men Luis had rejected had resulted in a fair distribution of the wealth. The rest was for him.

Although less than he had wanted, the reward was still more money than Diego had ever owned in his life. Even if he combined

319

all his life's earnings into a single pile, it wouldn't even compare. If he were careful and used his new wealth wisely, he could live as an honest man for the rest of his life. He already missed the thrills of being a thief, but not that much. Encounters with the sidhe had proved much more exciting, and he knew he would meet more of them while going after his brother.

Now Diego sat on a log near the Seelie Court's mushroom ring and waited for Erin. Looking behind the log, he confirmed for the dozenth time that his present for her hadn't disappeared. Yvret himself had arrived one afternoon and suggested a fitting gift. He couldn't wait to see the look on Erin's face.

When light came from the ring, Diego stood and shielded his eyes with his hand. Erin and Yvret rose from the center. Erin's large wings folded neatly behind her back.

As he studied her, he felt the color rise in his face. In a human society, her sandals and the skirts that showed everything lower than her knees would be scandalous, but in her new form, boots and long skirts would hinder the lowest set of wings. In fact, no one had known about the third set until Corinne had dressed her for bed. The new style of dress looked perfectly natural on her, but he couldn't help feeling a little flustered.

"Well done, my child." Yvret acknowledged Diego with a nod. "Still some trouble on that take off, but the rest was excellent."

"Thank you." She stepped out of the ring. "I'll have to keep practicing."

"You'll master the skill in time. You're already making much better progress than Kendall did. At the end of his first week, he still couldn't walk on his own."

She smiled and blushed at the compliment.

"Come back before nightfall. Sidhe activity is still very high around here at night, and I would hate to see something unpleasant happen to Diego on his way back to town."

Without another word, Yvret disappeared into the ground at the heart of the faerie ring.

When Diego's eyes met Erin's, she fairly glowed with the joy he saw in her face.

"How are you?" She adjusted the lay of her wings.

"I'm well." He pointed to the largest wings. "Are you used to them yet?"

She nodded. "Almost. If I stand up or sit down too fast, I'll fall over, but I'm getting better. I'm not sore anymore, either, and as soon as I can get a non-steel sword, Kendall will teach me how to use it and take advantage of my new skills."

"That's good. You'll pick it up quickly. You were a very good student for me, well for the one evening I taught you, anyway."

"I have something for you." She pulled something from her belt pouch. "Two things, actually. One's from Yvret."

He took the small disk she offered him. It looked like nothing more than a round, black stone. When he flipped it over, he saw an arrow etched on the surface. No matter which way he turned it, the stone twisted in his hand to keep pointing the same way.

"It points to Luis?" he asked.

She nodded. "The straightest way, which he warns is not always the most convenient or the best route."

Diego experimented with the artifact, turning it different ways and even trying to force the arrow to stay facing the wrong way. It was awfully persistent.

Then she gave him a long gold chain with a glowing, deep blue stone pendant. Until he tried hiding her gift in his cupped hands, he thought the light he saw was a mere reflection of the sun, but he soon found that the crystal shined with a light of its own.

She pulled one just like it out of her dress. "They'll help us keep in contact," she said. "And when I'm ready, I can come join you, if you want."

Diego slipped the chain over his head. "If I want? Of course, I want you there with me. You promised you would help me with Luis, if you'll remember. I need you there when the fighting starts. He might have more sidhe friends." He admired the stone for a moment then looked toward the hiding place of his present. "My turn," he said. "Close your eyes."

"Why?" she asked.

"Trust me. I have something for you, too."

He waited until her eyes were closed, then retrieved the rapier and dagger from their place.

"No peeking," he warned. "Hold out your hands."

When she had done as he asked, he placed the gifts in her covered arms.

"What is this?" she asked. "Sticks?"

"Open your eyes."

She did and looked wide-eyed at the ornate blades. "These are beautiful, Diego, but I can't."

"They're silver," he explained. "Well, the blade is silver over steel to make it strong, but the hilt and the handguards are all silver. There's no steel or iron in the scabbards, either."

She set them down and inspected them one at a time, admiring the scrollwork on the flat of the blade. "Thank you!"

"Yvret said you needed them, since you can't use the last one I gave you."

"You traded for these, too?" she asked.

He shook his head. "Part of the reward money."

In the morning, he would leave to start tracking Luis, but for now, he would forget all about that and spend the day with her.

Originally from Michigan, Cindy Koepp combined a love of pedagogy and ecology into a 14-year career as an elementary science specialist. After teaching four-footers — that's height, not leg count, she pursued a Master's in Adult Learning with a specialization in Performance Improvement. Her published works include science fiction, fantasy, and GameLit novels, a passel of short stories, and educator resources. When she isn't reading or writing, Cindy practices Wu style tai chi and Eagle Claw kung fu, collects hats, makes quilts, and creates dragons.

Cindy can be found on the web at: ckoepp.com

Other books by Cindy:
Remnant in the Stars
Lines of Succession
The Loudest Actions
Mindstorm: Parley at Ologo
Condemned Courier
Like Herding the Wind: Urushalon Part I
Into the Open: Urushalon Part II
Animal Eye
Bond of the Sword (cowritten with Travis Perry)

Anthologies
Mosaic
Medieval Mars
Avatars of Web Surfer
Victorian Venus
Hero's Best Friend
A Chimerical World: Tales of the Seelie Court
Aquasynthesis Again
Friends Like These
Rise and Rescue, Vol. 1
Rise and Rescue, Vol. 2
Warrior's Tribute
Spurs and Six-Shooters
When Your Beauty Is the Beast
Nightmare Collective, Vol. 2
Moonlight and Claws
My Voice Has Power
Mythic Orbits, Vol. 2
Misfits and Unusual Heroes

Comic books with Artist Rowell Cruz
Animal Eye